J. ELMER TESCH

JOHUOCIN
Shade of Liberation

PROMINENT
BOOKS

5830 E 2nd St, Ste 7000 #9983
Casper, WY 82609
USA

CONTENTS

INTRODUCTION

Johuocin stared at his mother lying in bed under a patchwork quilt she had sewn from old clothing and sackcloth. She had barely enough strength to pull it over herself the last time she had gotten up to stoke the fire. With her every breath, she was now wheezing from "winter's curse" and calling his father's name in her delirium. It was apparent she continued to love and miss his father, though he'd been dead more than seven years. It was with good reason. Johuocin's father had always taken good care of her and Johuocin, ensuring there was always meat on the table, wheat to make bread, and wood for the fire, even in the worst of times. Johuocin had realized what a good man his father was before he was ten. He was the only child he knew who had two pairs of leather shoes, one for chores and one for town. Johuocin was often distressed in the knowledge that many of the children he knew had none. He remembered the mixture of pride and guilt he would experience, seeing other children wearing hard, unforgiving, wooden shoes, or having to wrap their feet in burlap cloth.

After his father's death, Johuocin and his mother struggled to survive, causing Johuocin to become more resentful of his father's death and less concerned with how he and his mother survived. The years after his father's death filled Johuocin with thoughts of revenge and hatred.

His mother drew his thoughts back to her as she coughed, showing the pain of it was worse than it had been. She had found the energy to get out of bed and build a fire with the last of the embers from the night before. Unfortunately, it was also nearly the last of the split wood in the house, and Johuocin felt his uselessness to her as the wind howled outside, knowing he could do nothing to help her. There was enough wood for one more fire. He knew she did not have the strength or energy to retrieve more in her condition. It hurt Johuocin to think that this last fire may never be built. Despair filled him, knowing his mother's illness was becoming worse. Maybe the home his father built for them so long ago would keep her warm a while longer.

His father had been one of the finest stonemasons in the kingdom before the time of the new crown. Now he was gone because of the taxes that rose with the banner of the new king.

Because of the rising tide of taxes, an honest man could find it hard to feed his family, so it was that many of the folk were forced to do tasks without reporting the wage. Johuocin's father made just enough of a living to be suspect in the eyes of the crown, and local magistrates feared the king would suspect them if no others were reported to his court.

The only court of the land was that of the king, and if you were brought before the court, you surely lost your head. This was because the man who ordered people brought before the court was the king, and the judge was the only man the king trusted: himself.

So it was that Johuocin's father, Jorgan Mark, was brought before the court and proceeded to lose his life.

Some said that it could be the king was right. Some even said that what the king was giving was justice. Some even went as far as to praise the king. But those few never knew Jorgan Mark, never knew him as a man or a father. They never saw him split granite block so evenly that you would think a dwarf held the chisel. But many did, and they knew Jorgan to be a good man, unjustly punished.

Johuocin had never felt this cold in all his twenty-seven years of time in this world. The wind blew fiercely outside the hovel now. He knew snow would be piling up soon and leave no way in or out for anyone. That could be both good and bad. It was good because it was tax time again. (The old king, Aldwa, always stopped taxes after the last harvest and started again after planting; this king failed that mercy.) It would be bad, because without visitors to the home, he would have no way to help his mother.

His mother coughed again, hacking from deep within her chest and decreasing to a harsh rasp in her throat.

Without hope of shaking his chill, Johuocin placed himself over the embers in the fire, and there he was, without hope.

Then there was a loud rap on the door. Johuocin thought that perhaps the wind had thrown something against it. The rapping became persistent, repeating itself in groups of three. That was the knock of the king's guard.

Johuocin's mother, Riselna, lifted her head and tried to call out. She was too weak, and her head fell back to the small rolled blanket she used for a pillow. Johuocin rose from the fire and started across the room just as the door flung open from the force of a guard's boot. Johuocin, seeing a captain's rank on the soldier's collar, stepped into the soldier's body just as he had begun to yell, "Taxes …" He continued, "… will not be necessary here." The men behind him achieved the most unusual look. The two came running in, expecting some crossbows to be pointed at their captain's head. But they found only an old woman lying on her straw mattress.

"Calm yourselves," came from the captain's mouth. "I know this woman." After a momentary examination, Johuocin continued, "She looks to have a touch of the creep."

After barking a few orders to the soldiers to get the fire started and retrieve wood from the pile outside, Johuocin felt the warmth of the man's body run through him and the sharp feeling of guilt start to settle deep inside his soul. One of the two men that came with the captain returned to the house and instinctively began going through the cupboards and pantry. Johuocin let him go on about his business when he saw that the soldier was looking to prepare some food. Johuocin was now feeling the hunger churning in the captain's belly. It felt absolutely glorious to him—a hungry belly and the warmth of life flowing about him.

This gave Johuocin a reminder, though, and he remembered the deal he had struck with Bolac the wizard, as he was again able to go about caring for his mother while he was in the captain's body. Bolac had lived up to his part of the deal without question. In return for Johuocin's body at the time of its death, Bolac was to arrange it so Johuocin was able to avenge his father's death no matter how long it took. Johuocin agreed to this; however, he had not completely understood the wizard's patience in waiting for his payment. The wizard had poured a drink for them to bind their agreement, as was customary. He'd offered the cup to his guest first, as was also customary. Johuocin had drank from the cup, handed it back to the wizard, and suddenly felt a chill. He had been moving toward the fire to warm himself when he saw a body lying facedown in front of him. He recognized the Crolga ring in the man's hair. It was familiar because it bore the seal he had made in the spring of his thirteenth year, a dragon coursing toward the sky in a corkscrew fashion. He had turned to the wizard to scream his death in the wizard's face.

The wizard held up his hand and said to Johuocin, "It is done."

Johuocin would now not only have time to avenge his father, but he would have eternity to do what he would. To use his time, he would have to step into the body of another person who he thought would be useful in completing his mission, regardless what the mission was. Johuocin saw this as an opportune time to test this and began moving toward the wizard. Again the wizard spoke. He told Johuocin that he could not enter the body he saw before him, for the wizard was as Johuocin, and the body before him was a borrowed one. If this weren't true, the wizard went on, the wizard would not be able to see him. Bolac held up a mirror, and Johuocin saw no reflection except of those things behind him.

"Sir," asked one of the soldiers, "would you like one of us to try to feed the woman?"

Startled by the stocky little man, Johuocin turned the face of his newfound confinement up toward the man and waited for the question to register in his mind.

"No," answered Johuocin. "I'll take care of it. You men eat and take the horses into the stable out back. We'll stay here the night."

"Yes, Captain," the man replied giving Johuocin a strange look.

Johuocin discretely went through his pockets—the captain's pockets. He was looking for papers to identify him. Just as he was looking for whatever else the captain may have carried to give him a clue as to who he was, the inside of the captain's waistcoat displayed a coat of arms, a griffin diving hard to attack. Johuocin remembered the coat of arms but couldn't recall from where.

Then he found a paper, the orders for the captain, signed and sealed in wax by the king himself, just in case anyone had any questions about his authority. They read as such:

It is ordered that Captain
Orman Reglawr and two
soldiers of his choice from
the king's garrison collect
taxes for this quarter-mester
throughout the southeast area
of the kingdom of Eldwain.
Be it further noted that the
northernmost border of his
authority be the southern
edge of the Morlocrin Forest
and the westernmost border
be the River Swain. South
and east borders will run to
the edge of the kingdom.

His Majesty the King of Eldwain,
Eldwa the Centurion

CHAPTER 1

Moving On

As one of the men cleaned the table, Johuocin watched his mother and knew he would have to leave her soon. His hope was that the storm would hold out long enough to nurse her into enough strength to care of herself. Then Johuocin would leave as the captain and could send a neighbor to help her.

"We'll stay here the night. I'm not about to fight that wind again so soon."

"Yes, Captain. You want me or Merson to get the bedrolls from the stable?"

"No, I'll get them. I shouldn't expect you to go back into weather I find uncomfortable myself."

The two men were looking oddly at Johuocin. It must be strange, he suddenly realized, for the captain to do any menial tasks himself. But no matter, Johuocin was wondering how he was going to learn their names and a little about the men he would be traveling with. This would be the perfect opportunity. He would search through their gear while he gathered the bedrolls. Then he realized he hadn't taken a thoughtful look at them as yet.

The man who had answered him was tall and light haired, like the captain, with dark eyes and a square face. He appeared perhaps four or five years younger than the captain. The other man was much older, thirty-eight maybe, a little gray on the sides of his otherwise very dark hair. Much shorter and more muscular than the other men, Merson's leathery, tanned skin made him appear as though he had at one time worked hard, laboring in the open sun. In some ways, Merson's appearance put Johuocin in mind of his father.

"Don't get used to it," Johuocin, thinking to hide his deception, told them bitingly. "I want to check out the stable. If this woman dies, the kingdom may wish to place a constable here." Johuocin pulled the captain's coat close around his neck and walked out the door of the hovel.

The air was cold outside, but it felt good against the captain's skin. It reminded Johuocin of the warmth he felt as he inhabited the captain. It had been three months since

Johuocin had known the feeling of flesh, and he hadn't remembered what an asset it was. The lack of restraint in movement or entry as a spirit was no consolation in comparison to the warmth of occupying a body.

The wind had calmed some from earlier, and the snow had started to fall heavily to the ground. That combined with the cloud cover had caused blackness outside so deep that travel that night would have been impossible. Nothing but blackness and snowflakes met his sight. If Johuocin didn't know the lay of the yard so well, he would have gotten lost on the way to the stable. He remembered how his father stepped off every inch of the layout, dropping stone markers where every corner of each building would be. He remembered how he walked next to his father, trying so hard to look and be like him but running every third step or so to catch up to his father's stride. He recalled the strength and power in his father's arms and the scars on his hands from working with stone and chisels. As he remembered, tears began to flow and freeze to the face that was now his. With each breath he released, Johuocin cursed the king for taking his father from him. Revenge welled up in his core, and Johuocin felt the comfort of hearing his thoughts verbalized, even if they were in the voice of another man.

As he opened the stable door, he wiped his face with his sleeve and stepped inside. The stable was darker still than the yard outside. He reached up to the ledge by the door, taking down the lamp that had been kept there since his father first placed it. He searched the captain's waist pockets for the flint he had felt in his earlier search. (He was glad that the captain had taken care to wrap it in leather and oil cloth.)

As Johuocin looked around, he saw the three horses and two pack mules that the soldiers had brought. The horses were all very good stock, but one was markedly better than the others. He assumed this was the captain's horse. He began unsaddling the horses and going through the saddlebags.

The captain's bags had some maps, quills, some personal items, and a coin bag with what appeared to be the captain's initials, O. R., on it. It contained seven gold pieces, twenty-four silver pieces, and a few coppers. There was nothing more to give him clues concerning who the captain was.

The next bag was, by the age and wear of the leather, apparently Merson's. His full name was Merson Bennidact, according to his papers. In his coin bag there was a cube of granite. Johuocin knew this was a custom of stonemasons, to carry a sample of the first stone they had cut with precision in their purse. That would explain why Merson looked weather-beaten. Looking at the papers, it was clear he had been one of the king's guards for only six seasons. Merson had a scroll with a drawing of a woman and child in his pack, which was strange because if Johuocin understood correctly, the king's guard could not marry until they were of rank (lieutenant or higher).

The last bag belonged to the man resembling the captain. The papers identified him as Ouben Reglawr; he too had the same crest in his belongings. They were of the same family, brothers perhaps.

Just as Johuocin was putting the bag to the side, the stable door opened. It was Merson.

"Is everything all right, Captain?"

"Yes, Merson, of course," Johuocin said nervously, trying to avoid meeting Merson's eyes. "I was just delaying having to go out into the storm again. Help me unpack the mules."

"Aye, Captain."

There was silence as they unpacked the mules. Merson was a quiet man. He showed no desire for idle conversation and appeared to have something on his mind.

"There is some fine stonework in these buildings. They will probably stand for some time." Johuocin was trying to draw something out of Merson, anything that would help him understand the captain.

"Aye, I haven't seen work like this since before the new king. The dwarves used to do wonderful work."

"You don't think this was done by dwarves, do you?"

"I don't know. Before the new king we had a few human masons who did fine work, but very few."

"I know this wasn't. It was done by the old woman's husband, Jorgan Mark."

"Aye, I've heard the name. Rumor was his work was too good, and the king thought he should be paying more taxes."

Just then Johuocin remembered where he knew the crest of the griffin from. His father was contracted to do some work in the kingdom to the north of Eldwain after the dwarves could no longer pass through Eldwain to reach it. He traveled with his father as far as the Castle Eldwain, where Jorgan met an escort wearing the crest. Johuocin was in the habit of going with his father on most of his jobs at the time, but this one was too far and Jorgan didn't like to leave his wife alone for long.

"Yes, my father had him do some work for us when I was a child. I remember watching him as he would search a stone for just the right spot to lay his chisel. Then, down would come the hammer. The result would be some of the smoothest rock anyone could hope for without a stone planer." Johuocin was talking from his own experience of watching his father work.

"I would have liked to have seen him work."

After they had finished unpacking the mules, Johuocin picked up the bedrolls of the captain and Merson and started for the door.

"Captain." Johuocin turned when he was called. "Are we going to leave this here?" Merson pointed to a medium-sized chest. "We may not appreciate being robbed in our foolishness."

"Yes, you're probably right." Then he thought silently, *What do I care if the king loses a little gold?*

They each picked up an edge of the chest and carried it with them.

When they reached the warmth of the house, Ouben was stirring the fire, and Johuocin's mother was resting peacefully. It must have done good to get nourishment in her. It was the first time she had rested well in a week.

Johuocin was feeling the fatigue of the captain's day. He unrolled his bedroll and lay down by the fireplace. As he laid his head down, he felt something hard and bulky under the blanket. He reached under and pulled out three scrolls. He was too tired to investigate, so he set them aside and closed his eyes. Johuocin fell asleep, praying to the gods for his mother's recovery and listening to the wind once again blowing hard against the walls of the hovel.

Johuocin woke in the morning to the smell of cured pork frying and the sound of Merson and Ouben talking. They had not noticed he was awake, so he lay there with his eyes closed, listening, hoping for more insight into his new companions.

"It's after dawn," Merson said. "He never sleeps this late."

"Yes, it was a long day yesterday," came from Ouben. "He needed the rest; he's been pushing himself hard trying to meet the demand for a speedy collection. He started acting a little strange when we arrived here yesterday. No need for him to be awake anyway; we won't be moving in this storm."

"Aye, the weather seems persistent. Between that and the snow, we'd lose our way in the first league. I wonder how long it will last."

"It's hard to tell. No matter—we could all use the rest."

"The two of you could use the rest perhaps. You and your brother had a soft life before this. Common folk, myself included, have seen harder times than you will likely ever see."

"That's not a fair statement, Merson. You have no idea of what it was like for us as children. Your old crown was perhaps more gentle with his own people, but he was on a constant siege with our kingdom."

"You never lacked for food or rest, lad. It shows in your soft hands and fair skin." Merson poked a little at the younger man's light forearm and smiled. "But no matter, our concern now should be for your brother."

"I know," Ouben said as he released the offended look that was building in his face. "I've never seen him let anyone out of tax duty before. Or attend any labor he didn't need to."

"Aye, I found it a little strange. He was in a pleasant mood, though. I could get used to seeing that a little more."

"Don't count on it. He hasn't been pleasant since our father swore us into service to Eldwa."

"At least your father had the money to get him a ranking position. A great many nobles didn't have the sense or money to do that for their sons."

"I think Ory would have rather earned it."

"That could have taken years, and he's already seen thirty-one summers."

"Just the same …"

Then Johuocin sat up and cut his new brother off in a harsh tone. "Just the same I don't wish to hear that my father earned my rank with coin, no matter how well I do my job. And that's the only reason I work hard to fill the king's purse."

"Sorry, Captain. Ben and I didn't mean anything by it."

Johuocin got up and moved to his mother's side. He felt her head and moved to the table. Ben put a plate of food and a hot mug of asra in front of him. "As for the belay of taxes here, the woman is clearly sick; she probably doesn't have any money anyway. That and she is Jorgan Mark's widow. I'll claim our board as her tax."

"Who is Jorgan Mark, Ory?"

"It seems that I remember him doing some work for our father when you were about eleven." Johuocin was guessing at this.

"The outer wall around our home?"

"I think so." He was more than willing to agree with Ouben's memory since he hadn't actually been there and didn't know for sure that it was the case.

"Father offered him more than was promised, I recall, said it was better work than he'd ever seen, but the man wouldn't take more than agreed."

"Yes, he had pride." This was one thing Johuocin said with knowledge.

"I seem to recall something about having to travel the long way around to get to our home just so no one would think he was a spy," Ouben added.

Little more was said that day by anyone. The wind blew more fiercely than Johuocin could ever remember. The snow had stopped, but the air had become colder. Ben and Merson tended to the horses and mules and the pig and chickens that were there in the stable. Johuocin took the time to review the scrolls. One was nothing more than a tax record. Another was a diary the captain had been keeping. It revealed that the captain had the complete trust of the king, or at least as much trust as the king would give to anyone.

The third scroll was revealed in his diary as one given to him by his father, Sesnic. It was not to be read until he heard from his father again by messenger. In the diary it also gave the captain's reasoning for his choice of traveling companions—his brother because of the loyalty he would have from him if anything came up and a request from his father, Merson because of the circumstance that brought him to the king's guard. Merson had been a stonemason in the northern part of the kingdom. He was gone on a job three days away from home when the tax collectors came. His wife did not have enough money to pay the tax and promised the money when her husband returned. She was a beautiful woman, and the tax collectors said they would gladly pay it themselves if she would lay with them. Being a loyal wife, she refused. The men—if that's what you would call them—proceeded to rape her. Her son of seven summers came in at the end and seeing what had happened, took a pitchfork to one of them. The pitchfork was taken away, and the child was beaten to death. When his mother rebelled and attacked, she too was beaten to death.

A neighbor who did not wish to reveal herself at the time in fear for her own safety witnessed the incident. Merson at some point in their travels had told the captain about the incident and explained to the captain how he both had hated the woman for not helping his wife and pitied her for having to carry the memory of it for the rest of her life. Merson then joined the guard, found the men, and killed them. The matter came before the king, who said the killing of the soldiers were justified, but ordered Merson to pay the tax he was owed and continue in the service of the guard for forty years.

Now the captain, Ben, and Merson were charged with the responsibility of collecting taxes in the largest southern section of the kingdom.

*

Johuocin's mother was getting stronger, able to raise her head and look around, even sitting up in bed to eat her supper. However, she didn't speak even when asked how she was feeling and was clearly uncomfortable in the presence of the guards. In the middle of the night Johuocin woke to find her out of bed sitting by the table.

"Are you feeling stronger?" Johuocin asked from his bed on the floor. "You haven't moved much for the past two days."

"I'm stronger. Why are you here?" Riselna's tone was filled with bitterness, like asra root before it's brewed.

"We've come to collect the tax. Yours will be recorded as room and board to help us out of the storm."

"I'd rather pay the tax," she spat back at the captain. "My neighbors would not appreciate hearing I offered any kindness to you."

"Then perhaps it's fortunate for us you were next to dead when we arrived. I couldn't weather the storm further, and my men were near frozen."

She gave the captain a cutting glance. "Perhaps the people here would have benefitted had you stayed in the storm."

Johuocin had not realized how bitter his mother had become toward those who wore the king's uniform. She was a gentle woman before his father's death and became apathetic after. Now, with Johuocin, himself gone from her, perhaps she no longer felt anything but anger for anyone.

"You talked of Jorgan in your restlessness. Did you know he did some work for my father, Sesnic Reglawr?"

"You are not of Reglawr house. That family has been dead to the support of this crown."

"Things have changed somehow, Moth ..." Johuocin slipped and caught himself. "My father swore me into the service of the new crown."

"I don't believe that. Sesnic Reglawr wouldn't do such an abominable thing to his own children."

"Believe what you will. The truth cannot be changed."

With that Johuocin laid himself down and watched his mother as she moved to her bed supported by the wall. He was unaware that she knew the Reglawr family or how.

The next morning Johuocin made it a point to wake before dawn. The wind was still blowing stiffly, but the snow had stopped once again. If the wind let up, he would no longer have an excuse for the captain to stay, no excuse to take care of his mother. Johuocin would need to make a decision to stay uselessly to look on as his mother went about her life or to move on and remain in the captain, either to find someone else who would return to take care of his mother or to take some action that would forward his original intent of revenge. The other men were not far behind the captain in waking and were not surprised to find him looking over the maps.

"Get the horses ready," Johuocin barked. "If this wind lets up, we'll be moving on today."

"Aye, Captain." With that, Merson moved for the door.

"You go with him, Ben. I'm in a hurry to leave."

"I'm not going to stop the wind from blowing. We can't go anywhere 'til it stops."

Johuocin shot him a look that said he'd better go.

Mocking Merson's northern mountain accent, Ben replied quickly, "Aye, Captain."

While his mother still slept, he took the purse the captain carried and emptied it into the crock on the counter. This is where his mother always kept her money, and she seldom counted it before she absolutely needed it.

The gold was more than she was used to having, but by the time she found it, the captain and his men would be gone many days.

Johuocin thought hard on how he was going to exact his revenge on the king. He put his mind through many scenarios and could not find one that he felt comfortable with. Each time he thought he knew what he was going to do, he realized he would be implicating someone else by being in that person's body. He would have to think on the situation longer. But, time was the one thing Johuocin had plenty of.

By noon, or at least as best could be judged with the cloud-covered skies, the wind had stopped. Johuocin knew he must move on despite how he hated leaving his mother. He knew she would push herself too hard and wind up in bed again. He also knew he must act on the original purpose for his deal with Bolac. So as the captain, he gave the order, and off they went.

As they rode away from his mother's house, Johuocin began to feel that his purpose may be well served by impersonating a trusted soldier in the king's service. This situation might provide a base to form a plan of revenge upon the king.

CHAPTER 2

The Truth of It

The three trudged through the snow for what seemed an eternity, leading their horses by the reins. An hour after they left the home built by Johuocin's father, the wind picked up again and they could not see to steer the horses clear of trees and gullies. Therefore, rather than risk losing their mounts to injury, they opted to walk in front to guide them. Johuocin was sure that they had lost their way and the three would freeze in the snow before reaching their next destination, Cragfare.

Johuocin had been to the towns north and west of his home and could have easily led the party there in any weather. But Cragfare was south of his home, and his father had told him when he was a boy, "Never go south." Johuocin never asked the reason why; he had just avoided traveling south from his home.

As they trudged along, Merson called out the captain's name. Johuocin, forgetting who he was, trudged on in a state of worried pondering, concerned for what he had led the party into.

"Captain," Merson said, grabbing the captain's shoulder. Johuocin turned. "There's a light from that direction." Merson pointed to the direct right of the party. As Johuocin looked, he saw a faint glow at a distance in the blowing snow.

"Turn to it, Merson. We'll find out what it is."

As the party neared, the light became brighter, and there was a noticeable flicker. It was close to the ground, like a campfire.

Johuocin called out, "'Lo there, ahead?" No answer came. The party moved ahead more cautiously on Johuocin's signal.

As they neared, and the snow no longer impaired their vision so greatly, they could see that the light was coming from a cave, hidden in the side of a small knoll. Johuocin motioned for Ben and Merson to stay back while he went ahead to investigate.

Trudging forward to the source of light, Johuocin called out again, trying to sound more friendly than curious. Still no response came. Without hesitation he stepped forward into the light and into the front of the cave, leaving his mount tied to a bush outside the entrance.

Johuocin saw only a fire and a pile of evergreen branches by one wall. He could only see twenty feet further on before the light gave out, but Johuocin could tell the cave went steadily down and back by the sound of the wind lightly echoing its howls deep inside.

Again he called, "Is anyone here?"

A raspy whispered answer came from the back of the cave. "Yes, I'm here. What's your name?"

"I am Orman Reglawr of the king's guard. Who am I addressing?"

"My name is not your concern. You're in my cave. What is it you want, 'king's guard'?"

"Shelter. What can you offer?"

"I offer nothing. Get out."

"I have other business with you." Johuocin tried to draw out the unseen voice. "What business would that be?"

"I have been commissioned to collect taxes for the king."

"I have never paid this king's taxes, and I do not intend to start now. Be gone with you, soldier; I have no use for you or anyone like you. And I especially have no use for tax collectors, so leave while you still have your life."

"How do you expect me to take seriously a threat from someone I can't even see? I would think if you were a true threat, you would show yourself."

Just as Johuocin finished his statement, a short, stocky, powerful-looking figure jumped into the light. He was wielding a war hammer almost as tall as himself and appeared ready to give credence to his threat. A voice came from this small but commanding creature that shook the very floor of the cave.

"You'll regret not taking my invitation to leave, scum."

The appearance of a dwarf took Johuocin by surprise. Stunned, he stood staring at the little man as the dwarf ran to attack. Just then a crossbow bolt pierced the dwarf's wrist. A howl came from him and the hammer was dropped, but the little man kept charging. He made a leap for the captain and fell sprawling on the ground as Ben pulled his brother aside. Merson lunged on top of him and held a dagger at his throat.

The little man glared at Merson and said, "Cut me throat, ye worthless scrag."

"Nay, I'll not do it. Ye may be family."

"Ye aren't family, scrag. Mine wouldn't be caught dead in the throes with a mortal one."

"Nay would me mother if she weren't raped."

Ben and Johuocin looked on in dismay at the two as they had their conversation.

Neither could completely comprehend what Merson was saying, or why. Maybe it was a bluff to put the dwarf off his guard, but something inside Johuocin told him it wasn't any kind of a bluff.

"Even if it's so, you're still mortal bound, scrag. Let me up and regain myself. I'll not be attacking more tonight."

At that Ben raised his crossbow to the ready.

"Let him up, Merson," Johuocin issued.

"Aye, Captain. Are you sure?"

"Yes."

At that Merson sheathed his dagger and slowly got up from the dwarf's belly.

"What's your name?" Johuocin demanded.

"Granite Hammerhand."

"Dwarves are no longer allowed in Eldwain. What's your business here?"

"Now then, that's me own business, isn't it?"

"Let me remind you, Hammerhand, we would get a pretty reward from the king whether we take you to him dead or alive. He hasn't much taste for dwarves in his kingdom, and I would be just doing my duty by ridding him of what he doesn't like."

"What is your problem then, scrag? All ye have to do is your duty."

"Personally, I have no need for killing dwarves, unless, of course, they wish to excuse me of my own life."

"Then what's your real name?"

"I have already told you that."

Hammerhand looked over to Merson and then to Ben. Ben still had the crossbow trained on him. He turned back to Merson and asked directly, "What's his name?"

"Orman Reglawr." Merson then said some rough-sounding slurs that Johuocin didn't recognize and added, "Ouben Reglawr."

"Ahee, ye might've spoke like that when ye had me on the ground scufflin'. Captain, did ye know you're travelin' with a dwarf-kin at your side?"

Almost simultaneously Merson answered with a sharp, "Aye" and Johuocin answered with a quick, "No."

Hammerhand, agitated by this, raised his voice. "Well which is it, did he or didn't he?"

Merson and Johuocin/Ory looked at each other in confusion. Merson turned back to Hammerhand and guttered out a few words, in the language Johuocin could only assume was dwarfish, and that seemed to satisfy him. Johuocin was trying not to show his confusion and adapt a look of conscious pretense. Ben was just plainly baffled by the whole situation.

Hammerhand replied to Merson and then said, "I'll be gettin' some sleep now." He got up, wrapping his wrist, and went to the makeshift bed and lay down.

"Captain, may I have a word with you?" It was apparent that Merson was concerned about something.

"Ben, watch him closely. We'll take shifts tonight, you, Merson, and then me." Johuocin walked to the back of the cave with Merson behind him, curious if he'd given himself away.

Johuocin found an area with heavy dirt on the walls to muffle any conversation that took place. He turned to Merson, who had adopted a questioning look on his face. He wondered how much Merson had seen.

"Captain," Merson started, "you have to know already, Granite is one of the scouts from the east. I'm a little surprised he's this far west myself, but maybe they're counting on an early spring."

Johuocin was taken back. He was unsure of what his companion was talking about. Merson made it sound as if the captain should know something about Granite, though he'd never met him before. If this was true then Johuocin needed to find out what it was without drawing too much suspicion to himself. The only problem now, was how to do that.

"How far north are the rest?"

Merson gave him a queer look. "You know he couldn't tell me that, Captain. He was a little confused when you denied knowing I was dwarf-kin. For certain he was when I told him you knew. I myself am not certain why you denied it. After all, it's one of the reasons your father told you about me."

Johuocin wondered what he had walked into by taking the captain's body. The whole thing sounded like a plot of some kind. He needed answers, and he needed them now if he were to keep his own identity a secret.

"Why exactly do you think my father told me about you, Merson?"

"Several reasons lad, a few particular to your needs, and some that are personal to me. The most important is that I can interpret when you come to meet with the dwarf chieftains and teach you a little etiquette in dealing with them. They will not take kindly if you don't follow ceremony." Merson moved to look square into the captain's face. "Not doing so could undo all your father has worked toward."

The news stunned Johuocin, and he could feel himself struggle to keep the surprise from the captain's face. "Well, it appears that things are moving a little quicker than we expected. When were you planning to teach me this bit of ceremony you say is so important?"

"I'll do it as you ask, but the meeting won't be any sooner than planned. The winter solstice is very special to the dwarf clans."

"What will we express in this meeting?"

"Captain, did this last storm make you daft?" Merson sounded irritated at Johuocin's naiveté to the subject. "Your father explained everything step by step."

"How many will be there?"

"A chieftain and his lieutenant of each of the eleven tribes, including the chieftain of the Moramac tribe if they decide it's profitable to them. They'll be a little cautious, all of them." He felt as if Merson were warning him of arduous and possibly physical argument.

At that Johuocin decided to give the conversation a rest. Feeling bewildered by his assumptions and tired from the storm, he started to walk toward the front of the cave.

Merson caught hold of his elbow, "Will you be ready, lad?"

"Yes." But for the life he possessed, Johuocin didn't know for what or how unless he learned more of the truth.

That night Johuocin could not sleep. He believed he had grasped the thoughts behind the conversation with Merson. Sesnic Reglawr was mounting an attack upon the king with the dwarves as allies. He had the misfortune of stepping into the body of his son and lieutenant. This explained why Sesnic swore his sons into the king's service and purchased rank and position for his eldest. How was he going to use the situation to exact his revenge? How could he do so before others took his chance away? The solstice was only three weeks away. How was he going to learn enough to handle the position Orman Reglawr had set before him by his father?

"Ory, are you awake?" Johuocin turned over to see Ben standing over him.

"Sure, Ben, what do you need?" Johuocin was finding it easy to warm up to Ben. He'd always wanted a younger brother or sister as he was growing up and it felt natural to indulge his instincts.

"The dwarf; it was as if it didn't bother him that we found him. It wasn't that it didn't bother him to be found, but specifically, that he was found by us. Can you figure it?"

Did Ben not know what was going on? "Maybe I should talk to Merson. He might have found something out while he was talking to him."

"I have a funny feeling that he's here for a reason other than just finding himself here." Ben turned and walked back to the fire, staring at Granite as he came closer to the dwarf. Granite lay there rumbling the walls with his snoring.

By dawn the next day, the weather had cleared. Merson was standing at the front of the cave, looking out, smoking a morning pipe as Johuocin walked up beside him. Johuocin was still searching for a way to find out what Ben knew about the situation. Suddenly he spoke out loud, questioning himself, "I wonder if Ben knows anything at all."

"Aye, it wouldn't surprise me at all if he knew everything. After all, it seems to me you're forgetting everything, or at least acting like you are." Merson looked at the captain in disgust. "The chieftains won't take kindly to a confused or disoriented representative. They may want to take over the assault, and your father will never get his crown."

"Then you'd better start coaching me now, Merson." Johuocin adopted a cynical tone. "Because the truth of it is I might not be the person you think I am. And with the solstice not far off, maybe we should let Ben in on a little of this so he's not off guard when it happens."

"Aye, Captain, tonight we'll start." Then Merson showed a strong smile and a firm jaw that seemed to signal he was confident in his actions.

CHAPTER 3
The Veil of Rausche Laine

The three men saw Granite Hammerhand wake that morning with a smile on his gruff, wide face, having a look of total restfulness. As he stretched himself to shake off the night's sleep, he looked back across the fire at the three men enjoying a hot cup of asra.

"Well, I certainly appreciate the night's rest. First good night I've had in a long time."

By the way he started rubbing his wrist and met Ben's gaze as he spoke, it was apparent that he was taunting Ben, suspecting Ben had no knowledge of the current state of events.

Ben, who had been working on some cheer to shake off his confusion, began feeling his belly burn with angst. "I have no use for your good thanks this morning."

"Then don't listen, scrag," Granite said with nonchalance as he stood and began gathering his things to put in his pack.

"Where do you think you're going, short one?" Ben was aware that his companions didn't seem to think anything of the dwarf's preparation to leave, but he did.

"To do my job. If you ever want us ready, then you'd best stay out of my way."

"Want who ready?"

Merson jumped into the conversation. "Don't bother with it, Ben. We were going to let him go anyway." Merson hadn't had a chance to tell Granite that Ben knew nothing.

He saw Granite ready to come back with new words and stopped him with some words in the dwarven tongue.

Granite narrowed his eyes and went back to packing.

Ben, who had put his hand to his sword, stood baffled by the situation. He couldn't understand what connection there was between Merson and Granite but knew it was more than Merson's ancestry. "I want to know what's going on!" Ben pushed.

Johuocin knew what Ben was feeling. He was becoming familiar with the confusion of not knowing. "Ben, let it go. I'll explain the whole thing later."

At that everyone went to making ready to leave. Before leaving Granite pointed out the direction to the nearest town and said it was four hours by horseback. The town was called Rausche Laine.

As they traveled, the day was bright and good humored despite the interaction of the morning. Ben, seemingly recovered from his confusion and distaste toward the dwarf, was joking and laughing. Merson was riding with confidence and purpose in his knowledge of the task set before him. Johuocin was more relaxed than ever because he felt he had been presented with a way to learn what he needed to know without revealing himself. (He would ask Merson to explain everything to Ben, and he would quietly listen.) For Merson and Ben, the day itself was a relief from the storms of the week before, sunny and bright for the few hours of daylight they had for the time of year. For Johuocin, it was a glorious feeling of warmth and the familiarity of flesh. The time passed without notice until the three approached Rausche Laine.

Merson was the first to notice in the dusk of the early evening. "Captain, there in the distance."

"Well then, hot meals and dry beds tonight." Johuocin was happy to see many chimneys smoking in the village. It would mean an inn or two to choose from.

"Yes," piped Ben, "and clean uniforms for the morning."

Johuocin hadn't thought about that prior to Ben mentioning it. He had just been so happy to be in a body for the last couple of days that clothing didn't matter.

As they entered the village, they received many hate-filled glares. The people turned from them in disgust at the sight of their uniforms and mounts. The harsh reality of being seen as one of the king's henchmen drove through Johuocin like a wedge splitting logs on a dry winter night. He had never experienced anything like it before. He knew he would need to settle into the feeling if he continued in the role he was now to play.

Some boys were playing in an open yard near them. Merson yelled to them in a loud brusque manner, "You there, boys, fetch the town elders and tell them we'll be waiting at the inn here on the corner." He pointed to a corner building with a large wooden spoon hung over the door. The boys ran off in two directions into the town.

Carved into the door of the inn was a motto, "All who drink pay a price—but we will make your drinking nice." In the handle of the oversized wooden spoon that hung above the door, was carved, "O'bourn House." As Johuocin and his companions entered the inn, a hush fell over the occupants, and the four men sitting closest the fireplace moved to a different table. A man came from behind the bar and nervously greeted them.

"Hello and welcome. I am Kale O'bourn, the innkeeper here. May I offer you gentlemen a table near the fire?"

Johuocin looked around the inn. Everyone was avoiding his glance, making him feel uncomfortable. "Do you have rooms?"

The innkeep became even more nervous. "I'm sure I will have. How many will you need?"

"Two, next to each other," Johuocin said as he turned to his companions and motioned toward the door. As they stepped outside, he felt even less comfortable. It was as though they were being watched. He looked around and saw no one, but the feeling didn't leave.

"I'm going back in to get a table. Bring the chest in with you." Almost as an afterthought he added, "Watch your backs. I feel someone watching us."

"Aye, Captain. Is there anything else sir?" Merson had picked up his formalities again.

"Yes, do either of you feel what I'm talking about?"

"I do, Ory. It gives me the creeps." Ben too was looking around.

As Johuocin stepped back into the inn, the innkeep stepped toward him in anticipation of leading him to a table. "Can I take you to the table by the fire, sir?"

"No, take me to the corner table, and get rid of some of the light there."

The innkeep did as he was asked. He wiped the table down as the captain sat himself in the corner facing out. "I have maldo stew in the kitchen, sir. Is that all right for you gentlemen tonight?"

"Yes, bring three plates and three mugs of asra spiced with the best berry brandy you have." Johuocin stared at the innkeep for a moment as he watched him walk away. The innkeep looked nervous and unsure of himself, as if someone had just pulled a rug from under him.

As he waited for Ben and Merson to return from outside, the innkeep brought the asra as he had asked and said it would be a few minutes for the stew. Johuocin thought he remembered what the asra and brandy would taste like but had a difficult time not drowning himself as he guzzled the first mug as it actually touched his tongue.

As the inn began to empty out and the crowd thinned, the innkeep looked less nervous.

Ben and Merson returned with the chest and took a seat as the stew was set on the table. Merson was looking at the captain as if he had something to say, but the innkeep started to speak as he set down the plates.

"I apologize, gentlemen, for being so short with you earlier. The topic of discussion was the king's taxes just before you walked in, and none were too happy. Now let me introduce myself properly. I am Kale O'bourn; most folk here'bouts just call me Kale. I'll be happy to do anything for you that will make your stay easier, and your rooms are being made ready for you now."

"Thank you, Kale," Johuocin responded politely. "I'm expecting the town elders here soon. Be sure they are made comfortable when they arrive, and get them what they wish to drink. I want them cooperative with me so I can do what I must and leave."

Johuocin was still uncomfortable and a little unsure of his actions. He had never been the tax collector before.

"Yes sir, I can meet those wishes and would even prefer them to the treatment we received from the last lot that came through here."

As the innkeep started away, Merson caught his arm for a few questions he had. "Why are you being so cooperative and informal with us when it is very clear that the townsfolk can't stomach us?"

"Foremost, I am one of the town elders. It is my job to keep harmony a part of life here. Next, I am an innkeep by trade, and I pride myself on hospitality to all who walk through my door, regardless of who, or what, they are. Last, I do not believe that all men are strong enough to do what is right when there is an easier road to take by following the orders of a tyrant. It is not always their fault, though it is their responsibility." The last sentence had a bit of bitter scolding in its tone directed toward the three.

At this Ben jumped up and faced off on the innkeep. "Innkeeper, you'd be smart not to judge everyone by your feelings. Sometime it may cost you something."

"Sit down, Ben. We don't need any trouble here! These people may be our friends one day instead of our judges." Johuocin could feel the presence of someone watching him again. He looked around, but everyone had left the inn but them. When he looked back at Ben, he saw a cold, hurt look on his face.

"It's all right, Captain. The lad may be right. I do have a tendency to judge people by my feelings, but I'm seldom wrong, and never paltry, in expression."

Kale O'bourn was a very confident man in the things he expressed. If he felt threatened by Ben's outburst, he didn't show it. Indeed he showed just the opposite. He started to pull away from Merson's grip, but Merson tightened. "Just one more question, innkeep. Who's been watching us from upstairs?"

"The only one up there is my daughter. The rest of the place is empty and will be until you leave. She was making your rooms ready." At that Merson let go of the man's arm.

Kale walked away from the table, deliberately turning his back to the men as if to say they didn't threaten him. The three ate the maldo stew with the intensity of hungry wolves. It was heavy with pepper and onion, and the sauce had a smooth, pungent taste. They each had two plates heaped to the top. At this Kale smiled, though he had no use for the men, because he truly enjoyed seeing anyone enjoy his daughter's cooking.

Ben was the first to speak. "My compliments, sire O'bourn. You should have told us you were such a chef. I would have endured your scolding more gracefully."

"Thank you, sir, but it wasn't me doing the cooking. It was my daughter."

"Aye," Merson said. "We should have known there was a woman's hand in it. Could you ask her here so that we may pay our respects and thank her for a much appreciated meal?"

Kale turned his head over his shoulder, to the back of the tavern area, and yelled his daughter's name. "Riessa!"

Into the dining room strolled a girl appearing to be twenty. She was tall, with long gold and brown hair that trailed in wisps as she moved, blue eyes like star fire, and fair skin. She had a gentle appearance and a smile to match. The dress she wore was drab and unappealing except for the way it exposed the firm flesh of her upper arms and shoulders. The neckline was high enough to conceal the cleavage of her chest but low enough to expose soft, unblemished skin. The waistline was just tight enough to hug her flat belly and show the curve of her hips. Her beauty took Johuocin back. He stood and began walking toward her, staring deeply into her eyes. She was smiling and then became alarmed. Suddenly Johuocin heard a voice behind him. It was familiar but out of place. He turned to see the captain with a startled look on his face and mumbling in confusion.

"Where, what the hell? How did we get here?"

Johuocin jumped toward the captain and back in before he could say more. Then Johuocin realized what he'd done. He was concentrating on Riessa and forgot about the captain entirely, moving out of his body and through the table to reach her.

"Captain, are you all right?" Riessa moved toward him and took his hand. She was looking at the captain the way Johuocin imagined he had been looking at her.

"Yes, too much good food and spiced asra, coupled with your beauty, is a dangerous thing for a man. He could almost forget exactly who he is." Johuocin thought to himself, as he said it, that his words lacked any form of exaggeration.

She let go of his hand and smiled as she moved away. Kale glanced sharply at Captain Reglawr for his remarks. He had never seen his daughter react to a man's advances as she did with this soldier and tax collector. He did not want Johuocin to be confused about what he felt for him. He wanted the captain to see his contempt.

Merson, seeing Kale's anger, quickly spoke up. "Your cooking, Miss O'bourn, is most exceptional. I don't think I've had the pleasure of better since my wife died. Even then, I think, it was only her company at my table that made her cooking better."

At this, Riessa smiled and blushed, then achieved a very pitiful look. "Thank you for your gracious compliment, sir. It is seldom that one is compared to a loved one in such a kind manner. It makes me sad for your loss."

Ben, too, had to add his thought. He raised his mug to the others. "To the lady Riessa, whose cooking is only surpassed by her beauty." At this the three men held their mugs high and bent them to their lips to drink.

The front door of the inn opened, and two men walked into the tavern. Unlike Kale, who was a short man with a humble appearance, they were tall, powerful-looking men with anger in their eyes. They both wore the black robes of village elders, but neither had the staff that would have marked them as the village sovereign.

Kale introduced them immediately. "Gentlemen, these are the other elders of our community. Gorn Fustrum"—indicating the larger of the two—"is second elder and village blacksmith. Malach O'dall is third elder and village miller. I am the sovereign of the community and will excuse myself for a short time to prepare for our meeting. Won't you all please sit and Riessa will take care of your needs for drink or food until I return." At this he turned and walked away, leaving Riessa in attendance.

She quickly left the room and brought back a tray filled with eldcakes and asra. Setting the asra before each man and leaving the cakes on the table, she turned to the soldiers and smiled. "Thank you for your compliments, gentlemen. If you need anything else, please call." At that she turned and walked to the kitchen.

As she left, Kale returned in his black robe carrying the staff of the sovereign. It was wood with a pewter ball at the top with unique etchings on it—a man carrying a spear following a bear or perhaps it could have been the other way around. The two symbols alternated on the ball at its center ring and went all the way around it, the rest of the ball was polished smooth. As the staff moved across the room the ball rotated and it was hard to say who was meant to be the hunter or the hunted.

Kale moved to his seat and tapped the staff on the floor twice before sitting down. "Elders, these are the men who come to take our tithing to the king. We shall show respect to them as the king's agents, discarding any malice we have for what they do or why." Then addressing the captain, he said, "Sir, I have not yet received your names. Had I, I would have introduced you properly when Gorn and Malach arrived. I should have been more attentive earlier and asked then. If you would, Captain, please, introduce yourselves."

Johuocin stood and stepped into the light. "Excuse our appearance, gentlemen. It has been a long trail since we left the court and not a pleasant one. We need clean uniforms and a shave and look a bit unkempt to be presenting ourselves to the elders of any village, much less the fine men we have before us. However, it must be done as we have little time to waste due to our own delays." He paused as he stepped to the side of Ben and Merson. "I am Captain Orman Reglawr of the king's guard. These two are my appointees, Ouben Reglawr and Merson Bennidact. Yes, gentlemen, Ouben and I are brothers."

At that Malach shot a look of hatred at the men of the king's guard. "The king must place great trust in the two of you to allow two brothers to travel and collect his taxes together."

Ben jumped into the conversation. "Our father swore us into his service, and he is well aware that a Reglawr does not betray another Reglawr's faith or word."

"Which brings us back to the main topic," Johuocin broke in with concern as to what Ben may do if the Reglawr honor was attacked. "We will collect taxes for the quarter-mester starting at dawn tomorrow, right at this table. We will work until sunset, and thus it shall be until the tax for the village is collected. I expect your cooperation as the village elders, to ensure everyone pays their tax in the speediest manner so that we are not unduly delayed."

Kale looked to the other two elders and then back at the captain. "We've never been presented with this problem before, gentlemen. Just how do you propose we go about this?"

"Not my problem, Elder O'bourn," Johuocin pressed, knowing only he was in a hurry. He also had never been in this position and was not going to let it show. "However, I could send word to the king when I come to the next garrison and let him know how uncooperative you wish to be and why."

Kale O'bourn showed no worry over the statement as he shook his head in what could only be described as disappointment. His response indicated that he decided that it would not be such a problem. He was surely aware of the king's position on unwilling elders, as was everyone in the kingdom. They could be replaced, and the only way to do that was for the present elders to die.

"I will do this thing for my brothers, Malach and Gorn. You will collect your taxes starting tomorrow at dawn, but as soon as they are collected, you will leave this village."

"As was our intention, Elder." Johuocin confirmed.

Kale raised his staff high and screamed a shrill, lore-marred cry. "A-N-A-L-D-I-N-E-A-S."

The pewter ball began to glow an azure blue so brightly that you could not look upon it long. The images were so black as the ball spun, they seemed to be holes in time or space. Soon the entire room was filled with this light, and the images of the bear and the hunter were full size as they chased around the walls. It was still impossible to tell which was the hunter or the hunted.

Malach and Gorn both reached into their robes and pulled out medallions that hung around their necks. They glowed the same blue only fainter in light. The images on them were bear paws encircled by a spear. The two then stood and faced the soldiers.

Gorn said, "We all must leave Kale now. Go to your rooms upstairs, and do not come out until the first light of dawn. Of course you may do as you wish, but that is your choice."

Merson stared hard at the ball that sat on the top of the staff, and then looked to the captain. "Perhaps this is some kind of trickery, Captain. Or perhaps Kale wishes us to believe he is some kind of sorcerer?"

Malach stepped forward with his massive shoulders hovering over the top of Merson's head. "If you think we need to resort to trickery to intimidate you, little one, then that is your right. We have given our word as the council of elders, and this shall come to pass. Now, you may take our advice and retire to your chambers or do as you wish. That is up to you."

Johuocin, not wishing to take this conversation to a more heated point, said, "We will retire now if you would show us to our rooms. But I will expect an explanation in the morning."

Riessa appeared through the door from the kitchen, motioning for them to follow, and then turned to the staircase as they walked toward her, carrying the chest with them. As they reached the top of the stairs, Riessa lit a lantern on the wall there. She walked to the first two doors on the left and to the front of the building and opened them.

"These will be your rooms. If you need anything, please just knock on the floor and you will be answered. Our quarters are right below. Your animals have been taken to the stable next door and are being cleaned and cared for, and baths have been drawn for you. There is brandy on the table to help you sleep, and breakfast will be brought to you before dawn. If you have laundry, please leave it outside the door and it will be returned with breakfast." The whole time she spoke, the pleasant smile she displayed eagerly downstairs was absent. "Will there be anything else you need taken care of, gentlemen?"

Ben's eyes twinkled as he smiled at her with a flirtatious smirk. "A beautiful woman should not ask men such questions."

She returned his remark with bitter disgust. "There is a house six doors down for that, sir. If you are a man, perhaps you will brave this night and visit there. If you would not, then I suspect you are not man enough to make comments such as that to respectable women."

Johuocin was taken aback by Ben's indignant remark. "Miss O'bourn, I apologize for him as a soldier in my command, and I am embarrassed for him as my brother. If he could not openly see that you are a respectable young woman, he should at least show his appreciation for your hospitality. It will not happen again, and I ask, do not let it reflect on our future encounters."

The smile she had lost came back to her young face as she looked at the captain. "It's quite all right, Captain. I do understand the road you travel can get quite long and sometimes disorienting."

Merson had moved across the room to the window and opened the drape. An eerie blue light flooded the room. As quickly as her smile had returned, it left her when the drape was opened. She turned and left the room without further conversation.

The three men moved closer to the window to get a better look outside. The entire village seemed to be shrouded in the light, and the air itself seemed strained. Shadows moved through the light in a circle around the village, growing larger and larger until they began overlapping each other. Johuocin stepped back from the window and drew the shade. Still the strange light seeped in through the space between the window edge and the drape, making the men feel vexed and uneasy. It was then that the three men, in silence, decided to share one room.

"What do you suppose it is, Ory?" Ben was feeling the worst of it. Being young and having led the sheltered life of a sovereign's son was now starting to show full face.

"I don't know, Ben. I've never seen anything like it before. The only thing I do know is that it has something to do with Kale and his staff." This much even Ben had concluded, that and the fact that it was some kind of magic that they were unfamiliar with. "What do you make of it, Merson?"

"I don't know much of magic. My folk raised me to understand that a strong hand and a good hammer can shatter the skulls of your enemy or build great chambers to store your wealth. My memory of magic is limited to the old songs about the Eldwitch war, the war between the clans and the elven tribes. Only one song gives a clue to anything like this."

And then Merson began to recite the words in a low tone with a tic-toc tempo.

> As we stood upon the rock
> We hailed high to see the flock.
> The flock of elven shaft and feather,
> The flock of elven barb and tether.
> The rock repelled most every lance.
> On the rock we held our stance.
> Then the rock began to fly,
> From catapult that sent them high.
> Coming down on elven flesh,
> Spilling elven blood a'fresh.
> As we aimed for where they lurked
> An elven mage stood tall and smirked.
> As he chanted in midst of war.
> He brought about his elvish lore.

A sphere of blue began to form.
Our warriors began to swarm.
Leaving weapons all untended,
This is where our battle ended.
Our only choice was but to die,
And this is where our bones still lie.
Elven archers let go their shaft.
Elven mage and king then laughed.
On those hills our fathers lie
Left no choice but stand and die.

As Merson finished his song, his eyes looked moist and sad. It was clear that his attachment to the dwarves was more than just ancestry. The loss he felt was his own, not the loss of a people who shunned him as he took on a human appearance. At the sight of Merson's face, Johuocin began to feel the loss of his father, and his throat began to tense.

"Merson," Johuocin fought to restrain his own feelings, "perhaps we should fill Ben in a little on our situation."

Merson turned to the captain and began in a raspy tone that quickly but clearly was choked back. "Aye, Captain, the lad should know what lies ahead for us now."

"What are you two riddling about? You've been like this ever since the cave and the dwarf." Ben had a quizzical look on his face that would have expressed his confusion without a sound from his shaky voice.

Johuocin sat back to take advantage of his situation to learn more of the plan himself. "Merson, you explain it to him. I need to think."

"Aye, sit down lad. This might take a while." Ben sat down on the bed and braced himself by the post on the footing. It was clearly a shock to him to know that there was anything going on other than the fact that they were collecting taxes. Seeing the look on Merson's face grow stern in the reflection of the blue light as it seeped in from behind the drape made him more nervous, though he knew one had nothing to do with the other.

"Ben, your father has a plan to overrun the king. He swore you and Ory into service in an attempt to set him off guard. Your father instructed your brother to do what he can to gain the king's confidence. As you can see, your brother has succeeded beyond expectation so that he might not be suspected by the king to be a spy or mutineer.

"In a few weeks, after the winter solstice has reached its apex, we will be meeting with the dwarf chieftains in a conference to win their support on a southern front of attack. Granite Hammerhand was a scout for that front. The others your father has enlisted have done their job well in getting the messages to the Elder-king of the dwarves, Ironhand Pike. It will be important for you and your brother to call him by his dwarven name and title, Kinge Ischka Paok. If we are successful in our meeting, we will have the support of at least eight of the eleven clans. Full support is more than we can hope for or count on. Two at least we know we can count on. They are the tribes from the Irontree Mountains. They are the forest dwarves and known as the Ischtra Caszh. They are fierce in their battle tactics and love war above all else. They are, however, the two smallest tribes and are not on the best of terms with the others. The Ischtra Caszh live in the trees, as do the elves, and some of the tribes cannot appreciate their cultural differences. But they are great archers and scouts. They are rarely seen if they do not wish to be." Here

Merson paused for a breath and studied Ben's face for some kind of reaction, but nothing came, so he began again.

"There are four other tribes that we can at least give easy argument to, in order to enlist their aid. They are the Oschcra Cree, the Granite People, they are the tribes of Ischka Paok. They lost much of their trade and work when the new king came to power and refused their passage through Eldwain. They live in the caves of the Granite Hills, Angrat Sid …"

Ben stared. Now his eyes widened in amazement, and the shock of all of it began to sink in as Merson went on about the dwarf clans. Then he looked to his brother. "Ory, is this all true? Are we going to war with the king? Have we been sworn by our father only to turn in treachery upon our sworn sovereign? Does our father expect us to betray what he, himself, taught us? To 'live by our word for that is what makes us men.' Is that not what he taught us, Ory?"

"Yes, Ben." Johuocin was taken by surprise at Ben's objection to the assault. "But we must remember also the teaching of society itself. Blood first. First the support of family, then others."

Merson was gasping in awe that Ben objected at all to the whole situation. "Lad, I understand your shock of suddenly learning about all of this. You must understand that the king is nothing more than a spoiled tyrant. He does his people no good, and still he makes his demands upon them. Would you live under this for the rest of your life? Would you allow him to take your father's birthright because of your oath? If we don't stop him now, it will eventually come to that."

"Ben," Johuocin interrupted, "let me remind you of who you are. You are the second son of Sesnic Reglawr. You will be a prince of the Reglawr house if all goes well. Without that, all you are is one of the king's puppets. You are my brother, and friend above that. If you say we must betray our father, I will not have a brother."

"No, Ory, we are and always will be of the same blood," Ben said quietly, "and I will always honor the crest of the Griffin above all else. I was taken off guard and confused. Now we must be one in our efforts."

Just then the light from outside flashed and subsided. Merson went to the window and opened the shade to see the streets lined with torches. Then the blue ball of Kale's staff passed through the streets as Kale walked among the people there.

Johuocin could faintly hear what Kale was saying to them. "Be of heart. The time is not yet come, but we must complete a present task …" Then his voice faded, and nothing more could be heard.

"What do you make of it, Merson?"

"I don't really know, Captain, but I am sure we will get to the base of it before we leave. Tomorrow or the day after that."

CHAPTER 4

Riessa

That night the three men rested uneasily with the memory of the evening before. Kale's blue light continued in the back of their minds like a haunting menace, ready to swallow them. Ben had taken watch the entire night in reaction to the news of their intended revolution and his nervousness toward the light itself. All three men became fully alert when the sound of a knock came to their door just before dawn. They had all become anxious and unnerved by exposure to unexpected and unfamiliar elements. Ben, worst of the three, found his nerve bolstered by Merson's ability to maintain a face of calm.

Ben opened the door, and Riessa walked in, followed by two men carrying clean uniforms and buckets of hot water. Kale was not far behind the entourage, walking in with confidence as basins were being filled.

"Gentlemen, I assumed you would wish for a chance to refresh yourselves and put on clean clothing before you start your day." He had a sincere, calm manner about him and a very pleasant smile on his face as he gestured toward the water and clothing that was just delivered. "And if you would give your other laundry to my daughter, it will be returned clean before afternoon has arrived."

As Kale made reference to his daughter, Johuocin noticed that her eyes were locked on the captain's naked torso and stomach. Merson had also noticed and smiled with amusement as he tossed the captain a shirt to pull on.

Quickly pulling on the shirt, Johuocin turned his eyes back to Kale. "Yes, thank you for your consideration, sir. Not every town elder looks beyond the fact that we are tax collectors to see people with the same needs others have."

"Yes, well," Kale said with a touch of embarrassment in his face, "you might wish to thank my daughter for that. It was her idea to offer the opportunity before it was requested. Though I claim that service is my livelihood, sometimes I find it hard to be completely impartial. I am, in that respect, not without fault."

"I thank you just the same, sir." Then Johuocin turned back to Riessa to find her eyes fixed on some proclivity or curiosity, as she looked upon the captain. "And with that in mind, I must also offer you thanks, Riessa, for your kindness and thought."

Her eyes dropped immediately, as if she had just realized that anyone was talking to, or about, her. "Your thanks are well received, sir. You are most welcome." Her voice was soft and filled with self-gratification in the knowledge that she had the captain's attention. When she looked back to the captain and into his eyes, she concentrated there for what seemed an uncomfortable period of time to Johuocin. Then question fell over her face and she turned and walked out of the candle-lit room.

After watching his daughter leave the room, Kale, turned to the windows and pulled back the curtains as the sunlight threatened the horizon. Turning back to the captain, he looked into the captain's face quizzically. He excused whatever he was searching for and the others who had delivered the morning's unexpected service.

"Gentlemen, I don't wish to rush you, but the lines are already forming outside my front door to pay the king's tax. I would like to open my doors for the dinner hour if you could be done by then." Kale sounded preoccupied.

Johuocin moved to the window and looked out. The lines had not only started, but they were well down the street. He turned back to Kale. "Sir, it looks as if we are well ahead of expectations. We will stop an hour before sunset and resume in the morning if that will help you."

Kale narrowed his eyes and looked sharply at Johuocin/Captain Reglawr. "Please,

Captain, it would be preferred if you finish today, even if it goes into the dinner hour."

"Very well," Merson jumped in, "but we will have questions about last night when we are done."

"Yes, and I may have some questions of my own after talking to my daughter. If you are open, we will sit down to a late supper together and talk."

Kale sounded somewhat anxious and scolding, as he had the night before. Without giving a chance for response, Kale turned and walked out the door. The three heard his voice calling for Riessa as he descended the stairs into the inn.

"What do you suppose he would have questions about?" Ben was mumbling in drowsiness from his lack of sleep.

The three bathed and dressed in a hurry. Then Johuocin excused Ben from joining them in the inn so he could get some rest. The hot bath had taken any energy Ben had left, and Ben gratefully accepted the offer.

The rest of the day went very smoothly and quickly. No one argued the assessments or tried to make trouble of any kind. Though there were a few who could not meet the demand, it seemed that someone was always there, ready to assist with payment. Sometimes there was more than one, reaching into their pockets to pool their resources. The people of Rausche Laine were unexpectedly pleasant in view of the reaction to their arrival the night before. Merson and Johuocin exchanged many nervous glances that day, much to the amusement of Kale, who tended their every need for food and drink as the day wore on.

Ben finally came down from the room just after high noon and displayed his amazement at their progress. He had never seen an entire village line up to pay the king without showing any significant animosity toward the tax or its collectors. He had never felt so accommodated by anyone or anything in all his twenty-three years that he could recall, even in his father's house. It was an uncomfortable feeling for the young soldier. It is a very specific feeling: accommodation.

The entire register had been accounted for just before the dinner hour, and thirty-six names had been added throughout the day. As the last of the tax was collected and the streets cleared, the tensions of the three men had disappeared like fairy shadows in a spring breeze.

Kale had come back through the front door after following the last of his congregation out. He stepped into the back and returned momentarily. "Gentlemen," he announced, "if you would like to return to your room and freshen up before supper, Riessa will bring you some asra to help you relax while she prepares our food. It appears the dinner hour will be more quietly attended than expected. Many here left with empty pockets."

"Thank you for your hospitality, Sire O'bourn. We will take your gracious offer." Johuocin appreciated more the fact that he would have a chance to see Riessa once again.

"Aye, you have done more than necessary to make us comfortable." Merson's accent drew Kale's attention as if he had not noticed it previously. "It is sincerely my hope that our questions later will not offend you."

"And mine you, sir, and I do have questions." Kale gave all three a glance to assess their openness toward him. "Also my intention in this is not entirely unselfish. I wish to make my patrons, numbers as they are, a little more comfortable than they would be if you were in sight." At this he smirked and walked out of the room.

Johuocin caught Ben mumbling to himself. "Impish little twerp."

As the party relaxed in their quarters, the door opened and Riessa walked into the room. Her presence brought a bit of cheer to them all, but Johuocin could not turn his eyes from her. She had a very slight sway to her hips as she walked silently to the table and set down the asra and sweetbreads she had brought them. She looked to the captain and turned, walking to the door. Slowly she turned at the door and looked back to the captain once again.

"I do hope you are pleased," she said as she left, closing the door behind herself.

Merson turned to the captain, "Captain, I hope you're not feelin' what I think you're feelin'."

At that, the men looked at each other and sat quietly to enjoy the asra and sweetbreads.

As the night wore on, the men were not disturbed but for an occasional servant bringing in more asra or brandy. Ben proceeded to ask more questions of his father's plan to overthrow the Eldwain monarchy. Johuocin let Merson do most of the explanation, making a few comments himself as they touched on the few areas he was clear about. Johuocin was sure that Merson was blind to his ignorance of the situation, and he was able to learn most of what was necessary to maintain his facade as the captain. Just as they were finishing their conversation, a knock came at the door, and Kale walked into their quarters.

Kale was dressed in a blue and white frock, which was embroidered in gold at the seams in the design of leaves and vines with an occasional eight-point star to the inside or outside of the vines. Around his neck he wore a pewter chain, with a circular amulet hanging from it, depicting four figures in a crisscross pattern connected at their heads and running the inside of a pewter ring. The figures matched the head of his staff.

The chubby little man seemed oddly commanding and intimidating.

"If you would please," Kale announced, "dinner is waiting in the dining room at the table by the fire." At that he turned and walked out, not giving the men a chance to respond.

The men straightened their uniforms and joined Kale and Riessa, who stood behind their chairs before a fully dressed table with a large meal set out. The three men stood staring at the table in awe. Ben's mouth was agape. Each felt honored, confused, and underdressed all at the same time. Riessa was dressed much in the same fashion of her father. Kale had his staff with him and set it directly behind himself, where it stood without support. As the men joined them, each standing behind an empty chair, Kale spoke.

"Gentlemen, let me introduce myself with more accuracy. I am Kale O'bourn, first initiate of the fifth circle to the Master Oshan. I am also the bastard son of the Sea Gone King, Elbainen. My mother was a product of an Elven woman being raped by a sailor in at port. My grandmother moved inland after that, and my mother was raised here near the universities. My mother was a beautiful woman despite her origin and caught the eye of the king, so was wooed and bedded by him. I am the result. This is my daughter, Riessa, who, to the people of this area, is known as 'the Gifted One.' I apologize for not introducing myself in a better manner earlier but I did not see the need to do so, and now I feel it might answer some of your questions without your having to ask them."

"So, being the bastard son of the Sea Gone King makes you half-elf. Who and what is the Master Oshan?" Merson's curiosity stripped him of tact and decorum.

Kale motioned for the men to take a seat as he pulled out his daughter's chair. "Let's sit and eat, and perhaps I can answer as we relax and enjoy our meal."

As they all sat Kale began an evensong over the meal.

We thank the forces that exist
in our lives,
The forces that bring us
sustenance.
We thank the forces that exist
to be outside our lives,
The forces that show us our
fortitude.
We thank the forces that exist
to confuse us,
The forces that give us
understanding.
We thank the forces of chaos,
The forces that show us our
will.
We thank the forces of all
things,
For they are the creators that
serve us.

After he finished, Kale began passing platters of food around the table. The platters did not stop until everyone's plate was completely covered. It appeared that there were only five platters on the table, but some of their plates had up to eight different dishes on them. Johuocin counted only five platters but had seven dishes on his own plate. No platter had more than one dish on it, but as he counterchecked each dish from his plate to the platters, he found each one. The three men all looked very confused and disoriented. Kale looked at them with amusement as he started to answer Merson's question.

"Master Oshan is an arch-philosopher and the leader of our sect. It is our belief that all things are possible depending on your point of view to the subject."

Johuocin looked again at the table then to Kale. "Yes, I'm almost a believer myself." Kale's eyes twinkled a little and he smiled. "But does that make you an illusionist or priest?"

"Neither, it makes me a philosopher and believer. If I were an illusionist, I would see something different than you. But I see exactly what you see at this moment. If I were a priest, I might try to convert you to my way of believing, but I think you need to be what you are. Which brings me to my question of you, Captain; what are you?"

Johuocin looked at Kale with the curiosity deserved of such a question. "We are soldiers of the king's guard and tax collectors to the kingdom."

"No," Kale quickened, "a soldier belongs to his king, both in heart and loyalty. Merson is a man who belongs to no one, a man of perhaps lawful mind, but the law he follows is not that of the king. The young one, there," he pointed to Ben, "he is willing to be led wherever his brother leads and do as his brother expects. However, Captain, you are not so simple a case to see. My daughter says she cannot see your soul clearly. She is gifted, Captain, and can read the hearts of men, yet when she looks at you, all she can see is indecipherable entanglement. The clearest she saw you was last night when you met her. Then all she saw was confused anguish for a moment. So let me ask again, Captain, what are you?"

"I don't know how to answer that, Sire O'bourn. I know only me as I am in my soul. I don't know how Riessa is able to read a man's soul, and therefore I cannot know what you are looking for." Johuocin couldn't fathom what to say or what the consequences would be if they knew the truth of who he was. "I can tell you this: I am not in any way someone you need fear."

"Being a philosopher and a good judge of men has already told me as much as that. My daughter has also read in the other two your plans to overthrow the king, but you have intrigued my daughter, sir. This, before, has never confronted her. Still, she trusts you."

Johuocin looked to Riessa as she stared at him and did not glance away as she had each time in the past. He looked into her eyes and felt the regret for his deal with the wizard. He knew that no matter what he felt for her, he could not stand the thought of holding her close in another man's arms and that there was no other way. He also knew that he could not expose who he was just yet and had to find another explanation for her inability to see him or try to set her intrigue aside.

"Kale, I do not wish to lose your trust or bring on your scorn. However, I don't know how to explain your daughter's inability to see me. In actuality, I see a possibility that you could be a strong ally to us. At any rate we will be moving on in the morning, and you will not have us to contend with any longer."

"Captain, I too see a potential ally in you. I wish to strike a bargain with you. Let my daughter travel with you. It is her request. Another man will accompany her who will serve you well on your journey, while protecting my daughter. In return I will help you when I can." Kale was using a tone with his speech that was almost an order and not a request.

Merson was exasperated at what Kale was asking; he jumped in immediately with his objection. "No, we cannot let a woman travel with us at this time of year or with the duties we have ahead of us. She would slow us down, and it is too dangerous for her to travel with us now. That and how would we explain having her with us as we collect taxes from village to village?"

"I'm afraid that Merson is correct, Kale. There is no way we can allow this." Johuocin was fighting his own heart. There was nothing he wanted more than to take Riessa with him, yet he felt that nothing but trouble would come of it.

"Let me put this another way, Captain. As much as I hate to, if you don't take her I will send a message to the king himself informing him of your plot against his crown." This time Kale left no doubt that it was not a bargain or a request he was making. He had other things in mind. "Additionally,

Captain, Riessa could be very helpful in identifying the feelings of the people you come in contact with. The extra man also could only be an asset to you."

Merson stood up facing Kale with an accusing look, yelling "That's blackmail! Why would you put your daughter in that position? How could you even suggest to yourself that it's a possibility?"

Johuocin snapped at Merson, "Sit down!" Merson threw up his hands and shook his head as he did what the captain ordered.

Then Riessa called on Johuocin with a pleading look and squeaked out a very timid, "Please, Captain?"

Johuocin looked to Riessa, then to her father and back again. "I don't see where we have any choice. We can't afford to take a chance on letting your father notify the king. Not yet." The entire matter confused Johuocin, not sure whether he had given in so easily because of the impotent threat of Kale or the potent presence of Riessa.

CHAPTER 5

The Big Man

The next morning they gathered before dawn. Captain Reglawr, Ouben Reglawr, Merson, Kale, Riessa, and the man chosen by Kale to accompany them, Gorn.

As they stepped out of the inn, Ben asked a question that drew attention to the obvious. "Why are there only four horses?"

Merson and Johuocin looked up from pulling on their gloves. In the street in front of them they saw four horses, their two mules, and two more mules.

Gorn stepped toward the horses. He towered more than a full hand over the tallest of the four and was as wide as its chest. "I do not ride," he announced. He put his hand on the jaw of one of the horses and whispered something to it as he looked into its face.

"Ory, this will slow us more than traveling with the girl." Ben was appalled that Kale would expect them to not only travel with the girl but also with a man on foot—a man who appeared so large and slow that he would not even be able to travel the speed of an old mule. "Kale, you must convince him to ride or find a replacement."

Kale looked at the boy/man with a smirk on his face that made Ben detest him. "You needn't worry about Gorn. He will travel ahead of you and set your camps. If he slows you, leave him where he is lost." Kale turned then to Gorn and shared a laugh with him that angered Ben.

"That's exactly what will happen to both Gorn and the girl if they don't keep pace," Ben snapped out scornfully. Kale, Riessa, and Gorn all agreed with Ben. They had pompous grins on their faces as Gorn picked up a pack large enough for a mule and flung it on his back.

Gorn then turned to the captain and asked their destination. Johuocin told him it was Cragfare. Gorn turned back to the direction they had come from two days before. Without turning back, he began walking and said over his shoulder, "I will see you there."

Merson yelled after him, "I thought you were going to travel with us to protect the girl?"

"And so I shall, little one," he yelled back. "So I shall." And the big man just kept walking and laughing in his rich, deep voice.

"Kale," Johuocin turned to the elder, "I certainly hope all works out and we do become allies. Thank you again for your hospitality. We will return after winter solstice or at least send word of our progress."

"Travel safely and with care through Cragfare," Kale cautioned. "You will not be accepted well there. The folk are a less-than-virtuous lot."

Riessa stepped to her father and hugged him. Without a word she turned and walked to her horse, leaving Kale with worry on his face.

Riessa had dressed appropriately for their journey. She wore loose leather pants and tunic, with an oversized fur coat and hood that somewhat disguised that she was a woman. She wore a set of poniards strapped to her boots that looked well balanced. As she sat atop her horse, she reached into a pocket that was not evident in the cut of her pants and pulled out a set of riding gloves. Even in the oversized fur coat, she was small and inconspicuous. She appeared to be someone who could easily get lost in a crowd.

The four climbed on their mounts and turned to the direction of Cragfare. It was a clear, crisp morning as the sun came over the horizon. The group traveled in a disorganized fashion, with Riessa to the rear and center of them. Little was said among them as they traveled, and the mood was gloomy for such a good day. Time seemed to slow though they traveled well.

As the sun climbed high over their heads, they came upon Gorn sitting at the side of the road on a large boulder.

Johuocin stopped next to him. "Where have you been, Captain? I've been waiting for a while now."

"Waiting for what, Gorn? Are you lost?" Johuocin was being a little sarcastic, knowing that Gorn probably knew the area like the feel of his smithy's hammer.

"No, but you'll want to bury your collected taxes before going into Cragfare. They'll try to take it from you otherwise." Gorn looked at him sincerely. "The residents of this hamlet do not play when it comes to thieving, Captain. Many tax collectors have lost their lives here trying to defend their gold. Some have even lost it trying to give it away."

"It will take us hours to dig in this frozen ground, and we do not have the time. We'll have to take our chances."

"The hole is dug and waiting. It would take you no time to unload the chest and I will cover it and join you before you get to Cragfare."

Johuocin wondered how Gorn had gotten far enough ahead of them to dig the hole and be waiting. "Show me the hole, and then we will decide whether or not to take the gold."

Gorn led Johuocin off the road to a place behind some bushes. As he looked down Johuocin saw a hole that appeared fresh, and as though it had been dug with bare hands. "How did you have time for this, Gorn? Did you do this last night?"

"I did not know you were coming this way last night, Captain."

"Then did you do this alone? Or do you have an accomplice who intends to dig up the gold when we leave? I think we'll take our chances with the people of Cragfare, Gorn." Johuocin couldn't see how Gorn would have had the time to come so far and dig this hole by himself. As he looked back to the road, he saw how much Riessa looked like a thief and wondered about the two they now traveled with.

"Then, Captain, may I make another suggestion that may take you longer but might offer you more security?"

"What might that be, Gorn? Place the gold on your back?"

"No, Captain, just empty the chest and repack it with rock. Then pack the gold on your mules."

"That, I will do, Gorn. Then if the townspeople try to rob me, at least I will see who it is that wants to do us ill."

The two went back to the road, and Johuocin gave the order to repack the mules to Ben and Merson. Johuocin could see the relief in Merson's face. Merson too had a bad feeling toward Gorn's idea.

"Aye, Captain, it'll be done before you can see the sun move." Merson and Ben went to work.

It was not long before the group rode over a hill and could see Cragfare village. Gorn moved to Riessa's side and pulled out a staff that he had well concealed inside of his coat. It was the largest staff any of the three had ever seen. The length was about normal but it was at least three inches thick, and Gorn's massive hands fit comfortably around it. Riessa and Gorn fell to the rear of the mules and stayed there as they entered Cragfare.

The group stopped in front of the first inn they came to. A large wooden spoon hung over the door, and the handle was carved into the shape of a crimson faery soaring into the air. Over the door was roughly carved "The Crimson Faery," and a bloodstained broadsword was mounted to the front of the door.

Johuocin looked around him and saw people standing in the shadows of the town buildings, all watching to see what they do. "Merson, Ben, you stay with the animals. Gorn, Riessa, and I will take the chest inside." At that Gorn untied the chest and put it under one arm, holding his staff in the other hand.

As the three walked into the darkness of the inn, they let their eyes adjust to the dim light. Riessa kept her hood on as they walked through the room. They took a table that was in the corner. There were no windows in the room and only four other people in the place. Gorn set the chest down heavily and leaned his staff on the table next to his chair. The bar was directly across the room from them, and the innkeep stood behind it. Only ten tables were in the room and appeared to have been turned over and abused quite often. Johuocin motioned for the innkeep to come over. As he crossed the room, he stopped at the table with the three men sitting at it and whispered something to them. One of them got up and left the inn.

As the innkeep reached their table, he smiled with stained and broken teeth. "What can I get for you gentlemen today?" His tone was sugar sweet and untrustworthy. His appearance was that of someone who was no stranger to trouble, and he had a dagger tucked in his belt.

Johuocin finished sizing the man up, looked at Gorn, then back to the innkeep. "First some hot asra with brandy for us and my two men in the street. Then send for the town elders. Tell them I am Captain Orman Reglawr, and I have come to collect the tax."

"Well, sir, the asra I can give you and rooms if you wish. I can even get you some stable space. As for the town elders, I am afraid they are incapacitated at the time. It seems they had to leave us abruptly here about three days ago."

"Where are they?"

"It seems they reside in the skull yard on the other side of town. It was their wish. Offered the choice of two things, they said they'd rather die first." The man got a large grin on his face. "It seems that it happens to those appointed as elder in this place quite often."

"Then perhaps you could send word to the fair citizens of Cragfare that the tax will be collected here first thing in the morning."

"Captain, I could not do that. That is the job of the town elders, and I am just Corby the innkeeper."

"Then perhaps, Corby, I as the king's representative should name you the temporary elder of this town until the king himself can deal with it." A look of fear passed over Corby's face as Johuocin spoke those words. "You don't have to worry though, Corby. Nothing will happen to you while we are in town."

"No, Captain, that may not be necessary. Perhaps all I have to do is put out the word taxes will be collected."

"While you do that, tell the people of this fair village that I do need volunteers for the elder's position. I will not charge the new appointees a tax this quarter-mester, and anyone wishing to be town elder simply need not be here to pay the tax and I will take that as their submission to the post."

"Aye, I will indeed pass that message, Captain. I don't know, though, that you'll have any volunteers."

"I will be looking so forward to finding this out, Corby. But take heart, if I have too many submissions I will have to name you as elder because I like you. But don't tell anyone that because it would seem that I were playing favorites."

"Indeed I won't tell a soul, Captain. Believe me when I say that, I wouldn't want them thinking I were being favored by you."

"I truly believe that, Corby. Somehow I just know you'll succeed in getting my message across to the rest of the village."

As the innkeep left the table, Gorn laughed a booming laugh. "Well done, lad.

I truly think your tax will come quickly and thoroughly. That is unless the man has designs on the position he was offered." And again he laughed.

Gorn's laugh was so hearty it lightened the mood for Johuocin. The cheerlessness of the day had soon dissipated like smoke in the wind.

Corby returned with the asra as requested, nervously sat it down, and left. On his way back to the bar, he stopped and spoke with another of the men at the table across the bar. One of the men went to the bar with Corby and picked up two more mugs of the hot drink and took it out the door with him and did not return.

As Johuocin, Riessa, and Gorn warmed themselves by the fire, Riessa took off her coat and hood to reveal only a hooded cloak that did not reveal her face or gender. Gorn excused himself and went outside. A few minutes later Merson walked through the door.

"A bit dark in here, wouldn't you say, Captain?" Merson spoke quieter in his next words. "The two that left the inn a while ago are back. They're across the street with a few others, maybe five or six more. I don't know what yet, but, they're up to somethin'."

Johuocin saw a look in Merson's eyes he had not seen before. He wished he hadn't seen it now. "I'm going to find out from the innkeep where there is a stable. I want you and Riessa to leave here in that direction with the mules and your mounts. I saw a cabin just to the north of the village. When nobody is watching, you should head that way. If necessary we will meet you there. If not I'll send Ben after you." Then Johuocin yelled for the innkeep. "Corby!"

As Corby approached, he asked, "Where is the stable you spoke of? And also we'll need a couple of rooms for the night."

"Indeed, Captain, I've already been making arrangements for accommodations for you and your party, sir. The stable is just down to the end of the block and left. Do you want me to make, err, get someone to take your stock there?" The grin had returned to Corby's face.

"No, these two will take care of it. They know what I need from the packs."

"Aye, if that's what suits ya. The stable is next to the smithy's shop. Can't miss the smoke there."

"Thank you for your help, Corby, and keep in mind that we would like the rooms next to each other."

"Tonight you'll be so close to each other ya won't even feel the walls." At that Corby chuckled to himself and walked away.

Johuocin looked at Merson and motioned to the door. "Be careful." After Merson nodded, he added, "And quick."

Merson took a step and stopped, turning back to the captain. "Do you think they're after the chest?"

"And us, Merson. Now go."

Riessa was putting on her coat as she walked to the door. Her outfit seemed to fit into the surroundings of the inn. Johuocin was still not sure how far he could trust Gorn but had the feeling he was about to find out. He was also a little taken back by Riessa's appearance but couldn't find a way to completely mistrust her as he had Gorn.

Gorn and Ben came into the inn. Ben had brought the crossbows that belonged to him and his brother. They were cocked and ready.

"Put those aside. We don't want to bring any trouble that isn't here."

Just as Gorn spoke his next words, the men came from across the street and filed into the inn in groups of three. Their number had grown to nine. They sat in locations that cornered Johuocin, Ben, and Gorn. "I would keep them close, Captain."

Corby came to their table and put down more asra. "Could I get ya some grub, gentlemen? You must be a bit touched with the hunger by now."

"No thank you, Corby. We'll wait for our friends."

As Corby stepped away from the table, one of the other men stepped up. "That chest looks a little burdensome, lord. Could my friends and I take it and watch after it fer yas?"

"No, I think we can handle it, thank you." Johuocin stared at the man's face with contempt, wishing he had taken the chance of burying the chest when he had it.

"In a town like this, lord, that mi't be a bad choice of words." The man leaned back on his heels a little and moved his hands to his belt.

"You seem to be very helpful in letting me in on the dangers of this town. I'm Captain Orman Reglawr, and your name is …?"

"The tax takers just call me friend, Cap'm."

"I don't seem to remember that name on my list, Friend. Perhaps you could tell me your given name."

"That depends on what ya mean, Cap'm. People give me names all the time." Then he pulled out his dagger and held it pointing at Johuocin. "The one I'm known 'round here as is Sticker."

When he said Sticker, the two men that were sitting with him jumped up, pulling out their long swords, and stood next to Sticker. "Now, Cap'm, just push the chest over here."

As he was finishing his words, the man to his left fell face first in front of them with a poniard in his back. As they looked to the direction from where the knife came, they saw a small-cloaked figure with a whip in one hand and another poniard in the other. Riessa. As the figure stepped through, Merson rushed in, firing a quill at one of the men to the left of Johuocin and Ben, about to attack Ben in the same way.

As Johuocin looked back to Sticker, Sticker lunged at Johuocin/Captain Reglawr, only to be met in the face by Gorn's staff with a force that knocked him back ten feet, leaving his face bleeding.

The man to Sticker's right struck at Gorn with his long sword, slicing into Gorn's left arm badly. Gorn became enraged when he felt the strike and began swinging his staff wildly and breathing with such intensity that saliva flew from his mouth in every direction as he turned his head.

Corby turned, running toward the bar. Riessa caught him with her whip around his waist and pulled back as quickly as she struck, sending him spinning to the floor, where he laid like a lump of confused flesh.

The other five rushed to the defense of their accomplices, as Ben let a quill fly into the right shoulder of Sticker, who was up once again and moving toward his brother. Bleeding heavily from his shoulder and face, Sticker fell to his knees, letting go of his knife and holding his shoulder.

With a wild swing, Gorn crushed the skull of another man that he wasn't aware had struck anything or anyone. As the man went reeling across the tavern, slamming into the bar, another man, screaming, struck at Gorn's back with a dagger, leaving a long, deep gash from Gorn's shoulder to hip. Gorn opened his mouth wide, letting out a loud animal like growl. He turned to see the one who struck him and slammed the end of his staff into the man's chest. As the staff met its target, the sound of bones being crushed was plain to the ears of everyone in the room, and the man fell back, passing out in pain.

Merson took advantage of the momentary diversion that drew everyone's attention and ran to the front door and barred it. As he knocked another quill, he felt the sharp, biting sensation of a knife landing in his own left shoulder. He turned to see a quill from Ben's crossbow bury itself in his adversary's throat, leaving the man to drown in his own blood. Two of the three men still standing closest to the kitchen door, turned to escape. There they found Riessa in the doorway, striking her whip around the man to her left. As she drew him close and buried her poniard in his belly, the other pushed by her and through the door. Johuocin let a quill go, piercing the man's left leg, slowing his escape but not preventing it.

The last man, seeing no escape, lunged toward Johuocin to do what damage he could in his hopelessness. He caught Johuocin/ Captain Reglawr's left thigh as Gorn brought him to the floor with his staff. Ben rushed in holding a long sword to the man's throat as he rolled over.

When the fighting was over, Ben gathered the last of the surviving offenders into one corner. Corby, who had balled himself up and sat in the corner after Riessa's whip got him, helped Sticker and the others to the corner, where Gorn's last attacker lay breathing roughly and still unconscious.

Riessa was trying to calm Gorn and tend his wounds while Johuocin and Merson helped each other. Johuocin could not get the bleeding in his leg to stop and was feeling weak.

Ben went to the rear door and barred it. He knew they would need some time before they were ready for visitors. As he was heading back to the tavern area, he saw some movement in one of the back rooms behind a half-draped doorway. He decided to investigate and quietly moved along the wall until he reached the doorway. Standing next to the doorway, he drew his long sword and held it up.

In one quick motion he turned and flung open the drape, yelling, "Don't move! I'll slice you to stew meat!"

Merson and Gorn came running into the kitchen to find a flustered Ben red in the face as he looked into the next room at their mules and horses. Gorn once again broke into a booming laugh that shook the inn, and Merson joined in.

Ben turned and stormed past them, saying, "Piss off!"

That just made Gorn and Merson laugh even harder.

Ben entered the tavern still red, with Gorn and Merson talking about mule stew and how truly it must be a taste treat for Ben to want it so badly. Johuocin and Riessa, catching the drift of what must have happened, began laughing with the two jokers. As the laughter continued, Ben too eventually saw the humor. Letting go of his pride and embarrassment, he joined in.

The interior of the tavern had become a sticky mess that reeked of blood and death. The four remaining assailants became three as the man who last attacked Gorn died in a final shudder of pain, convulsions, and suffering that sent chills through everyone and caused Corby to beg for the man's death.

Johuocin was feeling the weakness of the captain's body as it continued to lose blood and knew he would have to vacate it before he passed out and found himself trapped in a sleeping victim, and even more useless than he might be if he were a wandering spirit.

Riessa was able to slow the bleeding, and soon it would be stopped but not soon enough to keep the captain's weakness from overcoming him. He was hoping that Riessa would interpret her insight into the captain as delirium.

Riessa set Corby to cleaning up the blood, with Gorn watching over him, as she went to the kitchen to fix something for them to eat.

Gorn unbarred the front door and took a look outside. The streets were deserted. Two by two he took the six dead bodies and threw them in a pile outside the front door, as a warning to those who would wish to try their own luck. Then he joined Riessa in the kitchen.

As Johuocin felt the captain slip away, he left the body and went to the kitchen. Gorn was nowhere to be found. Ben entered the kitchen with a worried look on his face and announced that his brother had finally slipped into sleep.

Riessa walked over to him and put her hand on his face to comfort him. "Don't worry about him. He'll be all right." Then she went back to cooking.

"Where is Gorn?" Ben asked as he looked around.

"He went out. He had something to take care of."

"Don't you think that's a little foolish? This town isn't going to be too friendly if they find him alone."

"Don't bother with Gorn. He can take care of himself. He has a special need that we can't help him with."

"What might that be? Apologies."

Riessa became angry with that and scornful with Ben. "Don't speak badly of

Gorn. He doesn't kill to defend those he doesn't like, and I think he killed plenty for you and your brother today. Just let him do what he must without question."

At that Ben walked out of the room.

Johuocin wanted to know for himself what Gorn's needs were and went out of the inn to find him.

As he went through the town he saw no sign of Gorn and caught no sight of the town's occupants unless he went into the homes there. The only conversations that Johuocin heard were about the events in the tavern earlier that day. They were stretched way out of proportion. He heard of ten soldiers coming out of nowhere to the aid of their captain, killing all but one of Sticker's band. Everyone but Sticker was dead, and he was wounded. No one knew exactly how many men the captain had waiting outside of town to come to his aid. They all were sure that it was a special detachment sent by the king to collect the tax that hadn't been collected for so long and to retrieve the tax money Sticker stole in the past. The one thing that reassured Johuocin about Gorn was the tale about the giant man who seemed to be the captain's personal guard.

Seeing no sign of Gorn, Johuocin finally decided to return to the inn. On his way he began feeling the guilt of using the captain's body again but couldn't figure a way of giving it back just yet without ruining everything or causing alarm. And now he had put the captain in a position where physical harm came to him, something that could have killed him.

As he arrived back at the inn, Johuocin spotted something strange. There was a shadow being cast in the moonlight that looked like a bear at the back door of the inn. As he came closer he saw Gorn tapping lightly at the door and the shadow was gone. The door opened, and Gorn went in. Johuocin followed.

Riessa had opened the door. "Are you better, Gorn?"

"Yes, thank you. Did anyone notice I was gone?"

"Ben."

"Did he ask? What did you tell him?"

"Yes he asked. I told him nothing."

"I am glad to have a friend such as you are, child."

CHAPTER 6

The Tithing of Sin

As the captain lay unconscious that evening, Johuocin roamed through the inn listening to the conversations of the other members of his party. Everyone was at a loss as to what would happen the next day. If he could get a message to them, somehow, about the feelings of the village folk or if the captain would wake long enough, he could give them some instructions. However, it did not look hopeful that the captain would wake any time soon.

Riessa had been talking to Gorn about the captain and the way she could see into his dreams as he slept. He was having thoughts about his father's instructions to him and seemed to be thinking about the cold of a past storm. All she could get from him that was important was that he needed to collect enough coin to support the needs of his father's effort. She thought that his dreams revealed a different persona than when he was awake. His dreams were more troubled, while his actions showed more confidence and comfort.

Ben was concerned about Gorn's whereabouts earlier in the evening. He was wondering if Gorn were part of another group who wanted to steal the tax money. He thought that would have given him plenty of reason to fight as he did earlier in the day. Merson tried to reassure Ben that he felt Gorn could be trusted even if he couldn't figure out where he had gone. Merson's big question was, "Where did Riessa become so skilled at such a young age as a female?" Both men laughed a little at the way she implied that she was above reproach as a lady back at the O'bourn House.

Johuocin tried to decide what it was he saw when Gorn returned to the inn that evening. All he could discern was confusion.

Ben had tied and gagged the three prisoners they had and moved them to the upstairs room where his brother rested. There he sat with his brother and watched them.

Merson had tried to sleep. The combination of his wounded shoulder and the tensions of the day prevented him, so he joined Ben.

As Johuocin roamed the inn, he entered a room where he should not be, but was unable to leave. Not because he was restrained by any power but only because he was taken by temptation for what was there. Riessa was bathing away the events of the day. She was more beautiful than he had ever seen her. Her skin was the color of alabaster. Her breasts were full and smooth, though they matched her size. Her hair was pulled up, and her neck was exposed. Her eyes more blue than he had experienced before. He yearned to touch her soft skin and feel the moistness of her lips. A pang of wanting ran through him as he was unable to turn and go from her. He cursed himself for his deal with Bolac, the wizard. He cursed himself for his trespass into the wickedness of wanting revenge. He cursed himself for coming to this room and to the temptation he knew he could not satisfy.

Without knowledge he moved closer to Riessa until he was next to her. She sat bolt upright in the tub of warm, clear water and covered herself with her arms and hands, looking around as though she knew he were there but could not see him. He moved away quickly, and her fear seemed to pass. Quickly and cautiously Riessa concluded her escape to relaxation, covering her body as she stepped from the tub.

Johuocin's thoughts ran wild as Riessa dressed herself. He thought of his deal with Bolac and how much he wanted revenge for his father's death. He thought of how much he wanted Riessa. Then he thought of the words he had heard his father speak a thousand times when he spoke of the poor deeds all men enact.

"There is a price to pay for everything."

Johuocin did not move as Riessa left the room.

As Johuocin sulked, he moved back to the captain's room. There he waited for any sign that the captain was going to wake. Just before dawn Merson convinced Ben to fetch a bedroll and get some sleep before the day overtook them without rest. Ben took his advice on the promise that Merson would wake him if Ory woke.

When the sun came through the window, the captain's eyes started to open, and he looked around the room. When he realized he didn't know where he was, the captain tried to sit up but was too weak. Johuocin moved back into the captain, knowing he would need to be quick and wary of the captain's consciousness.

"Merson?"

"Ben!" Merson shouted, startled by the captain's voice. Ben sat upright, and both men rushed to the captain's side.

"Merson?" Johuocin could feel he did not have much time before the captain fell back to unconsciousness. "I need you to collect the taxes here."

"But Captain, they'll not pay it without force."

"Yes, I know. Do we have any prisoners?"

"Aye. Corby, Sticker, and another they call Jundog."

"Good. Send out Corby. Tell him we have soldiers coming into town and if we have not collected enough tax to make up for the trouble they have caused in the past then yesterday's episode will look like we were being merciful."

"Who's to say Corby will cooperate?" Ben was feeling the sting of being ignored and expressed as much in his tone.

Johuocin corrected that. "You are. Be sure Corby understands that if he doesn't relay our message properly then we will make a deal with Sticker, his life for Corby's. Then, to let them see we are serious, brand this Jundog across the chest with a hot sword in front of them." Johuocin felt this was a kindness compared to what they would have done to one of them.

Johuocin left the captain just as he was about to pass out again. With the last of his energy, the captain looked at the two men with pleading eyes and whispered, "Ben …"

They both looked at the captain and back to each other.

Ben looked back at the captain. "It's one hell of a gamble, Merson. Do you think it will work?"

"We haven't got much chance of getting out of here alive either way if it doesn't."

Merson walked over to Corby and kicked him to wake him up. Corby's eyes opened wide as he felt the hard leather of Merson's boot. Gagged and bound, all he could do was fire a glaring look of hate toward Merson.

Ben walked over to Corby and squatted down close to his face as Corby lay there. "Listen to me, weasel. We are going to let you out of here. You are then going to pass a message to the rest of the people in this village." Ben then stood and walked over to the fireplace; pulling out his long sword, he buried the blade deep in the coals of the fire.

"You are going to tell them about the soldiers that will be coming into this town if they don't satisfy our tax. Also you will tell them they must satisfy us for the trouble this town has caused and the tax that was not collected in the past. If they do not do this, the soldiers will come and make yesterday look like the courting for a maid's favor. Everyone will suffer."

Merson saw the contempt on Corby's face as he listened to Ben. He saw nothing but rebellion in his eyes. "I don't know that the little scrag is willin', Ben. Perhaps we'd better show him, er, explain to him what we mean."

At that Merson walked over to Jundog and sat him up with his back against the wall. Grabbing Jundog's tunic, he ripped it open in the front and pulled it back over his shoulders to expose his bare chest.

"You see," Ben started again, "if you don't do this for us, we will ask Sticker to go out and bring you back to us. He will want to do this because he doesn't want to die, at least, not the way that we would kill him." Ben walked over and took the sword out of the fire. Walking toward Jundog, he studied the sword. "You see, Corby, we believe that anything done well takes time and thought." He watched Corby as his eyes widened in disbelief of what he was about to see. Then Ben kicked Sticker to be sure he was awake and watching. Sticker's eyes opened. Ben reached down with his dagger and cut the gag from Jundog's mouth and slowly moved the flat of the sword toward his chest.

Fear filled the eyes of the bound men. Jundog began pleading that turned into screams as the steel met his skin.

"No, please, AAAHHHHHHH ..." The screams died as Jundog passed out from pain, breathless and limp. The faces of the other two were filled with fear and disgust as the odor of burnt flesh and searing hair filled the room.

Riessa and Gorn came rushing into the room as they heard the screams. Ben turned to Sticker. "Now you make sure that Corby knows that you don't want to die like that." Sticker looked at Corby, leaving no mistake in Corby's mind that he would cooperate to the fullest extent.

Riessa left the room, sickened by the smell. Gorn viewed the situation with disgust. He looked at Corby, "If you cause them the need to do this again, I will personally find you and tear out your tongue for not saying the right words." Then he turned and left the room.

Merson looked at Ben as he excused himself and left the room. "I'll be back to help you move Corby out."

Merson left the room to find Riessa and Gorn waiting in the hallway.

"What are you two doing in there?" Gorn sounded angry but not surprised.

"Carrying out orders. The captain woke up long enough to tell us he wanted Corby released."

Riessa looked at Merson in confusion. She could see that Merson wasn't telling a lie, but, when she saw the captain she could tell he had no thought of Corby in his soul. "For what purpose?"

"To tell the village to pay their tax."

Gorn looked at Merson in disbelief. "Then are we to buy our way out of here when we have the coin? If we get the coin."

Merson motioned toward Riessa, "She can see inside our thoughts. Have her explain it to you." Merson didn't like what they had done any more than anyone else, but any chance of leaving Cragfare was better than no chance. Merson went back into the captain's room.

Johuocin looked at the captain and wondered if he would wake again soon. He had to leave for a while and did not wish to come back to chaos or have to explain the captain's actions as his own. And he did not know how Riessa would react if she could see into the captain one minute and not the next while he were awake.

Merson and Ben led Corby to the back door of the inn. There they untied his hands and shoved him out the back door, where Johuocin stepped into his body. As he moved out into the street, he acted as though he were disoriented. He was pulled aside almost immediately as he reached the other side of the street and carried into a storefront there.

"Corby." The man looked at him and shook him. "It's me, Stosic. Corby? Corby!"

Johuocin/Corby just looked at him. "Huh?"

"Corby? How many are there? Can we take them?"

Johuocin looked at the man in confusion and doubt. "The cap'm said 'e was early. Said the troops should'a been 'ere by now. Said if 'e don't c'lect the tax 'e should 'ave and enough to make up fer the others that didn't get it, 'e's goin' to 'ave the troops destroy the town and everyone who lives 'ere. Already killed Sticker an' mosta 'is men. We need to tell folk 'round 'ere. Maybe if we just dump it on the front steps they'll let us alone." Just then someone walked in the front door, and Johuocin/Corby jumped like he was afraid of something. "They're comin' after me. Quick, get out, save yourself and tell the others." Then Johuocin feigned passing out.

"Corby? Corby, it's just Earl." After shaking Corby and getting no response, Stosic relayed to Earl what Corby had said and sent him to tell the others.

Johuocin/Corby lay there on the floor quietly with Stosic sitting beside him, waiting for word of what was happening. From time to time another person would come in to confirm what they had heard. Some even reported the sighting of a few scouts from the large number of troops farther behind. Stosic would tell the story, and they would leave. As high sun approached Earl returned to tell Stosic that a chest had been placed on the steps of the inn and people of Cragfare had started emptying their pockets and purses into it. Hearing this, Johuocin left Corby's body and waited to hear Corby babble like a lunatic for a while.

Corby sat up at once. Seeing Stosic next to him and that he was in the store across the street from the inn, Corby sat startled. "How did I get here? What time is it?"

Stosic looked at Corby like he'd gone mad. "I pulled you in here out of the street. You were mad with fear. You told us about the taxes and it's bein' taken care of."

"What did I tell you? We have to pay them now. We have to hurry." Corby just kept rambling in fear.

"Corby, we're doin' that."

Just then someone came up behind Corby and hit him over the head, knocking him out cold. "It's fer his own good."

Johuocin left to go back to the inn.

*

Merson watched from the captain's window as droves of people came and dumped money into a chest that was placed there. Then he walked away from the window and down to the tavern, where Riessa and Gorn waited.

"I don't know how the captain knew, but it's working. They just keep putting money into the chest out front."

Riessa shook her head in bewilderment. "I've seen some of them. They're afraid of what their past behavior has brought down around their heads. Their souls are cold with fear."

Gorn sat quietly meditating and reflecting, but his concentration was broken by Riessa's words and he spoke. "Fear feeds on itself. The people of this village have been afraid of each other for a long time. It's easier to be afraid of outsiders. The captain's a smart man; he knew that without having any information from the villagers. Just from the reputation of this place and the welcome they gave us."

Riessa gazed off in the distance of another time. "You sound more like my father all the time, Gorn. You shouldn't spend so much time with him."

That brought a smile to both their faces.

"Has the captain woke again?" Johuocin entered the room as Riessa spoke to Merson.

"No, and he seemed disoriented the last time he did. He was askin' where he was and how he got here. It was hard on Ben. He's afraid he's going to lose him."

Johuocin felt the guilt of taking the captain's life from him. It had already been five days. He knew one day he would have to give it back to him, and the payment for Johuocin's time using the captain would be high. Johuocin also felt the guilt of the worry he was causing Ben. He knew the worry of losing a brother must be great, and Ben was too young to go through such grief. Johuocin knew he would pay that debt before he left the captain completely.

Johuocin went back to the captain's side before any more payment came due. He waited patiently there for the captain to wake. Ben also waited as the hours passed into night.

The days were getting shorter as the winter solstice was only seventeen days away, the one day that their schedule was up against. He also knew that the captain would have to recover for the meeting with the dwarf chieftains. In the captain's confusion, he would heal more slowly. He had no idea what had happened to him, and his spirit would not be in tune with the healing. He would not be able to fight for his life. The only thing that Johuocin could think to do would cost him some valuable time for gathering information. It would also separate him from Riessa. It would also be his payment to Ben. He entered the nocturnal detachment of the captain's sleep.

CHAPTER 7

Etiquette

As Johuocin/Captain Reglawr woke, he found himself in a brighter, larger room with whitewashed plastered walls, Ben sitting at the foot of his bed, sleeping in a tall, hard chair. As he looked around he saw finely painted pictures on the wall and a pitcher and mug on the stand next to his bed.

"Ben," he scratched out, "how about something to wet my throat?"

Ben woke up instantly, yelling his brother's name in excitement. "Ory! Ory, you're awake. You're all right."

"Yeah, I'm fine, now get me some water. I can hardly feel my throat." Johuocin was enjoying Ben's excitement at having his brother back.

Ben poured his brother some water and held the mug to his lips so he could drink. Johuocin didn't feel that weak but let Ben continue, knowing Ben was likely doing so as he woke sporadically in delirium.

"How long have I been out?" Johuocin asked, having no idea how long he'd slept or where they were.

"It's been five and a half days from the first night of our arrival."

"Where are we? What happened in Cragfare?"

"Ory, you wouldn't believe what's happened since you woke that next day. Do you remember waking?"

"Vaguely," Johuocin offered.

"I'll fill you in, in a minute. I'm going to get Merson and the others, just in case I miss anything." Ben rushed out of the room before Johuocin had a chance to answer.

When he returned, everyone was with him looking well rested. Riessa looked more beautiful than ever to him. Johuocin could not help but picture her as she sat in the tub that night. He could not resist the fire he felt in his soul. They all gathered around him, smiling.

"Merson, what's happened in the last five days? I don't even remember leaving Cragfare."

"Aye, Captain, you've been quite the worry for us all. We weren't sure you'd be joining us again." A smile found its way across Merson's face. "Welcome back."

"Thank you very much, but no one is giving me any information here. What's going on?" Johuocin went on anxiously.

"First I might warn you that you talk in your sleep. It seems you've lived an entirely different life in the dream world. You even mentioned seeing Riessa in a very compromising situation." Merson looked over to Riessa grinning, almost laughing. "The thing is she remembers feeling that someone was watching her." Riessa blushed, turning her face away and to the window, as he announced the last part of his statement.

Seeing her embarrassment, Ben and Merson chuckled a bit, until with a look, Gorn made it clear he was not appreciative of their amusement.

Johuocin was starting to worry what else he may have said. "So, now that you have all had a chuckle over my dreams, can you tell me what has happened and how we got where we are and maybe even mention the name of the place?" Johuocin felt his face warming up as he remembered that night.

As the smirk left Merson's face, he began the story of their arrival to the present. "We are in the hamlet of Skillcore. If there is something this place does not have, I don't know what it is. We left Cragfare two days after we arrived with what I believe was the bulk of their coin. The instruction you gave us the first time you woke was effective beyond our greatest hope. There were very few that found the nerve to test our ability or doubt our word about the soldiers coming into the village. Those that doubted us felt the brunt of Gorn's staff or Ben's crossbow.

The smith even supplied us with a wagon to move you.

"That night we found ourselves in the village of Almire. The people there paid their tax begrudgingly but without trouble. The next day we stopped in two small farm communities without problems except for one little thief who thought he would lighten our load. Gorn snatched him up and scared the thievery right out of him. We dropped him off at the monastery of Chinon on our way by. The monks there took him in and locked him in a room. We heard him screaming to be let out as we left. The next day we found ourselves here. This place is not on any of our charts, maps, or tally sheets. It is only by chance that we found it. We were taking a shortcut across the plains to Anshire when we came upon it. We wanted to get there quickly to get to a healer for you. When we first arrived, we thought this was Anshire, but when we asked to see the town elders, they said Prince Harishe employed none. We asked, then, to see the prince, and they have been catering to our every need trying to get you healthy enough for an audience with him. Apparently he will only speak to the leader of any group, and if you had died he would then speak with me. That is where we are now, and how we came to this time and place."

"This is all well and good, Merson, but do you realize that we have less than twelve days to solstice and I have very little of the knowledge I'll need to make it through that audience? If I do talk to this Prince Harishe, what am I to talk about? He is not in our charts and tallies. Am I going to tell a prince that he must pay taxes to the king? He apparently has gone to great trouble to remain undetected. I don't know if he will wish to be an ally to overthrow the king, or even if we should chance exposing that plan. Don't you believe that a prince will feel he is in line for the throne?"

Gorn spoke up here. "Harishe is definitely a foreign prince, Captain, judging from those we've met here. What about a supply source, Captain? If you have as many people as you think you'll have fighting this war, you'll need as many sources as you can find. And this one will have a good location."

"Aye, Captain, and it might also give you a chance to learn a little of dwarves. The place is teemin' with 'em."

Then Riessa caught his attention. "And you need a little diversion, Captain. If you don't relax a little you'll die of terminal responsibility."

Then, Ben had to put his copper in the kitty. "Ory, we do need some time to recover. Gorn took a couple of good whacks in Cragfare. Not to mention Merson and yourself."

It seemed everyone was begging to stay but him. He knew Ben was young and could use some fun. He himself did need to recover a bit before he could move on anyway. He didn't know why in the world he found himself giving in, but he did. "All right, two days," he said very seriously. "Merson you'll still have to prepare me for our meeting with the chieftains while we are here. And you, Ben, need to stay out of trouble."

"As for the two of you," he added, gesturing to Gorn and Riessa, "I have no control over your actions. You don't have to go when we leave if you wish to stay longer."

Excitement crept across the faces of Riessa and Ben. The other two just smiled in agreement with Johuocin's decision.

After everyone left the room, Johuocin lifted the bedcovers to check the captain's wound. It looked remarkably good by comparison to what he remembered. The wound wasn't dressed and looked to have been sealed by a hot iron. Johuocin decided to try getting out of bed. Stepping onto the floor, he felt the pain of healing muscle, but he could still walk on it if he leaned on a chair. He made it to the valet chair a few steps away, to get his clothes, which had been cleaned and pressed. There he also found a cane resting on the wall.

As he was making ready to leave his room, he heard a knock on the door. "Come in."

The door opened, and Riessa walked in. She was clearly surprised to see the captain up and dressed. "I came to see if you were up to joining me for dinner. I can see now that you are. Would you mind?"

Johuocin stared at Riessa and wanted her. He wished he could see her again as he had before. "I would love to, if you don't mind my reminiscing about my dreams."

Riessa blushed again, smiled, and took the captain's arm.

As they passed through the hall, everyone had a smile on their face and a friendly greeting on their tongues. It was a contagious atmosphere, and it was hard for Johuocin to keep his mind on the events he must face in the future. His worry about the meeting with the dwarf chieftains left him and was replaced by the light attitudes around him.

Riessa led Johuocin/Captain Reglawr to a large dining room in what must be the largest building he'd ever been in. It reminded him of what he imagined a king's palace must be like. He could smell the delicious foods around him as they passed by each occupied table. It seemed he could taste the quality of the wines as he looked at it in crystal goblets or saw it poured from jeweled decanters. He saw wealth dripping all around him like raindrops on a showery spring day. He saw three and four servants catering to the needs of a single table. Yet, as quickly as the thought of the expense of such luxury came to him, it left.

No sooner were Riessa and Johuocin seated than their meals were served to them. Though they did not order, the meal in front of each of them was exactly what they would have wanted if they had. Riessa giggled at the astonishment on the captain's face. Johuocin fought to keep his mind clear, but he was enveloped by the intoxicating luxury around him. He felt an urgency to accept his current situation and be pleased with it. He could feel a loss of control as Riessa smiled at him from across the table and looked at him with sparkling eyes that seemed to mesmerize him.

He felt the yearning to reach out and touch her. As they drank their wine, he looked into her eyes and was overtaken by the urge to kiss her lips, as they appeared increasingly more succulent with every sip. Still he found it in himself to resist the temptation, knowing it would be the captain kissing her and not him.

They finished their meal and were given more wine. Riessa began staring at the captain with intensity. "You don't have to resist your feelings for me, Captain. It was more than just intrigue that made me wish to come with you. I feel something about you that makes me wish to surrender my heart."

Johuocin was set back by Riessa's forward speech. He wanted to yield to his temptation. Still, he held fast. "I don't deny I am tempted by your beauty. My sympathy for your youth and inexperience holds me back." Johuocin fought the urge to yield with his lie. Knowing it was only the jealousy of letting the captain's body enjoy her that was true, or perhaps her enjoying the captain's.

"Captain, please keep in mind, I am in part elvish and hold my age well." Riessa smiled and looked at her goblet as she finished her statement. "My guess is that my age is greater than yours."

"Then perhaps it will be my own innocence and inexperience that will hold me back."

Riessa then raised her goblet in salute to a toast. "Then let us drink, to a man who knows the virtue of restraint and patience." Her eyes, however, revealed disappointment.

Johuocin/Captain Reglawr raised his glass, more in apology than a toast, and drank. He wanted so badly to tell Riessa the true reason for his restraint instead he excused himself. "I must go back to my room and rest. I think the wine and activity has tired me more than my body can stand right now. Thank you for your company and perception of my needs." He motioned for the waiter.

"What can I do for you sir?"

"May I have the bill please?"

"Sir?"

"I wish to pay for my meal."

"Sir, you are guests of the prince. If I let you pay, it would be my head."

Riessa smiled and looked at Johuocin in embarrassment. "I'm sorry. I forgot to tell you."

The waiter turned and walked away. Johuocin felt the heat rise through his face as he heard Riessa's words. Still he wondered why the prince would pay for their enjoyment. "Why?"

"We don't know yet. But it's like that all over town. No one lets us pay for anything, and they seem to know what we want before we ask."

Johuocin tried to think further about it, and his weariness overtook him. He and Riessa got up from the table and went toward their rooms. Once there, Johuocin had just enough energy to get into bed before he fell asleep to dream of Riessa.

In the morning Johuocin was wakened by a man he didn't know. The man pulled back his bedcovers and was poking at the captain's wound. Johuocin/Captain Reglawr flinched at the pain and tried to move away.

"Captain, it is good to see you. I am Acolyte Phyrna from the temple of healing. You are healing well. In a few days you will be ready to see the prince."

Johuocin studied the young man in front of him. "You seem young to do such fine work, Acolyte. I must thank you for your skill."

"No. It was not me that did this, Captain. It was the Curate Sola who did this. She is a fine physician. I am only her assistant. She will be the one to make the final decision that you are well enough to see the prince."

"When will I see her?"

"Soon enough, Captain." The man looked at the captain and smiled. "But be warned, though she is very skilled, she has no bedside manner."

Merson came into the room. "Good wishes, Acolyte. How is the patient?"

"Doing well, my friend. How are you?" The acolyte smiled.

"Well, thank you."

Phyrna poked around a bit more and turned to leave.

"Thank you for the warning, Acolyte." Johuocin smiled as he thought of Phyrna's warning. The acolyte left without response. "And good morning, Merson."

"Aye, that it is, Captain."

"It's time to teach me, Merson." Johuocin could see by the look on Merson's face as he said those words, Merson had other plans. "It is only eleven days to solstice, and I know nothing more than to address the chieftains by name and title."

"Aye, Captain, you must learn. But you can't learn on an empty stomach. Let's go get a bite first, eh."

"I'll be fine for now. We can send for some food in a little while. Merson, I must learn the etiquette I will need for the meeting with the dwarf chieftains." Johuocin could see the annoyance he caused Merson in pressing him to the responsibilities set before them.

"Captain, I came here to ask you to have breakfast with me and some of my friends from the clan I was raised with. I have already promised them I would be there. It would be an insult if I did not show up."

Johuocin thought of the pain Merson had shown when he first spoke of the clan who cast him out as a young man because of his size and human descent. He could not understand Merson's urgency to bond with these same people once more. "Then let them be insulted as they insulted you by casting you out."

"No. I will not." Merson threw his hands in the air as he walked out of the room, slamming the door behind him.

Johuocin was set back. Was the atmosphere in this place such that it took away your urgency and responsibility? Did it take away the sense of pride and decorum? He remembered Riessa's advances of the night before. As he thought about it, he realized it was out of character for her to do such a thing. Was this place so intoxicating that it changed the things about a person that caused them to be what they are? He thought about how even Gorn had found a reason for them to stay. Somehow even Gorn's seriousness and sensibility had changed. Johuocin knew he had to investigate this place more.

As Johuocin dressed, he heard a knock at his door. "A moment please." Johuocin slipped his tunic on over his head and limped to the door. As he opened it he saw Riessa and Ben standing in the hall laughing. "Come in. Did you rest well last night?"

Ben looked at his brother and laughed. "I didn't sleep at all. This place is constantly going. There is so much to do here, Ory. I came back here this morning to find Riessa on her way out and convinced her we should take you out to show you the town."

Johuocin was relieved. Now he would have a guided tour for his examination of the town.

Riessa moved closer to Johuocin and whispered in his ear, "Remember, that's not all I want to show you."

Johuocin smiled and blushed. Then he wondered once again if it was this place that stole her inhibitions. "Good, let's go see what this place is made of."

As they left the hotel, Johuocin could see people from every area of the kingdom he had ever visited. Some he recognized well as lords and ladies; others he saw were clearly commoners. He saw everyone here interacting as equals, as if it were a normal way of life. Johuocin even saw elves and dwarves walking together in fellowship and congeniality. The attitudes were good-natured and contagious. Johuocin found himself lost in the mood of the people, exchanging small talk with strangers as they passed, sharing eye contact and smiles with nobles as they passed through the crowds without an escort or concern on their smiling faces.

Johuocin thought as he watched how unusual it was to see nobles and aristocrats mingling with the population, smiling at those they met, making eye contact. He was sure he saw one of the nobles personally help an old woman with a load that appeared too heavy for her.

There were shops of every kind lining the streets, and the streets themselves were immaculate and paved with brick. There were street sweepers everywhere picking up the garbage people threw down, sometimes before it hit the ground.

Enveloped by the intoxicating mood of the city and its people, Johuocin found himself caught without a care. His heart beat rapidly when he looked at Riessa, and his mind wandered to a place that allowed him a feeling of surreal warmth.

As they meandered through the shops, if any of them saw something they liked, the storekeeper gave it to them with the explanation that it was being charged to the prince by his order. Soon the hours turned into moments as the party lost all track of time. The days and nights were separated only by the moon and short periods of sun. The captain's wound healed almost miraculously without rest. The three had become inseparable until somewhere on the third night after Johuocin woke. Riessa leaned over to Ben and whispered something in his ear, and Ben excused himself to make a visit to the local whorehouse. Riessa suggested to the captain that they return to the hotel, which they did. Johuocin thought about the time left before solstice and realized that he didn't care if he had the nine that were or a thousand more.

As they entered Johuocin's room, someone was lighting the lamp on the wall near the door. As the attendant excused himself, another came into the room with wine and goblets, poured the wine, and left. Johuocin and Riessa sat on the floor near the fire and drank the wine poured from a decanter that seemed never to empty. Johuocin had lost track of his actions as he leaned over and kissed Riessa for what seemed like an eternity, giving her a gentle but longing stroke with his hand down the middle of her back. He had not noticed before that the back of the dress she wore was completely open, and the sensation of his hand touching her skin caused him to lose all sense of being in the captain's body as he pulled Riessa closer to him.

Riessa gently pushed away from him and stood up. Walking over, next to the bed, she pulled the shoulders of her dress from her skin and let it fall to the floor. Johuocin was lost in her beauty as he saw the heat that radiated from her soft, sumptuous skin. He stood and began to walk toward her reaching out to touch her.

The sight that next met Johuocin's presence was a contrast so horrid that he tried to scream but heard no voice. The place in which he found himself was dark and dingy. The party sat in chairs around a table staring into an orb of some kind suspended by an ornate stand of gold and jewels. Tied in.

The party looked worn from the lack of rest and nourishment. A robed figure sat erect in one corner of the room, meditating, eyes closed. The party's belongings were piled around him.

As Johuocin held his position, knowing that he must have stepped out of the captain as he lost his senses, the robed figure stood and rushed to the captain's side. He raised the captain's eyelids and stared into the depths of his soul.

"Galeem!" he called, "Come quickly!"

Another man, tall and muscular with dark skin, came through the door of the decrepit hovel. "Yes, Master Harishe. What do you require?"

"The captain has gone daft. He babbles inside as if he were lost. The spell holds, but he is not as deep as he was. We must get him to rest."

Galeem went to a shelf and pulled down a vial. Opening it, he held it under the captain's nose. The captain's eyes closed, and he slumped into his chair.

"Quickly now, Galeem, move him to the bed. The wound may be infected."

The big man moved the captain to the bed and laid him down. Harishe opened the tear in his pant leg to see the wound. It had indeed been sealed and was healing. Johuocin couldn't understand why their tormentor would go to the trouble of keeping them alive, only to steal their belongings and starve them to death.

"Move him back to the chair, and wake me when his eyes open again."

"Master? Do the rest not amuse you?"

"They are simple and boring. They dream only of comfort and entertainment that is usual. This girl and the captain, they have piqued my interest. They both want each other, but the captain keeps fighting it. I thought for sure they would satisfy my amusement tonight along with their own." Harishe looked disappointed with his last words. "Tomorrow is another day."

The last words Harishe spoke struck urgency through Johuocin. If time had passed as he thought it had, there were only nine days to solstice, leaving only sixteen until their meeting with the dwarf chieftains. He left the hovel to look for their mounts and the wagon Merson had spoken of, if indeed there were a wagon.

Johuocin roamed the grounds of the hovel and stable, finding their mounts, mules, and the wagon. The night was clear, and the only evidence of a road was the path made by the wagon wheels days before. Those had almost been covered by the blowing snow of the last few days. Now Johuocin's only problem was finding a way to escape this desolate area and taking the party with him. They were too weak to move by themselves, and he had only two possibilities of escape.

The cold of emptiness began to invade him worse than ever before as he formed a plan for escape.

As Master Harishe slept, Johuocin entered the body of Galeem. Johuocin/ Galeem got up from his chair, where he

watched the captain for signs of consciousness. Quietly he left the hovel to make the
mounts and wagon ready for their departure.
Slowly and quietly Johuocin worked, loading
the mules and wagon with the belongings of
the five travelers, laying down a bed of straw
in the wagon. One by one Johuocin carried
out the party members, first Riessa, then Ben,
then Merson, and then the captain. Gorn
was so large that he had decided to leave him
for last. He found no way to lift Gorn, so
he grabbed him under the arms and began
to drag him from the hovel. As he pulled on
Gorn, the big man's foot caught the edge of
a chair and knocked it up against the table.
Harishe woke and was up at once staring at
Galeem with a mixture of fear and hate and
loss of loyalty. Johuocin dropped Gorn with
a heavy thump onto the ground as Harishe
raised his arms and turned into the most

hideous creature that Johuocin had ever dreamt of. The thing came at him, speaking with Harishe's voice, pleading, nearly begging for Galeem to give him some explanation that would excuse him from killing Galeem.

"Galeem, what have I done to turn you against me? We were more than master and servant, more than friends; we have taken care of each other in illness and heartache. We were family, Galeem. Why do you turn against me now?" The voice was crying, even wailing as the monster approached.

Johuocin was frozen in fear. He could not move or speak. He could not attack or turn and run. Finally the monster was close enough to touch Galeem. As it reached toward Galeem, Johuocin found the strength to turn and run, but it was too late; it had hold of Galeem. Johuocin left the body without knowing it, and as he did Galeem saw what had hold of him and screamed and struck at the thing. Johuocin turned and looked, only to see Galeem still screaming and striking, but the monster was gone. All that was there was Harishe. Still the terror in Galeem's eyes said he still saw the monster.

Harishe fell. Galeem came from his terror to see Harishe lying on the ground at his feet. Grabbing his chest, he knelt down beside him. Crying with heavy sobs, trying to catch his breath, he said, "Master, I lived for you. You gave my life importance." Then Galeem buckled over and sobbed some more. As he rose up, Galeem lifted clenched hands high in the air. Then Johuocin saw it. Galeem had a knife in his hands. Then he sobbed, "And now Master I die for you." And before Johuocin could enter Galeem to stop him, Galeem had brought the knife down into his heart.

Now Johuocin felt the guilt of losing a noble man his life. One who lived to serve another, no matter what the cost to himself, one whose only purpose was to do what was proper to his chosen profession. And in the end he did only that which was acceptable to his chosen path.

Johuocin had other problems now. His friends were in the cold. Already they were weak and consumed by their natural needs, and he had no way to help them as they lay in the cold, slowly freezing to death. He must do something to help them. What could he do?

CHAPTER 8

The Loss of Friends, a New Life Ahead

As Johuocin waited and thought through the early morning hours of winter darkness, he was aware of the changing color of his friends' skin. First the pale white look of weariness, then the red brought by the cold, and now as the sun was just below the horizon, the blue white accented by deep red splotches that is the preempt of frostbite. His helplessness was felt to the core of his soul and resounded back with the bitter cold of emptiness that was to be his burden when the guilt of life-piracy was not. An eternity of cold or guilt was his payment for the choice of revenge at any cost.

Johuocin was sure that the loss of his friends was imminent as he started across the plain in the direction from which the wagon wheels had made their mark. He thought of the captain and how he had confiscated life from him that day he had lost the hope of saving his mother. He thought of Merson and Ben and how he had just begun to know them. He thought about the mystery around Gorn and how he had found a man he could not dislike. Then he thought of Riessa and the passion she had inspired within him. As the sun showed itself over the horizon, these thoughts were a flood within him and distracted him from the riders coming toward him.

He found himself in the midst of the riders before he was aware of their presence. Then before he was aware of what he was doing, he entered the body of a man at the rear of the party.

Though he realized that the man must have been cold, to Johuocin, the warmth was overwhelming. The itching of the man's beard was glorious to feel as he bounced along on the saddled mule the man was riding. The man was missing many teeth in the front of his mouth, and the teeth in the rear tasted of rot. He was armed with a long sword with a chewed blade and a dagger fashioned from wood that would only be effective for stabbing his opponents. Johuocin felt a smile crawl across his face.

"What're you smilin' about, ya skank?" The man nearest to him was scowling at him.

"Nothing at all. What seems to be the knife in your back?" Johuocin felt the uneasiness of once again not knowing whom he had taken over.

"La-de-da, nothing at all, he says. You was complainin' as much as the rest of us a bit ago. So what's yer smile?" The man seemed just a little more than mad because of a smile. "You ain't gonna' be smilin' if we do run inta them soldiers them collectors promised us. I still think they're gonna show."

"So why are you here then?" Johuocin was trying to get some information out of his new riding companion as he realized this group had to have some contact with the party he'd been with.

"Why're you 'ere?" the man retorted in sarcasm.

"Because I want to be," Johuocin responded.

"Course it 'as nothin' to do with Sticker sayin' so, does it?" The man motioned with his head toward the front of the group, and there Johuocin saw Sticker leading the pack.

Johuocin realized then that Sticker must have seen through their bluff a couple of days after they left Cragfare and started out after the party. Sizing up the group, Johuocin could see that Sticker wasn't taking the chance of having another loss like the one he had back at the Crimson Faery. There were perhaps thirty to subdue and rob the already injured party of five.

"So, Sticker's the only reason you're here?"

"No, I'm here t'git me some o' that coin too. Just like you, ya faery dung."

Johuocin gave the mule a kick to the flanks and headed toward Sticker. Looking back to the other man, he called out, "Well I know something else too." And off he galloped through the crowd, digging his heels into the mule's flanks as he pushed it forward.

"Hey, Sticker? I know something about this area and someone who lives a short ways ahead," Johuocin was yelling as he came within ten feet of Sticker.

Sticker looked back to see who was yelling at him and turned back when he saw who it was. Johuocin was wondering how he was going to convince Sticker to speed up the party on the chance of saving his friends. It was at least a league to the shack that belonged to Harishe, and his friends may already be dead of the cold. His only hope was a band of thugs who wanted them dead.

"What might ya think ya know, Tom? You been stuck in that town fer years without so much as steppin' out of it fer a squat." Sticker didn't even look at Tom to give any credence to his words.

"Years back there were a feller who lived just ahead of here with a servant. He was up to some strange things; maybe he's seen the collectors." Johuocin saw only a scoff on Sticker's face as he spoke with Tom's voice.

"What sort of strange things, Tom?"

"He'd make you see things, things that wasn't there. He made some folks see a whole town." Johuocin could see a smirk crawl across Sticker's face. Sticker broke out in a loud laugh. "I'm not joking, Sticker. I saw it myself."

"Sure ya did, Tom. That's 'cause yer simple. Really it was just yer mind playin' tricks on ya 'cause ya were so far of home." Sticker wasn't laughing anymore. He could see Johuocin/Tom was serious, but he believed Tom was daft.

Johuocin couldn't afford any more time trying to convince Sticker of the shack. He had to do something quickly. "Fine, believe what you will. I'm riding ahead to find the place and warm myself." After he finished what he had to say, he kicked the mule and took off at a gallop.

Johuocin heard Sticker calling Tom back as the distance between them grew. When Tom didn't turn, Sticker sent two of the men to ride after him.

Riding mules themselves, the two men couldn't stop Johuocin before the shack came into sight. As soon as it did, Johuocin pointed and yelled. "There it is!"

As the two men caught up with him one of them said, "I thought you was kiddin', Tom. Ya never said nothin b'fore 'bout it."

"Sure, like I want someone to know I was in the habit of seein' things that weren't there."

The three men continued to ride quickly toward the shack. As they neared the hovel and stable of Harishe, Johuocin saw the wagon his friends were piled in and the open door that Gorn lay near with Harishe and Galeem in a heap next to him. Johuocin kicked the mule again, trying to get it to speed up. "There's the wagon we gave the collectors." The other two men hurried alongside of him.

When they were within a hundred yards of the hovel, the other two men slowed to a walk as Johuocin continued his gallop.

As Johuocin reached the wagon, he jumped off the mule and fell, finding that Tom had a bad knee that didn't bend as it should. He picked himself up off the ground and dusted the snow off. As he did that he realized the snow was wet, giving him an indication that the sun had warmed things up some. When he looked into the wagon, he could see more red in the faces that were there than he had noticed when he left that morning. He motioned for the other two to join him. They hurried to where he stood, looking into the wagon.

"It's them." The one who came up first was laughing. "They made it all the way here to freeze to death."

The second man answered "Sticker'll love it."

"I don't know." Johuocin was trying to think what he could say or do that would cause them to help him take Riessa and the others inside. "I thought Sticker would have liked to do it himself. Think of the way that they treated him in his own town."

"Yer right, Tom, he was looking forward to hurtin' 'em first. Too bad he's missed his chance."

"Maybe he hasn't. I think they're still alive. If we nurse'm a little maybe we can still give Sticker his fun." The man just looked at Tom with question in his eyes. "I mean if we take'm inside and start a fire and thaw'm out a little, maybe we can still do it."

"I don't know, Tom."

"Yeah, me either, Tom. They was a lotta trouble the last time they was healthy." The second man was a little worried. Johuocin saw mistrust in both their eyes.

"Maybe you're right. Maybe they'll die and get cold enough for Sticker not to know that we took away his fun before he even gets here. Even if he does find out we took away his chance for fun, what's the worst he could do to us?"

Both men looked at each other, then back to Tom. Then looked at the four in the wagon. The first man's brow wrinkled.

"Ya don't think he'd take it out on us do ya, Jense?"

"Ya mean, make us his fun?"

"Yeah. After all, we been trailin' these collectors fer three days now. He's been hearin' alla' us complain 'bout even bein' out here, and we all felt like he'd hurt us before lettin' us go back."

The two men fell right into the line of thinking Johuocin was hoping to create. Johuocin was counting on their fear of Sticker to feed the paranoia that he'd seen at Cragfare. Now all he had to do was start moving the party members into the hovel and the others would be sure to follow suit. That's what he did, starting with Riessa. Being sure to pull forward the hood of her coat to conceal her face, Johuocin picked her up with care.

As they reached the doorway, the other two men noticed Harishe and Galeem in a heap just inside the doorway.

"This is weird, Tom. No one's alive here but the collectors, and they's half dead. Who're these two, do ya 'spose?" Jense's eyes grew as he asked that question and looked around for evidence of someone else being there.

"The old guy, that's the one I was telling Sticker about. The other is his servant." Johuocin tried to sound curious as he spoke. He stepped over the bodies, being careful not to step on them or Gorn, who lay just beyond the doorway. "Bring the others. I'll look around and get a fire started."

Johuocin moved across the room and lay Riessa down on the bed, where Harishe had slept earlier, as he moved the party to the wagon that morning. He looked at the peacefulness on her face and tried to think of a way to protect her and the rest of the party from harm. For all he knew, he was going to keep them alive long enough to be tortured and killed.

Johuocin was starting a fire as they brought in the other two and moved the four inanimate men closer to the fireplace.

"This one's a little heavy, ain't he, Curly?" Jense was grunting as they moved Gorn to the fire. Once done with that chore the two men moved Harishe and Galeem outside and closed the door.

Johuocin stayed quiet as the other two talked and searched through the hovel for food and whatever valuables they could find. They were concerned about what Sticker's reaction would be to what they had done and hoped they had managed to make points with their leader. Curly suggested that they tie the hands and feet of the party in case they woke, and Johuocin couldn't refuse without sounding suspicious. Then Johuocin suggested gagging them, knowing the captain would be the first to revive because of the rest he had gotten. Johuocin had resolved that the power in the orb the party stared into earlier could only keep them awake if their bodies did not need the rest more than they wanted to enjoy the dream. If that was true, then the captain had really gotten the rest he felt in the dream. He had also figured that the more someone looked into the orb, the more power it had over them. As Jense and Curly studied the glowing ball, Johuocin was careful to keep his eyes averted from it. Then, reluctantly it seemed, they placed it in a bag. As they sat in the warmth of the hovel and ate what they could find in the cupboard, they heard Sticker and the rest ride into the yard of the hovel. Soon enough Sticker was coming through the door with his dagger pulled.

Sticker looked at the three men as they sat at the table and relaxed. "So you boys been havin' a fine ol' time while the rest of us've been ridin' in the cold." Then he looked around the room, and when he locked on the party lying by the fire bound and gagged and he smiled. "Looks like ya been busy."

Sticker turned and barked out a few orders for the men outside to set up camp in the stable. The group would be staying the night here, and in the morning they would be leaving for Cragfare.

Johuocin realized at that moment, though he was immortal, time was still a factor to all he would ever do. Not because he was limited by time but because everyone and everything around him was. Now he was faced with the limited time he had to save five lives he felt responsible for, five people whom he had, by chance, become part of their lives. One of which he had stolen life from, one whom he had fallen in love with, and three who he knew as friends. The sun had broken the crest of midday, and he had only a few short hours to find a way to give back to them what he had lost them. He had no idea of what Sticker would wish to do to the party, or how soon. He only knew it would be before morning, and in the body of Tom he stood little chance of influencing Sticker. He must act quickly or lose his chance to act at all.

Before turning to the three men sitting at the table, Sticker called out a name that sent chills through Johuocin. "Jundog! I have a surprise fer ya." Then Sticker walked over to the party and gave Gorn a full kick in the middle of his back. "Funny how they ain't so big when they're layin' on the floor. Shame killin' him though. His stick packed a curse of a whollop." Sticker was still rubbing his face in remembrance of Gorn's staff as Jundog walked up behind him.

Sticker turned Merson over to see his face better. "Do ya remember this one, Jundog? Don't look as cocky as he did in Cragfare, do he?"

Jundog pulled a dagger and started for Merson. Johuocin jumped up and grabbed him by the shoulder, spinning him around. Jundog put his knife to Johuocin/Tom's throat and grabbed the back of his head.

Sticker pulled Jundog's knife hand down. "Is that any way to thank a man for deliverin' a present?"

Jundog just glared at Tom. "What're ya stoppin' me fer Tom? ya take a likin' to collectors?"

"No." Johuocin was having a struggle within himself to find a reason for his action.

Then a cruel vision struck him, but it was all he had to go with.

"Well?" Johuocin had taken too long to think, and Sticker was becoming impatient.

"I think it would only be suited," Johuocin continued, "if the man were awake to see and feel Jundog do to him what he done to Jundog."

The two men stared at Tom for a while. Slowly a smile crept across Sticker's face, then Jundog's, as they all began to laugh.

"Yer just full o' surprises, Tom. I'm beginnin' to like the way you think." Sticker slapped Tom on the back as Jundog let go of him. "All this time I knowed ya, ya never showed yer good side."

Jundog took Tom's long sword and put it in the coals of the fire.

Sticker and the rest of the group were in a more jovial mood, knowing they would be going home the next day. One of the members of Sticker's vengeful band had found a cask of brandy in the stable and had been dispersing it to the crowd. As they drank they became more anxious for what they deemed as entertainment and were pressing for their leader to start the festivities. Sticker was putting them off, trying to wait for the members of the party to become conscious.

As day grew into evening, it became difficult for Sticker to hold them off any longer.

"It's time fer us to entertain the men, Jundog. Curly and Jense can take out the captain and the kid. Tom, you grab the little one on the bed. Jundog, you take out your prize. Try to wake them as you get them outside."

Until now Johuocin had been able to conceal Riessa's femininity. The pictures in his mind of what they were going to do to the others was gruesome, but he knew if they found out Riessa were a woman, the drunken crowd would violate her for hours. Johuocin's nervousness grew without restraint. He searched for a distraction or a miracle that would stop the atrocity that was about to happen. The others were already moving their victims out to the yard, where the events of inhumanity were to take their course. Johuocin saw no stopping the eventuality of their deaths. He would be a witness to all of it, and he knew it would have been more kind to let them die a frozen death. He knew he should not have led Sticker's band of marauders here.

The party groggily awoke, with some prodding and rough coaxing, fear filling their eyes as they saw Sticker's face. It took four men to carry Gorn out, and two more helped set him up against the hovel. Johuocin left the hood over Riessa's face as she woke. The captain woke once again, not knowing where he was or how he had arrived, and the confusion grew within him as he became aware that he faced his own death. Ben's eyes filled with fear that turned to tears of helplessness as he looked into the crowd before him, and then the tears stopped as he refused them the satisfaction of his anguish. Merson's fear suddenly turned to anger as he struggled against the ropes that bound his wrists. Gorn's fear passed quickly to complacency, as he became aware of the inevitable. Riessa sat shaking with her face covered by the hood from her cloak. Johuocin ached for the chance to relieve them of their tortured hearts, the remembrances of past mistakes, and their mental conjuring of their own futures that would have been, mixing with what it now would be.

Sticker stood in front of the crowd to speak to them. Raising his rough and scratchy voice, he said, "Now we start. We take back what they took from us. We have our coin. We have our pride. We've given'm back the fear they gave some o' ya. We can't take back the lives o' the men they took from our sides. We can't even take as many as they took. But we'll make'm feel their own deaths more fer it. Jundog wants his revenge first. So now he'll take it."

Johuocin watched helplessly as Curly pulled back Merson's shirt from his chest. Jundog carried out the hot long sword that was in Tom's belt earlier that day. He walked toward Merson and laid it across his chest as Merson fought back the scream he wanted to release. The odor of burnt flesh filled the air so thickly that even the cold could not stunt it. Merson passed out in his pain. Next they went to Ben. As they pulled away his shirt, fear and anticipation over took him and he passed out. The crowd laughed.

"We'll save 'im fer later when he can stay awake to enjoy it." Sticker laughed as he spoke those words.

Then they pulled back the captain's shirt, and the captain's eyes pleaded for an explanation that he would not receive before he too passed out in pain. Gorn struggled against his ropes as they neared Riessa. It was plain that his anger grew greater as they grabbed at her clothing to rip it from her. It became unbearable for Johuocin as he watched what was about to happen. Her clothing tore, her face and breasts were exposed, and the crowd fell silent with shock for what seemed an eternity, before giving a great cheer. Gorn started to bleed at the wrists as he fought the ropes even harder.

Sticker reached down and fondled her as she stared into the crowd. The only evidence of emotion was a tear running down her face. Gorn struggled until Curly hit him across the back of the head with a piece of firewood, knocking him out.

"Our moon just became a little brighter, eh, men?" Another cheer came up from the crowd.

When Johuocin heard that statement come from Sticker, it triggered something in his mind. He had no idea whether it would work or not, but he had to try. "Sticker, should we move her inside for now? Better still, should we move them all inside, make them watch?"

"I'm really beginnin' to like you, Tom!" Sticker replied in his excitement.

They moved the party inside and started to wake them all. As they got to

Gorn, Johuocin suggested leaving him to sleep, only because he might break the ropes. Johuocin wasn't ready for Gorn to wake yet. He wanted everyone to be distracted. They tied Riessa to the bed and stripped her of her clothes. Sticker started to undo his trousers, and Johuocin/Tom interrupted him with a suggestion.

"Maybe we should give the men outside something to entertain themselves with so they don't get impatient."

"Whatya got in mind, Tom? We got nothin' that'll take their mind off'n her."

Johuocin put his hands on the shoulders of Curly and Jense. "We found something earlier that might give their curiosity a stir." Johuocin/Tom walked to the corner of the room and picked up a sack. Reaching in, he pulled out the glowing orb. "Looks like a small moon, don't it?"

"What is it?" Jundog took it out of Tom's hands.

"Don't quite know. The old guy used it to make people see things I think." Johuocin knew there must be a lot of power in it but wasn't sure how it worked. He had to try something, anything. "It might amuse them out there for a while though. Long enough for us to have our fun before lettin' them in."

"Ya ain't failed me yet t'day, Tom," Sticker said with a hint of respect and a nod of reward to Tom. "Let's do it."

Jundog held it high in the air above their heads as they walked into the crowd. Near the fire, Johuocin took it from him and shined it a little. "We need to figure out what this is. While Sticker and the others are in there we're goin' to think about this thing, it might come in handy." When Sticker heard that, he and the other three that were inside went back toward the bed where Riessa was tied in the hovel. As the door closed behind them, Johuocin took out his wooden dagger and broke the crystal of the glowing orb. The light slowly grew from a small sphere to an explosion of color and sparks. He felt Tom's body fall and release him as he was aware of others falling or running. He saw screams on their faces, but no noise was there. Quickly he moved toward the hovel and inside. There he saw Sticker getting ready to mount Riessa. Johuocin stepped into Sticker and stood up. He reached down and grasped Sticker's dagger and cut the ropes that held Riessa's wrists.

Shock and confusion riddled Riessa's mind and face as she watched Sticker turn to his friends and grin.

Jundog and the others laughed. "Ya want'er to fight a little, Sticker?"

Johuocin didn't miss the opportunity. "Yeah, come watch'er hands if she gets too wicked." Jundog moved closer to the bed. Johuocin still had the dagger in his hand, and as Jundog got close, he ran the blade into his side and across his middle. Riessa grabbed the other knife from Jundog's belt and cut the ropes on her ankles.

Curly and Jense ran toward the two, pulling long swords. Riessa threw the knife she held, and it went into Curly's shoulder, causing him to drop his sword.

Jense went for the door to get help and instead saw nothing but chaos in the yard. He ran out the door and toward the stable. Curly ran out after him.

Johuocin/Sticker ran toward the captain, yelling, "I won't share you with anyone!" He felt the sensation of a sword being slashed across Sticker's back as he lunged toward the captain, making a false slash at the captain's face, missing him by inches. As he fell to the floor he rolled over and slipped out of Sticker's body, and he saw the hilt of Riessa's sword meet Sticker's head.

Riessa moved to Merson and cut his bonds and then closed and barred the door. Merson took Sticker's dagger and cut the others free as Johuocin slipped into the captain's body and woke Gorn.

Riessa grabbed the blanket from the bed and wrapped herself as Ben tied Sticker. Johuocin/Captain Reglawr moved closer to Riessa. "Are you all right?"

Riessa looked at the captain with hurt in her eyes that was directed at him. She turned away as Johuocin saw a tear roll from the corner of her eye, and he wasn't sure whether relief or sadness caused the tear. She went about hunting for the remnants of her clothing that were strewn about the hovel.

As Gorn recovered himself, he moved to Riessa's side and put his hands on her shoulders. The two exchanged a knowing glance, and Gorn left her and went out the door, motioning for Merson to bar the door behind him once more. Johuocin moved to the window and watched Gorn disappear into the darkness that had swallowed the yard outside the hovel.

The four left inside the hovel began hearing the most hideous screams and growling noises they had ever heard in all their lives. Soon the sounds faded into the distance as they stared at each other with reverential fear. All except Riessa, who sat upon the dirt floor with her head bowed in grief and sadness. No one spoke while they could still hear the terror outside.

Merson was the first to break the overwhelming silence within the hovel. As he did, Ben jumped, breaking his intense stare he held on the door. Merson's voice cut through the thick silence like the tooth of a dragon piercing tender flesh. "I'm going out to look for Gorn. He's been gone too long."

Riessa looked up. "Worry for yourself. You don't even know who is near."

Johuocin looked quickly to Riessa, wondering if she now saw him within the captain. Wondering if she now knew who or what he was.

Merson gave her a strange confused look. "You don't think that there are still some of them outside, do you? Not after what we heard?"

Riessa just looked at him without response and then placed her eyes on the captain.

Johuocin felt a chill as she dropped her glance once more to the floor. She knew. He didn't know what she knew or how, but he knew she knew something.

"Ben, are you strong enough to join me?" Merson asked Orman Reglawr's brother.

"No, but I doubt you're strong enough to go alone. Maybe together we can make it to the stable." Ben let out a laugh that ended in a light sobbing as he finished speaking. In looking at Ben the others could tell he was trying to lighten the mood within the hovel, but his words were just a little too close to the truth. Johuocin was able to muster a half smile and cast it in Ben's direction to make him feel his efforts weren't missed.

Johuocin got up and began rummaging through the pantry to find something to fill their bellies.

Merson and Ben opened the door and went out. Johuocin was torn, wanting to stop Ben from going, hoping it would stop Riessa from speaking of her newfound knowledge, yet wanting Ben to go, so Riessa would not speak of it in front of him.

After the two left the room, Riessa moved to Sticker's side to check him for consciousness. When she was confident that he was completely out, she turned to the captain/Johuocin. "What are you?"

Johuocin looked back into her eyes and saw the distrust that had replaced her previous interest in him. "What do you mean, what am I? I am a man. I am the captain of this party."

Riessa looked at him with disgust and anger and frustration. "You are the captain now. A while ago you were Sticker, before that you were Tom. Who knows who else you have been. I thank you for saving me from that atrocity. But what I am asking you is not who you are. I am asking what you are."

Johuocin was wrestling his mind for something to tell her, something other than the truth. Something she could believe and something that would relieve him of telling the truth about himself. He didn't want her knowing how hideous his actions were or why he was what he was. He wanted her to look at him as she had before. He suspected she would feel as he did. Stealing pieces of someone's life was more heinous than ending it all together.

Finally he settled his mind. He must tell her the truth, but not yet. "I am not evil, and I cannot explain more thoroughly than that now. I hope you find in your heart a way to trust me."

Riessa stared at him for a moment and then looked away. She moved toward the fireplace. Staring at the flames, she reached out to warm her hands, her eyes deep in thought, before she looked up again. "You must trust me enough to tell me more than I already know. Then perhaps I can try to trust you, or at least stay silent to the others."

"I am at a loss as to what you know. Tell me that and maybe I'll be able to find a way to explain." Johuocin could think of nothing that he could tell her, nothing that would not tell her too much.

"I cannot see your soul clearly. Or for that matter at all. I can see when you are in control of someone else only because they become blocked to me and their actions change. I believe you are not evil, because I believe you want me and have resisted taking me though you have had the chance, even if it were in some kind of dream. I also know you are not in complete control, because you have unintentionally left the captain, twice that I can account for, once at my father's inn, and once in the dream. That scares me, but if you hadn't left him in the dream I get the feeling we would still be there." She stopped and stared at him waiting for a response. The look on her face whispered she wasn't sure she wanted to know more than what she had told him but asked anyway.

He moved toward her and reached out for her hand. She backed away quickly, startled. Johuocin turned away, feeling the pain from her mistrust as it drove through him like an icy knife. "I can only say some of the things I do give me great guilt, but they serve a purpose. Some of that purpose, I'll admit, is selfish comfort. I believe this is where much of my guilt is born. I do have a goal, and I have not found another way to reach it other than to do what I do. When I am done, I will have much atonement to provide some people as repayment to accomplish, and this presents a great dilemma. My goal is certainly going to be the result of some if not many criminal acts, though I believe the result to be just. Though I would choose not to implicate an innocent person, it is an impossible task to accomplish."

"Who are you? Do you have a name?" She looked at him as if she were perplexed but intrigued by him. Wanting to know who he was. "If you change again, how will I know you?"

"I'm no longer sure exactly who I am anymore. I had a name once, but for now, I have to be the one I have taken and use that name. If you have any question that it's me, quietly ask 'who I shield?' I will respond saying 'the coursing dragon.' That was the shape of the Crolga ring I carved in my thirteenth summer, and I'm sure it is the last of myself that I will ever remember."

After receiving no response from Riessa, save the downward stare as she turned away, Johuocin went back to finding food for the group. He stood by the table peeling asra root so that he could brew it when Riessa came alongside him and placed her hand on the captain's arm.

Quietly she whispered to him. "Your secret will be safe for a time. But you must tell me the rest when you can." With that she looked and saw his chest. "We need to take care of that for the captain." Riessa then set about helping him with the task of preparing food.

*

As Merson and Ben crossed the moonlit yard, there among the trampling of human feet and the array of bodies lying across the open space, they saw claw marks in the snow and ice—the claw marks of a large bear. They began following the tracks to the edge of the yard and beyond. The tracks followed no specific path, but everywhere they led there was another body, mangled and torn, lying in its path. Some were even half eaten in the meatier parts of the legs and chest. The two came up on one body whose face had been completely bitten off. At that Ben became sick and began heaving bile from his empty belly. Seeing Ben, Merson could not help but join him. Soon the two were laying exhausted face down in the snow.

"Merson, where do you suppose the bear came from or why he was on such a rampage for human flesh?" Ben just barely squeezed out the last three or four words before finding himself too out of breath to speak more.

Merson mustered the strength to answer. "I don't know, lad. He should have been in hibernation." Then Merson stopped to breathe. After regaining himself, he started again, "I've heard stories about bears who've been woken from their winter sleep and gone mad, but not usually this far from the mountains."

Ben rose to his knees to stand. "You don't suppose he got Gorn, do you?"

Merson stood, taking on a look of urgency at the suggestion. "We'd better find out."

The two didn't travel more than another hundred yards before falling in exhaustion, passing out as their hunger and lack of rest overtook them.

They hadn't lay there long when they were woke by the hearty laugh of their friend Gorn, who picked them up and slung them over his shoulders as they once again passed out.

*

Riessa and Johuocin sat relaxing after eating some of the stew they were able to prepare, when Sticker woke struggling against the ropes that bound him, unable to make more noise than a grunt through the gag in his mouth.

Johuocin moved to Sticker and untied the gag. "Undo the ropes, ya mangy dog. I don't know what trickery ya used t'take me this time. I don't even remember anything past my gettin' ready t' enjoy that bit o' tender meat there." He motioned to Riessa with his head.

Johuocin glared at Sticker as he referred to his prior intention toward Riessa. "Speak more gently, lost soul. She might decide to run a knife through your gullet just because you're breathing after what you almost did. However, she's still wondering why you turned on your own men and started killing them before you went through with your intended plan."

"I wouldn't kill me own men. Yer tryin' hard t' sell it, but I ain't buyin'. What've ya done with Jundog and the others?"

"If I'm not mistaken, Jundog is laying outside with your knife in his belly. As for the rest, I'm really not sure. I'm sure someone will make it back to Cragfare to tell how you turned on everyone at the last minute to help the girl." Johuocin smiled at what he thought must be going through Sticker's mind. "I'm sure you'll hear all about it when you get back there."

"I didn't do it, and they'd never buy that story."

"Well then, I suppose we could probably let you go so you can start walking back then?" A look of indecision and confusion passed over Sticker's face as Johuocin suggested letting him go and Riessa laughed from across the room. "No, I think we'd better take you back ourselves just to make sure you make it safely. At least then you'll be able to tell 'your side of the story' before the soldiers find you."

Sticker, in his own paranoia, started to believe there was something to the story he was hearing, or at least he couldn't think of a plausible explanation to give the others back in Cragfare. "No, ya can't do that. Take me with you. I'll take care of your stock and cook for you. That is until we get to the next town, and then I'll go back m'self." Nerves rattled his voice as his fear fed on the thoughts spinning through his head. Seeing the look on the faces of Riessa and the captain, his eyes took on a pleading of their own.

Riessa, in disbelief of his allusion that they would trust him to cook for them, smirked and cocked an eye at him. "I don't think we can do that, and I don't think you intend on returning to Cragfare. If you're not going back, that means you'll be starting a whole new life. I'm sure we can find some way of helping you with that."

As she finished her statement, Gorn pushed through the door carrying one of his companions on each shoulder. He walked to the bed and dropped them as gently as he could next to one another. As he turned back to the others in the room, he found them staring at him in awe. He looked down at himself in the dim light of the candles burning on the table and found himself covered in blood. No one spoke as he walked back out the door and came back carrying two large pails of water. Without taking the time to heat the water or take the chill from it, Gorn stripped off his coat and washed the blood away as the others sat in silence, unable to speak.

After Gorn had washed out the fur of his coat and hung it by the fire to dry, Johuocin approached him in curious dismay. "What happened out there? How did you cover yourself in blood?"

Gorn looked at him with a loss for explanation. His eyes were sad as the thought of what must have happened ran through his mind. Then he looked away.

As Johuocin stepped closer to Gorn to demand an answer, Riessa pulled on Johuocin's arm and drew his attention. "Leave it alone. He can't tell you what he just went through." Then more quietly, "He must not tell you."

Regaining his senses enough to speak, Sticker could not resist tossing his coin into the fountain. "She gonna stop ya from findin' out what kinda' killer gets blood all over 'is face while 'e's killin' Cap'm."

At that Riessa walked over and kicked Sticker in the head, sending him rolling into a wall and leaving him unconscious.

Seeing this, Gorn averted his eyes from his friend. "I'll tell you as much as I can, but I don't think you'll like it much."

Riessa stopped Gorn from speaking any further with a raise of her hand. "But he'll only tell you if you share the rest of your secret with us." She glared at Johuocin as if she knew he would not press the issue.

Johuocin felt as if this were a challenge to him and also saw it as a safeguard to a secret he could not burden alone any longer. He felt both Riessa and Gorn would be dependable advisors when needed. He made the resolution to chance his judgment to trust the two before him. "Agreed."

A look of shock and disbelief came over Riessa's face as he accepted Riessa's offer. She knew then that she had underestimated his burden.

Gorn looked at the two of them in confusion as he took a seat by the table. "What is this deal the two of you are pledging over what happens to be my privacy? It's something I will share as I see fit," he looked at Riessa sternly, "and not yours to make deals with or purchase other secrets."

Riessa turned her eyes in harvested shame. She knew Gorn was right. She knew she had no right to use Gorn in such a way. "I apologize to you, Gorn. I release the captain from his ill-obtained obligation. It is myself I serve."

"I did not mean to shame you, little one, only to correct a poorly chosen claim."

"You are a loving friend, Gorn. Thank you."

Johuocin heard the comfort they gave each other as they spoke and was certain he could trust them with his own unkempt secrets. He also knew he must first ask for their help rather than push them into it without warning.

"I would like to keep my part. But I must tell you that it also will be a service to me if you would act as my counsel in this.

Before I speak of it, I must ask you if you are prepared to do that, and if you are willing to let me burden you with my self-inflicted curse. If I tell you, however, you will become part of this whether you help or not.

"However little I know of you, I trust you and value your courage, your strength, and your discretion."

The look on Riessa's face told him there was no hesitation to wish to know his secret, regardless of cost. Gorn was puzzled and concerned what his secret could be that it was so demanding of those around him. He could see the calculation in Gorn's eyes as he weighed the possibilities, and still he knew Gorn would not be fully prepared for what he would hear.

"Captain." Gorn captured Johuocin's attention with his soft deep voice. "I am not one of the world. I cannot begin to guess what it is that would make your secret so demanding, but I have learned much from Riessa's father over the years and I will not be so bold as to deny that it would bind my service to you simply by speaking of it. At the same time, I cannot begin to think what would bind me so thoroughly to this."

Johuocin looked at Gorn with shame for his own predicament. Then, looking away, he gave the binding element a name. "It would be your concern for the innocent and naïve, as well as your willingness to punish the guilty."

Gorn conceded to Johuocin's knowledge of him and the insight that Johuocin possessed. "Then tell your tale, though I may not serve you well."

Riessa jumped to the quick. "Yes, Captain, tell us who you are."

"First let Gorn speak his own secret. After, I will need a while to collect my thoughts."

Johuocin listened to what Gorn lay out before him, his story of battling a lycanthropic bear, and then being bitten and surviving the struggle by killing his attacker. He told of the effects of his wound and the burdens it placed upon him. He told Johuocin of his battle with the disease it inflicted upon him and how his final survival of the infection caused him to ever battle lycanthropy, at the last, a ware-bear. Now every night as the moon hits high, he must go satisfy the needs of his counter-self, the killer bear. How, when he was angered or in pain, he must fight an inner struggle to keep the bear within himself. How letting go of the struggle, he could turn at will into the bear. Gorn's final portion of his tale was about the path he followed the night before and how he tracked every member of Sticker's party and killed them, mutilating and eating the flesh off their bones, trying to satisfy the hunger that was built up while he was in the dream. Then he looked at the captain in relief, for Johuocin did not show disgust or recoil from his presence.

"Captain, you are truly an unusual man not to judge me for my odious tribulation. You have made a friend in me for giving me another to share my burden with, without fearing judgment."

"Truly you have made two friends, for you have shown compassion to one who deserves it." Riessa's eyes softened as she spoke those words. Then she reached out her hands and touched the hands of both Gorn and the captain.

Johuocin saw their sincerity, and his heart filled with self-disgust. He dropped his gaze to the flame of the candle on the table before him. "You'll soon understand why I can't judge Gorn. He came upon his dilemma by chance and survival; I came upon mine with a vengeful heart. If you hear my tale and no longer wish to offer your friendship, I would not blame you. Just please don't condemn me for my mistake. I assure you, I have already condemned myself."

The two sat quietly as Johuocin got out of his seat to check the others for consciousness.

As Johuocin related his story from the time of his father's death to the time he sought out the wizard, Bolac, Riessa and Gorn empathized with Johuocin. As he told of his deal with the wizard Bolac, they became appalled at the wizard for taking advantage of Johuocin's naive nature and the lack of honesty with which he pulled Johuocin into the trap that was triggered on Johuocin. Then they became dismayed at the way Johuocin let himself be manipulated into the situation by the wizard, knowing the insight he has demonstrated since they had met him. Then as Johuocin described his stepping into the captain's body and the way it affected the captain, taking pieces of his life, leaving the captain with no memory of the time that he was inhabited. They became disgusted with Johuocin and his ability to justify to himself that he had no choice. Then Gorn began to empathize with Johuocin, realizing that if it were not the captain, it would be someone else, knowing that he did not have a choice in how he used his time. Gorn knew instinctively that it tormented Johuocin more than anyone that he must do this. Then as Riessa saw Gorn soften toward Johuocin, she knew what Gorn felt was honest and right. She respected Gorn for his wisdom and Johuocin for his courage in telling his story. As Johuocin finished his story, Riessa and Gorn joined hands and reached out to Johuocin to join with him and offer their support. Johuocin took their hands as Gorn said, "The road ahead may be long. May our path be lit by wisdom."

Riessa squeezed the captain's hand. "Your secret is safe with us."

Just then Sticker's voice rang out through the dimly lit hovel. "What secret might that be?"

Gorn turned quickly and shot a look of hatred toward Sticker. "What have you heard, friendless one?"

"Plenty, and me friends'll return. Seems to me ya have a new problem now."

"You didn't wake in time or you would know your friends are all dead. Killed by bears. As for the other problem, I think I have a solution for that." Gorn smiled at the last bit of information he gave Sticker.

"Ya wouldn't kill me while I was tied. I'd stand at least a fair chance if I weren't. So do what ya hav'ta."

Still smiling, Gorn stood and put on his coat. "I'm not going to kill you, Sticker. You're going to be rehabilitated. You will make a great addition to the efforts of the Chinon monks, and I think they'll appreciate your stories of madness while they cure you."

Sticker's eyes widened as Gorn spoke. He was fighting to object, but all that would come from his mouth were stutters. Finally, as Gorn packed him across his shoulders and left the hovel, he managed to screech, "Nooooooo!"

Gorn laughed as he turned to Riessa. "I'll be back by midafternoon tomorrow." He turned again and was gone.

After Gorn had left, Riessa and Johuocin turned their efforts to tending Ben and Merson, cleaning and tending the wounds of the two as they slept, feeding them when they woke.

CHAPTER 9

An Unexpected Escort

As Gorn walked away from the hovel of Harishe, Sticker struggled and pleaded for his release. Even Sticker, in his secluded life as the master of Cragfare, had heard the rumors surrounding the Chinon monks who were notorious for curing men of ill deeds. The monks never left the walls of their monastery in search of those who needed help, but if someone were brought to them, they most certainly took on the responsibility. Those who survived the efforts of the order became part of the order; those who did not were considered blessed as they passed to the netherworld. Neither option seemed attractive to Sticker, but the more Sticker objected, the louder Gorn laughed and the faster he ran.

Finally after nearly ten hours at a full run, Gorn arrived at the secluded monastery of the Chinon. High walls of a cliff side revealed only a single door with a sash hanging to one side. No windows or casements were apparent anywhere in the barren stone wall that exhibited the single normal-sized door. The door was not ornate in any way, but the simplicity made it an awesome sight as it opened to the base of a sheer, stone cliff side.

Gorn reached out and pulled the hemp sash that hung from a rod that protruded from the wall. As he pulled he felt the springs of a counterweight pull it back. Then he waited patiently by the door as the dark winter night closed in about him.

Just as he was growing impatient of waiting and darkness had completely engulfed the horizon, the door opened and two hooded figures stepped out. Without a word they took hold of Sticker and pulled him through the doorway into the long, torch lit passage behind them. As the door began to close, Gorn could hear Sticker begin to scream his objections to being imprisoned without so much as a how-do-you-do. Gorn chuckled one last time at the pointless objections of the newest member of the Chinon monastery, shaking his head before turning back to his path of return. Though he felt his actions conflicted with his beliefs, it was fair to say that the monastery was a kindness in comparison to allowing Riessa to decide Sticker's fate.

*

Ben woke to the smell of stew bubbling by the fire and seeing steam rise from the kettle. His stomach grumbled its objections to the emptiness it felt, and he did not notice Riessa walk over to help him get up from where he lay. He jumped, startled, as she touched his arm. There was a look of terror in his eyes before he had the chance to focus and recognize Riessa.

"Calm yourself, Ben. It's me." Riessa was very quiet and reassuring as she helped him to the table.

Ben didn't say anything as she put food in front of him, and he started to eat like an animal that had been starved. The noises he made as he ate were anything but polite, and he released a large belch as he finished his third plate. He stared at the fire as he slurped from his cup of asra, still and in silence, not acknowledging Riessa except as he wanted more to eat or drink. Johuocin/Ory had gone outside to clean up the yard and surrounding area in case anyone happened by. After about an hour of silence from Ben, Riessa became worried and opened the door to call Johuocin. Just then Merson woke and called from the other side of the room.

"What happened?"

Riessa turned quickly to look at Merson. Softly, she answered, "Gorn found the two of you passed out in the snow and carried you back here."

Riessa moved back to Merson and helped him to the table. When Ben's eyes locked on him, Merson smiled and Ben laughed. Then it was Ben who took over and shakily got something for Merson to eat and drink. As he sat down again, tears started to roll down his face, and he sobbed. Relief hit Riessa's heart, and she joined Ben in his release of anguish, sitting next to him to watch Merson eat.

As Merson reached for his cup of asra halfway through his third plate of stew, Johuocin reentered the hovel. Seeing the two men up and about had a cheering effect on him after his ordeal of moving the dozens of dead bodies from the yard into the stable. He had piled them into a single stall, layer upon layer, with straw between them to catch the blood that would drain from them as they thawed.

Looking upon Johuocin, Riessa's face was engulfed in distaste as she ran her eyes from shoulder to foot along Johuocin's body. He looked down to inspect himself, only to find he had been covered in blood by his task. "A bit of a mess, isn't it? I'll go find my pack and get some clean clothes." At that he turned and walked out the door.

Merson looked around and interrupted his exit, "Where is Gorn?"

Riessa and Johuocin looked at each other, and smiles came to their faces. Riessa, giggling like a young girl, said, "Making a delivery." She and the captain broke into a full laugh as Johuocin turned and continued his trek out the door.

Ben and Merson exchanged a curious glance, and Ben could not contain his questions. "Did we miss something in our slumber, or have the two of you begun to share some kind of strange secret?"

"A little of both," Riessa answered. "You missed Sticker departing with Gorn on a journey to the Chinon monks." Her smile grew with her last words.

Merson and Ben began to laugh at the vision the words conjured, of Sticker being rehabilitated.

*

As Gorn was traveling back along his path toward the hovel, the moon lit his way. Slowly as the bright orb rose higher and higher above him, he could feel his senses heightening, his sense of smell becoming filled with everything around him. His eyes saw the heat the sun left upon the rocks. His ears picked up the tiniest rattle of nervous animals breathing as he passed. Gorn knew what was happening and decided not to fight it. No one was around to witness his transformation from man to bear. He just continued on his way, loping over the very plains he had experienced that morning as the sun came up in the eastern sky. He knew soon that it would overtake him and he would have to stop and hunt. He would have to satisfy the needs of the bear and ignore his own needs, the need to return to his friends, the need for rest.

*

As they discussed the events of the prior days, the four occupants of the tiny hovel relaxed and became more at ease with their situation. There were a few uneasy moments for Riessa when she would blush and turn away as they discussed their time in the hamlet of Skillcore. She was not put at ease by the logic of Merson, who would say time and time again, "It was only a dream, lass," as he chuckled under his breath, "no matter how real it seemed."

Johuocin too felt the uncomfortable wall of remembrance at some points of the recant. For instance he had not known she sat at his bedside in the hamlet, wetting his brow with cool rags. He also did not know that Gorn had left them at high moon in the hamlet, which meant that Harishe was indeed aware of Gorn's problem and secret. Then he remembered talking to Merson about his meeting with the dwarves. If Harishe had lived, that could have been dangerous. He would have certainly tried to sell the information to the king.

Merson looked at the captain sternly as they finished talking of Skillcore. "When is Gorn due back?"

"Tomorrow before sunset. Why?" Johuocin had a feeling he knew why Merson was concerned. By the time Gorn returned, they would have less than seven days before the winter solstice. Seven days later the meeting with the dwarf chieftains would take place. If all went well, war would be waged with the support to reinforce a takeover of the oldest hierarchy on the continent.

"We must move soon, Captain. The days are short, and soon the darkness of the winter solstice will be here." Merson sighed as he let out his words. "I still must tutor you in dealing with the chieftains. You still have not heard from your father."

"Yes, I know," Johuocin snapped, "and we all need attention from skilled healers, and we all need rest, and we all need to forget a lot of what we've been through."

Frustrated, Johuocin slammed his hand on the table and brushed away the imaginary item that sat on its corner. "So, why don't we just cut our losses and let the demons take us!" As he screamed those words, he walked over to the fireplace and leaned with both hands on the hot mantle, saying, "Even now my choices are failing you, Father."

Ben stood and walked over to his brother, laying his hand on his brother's shoulder. "Ory, we still have time. We can start to plan now."

Johuocin thought about the convenience of Ben and Ory's father having so much to do with their situation, considering his remark.

"Plan what? We don't even know where we are or how far we have to go. Or have you become an oracle in the last few days?"

Johuocin was on the verge of just walking away. If he had not caught sight of Riessa at that instant, he would have. But as he did, something deep inside of him pulled together. He softened and knew he could not bear to lose any more of her respect than he felt he had already.

Merson was the only one in the room with a clear head. Whether it was age, wisdom, or logic didn't matter. He was the only one who had an idea. "This man who lived here, he had us under some kind of spell. That means he was a wizard of some kind."

Riessa looked at Merson quizzically. "What good does that do us now? He's dead."

"Sure he is, lass. But he didn't take his things with him. And if he didn't take his things with him, that means they're still here. If he were a wizard, he'd have himself some star charts." There in front of all of them stood Merson, with a smug little grin on his face.

Johuocin felt dumbfounded by his reasoning. "So because this Harishe had star charts, we get to play riddles until we're blue, or have you got an answer?"

"Well, elves use the stars for everything, from telling them when to go to battle to where they stand on a map." Again Merson stood and grinned, but everyone's eyes fell on Riessa, and Riessa just looked at Merson in confusion.

"Don't look at me," she said. "I was raised as a human. I am only half-elf."

"It was a good idea though, Merson." Ben let out his disappointment.

"Still is, lad." Merson maintained his smug look. "I was raised by dwarves. Our mortal enemies were elves. When you have an enemy, you try to think like they do. If you want to think like them, then you learn like them." He stood and chuckled. "I can read star charts."

*

As the sun rose over the horizon, Gorn stopped to check his progress. The peak of the Mountain of Chinon was still visible behind him but displayed his progress well. Had he not seen the distinctive, needlelike mountain as they traveled into the illusion of Skillcore, he would not have known his path. He looked to the sky. As the stars disappeared, the blue overtook the black, announcing a clear day.

The days were short this time of year. In another hour the sun would be at its peak. Gorn would have to pick up the pace of his travel in order to reach his friends before the dinner hour. He knew they were on a schedule of some kind, and he could not fail their purpose.

He started to move forward to the hovel once again. Encouraging the pain in his legs to call on the strength of the bear, Gorn began picking up speed as he climbed toward the top of a small hill. As he picked up speed, the pain increased. His long, arduous journey was beginning to wear on the muscles in his thighs. He knew he should not have stopped to look back.

As he crested the top of the hill, he saw to the southeast a group of riders on the high road two miles away. He could not tell who they were, or how many. If it were not for the sharp sense of smell, the eyes of the bear would not have seen them at all. Soon he saw them leave the road headed in his direction. The thoughts of his discomfort left him, and he found the strength to move with more speed.

*

Johuocin and Merson worked together on fixing a route to the nearest dwarven city, Korfri. There they would meet with some of the Oschcra Cree. Merson had found the star charts in the hovel behind a loose stone. His face filled with laughing arrogance as he pulled them from their hiding place.

In the meantime, Riessa and Ben worked on getting the stock together and hitching the wagon. The group had already decided that they would leave as soon as Gorn returned. While Gorn had not had the rest and comfort they had, Riessa had volunteered him to sleep in the traveling wagon as they moved.

"Merson." Johuocin looked up from the maps they were looking at. "My father still has not reached us with his message. I think we may have been occupied here too long. My fear is that they could not find us and returned to my father with that news."

"I would say that is a good possibility, Captain. Isn't that why we are charting for Korfri, to locate the meeting?" Merson seemed disinterested in the topic of their discussion, looking up only momentarily at the captain.

"I do have the scroll that I was to read upon seeing my father's messenger. Perhaps we should read it now."

"He would not have put the location there, Captain, but, it may be a good idea to find out what is in it. It will be there when we are done with the charts."

The two went back to their maps and charts to lay out the rest of their trip. If they stopped briefly in Villanek Elna, a religious colony to the south, they might find some skilled healers and stock up on supplies.

*

As Gorn traveled along his path, he occasionally looked to the rear. He saw no sign of the riders. He traveled as quickly as he could, knowing they would follow his path had they spotted him from the road they were traveling. And he also knew there was little reason for them to leave the road had they not seen him. His speed was greatly diminished by his fatigue. He wished he were fresh and rested as he had been the day the party had left Rausche Laine. Then there would be no worry as to his maintaining the lead he had on the party behind him.

He heard a bird call from above him as he ran. Gorn looked up. A falcon traveled comfortably at the speed he ran. He tried to increase his speed, but the falcon only paced as he moved. His intent became merely to maintain the lead he had on the riders.

For hours Gorn ran constantly with the falcon intent above him. Finally he saw his destination before him in the near distance. A column of smoke rose in front of him, behind a few small hills. As he spotted the smoke, the falcon turned away and went back in the direction from which they had come so far together.

*

"We have only to wait now, Captain." Merson stood up from the table, moved to the window and peered out. "Gorn should be returning soon if he is not lost."

Riessa stirred the pot of stew near the fire. "He will be back, and probably tired and cold. We can leave after he has a hot meal."

Johuocin stood and walked over to the captain's pack laying in the corner of the hovel. Reaching into the front pocket of the pack, he pulled out the scroll with the griffin seal. Staring at it, he slowly moved back to the table where Merson had been sitting. "It's time we took a look at this," he said as he set it on the table and stared at it, feeling the guilt of the invasion. He knew it was nothing he had not done before, but now, he was aware that Riessa was watching, judging, him.

Merson walked back to the table and sat down, pulling out his knife, he reached out and creased the wax with the edge of his blade. Giving the scroll a flick of his blade, it rolled open in front of Johuocin.

As Johuocin looked down at it, he began to read aloud the words written by the captain's father.

Orman, my son,

As it is that you are reading this letter, my hope is that everything is well and my messenger has reached you. If he has said I have "fallen ill," then our plan is to proceed as is written in this scroll. If any other message is given to you, you must do what you can to make other arrangements and send a messenger with the details. As you have opened this scroll, your first priority is to inform Ouben of everything that has happened or has been planned. Tell him I felt it was best for everyone that only as many people as were absolutely necessary were to know about this for securities objective to survive, his safety as well as the mission's success.

I trust that Merson's coaching for the council was adequate and that he was able to school you in the manners of the presentation and protocol to these chieftains. They are vital to our plan if we can make them our allies. We will need as many of the eleven tribes as we can muster. Any less than seven of the tribes will cause a failed attempt.

The forest dwarves are our strongest surprise element of the attack and must be set to leave the last of all enlisted. This will be a hard argument to them. If they crave war as much as they are rumored, they will want to be first into battle. You cannot let that happen. Make them understand that they will be the strength of our attack upon the Castle Eldwain. They must move undetected, regardless of their number, through the Morlocrin Forrest and along the River of Sleep. That, in and of itself, may be a battle harsh enough to exhaust them. They must not leave until the eastern and southern fronts are detected and moved upon. A minimal number of troops must be remaining at the castle when they arrive.

Remember, Eldwa's armies are great in number. We must have strong fronts to the east and south to prevent the king's front from retreating any of its forces to another front. From where the battles begin, the tribes must advance only if the king's forces weaken or retreat. If that happens, they must hit fiercely to keep the main battles away from the castle. They also must retreat if they make too much prog-ress—slowly enough to draw back the king's army without drawing suspicion. With the king's army numbering over twenty-five thousand, we must keep them busy on as many fronts as possible. The north will be advancing as quickly as it can to overtake the castle.

The wealth and land of Eldwain will be opened from all sides when the battle is over and the king is dead. But only as to who will control it. It must be made clear that no citizens will be displaced without voluntary submission. The fronts to the north are already in agreement to this.

The information given to you by my messenger is written as we played when you were a child. I hope you remember the war against the gophers. I say this in jest, but your youth taught you many things.

Good hope and strong voice,
Your father, Sesnic

There at the bottom of the page was the griffin stamped over Sesnic Reglawr's signature.

"There it is, little of what we must know." Johuocin shuddered as he spoke in reference to the written words of the captain's father. "I wonder if it will be enough."

Ben looked at the man who was his brother and smiled. He always trusted Ory to find strength and make do with what was available. He knew the bond between his father and Ory and knew how much alike they thought. "The messenger still might find us. Even if he doesn't, you'll know what Father would have planned close enough to make it work." What Ben didn't know was that the man he was looking at had no such bond with Sesnic Reglawr. Johuocin and Riessa exchanged a distressed look.

Merson looked at the captain. "We'd better get back to tutoring you for the meeting of the chieftains.

*

As Gorn crested the hill that put him in sight of the hovel, he looked behind to see if the riders had caught him yet. There was still no visible sign of them but he did not slow as he ran across the area in front of the hovel, barely noticing it had been cleared. He slammed himself against the door and burst into the hovel, startling everyone in it. The sun still had not set, and Gorn was hours ahead of the time they had expected him.

Riessa recovered excitedly, anxiously, curiously, saying, "You're back early. What's wrong?"

Gorn, too out of breath to speak, unsuccessfully tried to motion for the party to hurry and leave. As he saw his attempt fail, he closed the door and fell back against it to catch his breath.

Johuocin and Ben helped him over to the table to sit. "Merson, get the horses ready to leave. Riessa, get some food for Gorn and help him get his coat off. He needs to dry out a little before we leave. He's soaked with sweat."

Johuocin, like all the rest, had sensed Gorn's urgency but was the only one nervous enough to act. Looking around, he saw no one moving. Frustrated, he raised his voice. "Now! I think we're in a hurry." As he yelled, everyone began to move. "Ben, help me gather what's left to go." Even before he could finish what he was saying, Ben had started to pack the remaining items about the hovel.

As Gorn caught his breath and shoveled what food Riessa had put in front of him into his mouth, he began to tell Johuocin what was happening. Soon he had finished both what was on his plate and what he had to say. He gulped down a mug of hot asra as Riessa put down another plate of food in front of him.

"You don't know who or how many are following you?'

Johuocin was curious. Maybe this was the messenger from Sesnic Reglawr. "Maybe we should wait and see who they are?"

Just then Merson returned from outside. "Ready to go, Captain." He realized almost immediately that no one had acknowledged him. Instead, they were intent on Johuocin and Gorn.

"You'd better make up your mind soon, Captain. They weren't far behind me. And they were traveling fast." Gorn stared at Johuocin.

Merson saw the dilemma in the captain's expression. "If you're thinking it's your father's messenger, Captain, it's not likely if there are more than two or three."

Gorn got up and put his coat on. "And there were definitely more than that, Captain. I would not have seen them at the distance I did."

At that Johuocin stood and put on his coat. Riessa and Ben followed his lead. "Let's go."

The party moved away from the hovel toward the colony of Villanek Elna. Their plan was to stop briefly there to buy supplies and clothing before going on to Korfri. They would probably not have time to find healers, though they still were in poor shape to travel.

The wagon was heavy, and in the snow it was hard to get the horses up to any speed. Though, once they were moving well, the wheels seemed to cut through the drifts without any problems. Daylight was still handy when they heard the shouts of the approaching party closing behind them, and the screech of the falcon overhead. Ben and Merson dropped from their horses and lay prone in the snow to each side of the wagon with their crossbows at ready. Their horses moved on without them alongside the wagon as any well-trained military mount would. Riessa moved the wagon forward as Gorn jumped out and Johuocin pulled his mount away and faced the oncoming party, riding up next to Gorn and stopping just beyond where the other two lay in the snow.

As the riders came closer, Johuocin counted ten of them. Four with short bows, three holding swords across their saddles, one with a sheathed short sword and a mandolin on his back to the rear, and two not showing weapons of any kind and hoods flying in the wind. They spread out as they came even closer, the four bow men to the outside, placing arrows at the ready. Then the large man next to Johuocin began to laugh. His laugh was deep and hardy and seemed to roll over the hills and bounce off of the crisp air of the day. It engulfed the entire area and having its usual contagious effect on the other members of the party of five, even through their confusion and worry. Then all at once everyone noticed how the horses dwarfed the riders, making them seem small and insignificant, or perhaps just less threatening.

"They are children, Captain." Gorn's booming voice carried over the hills at the announcement. The entire party joined his laughter.

The riders came to a halt. The laughter stopped as the bowmen let go their arrows and had another knocked before they landed each one three inches in front of the four men who were ready to fight just minutes before. Johuocin had an arrow plant itself in the yolk of his saddle.

As they surveyed the riders, all appeared to be between the ages of eight and eleven. The rider with the mandolin came up through their midst, a little forward of the rest. He was wearing a colorful outfit of red and green and yellow, and a smirk on his face of arrogance and pursuit.

"I am Alsie," he announced. "Which of you is Harishe?"

Johuocin looked at them in wonder and apprehension, not quite knowing what to think or do or say. "Why do you want Harishe?" he called back.

"He has something we want." The determination in the boy's voice was strong. "If he will give it to us, we will leave and not harm anyone."

"We do not have Harishe," Johuocin reached down and pulled the arrow out of his saddle, throwing it down to stick in the snow. "If we did you could gladly have him."

"Is that not his servant standing next to you? We have heard of his size. There seems to be an illusion about you. Are you Harishe?" The boy had an accusing tone to his voice. Johuocin could feel the boy looking at him, placing the guilt for all the atrocities he had performed and making Johuocin feel the transgression and criminality of all his actions.

"I am Gorn. The one you have mistaken me for lays dead in the stable of the hovel." Gorn's voice again carried over the space surrounding the two parties. This time there was no laughter or amusement to be felt. "Next to Harishe. Next to the many dead in that place."

Alsie looked at Gorn in astonishment, anger, and disbelief. "You have not killed Harishe. You could not kill Harishe." He looked at Johuocin. "He is Harishe." At that he screamed, drew his sword, and charged Johuocin.

Johuocin gave his horse a kick in the flanks and turned to avoid the attack. The boy passed and stopped his horse; turning back to the captain, he sheathed his sword again. "So, if you are not Harishe, who are you?"

Johuocin was confused. Why did the boy charge him if not to attack? Why didn't Ben or Merson fire on him? "I am Captain Orman Reglawr. How did you know I was not Harishe? And how did you know my men would not fire on you?"

"Captain, Harishe is a coward and an illusionist. He would have let me see him as something to be frightened of. Your men did fire on me." At that Alsie pointed to two arrows that had fallen to the snow, with two other arrows piercing their shafts dead center. "As far as the others not attacking when I did, I only scream when I don't attack." The boy's voice had adopted a sad tone. "I wish you hadn't killed Harishe though."

"What did you need from Harishe?"

The boy turned his horse back to walk slowly toward the captain.

"Perhaps nothing, perhaps something. I don't know." The boy pulled his mandolin off of his back and began to play. Two of his companions rode to the wagon and brought back the horses to Ben and Merson. "Where are you going?"

"Villanek Elna." Johuocin volunteered the information without defense as he listened to the music playing softly on the hypnotic instrument.

"Very well, we will ride with you. I will tell you a story and play you some music to apologize for our indiscretions."

CHAPTER 10

The Tale of the Ten Children

As the parties moved toward Villanek Elna, Johuocin made introductions for the five. He told Alsie what he could of Harishe and Galeem, and the adventure into Skillcore, the dream city. As they traveled, Alsie played, and the time passed quickly. The music had a natural magic to it. Everyone became relaxed and hardly noticed the wind bite at their faces and legs. The story of Skillcore restored happy faces to the children, who seemed much too serious and burdened for their years.

Alsie started to sing a lighthearted tune when Johuocin had finished his story. But Johuocin interrupted. "Wait, you haven't introduced your friends yet. Or told us why you were seeking Harishe."

"That might be a long story, Captain. More so than we have time. As to introductions, these two nearest me," Alsie indicated the two with the hoods and no apparent weapons, "they are my younger siblings, Anitae and Otinoe. They are born twins to my father's wife. Our parents are dead many years. The archers to the front are Minac and Soral. They are siblings of my brother and sister, Anitae and Otinoe, and cousins to me. Their father died by the hand of a Minotaur king in the south. They are cousins to my cousin Finat, who is the tallest of us, and a fine swordsman. The other two swordsmen are Koreal and Avalaes, the older siblings of Finat and cousins to Anitae and Otinoe. The two other archers are Riman and Domatis. They are the older siblings of Koreal and Avalaes and also my cousins and the cousins of Finat. Riman and Domatis are also cousins to Minac and Soral. So as you can see, Captain, we are more than friends; we are all family. I am the oldest, and Finat is the youngest."

Gorn studied the child as he canted the present branches of their family tree. He was having a hard time himself distinguishing how so many could be so closely related or so distantly related from and within the same family homes. He was able to conclude that there were only two households and still there were cousins of cousins in the same home with the same parents, or at least parents who were related in some indistinct way. How many parents were there?

In his confusion Gorn said aloud, "Where are their parents?"

Finat ignored the fact that the question was not directed at him. "Dead. All of them."

Gorn, startled as he realized he had spoken loud enough to be heard, asked without pause, "How long ago?"

"Two score and three summers at the day of winter solstice." The boy glared as Gorn chuckled to himself and then looked up at the young rider from his seat in the back of the wagon.

"No boy, your parents, not your grand-parents." Gorn continued to smile as tears welled up in the boy's eyes.

Alsie looked at Gorn and stopped playing. The silence of the night overtook them. Seriously. Contemptibly. "As Finat said, two score and three summers ago. Do you think he would joke about the death of our parents? Do you think that we are too young to be alone so long? Or is it you think our experience and skill is not great enough to be so long in this world?"

Gorn was more confused than ever. Maybe he was losing his touch for looking at the world without judgment. Losing his philosophy. "But how?"

Ben, Merson, Riessa, Johuocin, and Gorn all turned their attention to Alsie at that point. They were not going to miss the account of how ten children had remained children for over forty summers. Two summers ago, only two would have even listened to the story with anything more than skepticism. Over the last few days, they had learned not to discount anything as impossible.

"As I have said before, the story is a long one. Perhaps longer than we have time." The boy, Alsie, tucked the reigns of his horse under his leg and began to play again. "I will tell it as it is told where we come from, it is a small village nine days south of Eldwain called Lonely Valley. There, among the mountains of Sol Daieneo, there were few families and more miles between them than you could walk in a day. Horses were scarce, and the Ocre, the faery folk, wished to drive away the humans from the mountains. They claimed it as their territory and did what they could to discourage us from existing there. They could not do evil harm to us. That was their way of life, to protect nature and not harm life. All they could do was mischievous harm. Our fathers would plant corn in the fields and trees would grow. They would plant asra root, and rocks would prevent us from digging it out. So, many families conceded and moved to the valley. Only the three families from which we were conceived remained on the mountain. They were the families that harvested only what nature would give them. The Ocre did not object to this and left us alone.

"The community elders continued to visit our families from time to time and conceded that it was the perfect situation. Within the three families were four male children and four female children. These were our parents. It was assumed that they would match up according to ages and all would be fine as their lives continued and they had children, us. My parents were the first to marry and promptly went about conceiving a child, me. Upon hearing of my birth, the elders came and blessed the event. A large celebration was planned, and many of our neighbors came from the valley to witness the blessing and offer their own in the form of gifts. The Ocre caused no problems as they saw that the people were going back to the valley where they had made their homes. The same continued as first Riman and then Domatis were born. The families were very happy as they saw so many male children were born to them. As yet though, no others were married. Then the winter after Domatis was born, there was an illness that came to the mountain. All the families became very ill and could not cope with the sickness. The Ocre, though there was no great love between the faeries and our families, were satisfied with the fact that no other families were coming back to the mountain. They offered herbs and natural cures that helped us greatly. Still, my mother and the father of Riman and Domatis, brother and sister, died of the illness.

"This left my father and their mother, also brother and sister, widowed and alone. Their grief was great, and no one could comfort them. In their year of mourning, no one married so as not to remind them of their loss. Brother and sister from the family not directly affected by the loss took on the responsibility of helping our parents with their families, brother helping the widow, sister helping the widower. No one was surprised when they expressed their plans for marriage and planned the weddings to take place on the same day. There was a large celebration as the faeries looked on. Some even brought gifts.

"The couples were happy as they continued their lives, and my father's wife soon conceived and gave birth to twins, Anitae and Otinoe, one girl and one boy.

"Soon after, Riman and Domatis also had a new brother, Koreal.

"Hints were given to the last couple remaining to marry. The elders were lecturing them on the benefits of sharing their lives. But they could not find an attraction to each other. They tried to court one another. They tried to help one another, but alas, no word of marriage could come to pass their lips. It was rumored that even the Ocre tried to play a hand at making the fire spark between them. Nothing.

"Finally, the families had a party to try and find suitable mates for the two. The Ocre became angry at the thought of bringing more humans to live on the mountain. They caused a horrendous storm of cold wind and rain in the midday of the party. If that was not enough, a tearing dust storm started the next day and continued for five days. My father fell ill with a bleeding lung from all the dust and soon died.

"Out of the guilt of having angered the Ocre, his brother took his place in providing for our family, and soon loneliness and need of a woman overtook him and he married my father's wife.

"The next season, the mother of Riman, Domatis, and Koreal, died giving birth to Avalaes.

"The last remaining to marry took on the responsibility of raising the infant and his three brothers, also caring for the father of the four. Soon she fell in love with the children as she cared for them as her own, tending their every need. Her parents passed away, and she spent all of her time with the family she had adopted as her own. The children's father suggested they be married so as not to upset the elders who would look on them with distaste and arrogance. They married, and the Ocre were satisfied no one new would come to the mountain.

"The Ocre became helpful to them. Now only two families remained on the mountain. All the others had left or died.

"A third winter had passed and spring was about to blossom when my father's wife gave birth to Minac. She was strong and healthy and a sturdy woman. She was able to continue her everyday chores, taking only an hour of her time to give birth. The seasons passed quickly, and the next winter she gave birth to Soral.

"Soon after, my mother's sister, the last to marry, gave birth to Finat. He was born on the solstice. His mother was not so strong. After near death with the birth, she and her husband decided not to have more children.

"The next years were uneventful. The Ocre became commonplace in our everyday lives, helping us with harvest and illnesses. They were even friendly.

"As Riman and I passed through our eighth summer, our parents started talking about what we would do when we came of age and wanted our own families. Then stopped, acknowledging that there were many seasons to pass before that happened.

"Two summers later word was received that there was a war to the south. Minotaurs were invading at the coast from the Isles of Banalor. My father's brother enlisted in its defense and was reported to us dead by spring, killed by a Minotaur king as he himself delivered a fatal blow to the invading monarch.

"Now the talk of our coming of age became constant. As spring wore into summer and summer to fall, the faery folk became more secluded to us, helping us harvest only when they had questions. They had become concerned once again that more humans would come to the mountain. Even though the elders had stopped coming but once a year, they had not thought about the children getting older.

"As winter wore on, we were content. Harvest had gone well, and a profit was made. We had plenty of food to get us through the winter and enough dead wood was gathered to keep us warm.

"At solstice we were all gathered together in one home. We children were all playing with the toys given us by our parents and nibbling on the leftover food from our solstice feast and sweet meats laid out for us.

"There was a knock at the door. It opened by itself, and a small whirlwind flew in. Circling around the room carrying leaves of many colors, then it stopped in the middle of the room, and the Ocre king himself appeared carrying a small box. The box was ornate with its designs of spring flowers and fall leaves, star-riddled skies, and snowy fields. All these things seemed to blend together like the changing seasons. We all looked on in awe and giddy happiness at seeing the box and the Ocre king himself.

"'Greetings,' he said in his enchanting little voice. 'I have brought you all wishes for being the neighbors you are. I certainly hope they satisfy.'

"'Wishes?' my mother's sister asked. 'What kind of wishes?'

"'Any kind you can wish, of course. That is what a wish is.' He smiled widely as he answered her questions. "All you do is make the wish and I will open the box when everyone is done. I can only open this box once a year, but it will grant everyone's wish that is near."

"'That's wonderful,' said my father's wife, smiling in delight. 'Will it give exactly what is asked for?'

"'Indeed,' he said, cocking an eyebrow. 'You must wish exactly. Come, you be the first to wish.'

"'No. Let my brother go first. He works so hard for us.'

"'All right then,' he said, turning to her brother. 'Make your wish, good sir.'

"'I wish,' he said, smiling, 'I could be as strong as granite.' He paused and looked at his wife. 'That might make my work a little easier.' They laughed.

"The king turned to the man's wife. 'Your turn, madam.'

"My mother's sister looked at the king and then to her husband. 'I wish,' she said, 'that we will always be close at heart.'

"The king turned back to my father's wife. 'Are you ready now?'

"'I have always been seen as a sturdy woman. I wish that people would see me beautiful and delicate.'

"Then he turned to us children. Smiling as he walked toward us, he said, 'You each get a wish too, you know. My gift is for all of you and each of you.' He looked at each of us as we giggled and lowered our eyes. We were so foolish and young. 'Who will go first?'

"Riman, Domatis, Minac, and Soral all at once remembered the games we played the summer after hearing about my father's brother. 'I wish I could be a great archer.'

"'Done, done, done, and done,' he said, looking at them each. 'Who will be next?'

"Koreal and Avalaes, getting caught up in the thought of war games, blurted out, 'I wish I could be a great swordsman.'

"'Also done,' he said, then quickly, 'next.'

"Finat, the youngest, who so despised being small, blurted, 'I wish to be a bigger, better swordsman.'

"'A fine choice, well done.' He turned to the twins.

"Otinoe was ready to speak but wanted his sister to go first. He was always the instigator. He would think of things to get into and convince his sister to go first. Then when they were caught, he would use that as a defense.

"Anitae, a softer, gentler, more giving child, would take the blame and smile her way out of trouble. She was not ready yet.

"'Let me come back to you two.' He began to turn to me but was interrupted by Otinoe.

"'Wait!' he pushed out. 'I wish me and my sister would never get caught at anything we shouldn't do.'

"'Fine,' he said with a bit of a smirk and the raise of a brow. Then he turned to Anitae. 'Ready?'

"'No, not yet. Thank you sir.'

"'Fine, it's you then,' he said, turning to me.

"'I wish to be a bard.' I thought about the stories I could tell to all I met, enhancing it with the music I played and yet, not being defenseless. I remember looking at the little king with a hopeful look, wanting so badly that he grant the wish I had wished.

"'Done,' he said. 'My subjects have not underestimated you one bit.' Then he turned to my sister. 'You are the last, small one. Ready to make your wish?'

"She only shook her head.

"'Then I have a wish of my own. I wish you all get your wishes. And I wish you get the things you need to practice your choosing and a horse for each of the children. Just because you are children and you deserve to be treated kindly.' He looked at Anitae again. 'Now don't you wish you could all remain children forever?'

"She nodded just one shy little nod.

"That's all it took. He said, 'Done!' He opened the box turned back into the whirlwind and flew out the door.

"When we recovered from his departure, my sister stood there with her head down, saying, 'That wasn't my wish. I didn't get to make my wish.'

"I walked over to her and raised her chin. A tear rolled from the corner of her eye. I asked, 'What was your wish, little one?'

"'I was going to wish for my daddy back.' And a tear rolled from the other eye.

"As we looked around the room, we didn't understand at the time. There stood a granite statue of my father's sister with her husband and a potted wild rose. Now, of course, we do understand. It was their wish, but you must wish exactly. Granite is as strong as granite. To be alike is close at heart. Nothing is as beautiful and delicate as a wild rose."

As the party listened to Alsie play his mandolin, they pondered the story he told. Riessa had a tear in her eye for the little girl who was tricked out of her wish and into another. Johuocin, for the first time since he met with Bolac, felt worse for someone else than he did for himself.

They rode in silence for a time before the party of five could recover from the tale of the ten children.

"So, lad, why is it you were looking for Harishe?" Merson turned to the boy bard. "What is it you were hopin' to find?"

"I thought it was obvious. We want another wish. And who would have one if not a wizard?" The boy was smug as he answered Merson. Or he was lost in the sadness of that day so many seasons past. "Really, we want two." He smiled at Merson and looked to his sister and winked.

When she saw Alsie wink, she wiped her face and giggled.

"Now let me sing you a song about the same story so dreary. I discovered it in my heart ten years after the fact when we were enjoying our adventures more than we were dwelling on the fact that we were still children lost to time." He began to play a lighter tune and pace, as if he were trying to find the right mood in the cold wind of the early morning hours. He began humming the tune to warm his voice to carry. His tones were strong and light, as contagious as Gorn's laugh, making you wish to hum along with him. But his voice was so beautiful it made a person feel inadequate to do so.

He began to sing the words to his tune. The tune itself sounded familiar and unidentifiable.

> None had come, none had gone.
> 'Twas their mountain we were on
> On the mountain, high and
> strong,
> A battle, quiet, grim, and long.
> Humans driven from their
> home,
> As faery folk changed wind
> and loam.
> To the valley, go they would.
> Three families, on the
> mountain stood.

They took what nature there
would give,
And on that gift they all would
live.
The Ocre soon would grant
their being,
From the harvests they were
seeing.
These humans tore no land
or tree.
They let the wind and streams
flow free.
So there the mountain war
would die.
But faery kept an open eye.
To see that none would wander
back,
To set up house or seed their track.
So here begins another tale.
One in which the peace will fail.

The children now began to
marry.
Four of eight, the rest would
tarry.
From these four, three sons
were born.
But, soon their families were
forlorn.
For illness came to all the folk,
And two had died when fever
broke.
(The Ocre came to break our
fall,
but came too late to save us all.)
Brother and sister left to fend,
When sister and brother found
their end.
As brother and sister mourned
their dead,

Through aid and caring, a love
was fed.
As the widowed married anew,
Six were married, leaving two.
The newly wedded were
quickly blessed.
The three new children gave
no rest.
Now families set to fan a flame,
To the last whose age had came.
But the two had no desire,
No spark of kindness turned
to fire.
The Ocre tried their very best,
But all their nature failed the
test.
They filled the glades with
pretty flowers,
Built fall whirlwinds into towers,

Chased clouds away for starlit
    nights,
But still the two had missed
    the sights.
They tried to court, each the
    other,
But felt to each sister, brother.
Then the families held a ball.
Summers day had turned to fall.
Ocre, faery, vexed to view
Valley folk court the two.
So after all had left that day,
Faery folk set dust to spray.
Five days it blew across our lives,
Cutting lungs like tiny knives.
As the dust stole children's grins,
So it took the life that fathered
    twins.
The brother of the father took
    widow for his wife,

And to the other family was
born another life.
As life comes into life it needs
room to exist,
So as life came into life, the
giver did desist.

Now there was but one to marry, giving
care behest of mother.

So it came to her consent, to
marry sister's brother.
Now all the eight were surely
wed,
But four of eight were gone
and dead.
All three families turned into two,
And that is what the faeries knew.
Soon three infants came to light

Conceived on peaceful, starry
night.
Peace reigned over mountain
life
As neighbors gave no heed to
strife.
Ocre came into our presence
Giving life an easy essence.
For years they helped us in our
work,
Never would they spy or lurk.
Harvests would be rich and
heavy.
In spring the Ocre built a levee.
But time passed on and children
aged.
Soon there was a question waged.
What of marriage for the young,
What of romance to be sung?

For this the faeries were
undone,
For, nine were boys, and girls
but one.
And family, not just some but
all.
So, faeries planned to make
us fall.
Then war was waged at
southern sea,
Minotaur king made parents
three.
Three now left to raise the ten,
Faery, Ocre, watched for men.
None had come, none had
gone.
'Twas their mountain we were on!
Summer, fall, and harvest came,
Faery help was not the same.

Winter came with cupboards
packed.
Solstice came of not we lacked.
Then he came, the Ocre king,
Holding out that cursed thing.
A wishing box he said it was,
Opened up this year for us.
So wish we did, without suspect.
Our memories we did neglect.
Beginning with parents, all too
eager.
Making wishes unclear and
meager.
Strong as granite, close at heart,
Beautiful and delicate, true at
part.
Then the children, quick to shout,
All but one made wishes stout.
First four bowmen, best of
many.

Then three swordsmen, one
bigger than any.
Then the one made a wish for
two,
The twins would be stealthy
true.
Still the one could not make
her choice,
She knew her wish but lost
her voice.
Then the eldest made his
choosing.
A bard, he says, no confidence
losing.
Then back to the girl the king
did turn.
He wished for us horses, and
tools to help learn.
He said to the girl, "Are you
ready to choose?

"You are a child with nothing
to lose."
Still too shy to wish her dream
The king went on, smooth as
cream.
"Children are special in every
way.
They always say what they
mean to say."
He looked at the children with
a sparkle in his eye,
And turned to the girl. "Are
you still too shy?
Don't you wish you could be
children forever?"
She nodded in answer like
pulling a lever.
"Done!" he snapped as he
opened the chest.

Then out he went from our
    solstice nest.
Then as we looked, our parents
    were gone,
Leaving statues for two and a
    flower for one.
Then as the clouds in our eyes
    had expired
The little girl stood where her
    dreams had aspired.
A tear rolled down from her
    eye on the right
And both eyes were wet and it
    rippled her sight
"I just wanted father," was then
    what she said.
As the other eye teared and she
    lowered her head.
As he finished his song, the
    party felt the loss of the

little girl once more.
Silence was the only thing
to meet the air as they
traveled on until daylight.

CHAPTER 11

The Ruin of Rest

The rising sun came up behind them as they crested the hills near Villanek Elna. In the distance they saw ruin in the place they were to stock their supplies and trade their stock. Save perhaps two or three active smokestacks, the place they were headed appeared deserted. The places of worship were in ruin, drifted over with snow, and the evidence of civilization had been camouflaged by the season. The spirits of the parties that traveled there were dampened with the acknowledgment that hope of replenishing supplies was gone.

Johuocin let his mind wander into the dismal corners of his eternity as they rode into a place that once was. How many times would he see this in a lifetime that would not end? How many times would he visit places that were no more? Would he be there even to see the fall of his father's own stonework?

A silent communication passed through the party as eyes shifted from one person to the next. They felt an eeriness as they rode into the streets that were no longer traveled by villagers who once lived there. The feelings Johuocin was experiencing were intensified by the sight of children raising their guard, with weapons being set ready, and small hands on the hilts of swords. Knowing the children were older than he was had no effect on the sight of it.

The parties headed for a small home near the edge of the fallen village, a small cottage where smoke drifted slowly from the chimney.

"There doesn't appear to be much life, or that many provisions will be found here, Captain." Merson broke the silence that haunted the two parties since the lightless hours of morning.

Riessa was relieved at the sound of someone's voice, and she answered him in Johuocin's stead. "Let's see what life is here before we freeze to death. We can deal with starvation when we get warm."

"I don't think we have to worry about starving, lass. As the mules die, we can always eat them." Merson looked over at Ben and winked. "I'll bet Ben here makes a great stew.

He may kill one before they die on their own. I've seen him threaten stock before." Johuocin and Gorn laughed as Ben looked at them with disgust in his embarrassment.

"That's not playing very fair for a man your age, Merson. That was an honest mistake, made in an attempt to protect the rest of you." Ben tried to sound hurt and defensive as he put out those words, but he couldn't control the grin that came from laughing at his own humiliation as it crept across his face.

Gorn, seeing that they were leaving the tagalong party out of the humor, tried to fill them in on the incident in Cragfare. Much to the chagrin of Ben, they laughed again. Finat offered to cover Ben's back if the party actually came to that.

Ben, forgetting the suspended ages of the children, said, "I'd like someone a little older at my back, thank you."

Johuocin couldn't resist comment, though he knew it would annoy Ben. "I'd like to remind you, even the youngest of these children is thirty years your senior, brother." At that Ben nudged his horse and went a few feet ahead of the caravan.

"That was cruel, but true, and a reminder to me," Alsie added with a remorseful but unhurt tone. "Will you be headed north or east when you leave here?"

"East," Merson muttered without thinking.

"There is a place southeast of here," Anitae spoke up, "I would say about two days. You could get supplies there. We'd heard a sorcerer was known to be near there, and that is our destination now that there is no Harishe."

"No, we must head due east if we are to be where we must by solstice. We must head through the mountain to reach our goal.

Around it would take two more days than we have." Merson reverted to his goal-minded self as he thought about the travel they had ahead, knowing it might take the extra two days through the mountain anyway at this time of year. He knew they must shed the wagon as they headed into the mountain, and he hoped they would not have to leave much else behind, but he knew that this was only a hope. The stock had already been burdened beyond safe limits for the travel they had been forced into.

As they came to the hovel where smoke streamed high above the stack frozen in the still air of the valley, Johuocin and Riessa were the first to dismount. Gorn began to climb from the back of the wagon when Riessa motioned for him to stay.

Johuocin/Captain Reglawr looked back to the party as the two went to the door alone and knocked. As quickly as they knocked, the door opened. A woman stood in the doorway (or at least what appeared to be a woman). She was round and wearing a glorious array of color and a hooded shawl that covered her face. Her hands were old and scarred by a lifetime of work.

Sarcastically, with suppressed anger, she spat, "Welcome to Villanek Elna, refuge before the gods." Her voice was as bitter as the words that flew from her mouth. "What do you seek here in this sanctuary from evil and harm?"

Riessa looked at the woman who stood before her. She was strong and defiant and sarcastic in her words, yet Riessa saw a soul that once carried those same words the woman spat out with tenderness and belief. "Dear soul," Riessa began, knowing only that which she saw, "we came here in search of supplies to continue our journey. We despaired at the sight of your village, as we had expected it to be a thriving community. If you could tell us, is there a place where we may seek out such things anywhere near here?"

Turning to the captain, she hissed out, "Ask this one who dares to come here asking help and assistance after his kind brought this ruin down upon our backs like a boulder from a mountain rolls over a tree. Not doing the evil thing, but acting as the rain that dislodges the boulder. Taking away the support from under it, slowly, until it has no place to rest. So it rolls along its way, leaving that which was under it and protected open to the elements and vulnerable."

Johuocin was taken off guard, not realizing who he was or how he dressed. He felt the hurt of being under attack for something he knew nothing of. He felt the woman's eyes burn through him from under the shroud of her hood where they were hidden by the darkness. He felt the burning in his cheeks from shame of things he didn't know. He felt himself flush with that burning.

The woman pointed an accusing finger at him. "Yes, you and your kind, always tapping our shoulders for more coin. Leaving most of us without anything to make offering to the gods, taking the lives of those who still managed to make sacrifice at the altar, accusing them of doing task without report. Finally, with nothing to offer, we offered all we had left."

Her voice became harsh and raspy; she reached into her hood with a towel from her pocket. Her hood slipped back as she wiped tears from her face, enough for Johuocin to see the scars left there, as if by her own fingernails from her eyes down her cheeks to her jaw. A multitude of scars so deep, they left her face hideous and disfigured. Quickly, seeing the look on the captain's face, she pulled the hood back in place. "We offered our children, our hope. The gods took them and sent to us their vengeance and wrath. In their disgust for us, they dealt their destruction as we froze in fear to watch it happen."

She stood there with her finger pointing at Johuocin once more. One moment he was hot with shame. The next, he was cold, as if he no longer had any hope himself. He felt as he did outside the captain's body. Then he realized he had lost control. The captain had fallen to his knees, and Johuocin still stood.

From the road in front of the hovel the group watched without hearing anything that was being said. As the woman pointed her finger at the captain, they could see him flush red. They saw him start to breathe in deep gasps, his chest visibly rising and falling, even through his heavy winter coat. She dropped her hand and wiped her face, and the look on the captain's face turned to one of pain and loss. When the woman raised her hand to point once more, the captain gasped, trying to recover his bearing, and Riessa, seeing the captain was in confusion, stooped to help him up and calm him. Merson lifted his crossbow and fired at the woman, knowing that she must be a sorceress or witch, casting some kind of spell upon the captain. The venerable children must have been of the same mind as Merson, for as he shot his quill, Minac let go a shaft of his own. Minac's arrow dropped that of Merson's and planted itself in the wall of the hovel. Otinoe rushed in with his horse, throwing his saddlebag at the woman, knocking her down in the doorway of her home. Otinoe jumped from his horse and rushed toward the woman. Riessa turned from the captain, who fell to the ground, and she blocked Otinoe and pushed him over. Riessa rushed to the woman's side, helping her up as she blocked any further attacks from the onlookers from the road. Ben ran up on foot to aid his brother and captain. Riessa turned glaring at the party as she saw them coming toward the hovel on foot, running.

Things were happening so quickly around Johuocin that he could not move, or think to. The words of the woman were setting his memories in motion. "Taking lives for task without report," that was his father's doom. His father, who meant so much to his mother and him, his father, a man who deserved to be avenged, a man, who in losing his life, inspired a deep hatred for the king in at least one person. A person who blindly sought out vengeance for his father's death and created in him a self-spite for what he did to achieve his goal. One person so blindly goal-minded toward vengeance that he allowed himself to be made into someone worse than the king himself, taking pieces of another man's life and not just coin from his purse. Taking something that could never be regained. Guilt for his sins enveloped him, closing him off from everything around him.

Johuocin found himself fading into memories of his father and mother together in a happier time—memories of himself as a young boy, imitating the movements of his father, stepping off the measurements of the buildings around their home and yard. His father's strong, smiling face as he tried to teach Johuocin the art of carving stone to fit the walls of those buildings. His father's strong hands working so gently on a piece of wood, to show Johuocin how to carve a Crolga ring for his hair, helping teach Johuocin so he could enter manhood in his thirteenth summer with something that was truly and only his, remembering his father's pride in showing the ring to those that came for the celebration. Remembering how perfectly that ring was carved, the form of a coursing dragon flying straight to the sky as if wrapped around a tornado funnel in a corkscrew fashion. It was only two inches from the point of its tail to the tip of its snout, but every detail clearly marked—as clearly marked as the memory of his father's death was marked in his mind.

*

Riessa saw a change in the captain as he fell, and she bent to help him. She saw a quill fall into the snow and heard an arrow hit the side of the cottage. Before she could look up to see what had happened, she saw Otinoe rushing toward them on horseback as he threw his saddlebags toward the woman, knocking her down. Riessa turned away from the captain, dropping him back to the ground. She helped the woman up and blocked her from further abuse, knocking the boy warrior to the ground. She turned then, glaring at the others as they rushed in on foot, and held up her arms, boding them to stay back.

"What is the matter with all of you?" Riessa yelled. "You are visitors here."

"What's the matter with you, lass? Didn't you see what she was doing to the captain?" Merson was yelling as he tried to push past Riessa while pulling out his dagger.

Gorn caught hold of Merson's collar. Holding the small man back with little or no effort, he looked to Riessa with an unspoken question in his eyes. He too was confused by her actions. "Hold off, small one," he said to Merson. "Ben, how is your brother?"

Ben looked up from where he was kneeling, holding down Orman Reglawr, "He's babbling and confused. He doesn't know where he is or how he got here." He looked back to his brother, who was starting to calm down. "He wants to know who the others are, Merson." Confused, concerned, and disheveled, Ben looked to Merson for answers.

Gorn and Riessa looked to each other, and then Riessa looked at everyone around. She turned back to Gorn, shrugging her shoulders and shaking her head.

Alsie came forward, walking closely past Gorn. The sight of this accentuated the big man's size. The top of Alsie's head did not even reach Gorn's belt, diminishing the effect of Alsie's command. "I must talk to the woman. What is her name?"

Riessa turned to the woman and lowered her head apologetically. Raising her face to look at the woman, she felt the compassion she felt as the woman told the story of her children. "Dear lady, please forgive us for our behavior. Though not a long road it has been a trying one. Many things have raised our fears, making us wary and quick with improprieties. In your words, you have expressed great loss. Those who did not hear them think you may have harmed our captain in a way other than shame. That is why they wished to assault you, and that is also why you are not dead. Please forgive us and let me introduce ourselves. I am Riessa O'bourn. The big man is Gorn Fustrum. The captain's name is Orman Reglawr; with him is his brother Ouben. The other soldier is Merson Benidact. The others are not as familiar to me but I will try to get their names correct." Pointing to each as she went, "Alsie, he speaks for them, Finat, Minac, Soral, Riman, Domatis, Koreal, Avalaes, Anitae, and Otinoe. The last was the one to knock you over, but I believe he did that to stop you, not to harm you." Then Riessa put out her hand, which the woman took in her own. "And what is your name, dear one?"

"Marie." She let go of Riessa's hand and looked past her at the venerable children, "Marie Odure. Bless you for bringing home my children, miss. All of you please come in. Warm yourselves."

The woman reached out for the children—to touch them and caress them, to welcome them home. Riessa put her hands on the woman's shoulders to stop her. She could read the woman's soul, as it rejoiced at the sight of the children.

*

Riessa could hear the belief in the woman's voice as she spoke of these children being hers. "Marie, these are not your children. They belong only to themselves, and to each other."

"Of course they do, precious one. That does not change the fact that I am their mother. Every mother understands that her children must grow into themselves. That's part of motherhood." Her voice was soft and kind.

Riessa, filled with sorrow and compassion, saw what it had done to the woman to lose her own children. Her heart beat wildly as she began to feel some of the pain the woman must once have felt. She let go of the woman and went into the hovel, where she watched the faces of the children as they passed through the door. They were filled with the compassion and understanding that comes only with the experience of such great loss. She watched from a corner of the cottage as they continued their charade in consolation to the woman. Otinoe sat away from the crowd of aged children as they gathered around the woman. Whether out of embarrassment or shame for his action outside, it was hard to tell. Riessa could see a longing in his eyes to be in the crowd—to be stroked and fondled and hugged as he had been by his own mother before the fairy king had done his deed of mischief and vengeance.

As suddenly as Johuocin had slipped into memory, he found himself in silence. No one was near him. The wagon and horses still sat by the road. The door to the hovel was closed in front of him. He moved forward, passing through the door into the hovel. He saw the captain sitting by the fire with Merson and Ben trying to calm him and help him regain his wits. The woman was sitting with the children, all but Otinoe, who sat away, looking on. The woman was weeping as she fondled the children's hair and shoulders. Riessa and Gorn sat in another corner alone, clearly concerned about something.

Johuocin passed through the cupboards and pantry to discern what supplies the woman had that would be useful to the party. She didn't have much, but it would get her through the winter. What was there would take the group through three days of travel. As he came from the pantry, he looked back to the captain, who was still confused but less alarmed, sitting in a chair, elbows to knees and face in hands, contemplating what could or might have happened. Ben and Merson were trying to reacquaint the captain with the most recent events, of which the captain had no memory. Riessa and Gorn were sitting to one corner, whispering between themselves, as Riessa's eyes looked from one person to the next. Johuocin knew she was looking for him. He knew she was wondering whom he would invade next and why he left the captain. The "who" he still did not know. The "why" he did not know if he could reveal to this strong-minded and beautiful woman, this woman whose beauty had caused him to leave the captain's body, out of infatuation in Rausche Layne and out of awe at Skillcore. He also knew that he must, simply because he had asked for her trust and he could not betray that. As suddenly as he had found himself outside of the captain's body, he realized that the unbearable cold of his eternal freedom had overtaken him. It was a cold so deep that if it were outward instead of inward, it would touch the sky itself or perhaps even the stars that warmed its blackness by night.

The captain stared in wonderment as Merson and Ben recounted the events of the days past. From coming to this place, where he gained confusion, the meeting with the venerable children, then, further back, to the time at the hovel of Harishe and Galeem, their battle with the party from Cragfare. To their adventure in the pretended hamlet of Skillcore (the captain remembered something of seeing Riessa in such a place. Disrobed with fine clothing at her feet, a goblet in his hand, and his head filled with the same confusion he now experienced). Then they recounted Cragfare and his brilliance in using that town's own fear to defeat them.

Each time they recounted a story, the captain just gave a blank stare at its conclusion. The entire while, his mind swam in confusion. The scars and wounds of the events he carried as proof that he was there; still there was no memory of the occurrence of infliction. So they continued back.

They told the story of Rausche Laine and the O'bourn House. (Here again the captain remembered seeing the girl they refer to as Riessa, and his mind in confusion as the beautiful girl stood before him.) Then they told of Granite Hammerhand and Ben's learning of the plan to defeat the king. The captain's eyes grew as they spoke so freely of it, with Riessa and Gorn so near. He tried to hush them and was stopped by Ben as he reminded his brother of their knowledge of it. Then they told of the delay at the Mark home and their travel through the storm. As they started to go back further, he stopped them, starting to remember what was an uneventful journey to that point in time. Merson and Ben felt themselves relax as Orman Reglawr was able to relate to them the journey they began only weeks ago that seemed so distant to them now. The captain too relaxed a little and smiled a wide smile as he realized that what he was saying was familiar to the two, and not imagined by himself. He began to speak of familiar times in his excitement. Memories of childhood and his father's habits, how his father would sweeten his pipe with cherry wine. How his mother would sing to him every night before bed. How she died not long after Ouben had turned through his fourth summer.

Then he turned to Ben, "You were her pride, for the healers told her she would not give birth again after I was born." Tears filled with memories of his mother. "Did you know?"

Ben, looking off at the old woman, softly replied, "No."

Johuocin listened to the brothers' talk a little longer and knew he could not interrupt their bond again. He also knew he could not invade Merson. The party needed his knowledge of the dwarves and his balance of mind. Riessa's alliance of trust was essential to him. He needed her. Gorn also knew who he was; also, he had a physical affliction that would complicate his presence there. Johuocin could not duplicate the prowess of the venerable children, nor could he bring more strife and confusion to their search for help. This left only the old woman.

She would be defenseless if trouble arose. She may not be able to handle the travel. And Johuocin didn't know if he could be and act like a woman. Also, to consider, would the party allow her to go with them? He had no other choice. His reason began to fade as the cold grew, and he could not afford to lose control and become irrational.

Johuocin wanted to let Riessa know of his plan to enter the old woman, Marie, before it actually happened. He waited, looking for his opportunity, hoping that the cold would not overtake his senses before it came along. The bitterness of the cold seemed so much harder to tolerate now than it had been before he first entered the captain at his mother's home. His tolerance of it became more exhausted, it seemed, each time he entered a new body. Was his own willpower so weak that he actually began to lose his distaste for taking hold of another person's life and fate? Was it becoming, to him, as the liquor, tonics, or degenerate fornication was to the deviants of society's gutter dwellers? Again he began to lose concentration of his thoughts as the cold took hold of him once more.

The brothers concluded their talk as the captain laid out his bedroll at the fireside. He was going to rest, as the day's events had tired him so. Johuocin saw his chance to talk to Riessa and entered the captain's body once more as he lay down and closed his eyes. Once again as Johuocin/Captain Reglawr he was flooded with the warmth of a human body surrounding him. He raised himself on one elbow and turned toward Riessa, motioning to her to join him by the fire.

Riessa looked to him in disfavor. She no longer could see the soul of the captain clearly, and it was obvious she knew Johuocin had entered him once again. She crossed the room intently, glaring at him. Johuocin could see that she was about to admonish him for taking the captain over once again. He silenced her by holding up his hand, saying, "Wait.

"It's only momentary," he continued in a low whisper, "I had no other way of talking with you. I must have a way of communicating and being seen by you. Unless I miss my guess, the woman there," he pointed to Marie, "is very troubled, to the point of being near madness. She needs to get to healers, and I need to be seen. We need food to travel with, and she has very little for a party this size and if we take it and leave her, she will starve. There is no better way to accomplish our goals than me taking this woman from her misery for a few days."

"There must be," Riessa interrupted him. "Can you not travel without her?"

"Yes, but the cold of emptiness is becoming too much. I lose track of my thoughts."

Ben came over to Riessa's side. "Are you all right, Ory?"

"Yes, Ben, I'm fine. I just remembered something more about our trip and wished to confirm it before falling asleep."

"What did you remember Ory?" Ben was elated that his brother's memory was returning.

"It's private, little brother. Hope you understand?"

Ben smiled and looked at Riessa. He winked and stood. "Your secret is safe," he said as he walked away.

"What did you say that for?" Riessa chided. "I don't want people thinking things went on between us."

"But they did in a way. Remember Skillcore?" Johuocin said, using her own tone against her.

She blushed and looked away. "Still, that was not real."

"Fine, I apologize. That continues to leave the subject unclosed. I also believe I could enlist the aid of the venerable children by being Marie. They could be very useful. Remember our surprise at seeing our attackers?"

Riessa was silenced in thought for a few moments. Then looking at the captain, she said, "Very well, there is probably some merit to what you are suggesting."

"Very well!" Johuocin had taken offense to this woman who was suddenly giving him permission, it seemed, and to do something he was merely informing her he was about to do. "I was not asking your approval. I just thought it would be helpful if you knew my plan before I acted. I thought that would allow you to understand my intention and aid in the situation."

"Fine!" Riessa spoke a little too loud and forcefully for the rest of the group not to hear. She and Johuocin looked up at the rest. They were looking at them but immediately looked away when their gaze was met. Ben and Merson went back to their conversation with a little bit of a smirk on each of their faces, no doubt sharing a small jest about a lover's spat. Riessa resumed the original modulation level in her voice, but some annoyance and anger still existed there. Her expression itself told everyone who saw her that she was cross.

"I was only offering my opinion. I do have other things to tend to, though, so, if it's possible, don't ask for my help."

"Fine. Though your help could have been useful, I'm sure I can handle it. Please do inform Gorn. I would like him to be aware." Johuocin tried to be perfunctory in his tone so as not to react to her chiding.

Johuocin rolled back over to the position the captain was in when he entered his body. When he was comfortable and Riessa had walked away, he removed himself from the captain's body. The cold once again enveloped him, but not the bitter, unnerving cold he was experiencing just before entering the captain. He found himself once again able to concentrate and observe what was going on about himself without distraction. In his relieved state, he took the time to observe. The children yet were gathered around the old woman, who reached out occasionally to caress one or the other of them as she smiled with joy at the sight of them. Ben and Merson sat quietly watching the old woman and the venerable youngsters. Riessa and Gorn had begun to inspect the contents of the woman's cupboards and larder, quietly talking with each other. From time to time, Riessa would look back to the old woman and then to Gorn with a look of contradiction, which he assumed was in regard to his whereabouts.

As the cold began to increase within Johuocin, he decided to affect his plan of action before it started to become a problem.

Johuocin moved to the woman and took control of her. Warmth flooded him. He sat silent for a moment and felt the woman's tears run down her face. Then he reached up with her hands and wiped them dry, remembering the hurt she expressed at the door of the cottage and the memories she had brought back to him, and her tears became his, tears of sadness and joy, for pain and warmth. He then looked across the room at Riessa, who looked both sad and relieved as she looked back to Gorn and nodded.

Johuocin/Marie stood and looked around. "I must fix you all something to eat."

As Johuocin got to where Riessa and Gorn stood, Riessa reached out, saying, "Let us help you." Then more quietly to reach only Johuocin, "I am embarrassed for my behavior and words earlier. Gorn has reminded me that as a friend and advisor, sometimes, it is only to listen." She looked at Gorn with false scorn. "Sometimes I truly resent his wisdom."

CHAPTER 12

A Mother's Assurance

As Johuocin went about fixing a meal for the group, he felt uncomfortable with his new anatomy. It was clumsy for him as he moved from cupboard to counter. He found himself having to reach around the ample breasts of the short, round woman to do what otherwise would seem natural to him and also having to stand back further from the preparation table so he could observe what he was doing and having to ask for help in reaching things that would have otherwise been within his grasp without a problem. The woman Marie was short, shorter even than he would have guessed by looking at her, and a little heavier than he had thought. Having his thighs rub together where he had always known the feeling of a scrotum made him nervous, almost paranoid, at times. Then he would remember who he was, or who he was supposed to be at the time.

Though he had bumped into almost everything in his path and spilt so much (generally making a mess of things), he was able to get the meal together with the help of Riessa and Gorn. He had given no thought of the mess he had made of Marie.

As he turned to the table to put out the pot of vegetable stew, he found Riessa standing in front of him with Gorn behind her. While Riessa seemed to look a bit taller to him now, Johuocin had not noticed (until now) that the big man had become a giant. It appeared through the eyes of Marie that Gorn was at least twice Marie's height, though in reality he was probably only one and a half times her stature.

"Marie," Riessa began, looking at Johuocin/Marie with a peculiar simper on her face, "it must be wearing to fix a meal for such a large group when you're out of practice. By the looks of you, I would guess, you would like to change your clothes and freshen up a bit."

As Riessa spoke, Marie's eyes grew as round as the small saucers that could be seen in fine tea rooms. Marie's mouth opened a little as her jaw released in shock. Johuocin had not thought about that aspect of inhabiting Marie's body. He was now responsible for dressing, bathing, and the overall general hygiene of a woman. Moreover, a woman he did not know at all. He had fallen short in his sight of consequence, and if he had found her at the wrong time or did not hurry to move the party on and find a more suitable body to invade, he might find himself responsible for "the Visitor." Johuocin had heard terrible stories from other older boys in his youth, and more stories later, less terrible. At this point he really did not wish to find out which were true, at least not in this way. Johuocin hurriedly handed the pot of stew to Riessa.

Quickly giving credence to who he was at the time, he said, "Oh no, I cannot leave my children so soon or for so long, dear." Johuocin looked up to see the smile grow on Gorn's face as Johuocin spoke. Turning quickly back to the venerable children, he heard the infectious, booming laugh the big man carried in his chest being released.

With the sound of the big man's laugh, the captain woke from his slumber. Johuocin went immediately to the cupboard and put tea leaves and a little spice into a mug and added hot water from a kettle next to the fire. Next he would have to get the captain alone to suggest he pretend his memory had returned to regain the confidence of Ben and Merson. By the time the tea had brewed, Ben and Merson had already brought the captain some of the stew and were sitting with him.

Johuocin took the tea over to the captain. "May I offer you some remedy to your problem, Captain?" Nervous for what he was about to suggest to the captain and still not use to hearing a woman's voice when he spoke, Johuocin continued, searching for words. "I have overheard some of the others talking about it. You seem to have lost your memory, parts of it anyway. I've seen this before. It's not a very common situation, but I've dealt with it myself when the children were gone from me."

The captain looked at the old woman oddly. "I'm sorry, madam, I don't know you, and there seems to be some reason that my comrades did not trust you." He indicated Merson and Ben with a motion of his hand. "I don't know that I can trust a remedy from a stranger, especially one who was mindless when her children disappeared."

Johuocin was at a loss in what to say. He needed to speak with the captain alone and he needed to gain his trust in some way for that to happen. "Do you think I would poison you, Captain, with your friends here to take their revenge on me? Even now, when you have brought back my children to me?"

Johuocin knew that the last question would either win part of his confidence or confirm his suspicion that Marie was indeed a lunatic. Johuocin also knew from what he had seen in his life that more times than not, men would not fail in chivalry when a woman cried, even an old woman as unattractive as Marie, as long as they thought it sincere. So for the first time as an adult, Johuocin searched himself for the means to cry and found it in the memory of the loss of his father. As a young man, he was not allowed to cry in front of anyone, and so it was he found the tears.

"I admit, Captain, there are other reasons for my helping you."

Johuocin was right about the question he posed last. The captain thought about the question. With the sincerity of the weeping that Johuocin produced thinking of his father's death, it had accomplished both. As the captain looked at the woman, thinking of her anguish and seeing her lunacy in believing these were her children, sympathy filled his heart as he reached out and took the mug. Before drinking, though, he wanted his own question answered—the question of her hidden agenda.

"What other reasons might those be?"

Ben and Merson stared at the captain as if he had lost his mind. This woman held tax collectors and the king responsible for the loss of her children. You could see in their faces that they did not trust the woman's motives. Johuocin looked at the captain and then to the companions he had near.

"I would need to speak with you alone about this. You are the one who can help me, no one else."

"You may trust my men, madam. We have shared greater troubles." The captain was at a loss as to what he could not let them hear. They, after all, knew more about him than he did over the last days. "Speak of what you must."

"I cannot, Captain. You may tell them after if you wish. But I cannot speak of it in front of those who do not trust me."

"I offer apology, madam, but if you wish to speak, then do so with their presence."

Merson and Ben gave Marie a look of arrogant approval for the captain's decision. Johuocin could see the captain was a natural leader. One who put trust in those closest to him and therefore received trust in return. Perhaps the captain would not need his suggestion to return their trust and regain his leadership. Already Johuocin felt that the captain had taken charge once more. His speech, while polite, was direct and confident. Even as he sat on the floor, his good leg crossed beneath the other, his posture was straight and almost stiff. He commanded an ability to maintain eye contact when he spoke or was spoken to. Johuocin could see that this man had presence, and would have, no matter where he was. Orman and Ouben Reglawr were as different as two sides of a coin when it came to personality. Johuocin felt he had done this man or his companions a disservice by invading him. Once again Johuocin felt the guilt of taking away part of the man's life and was not consoled by having now taken over another, knowing that one day Marie would also be missing pieces of her own life in her memory.

Still, this left asking the captain to take Marie with him. "Very well," Johuocin said, hearing Marie's voice trembling, "I must still ask. Will you take the children and me to another place? A place where there are people and supplies. I do not have enough food for all of us for the entire winter."

The captain, though having been made aware their supply situation, still made no promise, and did not allude that he would indeed take Marie with them. He merely told Marie that he would talk with his men in private about this and sent her away.

Johuocin returned to what Marie had been doing before he had invaded her. He gathered the children around him and continued to fuss over them.

The captain, Merson, and Ben sat watching, as Marie seemed to become completely engulfed in the presence of the children once again. They looked to the kitchen area to see Riessa and Gorn cleaning up after the meal. The three finished what they had been eating when Marie had come over to talk.

The captain looked at his brother and his friend. "Well, gentleman, any suggestions or comments?"

"Aye, Captain, we need her supplies, and we can't leave her to starve." Merson was the first to speak. "I think it's better that she go as a willing traveler than a reluctant companion."

"My question is, can she make the trip? It is the dead of winter out there, do we know how long it will take to get to our next destination?" The captain felt good as he asked the questions. He thought it felt as if he had just woken out of limbo, and he once again had a direction and a path.

"Merson said earlier that it would be three or four days to reach the dwarven cities. But we still don't know where we need to be," Ben said. "We've been slowed down so much already. We should have met with the messenger but never did."

"I'm still unclear as to how long it is until solstice. My memory still is not the best, and I've lost track of time." The captain was nervous about saying this last. He did not know, if even they knew.

"Captain, we only have six days left before solstice! The daylight comes late and is gone in an hour! The sun barely crests the southern sky in these days we have left." Merson fought hard not to sound anxious about his captain's confusion. He knew that his rambling about the sun's habits gave him away. "I apologize for the outburst, Captain, but we have only six days to be at a place we do not know yet."

"Six days? We can't take the woman if we have so little time. The pace and the cold will be too much for her I'm sure."

The captain sounded concerned, but his voice rang throughout the cottage like organ pipes in a vast temple. The occupants fell silent as they turned their eyes to Marie. The captain stood. "I'm sorry, dear lady. With this weather and the little time we have, we must already perform a near-impossible task. We would only be endangering you further if you traveled with us. Honestly, we would also be slowed by your company."

Johuocin once again was taken aback by the captain's refusal. He had not realized the advantages he had as the captain of the party. It was always assumed by him that the others would follow his suggestion and orders. He had not yet been in a predicament as menial as this, to have to ask permission from an authority that thought only with premise of calculated risk. His frustration became heavy in him. Now knowing that as Marie it was acceptable, and somewhat advantageous, he called up the tears that made some progress earlier. Crying, Johuocin looked about the room. The children took the greatest sympathy to their faces.

"You must take us, Captain," Johuocin said, motioning to the children around her. "Here we will surely starve."

Finat Sood and moved next to Marie. He looked up into her face with sorrow and pity. "We will travel without them, Mother," he said softly, with the pity riding his voice like smoke from a distant fire, letting the old woman live her fantasy as if it were all she had left. "Your children have become very skilled in their absence. We no longer need protection from others. Indeed, it is quite the opposite with those we disfavor." Finat's anger shot at the captain as he spoke and looked to him as a monster. And Finat knew what he said was true.

Johuocin looked at Finat. "Is this true? Have you really grown so without me?"

"Yes, Mother." Finat looked back to the captain. "I will need your wagon, Captain. This woman cannot sit astride a horse. Take your things from it and pack your mules. We will be resting here this night and leaving before the sun shows."

The captain looked at Finat with disbelief. A child or even a small man before this had never dared give him instruction. He had never seen these venerable children wield their weapons before and felt them as no threat. He knew, however, they must travel without the wagon to make any time at all, but his pride was bruised. He used his injuries to justify his need for the wagon.

"Small sir, what makes you think I will give you my wagon when I myself am injured and may not travel well by horseback?"

"I did not ask you to give it to me, Captain. We are taking it. Though, in consideration for your injury, we do have something for you in trade, but in my estimation, you will continue to stand in our debt to some degree. That is, if you choose to accept it."

The captain was livid as Finat's words came at him like a command. "You will take it and I will stand in your debt? I suppose next you will say you will kill me and I will thank you for it."

"We would take it much as you did, if I followed what was said of your journey. Would you rather we take it and you not find out what we have to offer?" Finat looked at the captain with complacency.

"Captain," Merson jumped in, knowing the captain's pride was the only obstacle between Finat and the captain agreeing on the loss of the wagon, "you should at least find out what he has to offer."

Riessa came toward the captain. "Captain, the wagon will only slow us down anyway." She had seen what the captain was bothered by, and she also knew that Marie's physique would not sit a horse well.

"Yes, it will slow us, as much as our injuries. I will not take threats from anyone, much less someone of his size, injured or not," the captain snapped at Riessa.

Alsie came forward holding his mandolin in his arms. "Please accept my apologies, Captain. Not for my brother or his words, for they are accurate. We all stand together on this. I apologize for his lack of persuasiveness.

He should first have asked for the wagon and allowed you to respond." Alsie's voice was soft and soothing. The tension in the room melted away as he spoke.

The captain was given a graceful exit to this exchange as Alsie took charge of the conversation.

"Very well, what is it you have to offer in trade?" The captain's expression changed little. Only through a conscious effort on his part was he able to recompose himself.

"We," Alsie continued, "have some herbal potions given to us by the Druids of Allaknok. They are healing brews, Captain. You have sustained some injury in your journey that they could give aid to. One of these would bring a price that would buy and sell your wagon and its stock many times over. We had already decided to share some of our fortune with you before this sparring of words took place. We will give you each one dose, and two more for you to carry in apology." Alsie looked back at his brother before continuing. "However, Captain, my brother is right. You will still feel your debt to us is not fully paid with your forfeit of the wagon, as will we."

"How do we know that what you offer is not poison instead of cure? That would leave you with quite a ransom at our death. What do you have to gain by our living that you would not have more by our death?" The captain stared into the eyes of the small bidder.

Alsie reached under his cape and behind him. As he did so, Ben stepped forward and drew a knife from his own boot. Alsie quickly pulled out his hand, and in it was a purse. Holding up an open palm to Ben, he carefully spilled some of its contents onto it and knelt to the floor, where he emptied his hand and the rest of the contents of the purse. The eyes of the five opened wide at what they saw, for there on the dirt floor of the cottage laid a small fortune in jewels of every color and size.

"Each of us has a purse such as this, Captain. We do not need the gold you have gathered in the name of the king. We have offered the potions instead of wealth because that is what you are in need of to travel without the wagon or even to advance your journey with less trouble. We had decided this before we needed the wagon but did not offer more than the potions, for they are very valuable. As for what we will gain by your living, only our own self-respect. What we have gained and wish not to lose is the compassionate love of a mother, even such as it is." Alsie looked back to Marie. "She is why we need the wagon, Captain. If you would rather have coin for the wagon, that is what we will give. The choice is yours."

Ben still stood with the knife in his hand, but his mouth was agape and his eyes wide as he stared at the jewels spilled upon the floor. The captain was himself taken aback by the words Alsie spoke with such clarity and lyrical tone, stunned by the display of wealth in front of him. Merson, Riessa, and Gorn looked on at the children as if they had for the first time realized their actual time of existence and the anomaly they represented.

"We will accept your original offer, Alsie." The captain's look softened with his voice. "I apologize for my suspicion and lack of trust."

"No need, Captain." Alsie spoke mat-ter-of-factly. "There are many who one must not trust. We do not know each other and must be wary. I, for instance, do not think I fully know who you are. But I follow my instincts, sometimes to my own undoing."

Finat at that time went out the door and returned with a small coffer made of wood. As he set it down in front of the captain and opened it, he revealed its contents of clay bottles with pitch-sealed corks. They were neatly arranged in rows and columns by dividers of stiffened canvas. Seven by ten, they filled the coffer except for one row and two spaces. Alsie told the captain to take out seven of the small containers, which he did. The containers were not more than a quarter hand high and as round as a thumbnail.

"Captain," Alsie said, with a sound of concern in his voice, "I would suggest that you not all take a dose of the cure at one time. They will cause a feeling of sleep to come over you. That is one of the ways in which they work. Anyone who takes the cure will experience a feeling of high energy while they are also in and out of sleep. The effect lasts about a half a day, and then a feeling of complete restfulness and health will come over you. At that time all that will be left of your injuries will be scars. If your injuries are only minor, such as Merson's, drink only half the dose and save the rest for need. One more thing—we were told that once any person puts his or her lips to the bottle, this is the only person who can use the remainder of the potion."

"I have heard of such potions before." The captain spoke with hesitant awe. "If indeed these are those potions, they are very rare, and as you said expensive. I wish to know how you acquired so many. It's said that the healers don't part with them easily or in any great quantities." The captain eyed the box of potions in Finat's hand.

Anitae then came forward and knelt down in front of the captain to look him in the eye where he was sitting on the floor. "Sympathy and trust go a long way, Captain. We are often pitied by those who wish to help us but cannot. I do not deny that sometimes we use that unwanted pity to our advantage. A little girl's tears are often effective to the unwary sympathy of a caring heart." A tear rolled down the face of the little girl as she sniffed and let out a small sob. But as quickly as it came, she wiped her eyes and smiled, and it left.

The captain couldn't deny he felt a momentary tug at his own heart as it happened. "So they are."

The captain handed a bottle of the precious liquid to each of his four traveling companions who had come so far, not hesitating with the two people he did not really know. From what had been told him by Merson and Ben, Riessa and Gorn, had been honorable companions in the journey they had shared. Though still unsure of their motivation to travel with them, the captain did not hand either of the two a second vial to carry. "As it is that I and Gorn are the two with the most serious wounds, we will be the first to take the dosage. Then Ben and Riessa, followed by Merson."

Gorn looked at the captain with contention. "I will not take the dosage until we have reached Korfri, Captain. I must be alert and ready if we come into danger. I must be ready to defend Riessa." Though that was not what kept Gorn from taking the dosage. He was afraid of his problem being revealed if he were not aware when he traveled through the darkness of winter.

"I am not badly hurt, Captain," Riessa said, adding to Gorn's upset to the captain's order of sequence. "My wounds will heal on their own I believe. After all, they are only rope burns, scratches, and bumps compared to yours. Gorn is the one who is hurt as badly as you, but you cannot force him to take the potion if he has made up his mind. Merson or Ben may take theirs with you."

"Merson must get us headed in the right direction before he takes his dosage. He can read the star charts and knows where Korfri lies." The captain had thought to keep himself, Merson, and Ben on equal or greater footing with the new companions who traveled with the original three. He did not wish to seem mistrustful but also, he did not wish to compromise his mission. Then remembering that he mentioned Korfri in the presence of Alsie and the rest, he had done just that. The pain of his injuries was getting to him. "I will take mine, then Merson, then Ben. The two of you can take yours when you are ready. At any rate, we must leave within the hour." The captain turned to Alsie. "Would you give us help packing our mules?"

"Of course, Captain." Alsie was curious as he looked at the captain, who showed so little trust even to those who traveled with him. "But did you know that Korfri is a dwarven city? I don't think you will be very welcome there in the king's uniform. If you waltz into that city like that, you will have reason for your distrust toward others."

Indicating his awareness of their destination, the captain responded coldly, "I am not in the habit of bringing strangers into my confidence. I am not about to start now. I do, however, appreciate your help.

"Merson, see to the preparation. I am going to drink this potion now. If it is necessary, strap me to the back of my horse."

"Aye, Captain." At that acknowledgment Ben, Merson, and Gorn went through the door, followed by Finat, Otinoe, Riman, and Domatis.

Alsie, aware of Otinoe's curious nature, called to Minac and Avalaes, "Send Otinoe back in here, and the two of you stay to help. I do not want any problems with property disputes." Otinoe returned looking rather dejected.

The captain took out a knife and pried open the pitch-sealed vial. Before drinking, he turned to Riessa and raised it high in salute, looking at her without emotion as the potion started to take effect and he began to sleep.

Riessa watched the captain as he began to sleep. She was suddenly aware that she had once been attracted to this man when he was occupied by a different soul, and now she was simply amenable to his cause. Her intrigue with the captain left as his personality reflected his own soul. Indeed, her intrigue had shifted to Johuocin. Now it was less attraction, but still the intrigue seemed to create an attraction. This realization made her feel uncomfortable and unnatural.

Riessa swung her attention now to Marie, who sat with Alsie, quietly watching the others divide the provisions. It seemed she had caught Marie's attention as she looked over.

Marie patted Alsie on the hand and stood up, excusing herself. She walked over to Riessa and sat down beside her on the bed.

"You should take part of the potion, Riessa. It will help you. Alsie has assured me it is not harmful." Johuocin filled the silence with concern as she spoke.

"No, I must be awake for Gorn if the need arises. He fears it is time for him to hunt again. His scars will heal quickly if he does, and his energy will return. He tells me he is more tired now than anything."

"You are going on with the captain from here?" Johuocin knew she would continue with the three soldiers but still felt the pang of loss inside.

"I must. My senses will be needed by him." Riessa fell silent for a moment. "You were the reason I started this journey, though that is not what I told my father. But now I see a need for me to be at the dwarven council meeting. The captain is arrogant but vulnerable to mistrust. If he attacks the honor of one of his supporters, it could be disastrous."

"That I feel is my fault. If he didn't have blank spots in his memory, perhaps he wouldn't question the honor of others so much."

"Or maybe he would. He has been in the service of the king for some time now, and his own allegiance is in another place. I'm not saying it's misplaced, just that it may create its own questions."

"Perhaps."

Merson entered the cottage once again. "We're ready. We must leave now." He looked at Riessa as he said this, and then to the captain as he saw him slowly standing to his feet.

"Get me to my horse, Merson, before sleep has a chance to overtake me again. Tie me in my saddle so I don't fall."

Riessa went to Marie. "Good luck, wherever you find yourself." Then she spoke to Alsie. "Let the wind be at your back. I hope you find your wish."

Alsie smiled. "Good travel, Riessa. It was a pleasure to meet such a kind soul."

Johuocin/Marie excused herself from her children and walked a few steps with Riessa. "I hope we meet again."

"Where will you be going?" Riessa asked.

"I don't know yet. Just remember, 'The Coursing Dragon.'"

"Yes." At that Riessa mounted her horse and pulled her hood over her face.

Marie walked back into her cottage, followed by Alsie, who she had not seen walk out. After having more of the stew that was made earlier, the group laid down for a good rest in a warm home before starting their journey.

CHAPTER 13

The Stars That Shine

As Merson looked to the skies for the spark of light against the darkness that would guide them to Korfri, he set his prayers to the wind that kept them clear. He pushed the party onward in the general direction of travel until he could focus on his mark. The wind was chilly, but high, and moved the few clouds that persisted across his living map. Checking the sky against the map in his hand was tedious and slow as the wind would blow and sway the paper and the focus of the lantern held by Gorn. The big man would hold it high and look on as he ran alongside Merson's mount.

Gorn, too, looked on at the map, finding a point of reference and losing it in the jostle of light and paper as the wind would gust. The situation only frustrated him, aggravating a condition of his disease. Hunger began to gnaw at his mind and belly.

Riessa pulled her hood forward and held the collar high on her cloak as the party trotted into the light gusts of wind.

Ben rode beside his brother to prop him and prevent the ropes that secured Ory, from pulling harshly at his wounds. The captain had nearly fallen twice as he found himself in and out of sleep before Ben had come to ride alongside him. Ben's concern for his brother blanketed his concern for the mission. The way his brother was now acting was how Ben remembered his brother becoming, slowly, over time.

Before they were sworn to Eldwa, Orman Reglawr was a different person, more jovial and relaxed. His sense of purpose just as strong, but without the constant wariness of all he came in contact with. Also, next to him now was the brother he remembered of the last few weeks, a man entirely different, a man who made decisions by the seat of his pants, always landing on his feet. He was like a cat that's been knocked on the head once too often, wandering aimlessly about, but always knowing what needs to be done to secure the next meal.

For a time the party traveled in silence and Gorn put aside trying to read the map and concentrated on holding the light as steady as possible as they moved forward.

The moon that created such havoc for Gorn was high in the sky now. The hunger that came with Gorn's disease burned within him once again, reminding him of his growing contempt for the winter seasons. It was the time when the moon pulled at his disease, increasing its control over the large man. Soon, low solstice would be upon them, upon him. He often thought of how he wished to curse the one day of the year that had carried so many fond memories of his past, memories of a time before his malady. The day that had once been the most joyous of all for him had become the most torturous, as it was the day the moon traveled alone across a backdrop of stars in the sky to celebrate its victory over the sun's dominance. Now he ached for high solstice, the day there was no moon, the day the sun reminded the moon that without him, the moon would rarely be seen.

Merson slowed his horse until he came to a stop. Looking at the sky, he asked Gorn, "What do you see up there, my friend?" He pointed up and to the right of where they faced.

Gorn looked up and then back to Merson. "I'm sorry, Merson," he apologized. "I cannot read the stars. I have tried to look over the map, but I can't seem to match it to the sky."

"No man, closer than that," Merson retorted. "Not the stars. There is something there flying. I started seeing it about an hour ago and have been catching glimpses of it ever since, just circling above us."

Again Gorn looked. Finally it caught his eye. It wasn't very large or very high. Handing the lamp to Merson, he ran ahead in the darkness to see if he could get a better look. Unable to see much more, Gorn tried to let the moon's pull on him take control so he could use the sight of the bear. The moon was too strong, and he lost control of the change. He called to Riessa, in a gruff voice, letting her know he was going further ahead. Riessa recognized the sound in his voice and realized he was changing. She moved toward Merson to move him onward as Gorn's footsteps could be heard running heavily into the distance.

Riessa reached out for the lamp in Merson's hand.

With a queried look in his eye, he handed the lamp to her. "Where is he going? We're in the middle of nowhere. What if we change direction?"

"He'll find us. Do you have your direction now?" Riessa offered no explanation of Gorn's going.

"Yes, but we have a shadow above us in the sky."

Riessa looked up and spotted the object immediately. Her half-elven vision left no mistake as to what was there. "It's a bird. Perhaps Gorn is trying to lure it away. Or maybe he is trying to see if it belongs to someone."

Riessa's "'perhaps" and "maybe" didn't begin to answer the questions on Merson's mind but he knew they must move on quickly before the party lost the use of the stars. "I hope he knows what he's doing, lass."

"I'm sure of it." Riessa looked back at Ben as they traveled on. He was still too preoccupied with his bother to notice Gorn's departure.

As they traveled along, Merson reached into one of his saddlebags and pulled out a small globe. It was half filled with water and had a small piece of cork floating in it with a needle of some kind attached across it. "Lass, as we pass into daylight, pay attention to the direction of the metal piece on the cork. We must keep it at that angle as we travel."

Looking curiously at the globe, Riessa nodded.

Gorn ran far in advance of the party as he transformed into the bear that was his cursed companion. Searching for his next quarry, he heard the bleating of sheep come from the direction of a small clump of trees to the right of his path. That would be his destination with the hope that no one would be there to see him. As he loped toward the trees, he found the strength within to pray to the seven forces of philosophy.

CHAPTER 14

Not the Children

Johuocin woke to the sound of Alsie's voice in a quickening beat and soothing tune. As she looked over at him, he smiled back at her with the twinkle of a child's eyes behind it.

Alsie sang:

> Before the sun
> we rise and wake.

In our care
a mother take.
From this place
we go in stride
To seek the dream
and gain our pride.
Revenge we left
a score of seasons
In our path
we seek the reasons.
Reasons for
our lives' existence,
Reasons for
our charge persistence.
Perhaps in finding
greater ground,
There our quarry
will be found.
'Tis only this
for which we wait

To find ourselves
at close with fate.

As Alsie finished his tune, he went on playing his mandolin. With the clearest tone and soothing voice, he walked through the hovel, waking all who were there. "We must be on our way within the hour. The moon is bright in the sky and on the snow beneath it. We will travel far today and see our way through the darkness of our days to another place."

He smiled at all who were his family as he placed his mandolin upon the mantle above the fire. The others rubbed their eyes and returned the smile. All but Finat, who rose to his feet, putting on his coat. As he walked across the room to the door of the cottage, the large boy refused eye contact with anyone. His expression was glum and emotionless. Alsie's eyes lost their sparkle as Finat went into the cold.

Alsie's gaze went to Marie. Again his smile returned until he saw the look upon Marie's face. "Don't worry, Mother, he is only thinking of a time long past. He'll be fine at the pass of solstice."

Johuocin was reminded that solstice would soon be upon them. The party of venerable children would certainly not wish to be in the elements on horseback at the passing. "Where will we be off to?"

"There is a village to the south of here, Khibanhahm. That is where we will get supplies and rest through the holiday. We have been there before. They are a very kind and friendly village and know us as friends," Alsie said with fondness in his voice. His eyes were focused on places other than where he was, and they softened his smile. A tear rolled down his face as he too left to help Finat outside. From the look on Alsie's face, Johuocin believed it was a tear of both joy and sorrow.

"Why the tears from that one?" Johuocin asked as she saw the kind smile on Anitae's face.

Anitae looked up at Marie with a regretful smile. "It is hard to explain to you, Mother."

"Try, sweet child."

Anitae thought for a while on how to tell the story without confusing the woman before her more than she was already—the woman who thought they were her children. "You see, Mother," she began slowly, for her stories were never as clear as Alsie's, "we have traveled much before finding you. We have spent many years trying to find our peace. In our search we traveled through Khibanhahm. In our search"—here Anitae paused and dealt with the confusion of relating their age without upsetting Marie—"please understand, we did not age in our search nor could we hope to. It is part of the reason for our search."

"Child, please tell the story as you remember it. Try no longer to spare me." Johuocin wanted to ease the tension of the children's minds with her. She must, or she would not have their friendship. "I do realize now that you are not the children who were taken from me. But for me to be with you helps me. I do not know if I will always remember this, but for now I do." Johuocin added this last to camouflage his leaving of Marie as he knew he one day soon must do.

Anitae and Otinoe both came closer to her then. They each took one of her hands and softly smiled. The other children also gave Marie a sign of their awareness and attention.

As Anitae then continued her story, Otinoe sat with her as the other boys went about preparing for their journey.

"We rode into Khibanhahm just before high solstice five summers ago. The season was warm and forgiving to travelers and those who live in the street. We were in search of a healer for Minac, who had taken an arrow from a band of thieves in the forest to the west of Khibanhahm. Minac was badly hurt and covered in blood—"

Here Johuocin interrupted. Not because he had wanted the answer to his question, but, because he felt that it was a question a mother would ask.

"Why would thieves attack a group of children? I have never heard of such wickedness."

Anitae held her hand to Marie's mouth. "That is another story, Mother, best told by Alsie." Then she returned to her story. "Minac was covered in blood as we rode into Khibanhahm. An innkeeper who was in his front doorway ran into the street to stop us and ask if we needed assistance. To him we were just a group of children with one of us badly injured. Alsie came forward and asked where we could find a healer or if the town had one. The innkeeper, Hafer Lotzman, urged us off of our horses and into the inn while he sent for the healer.

"Master Lotzman said the healer was very skilled but to expect a lot of mumbo jumbo and other nonsense because he also fancied himself a minor magician.

"To that end the innkeeper suggested a bit of lunacy in the healer's mind." Anitae let out a small giggle. Then remembering

Marie, she gained an apologetic look. "I'm sorry. I didn't mean to—"

"It's all right, child," Johuocin/Marie broke in. "We all have a little bit of lunacy in us."

At that Anitae agreed with a small look of chagrin and a nod.

"When the healer arrived, he was wearing long white robes and a droopy pointed hat with a crescent moon embroidered on it. The door had opened and momentarily we saw him outside. Then a large puff of smoke entered the doorway, and as it cleared, the healer was standing where the smoke was. He waved his hands in front of himself to clear the smoke, which he seemed to be choking on and a girl came running around in front of him, shouting, 'Ivan, healer and magi, here to serve.'

"He was quite a sight. He pulled on the girl's sleeve, and the two turned so as not to see us and he was trying to whisper to her, not successfully, I must add, 'No, Avilla, how many times must I tell you, it is "magi and healer."' At that the girl turned and started again. 'Ivan …'

"Distressed and embarrassed, he stopped the girl. 'Not now, Avilla. It's too late for these. Next time.'

"The girl hung her head. 'Yes, Father,' she said as she rolled her eyes.

"The healer crossed the room, waving smoke from his face, as it had filled the room quite thoroughly. He looked at the innkeeper. 'Sorry, Hafer, it was the quickest way to get here.'

"The innkeeper rolled his eyes at the healer and shook his head. 'Not now, Ivan. The boy is seriously hurt. Do what you do best. Help him.'

"The healer looked over and saw Minac. Rushing to his side, he asked how it had happened. He was suddenly very concerned.

"Alsie spoke up. As is usual in these cases, he was the storyteller. 'A hunting accident.'

"After looking the wound over a bit and pushing this and probing that, Ivan turned to his daughter. Or at least where he thought his daughter would be. 'Avilla, where did you go?' Then he saw her. Standing next to Alsie, with her eyes fixed on him. Of which Alsie was quite unaware, he himself being fixed on, and concerned about, Minac.

"'Avilla!' Ivan was quite taken back. He had always had his daughter's immediate attention.

"At the calling of his daughter's name everyone became aware of where she was and what she was doing, including her.

"She blushed as she turned back to her father to attend him. 'Y-yes, Father?'

"'I need some things from home.' He quickly gave her a list and watched her strangely as she left the inn. Then he turned a rather intense eye to Alsie. After a moment he shook his head and focused once again on Minac.

"'Have you a room for the boy, Hafer? He'll not be going far for a few days. If this arrow had been a little left, he would have drowned from the inside out. I've seen *that* happen before.'

"'Of course I do, Ivan. He can stay in my personal quarters.'

"'Very well. I'll be over daily to check on him.'

"The innkeep then turned his attention to the rest of us. You children haven't been hunting the beast, have you? Because if you have, I'll find each of your parents and be sure they give each of you a sound beating.'

"'We are orphans,' Alsie said. 'We have not heard of any beast. We were hunting for need.'

"The innkeeper Lotzman looked at Alsie very strangely. He looked us all over very closely. 'All of you, orphans? Have you no families that would take you in?'

"Alsie shook his head and stood a bit taller, as if to defy the innkeeper's questioning. 'Sir, we have become quite capable of taking care of ourselves. We are the last of our families and are all related to one another. We do very well for ourselves and expect or desire no sympathy or pity. I am Alsie, the eldest, and we have come here for help for my cousin Minac.' Then Alsie went on with the other introductions, giving our names, relation, and age at the point where we did indeed stop aging.

"The man stood there stunned by what Alsie had said but became shocked at what he said next.

"'We have been on our own for years. We shall continue on our own for many more.'

"'Y-y-you are very young children. Do you not want to belong to families that could protect you and care for you?' Mr. Lotzman was excited with concern for us. He could hardly contain his words as they flew from his mouth. 'We have many families here who would take you in as their own. Many farmers who would love to have a child to help them with their work.'

"Finat, who angers the easiest of all of us, stepped forward to speak his feelings. 'Innkeeper, we are not farmers. I am the youngest but largest of all of us. I can use a sword better than the most skilled in this town. We do not need protection or care from anyone. Just because we are children does not make us helpless.'

"Hafer Lotzman looked at Finat in shock, as did the healer, Ivan. Neither could believe the forwardness of this boy, who stood in front of them and addressed them with little or no respect. Mr. Lotzman gained the sternest expression and waved his finger at Finat as he spoke harshly against his tone. 'Young man, watch your temper while addressing me or I'll address your little round behind with the flat of my hand.'

"Finat stepped forward, putting his hand on the hilt of his sword. Alsie stepped between the two, remembering that the last person to shake his finger at Finat promptly lost it at the edge of Finat's blade. After admonishing Finat with a look that could have made a dragon faint, he turned back to the innkeeper.

"'I must apologize for Finat,' Alsie said, speaking through his teeth, then relaxing. 'You see, we have become very independent, and Finat, being the youngest of us, takes more offense than the rest of us to authority. Unfortunately, most adults we meet take authority of us upon themselves. That is,' he paused, 'after learning our circumstance.'

"As Alsie finished speaking, Avilla returned with the necessary ointments and bandages. After handing these things to her father, she once again returned her gaze to Alsie. He was very uncomfortable with that, especially when her gaze did not leave him until her father took her by the hand, leading her out of the inn.

"(Of course after this experience, Alsie decided that we should not have to seek out the medical attention of a healer anymore. After leaving Khibanhahm, we sought out the druids in the south to gain possession of the potion we shared with the captain.)

"The innkeeper must have gotten some sort of message from what Alsie had said, because after moving Minac to his private quarters, he offered to throw out some of the hunters staying there to make room for us.

"Alsie politely declined, to the satisfaction of Finat, saying that we would camp outside of town. Mr. Lotzman was not happy with that at all. (One could see it in his face.) But he accepted it in view of earlier circumstances.

"(Personally, I'd have rather stayed in the inn, where I could have gotten a proper bath.)"

At this point in Anitae's story, Alsie walked back into the cottage. "Ladies," he looked to Marie and Anitae, "we must be moving out soon. Please make yourselves ready."

"Of course, Alsie." Johuocin/Marie stood. "We will make a quick hot breakfast, and then we will dress." Then she stood and took Anitae's hand, heading for the cupboards.

As Alsie picked up some things and left the cottage once again, Marie encouraged Anitae to continue her story as they made porridge.

"Well," Anitae resumed, "as the next few days went on, Avilla made it a point to be wherever she thought Alsie would be. Minac was recovering well, and we thought we would not be in the village much longer. The days turned into weeks, and Alsie seemed to be finding reasons for us not to move on. More and more of his time was being spent with Avilla as we stayed. The two were laughing and playing together constantly. Avilla's father, Ivan, was becoming concerned about his daughter's absence from his side. After all, as he put it, 'How could one announce oneself without sounding arrogant?'

"Personally I thought he was jealous of his daughter's attachment to Alsie.

"In the time we were there the beast we had heard of still had not been caught or killed. It was terrifying the farmers and had been killing their livestock. It had even become so bold as to attack the stock in the barnyards.

"The ones who had seen the beast described it as winged and covered in fur with scales on its belly and legs. It would be seen disappearing into the sky on wings so large that it would shadow the stars. No one had seen it in the daylight.

"Then one day as we were eating the midday meal at the inn, a farmer came crashing through the door. He was yelling at the top of his voice for everyone to meet in the town square. Then he ran out. Everyone in the inn rushed out behind him.

"Minac had progressed quite well in his recovery at this time. We ourselves had devised our meal, as a meeting of our own to convince Alsie it was time we resumed our journey. After everyone else had gone, Alsie too set down his fork, and we followed.

"When we arrived in the square, an emotional woman was screaming and crying about her daughter being taken by a beast. A large beast, one and a half times the height of a man and twice as long as a wagon, had grabbed her daughter with large, spiny claws. Its wings made the sound of blankets being snapped in the wind as the beast screeched and flew high into the sky until you could no longer distinguish the deep red streaks in its black fur coat. In the sky it headed toward the Forest of Fear the Abranas Forest. That was where Minac was wounded. This was the first time anyone had seen the beast in light of day. Indeed the beast had become smug and defiant. The beast having stolen a child in the bright light of the morning sun, when known only to have fed on poor dumb beasts of the field and farm, emphasized its impudence.

"As the woman was just calming down from her telling of the beast, and wailing at the loss of her daughter, Finat and I spotted Ivan peeking out from behind the corner of the general store. Suddenly smoke filled the air in front of the store and through it, coughing and wheezing, came Ivan with Avilla in the lead.

"Ivan, healer and magi, here to serve!" Avilla announced in her very largest voice. Again we were to witness Ivan pulling at his daughter's sleeve and turning from the crowd. (One could not hear him, but we all chuckled in knowledge of what he was saying. Or at least most of us were.) Some grumbled in distaste of Ivan's foolery at such a serious report as this. The shopkeeper we had come to know as Master Imil stepped forward.

"'Ivan, we have no time for such things as your pretense of illusion right now. This is a serious matter.'

"Master Imil was quite cross with Ivan and had embarrassed him to a great degree. All who were in the square saw the redness crawl over Ivan's neck and face. Ivan stood as tall as he could (which was almost as tall as an average fellow), and looked about nervously.

"'What are you talking about?' Ivan snapped as loudly and angrily as he could. 'I watched the entire announcement in my crystal oracle and chose the quickest way to arrive here. The reason being is that I know what this thing is, this beast. I can kill it or tame it. I am its nemesis. I am who it is truly after, for he wants my power. And the only way he can have it is to devour me. He needs to devour a great wizard or he will not grow beyond his youth.' Then he paused as he looked into the crowd. He glowered at them all in defiance of their denying he was a great wizard. Then he announced what the beast was. 'A dragon! That's what it is, a dragon.'

"A few short gasps came from the women in the crowded square. It was then, silence befell the crowd. Suddenly and simultaneously the silence was broken.

"The crowd laughed uproariously as many pointed at Ivan. Avilla herself looked hurt for her father, and she looked astonished at what he had just announced. Someone from the crowd yelled at her to take her father home and tuck him into bed before any other legends decided to come after him. Avilla looked back to the still-laughing crowd, then back to her father, her father who stood defiant of the crowd but with a look of humiliation in his eyes.

"'I will show you,' he yelled as he shrunk a little from the crowd. 'I will bring back the forepaw of the beast, and in it will be clutched his own two eyes! I will leave now and not return until I have won my battle!' he stammered and rattled on as he turned from the crowd and walked away. Then he hollered, 'Come, Avilla, you must help me make ready.'

"Avilla burst into tears as the crowd hailed up another round of laughter, and then she turned and ran in the opposite direction of her father.

"'Avilla,' he yelled once more, turning, only to see her running away from him, her long blond hair trailing behind her in the wind. He turned back to his destination, and one could see him slump over and hang his head as he reached up to wipe his face. Then he disappeared around a corner slowly. Then the smallest puff of white smoke came out from around the corner he had just turned.

"I saw something fly from his hand just before the smoke appeared.

"I wanted to run after him, help him some way, tell him they weren't really laughing. When I turned to tell Alsie I was going, I saw Alsie pushing through the crowd to follow Avilla. I went after Ivan.

"Finat later told me that he was looking at the woman who had lost her daughter to the beast the whole time. She did not laugh or look repulsed by what Ivan was saying. She only stood there and gained a look of fear at his words and wailed all the more as he had finished his announcement.

"Otinoe was close behind me as I arrived at the home of Ivan. His door was open, and

I could hear him babbling to himself in a raspy, sobbing voice 'I will show them, Avilla, I promise. They will not laugh when they see me again. They will see me as the great source of power that I am. Then it will not matter if I am announced or not. They'll see.'

"I called to him as Otinoe and I walked through the door. 'Ivan?'

"'Who's there?' he barked. 'Someone else to laugh?'

"'No,' I said, 'someone to help, or at least tell you that you don't have to go.'

"'I must go now,' he said. 'Even Avilla is embarrassed by me.'

"As he said those words, Avilla ran through the door with Alsie close behind her. She heard the words her father said and stopped dead in her tracks, as if she had hit a wall. A look of pain overcame her features that expressed her urgency and embarrassment the moment before. A tear rolled down her face as she covered her mouth with her hands and sobbed.

"Her father, seeing this, became quiet and went about his packing without acknowledging her pain, and without the anger and self-pity that spewed from his mouth earlier. He almost achieved a self-righteous look, but with more defiance than conviction.

"Finally, through her sobbing, she managed to speak the words that would force her father to carry out his impotent plan, if for no other reason than to defend his egotistical honor. 'Please, Father, do not go. I do not know where I would be when you do not return.'

"Ivan looked at his daughter with loss. He looked as if he had lost the faith of his one believer, his one adherent. Then with the voice of one who had nothing more to lose, he said this to his own heart more than to Avilla. 'I have two feet that may follow only one path. I have taken the first step, and the abyss opens behind me. I may not turn back for my heart has begun to pour out in front of me, and I must reach out to catch that which is spilling from it or fall into the abyss with an empty heart.' At that Ivan picked up his pack and pushed past us who were there, head raised high with doom deep in his eyes.

"Avilla fell then to her knees and closed her hands over her face.

"Alsie motioned to Otinoe to gather the others and our gear. No sooner had he walked out the door than he returned. Finat had taken it upon himself to get all things ready for a hunt.

"Always the first to enjoy a good chase, challenge, or choke, that is Finat. Always ready to prove power.

"Without a word to Avilla, we left the hovel and the village to follow after Ivan. Distantly and discretely we followed without detection. As we came upon the Abranas Forest, Ivan stopped and turned back toward the village. Then after taking a few steps, he turned back again. He did this several times while shaking his head and flailing his arms in the air. Suddenly, through the distance, we could hear his voice as he turned to the forest once again. 'No, I will not face them without daring my pledge. I will face you, serpent, there. Fate may take its payment. But I will not return weaker in spirit than they are in faith.'

"Ivan reached into his pack and pulled out a wand of sorts. He held it up and started turning from side to side. For perhaps an hour he did this when the tip of it began to glow. It stopped as he turned to his left and began again as he turned back toward the right. As it reached the height of its luminescence the third time he turned, he began to walk in that direction. Later we found out that what he carried and waved was not a wand but a stick, with a shard of stone at the end of it that was the deepest red color any of us had ever seen, deeper red that even the finest of rubies.

"He continued on his path, raising the stone now and again to check his direction. Where it glowed its brightest, that was the path he would follow. As the forest grew dense it became impossible to follow on horseback. We tethered our horses and started to go on foot, following a path that had never been made. Dusk started to come upon us as the sun drew its last breaths of the day, and it became easier to follow Ivan's stone than to follow Ivan. Then as the sun dropped and left no light, the light of the stone disappeared also. We moved forward quickly to see if we could spot Ivan himself. In the darkness it seemed an impossible task. It seemed the faster we tried to move, the less progress we made through the thickets of the forest. It was so dense and dark, Alsie would not allow any torch light, as we did not want Ivan to know of our presence, so on we struggled.

"Soral let out a high yelp, as he seemed to disappear from Minac's sight. Then he was back again, limping on one side. He had hit a large rock with his shin and tripped, falling into and below the brush that we pushed our way though. The rocks became more prevalent. Then the rocks in our path were boulders in our path. The path became a hill until right before us was a flat wall of stone.

"Brush was high at its base, so high in fact that it would probably have been eye level with Gorn. There was no way to climb the face of the wall, and still there was no sign of Ivan.

"Alsie split us into two groups; himself with Koreal, Riman, Domatis, and me, Finat with Otinoe, Avalaes, Minac, and Soral. Each of the two groups was to follow the edge of the wall we had come to looking for Ivan, and still Alsie insisted on no torchlight. (We were not even sure that we had followed the same path as Ivan.)

"Off to either direction the two groups went. The path became easier as we followed the wall, but still no sign of Ivan. Minac and Otinoe came up behind us. Otinoe, the constant joker, roared like a beast. He scared the wits out of us, and we all turned, weapons ready. Minac started yelling as he backhanded Otinoe across the shoulder, 'It's us, it's us, and don't let this idiot get us killed.' We lowered our weapons, and Otinoe began laughing. Everything was a game to him. 'What's the matter? Getting a little spooked?' he said. Alsie just glared at him, and Minac told us about a cavern about four hundred paces from the place we separated on the other end of the wall. He told us Finat thought he saw footprints in the dust.

"When we arrived at the cavern entrance, we all went in together. There was rubble everywhere; most of us had tripped at least three times before Alsie gave up on the no torch light thing. But almost as soon as we lit the torches, we extinguished them.

"It was unbelievable. The walls of the cavern had huge claw marks all over them. Huge chunks of solid rock had been torn from the wall by physical force without the use of any tools or even the aid of a cracked surface. We all quivered at the thought of how powerful the beast that did this must be, and at the thought that this beast may be the same that was to be our quarry. It never sounded to us that the beast was this large in any of the descriptions given.

After trying to go on without the aid of any light, Alsie decided that the risk of some light was a must or we would make enough noise to attract attention anyway. So two small candles were lit, it was enough light to get our feet past the rocks. As we walked along, we could see that some of what we had been tripping on was not rock at all but the skeletons and bones of animals that had been carried in by the beast to feed upon. Further on we discovered the remains of human prey, some of which had not been completely devoured, some of whom we recognized as those who had been chasing us before our arrival in Khibanhahm. We could only recognize them through the clothes that lay torn and scattered about them. Their gear and weapons were gone, or at least not anywhere near. And even though it appeared that the beast did not decide to dine on their faces, they had been there long enough to decompose beyond reasonable recognition. Between the visions of the walls and the skeletal remains and the stank, damp smell of rotting flesh, our thoughts grew more and more uneasy. No one said a word, but we all felt the tension.

"Then as we moved through the cavernous tunnel, going deeper into the darkness ahead, there was a great flash of light. We all heard Ivan yelling strange words at the top of his lungs. We all lit torches and ran toward the sound of Ivan's voice. Then a high-pitched screech filled the tunnel. Pain ran from our ears clear down our backs as the screech echoed on. In the background we could hear short bursts of Ivan's yelling voice, and then as the screech quieted, the sound of falling rock started to fill the tunnel, and Ivan let out a scream of pain. The screech began again but in short, varied bursts. The flapping of large, leather-like wings cut through the other sounds.

We ran into a large cavern, so large that the entire village of Khibanhahm could have fit into it. In the center was a pile of weapons, armor, and other indistinguishable items. There on the other side of the cavern was the beast, flapping his wings and coming slightly off the ground beneath him with each effort. Fur-covered scales were visible across his back as we came up behind him. He was still unaware of us. As we came within twenty paces of him and behind him, we saw glimpses of Ivan.

He was sitting up against the back wall of the cavern, legs sprawled out in front of him. He was holding a scroll up and reading from it as the beast moved left and right about him. He had two large slashes across his chest, as if the beast had narrowly missed his victim's end.

Minac, Soral, Riman, and Domatis each knelt with arrows knocked. Riman yelled for the four to aim at the back of the beast's neck. There his scales had risen in anger as he loomed over his target. They let arrows fly and had knocked another before they hit. As they hit, the beast swung around. His head flailed in anger and confusion as he did so. His face was burned, and he appeared blinded. The four let go the next arrows, and one caught the great beast in the eye, another in the throat. The other two hit the chest and bounced away as if they had hit rock. The beast tried to screech in pain and could not. His tail waved wildly, catching Ivan and throwing him clear of the area where the beast continued to grapple with the pain and confusion that controlled him. Finat yelled at Otinoe and me to throw elven throng razors at the wings of the beast when they opened.

"'Now I know what they were made for.' Anitae reached into her coat and pulled out the weapon. It was an awkward-looking instrument. It was made up of two circular blades connected only by a yard of fine-spun wire wrapped by another wire of the same gauge to give it strength. The blades were razor sharp at the edges, but the center was heavy and thick. 'All you do is swing it upward from the ground toward your target. The blades will both strike, and the wire will pass through the target, pulling the wire through.'

"Anyway, he then yelled at the four to strike their arrows at the juncture of the wings and torso. The arrows didn't strike deep, but they caused enough pain for the beast to spread his wings in anguish. My brother and I threw our blades at the beast, and as they hit, they tore large holes in his wings. Again he went wild, and again we threw another set of blades. Again they struck their target with the same effect. He went wild. The beast flapped his wings rapidly, more rapidly than I would have thought possible. Dust rose up around us all, and we couldn't see farther than the ends of our arms. The beast was hissing loudly and moving about. We heard a thud as Koreal's scream moved away from us, through the air above, then to the ground behind. Still the beast was before us and was beginning to tire. His hissing stopped, and he moved more slowly. The dust around us started to settle. The beast fell with a great rumble that filled the cavern. The archers of our group began sinking arrows into every vulnerable spot they could find as they surrounded the beast. Still he breathed and hissed lightly.

"From across the cavern, Alsie, Avalaes, and I heard Ivan. We could hardly believe our ears. In a hoarse, worn voice he was saying, 'Stop, stop what you are doing before he dies.' Over and over again he repeated himself until Alsie ordered the archers to stop.

"Alsie and I ran over to him, and my brother and Avalaes went to find Koreal. As we reached Ivan, he was still whispering to himself, 'Stop.'

"Alsie bent over him. 'Why must we stop, Ivan? What is it?'

"Ivan just continued his whispers. His eyes closed.

"Alsie repeated his questions with no response. Finally Alsie took Ivan by the shoulders, shaking him with all the strength he had left of the day, again repeating his questions.

"Ivan's eyes opened slightly. 'No time to explain,' he said. 'The girl must cut off his mane while he still lives.'

"Alsie and I both looked at him like he had lost all reason. Alsie asked him, 'Why?'

"Ivan held up the stone on the end of the stick. It flickered with light. 'No time,' he said. 'He's dying.' Then Ivan fell limp, and his eyes closed.

"Alsie looked up at me and said, 'No!' Then he stood up and walked toward the beast as he drew his sword. How he knew what I was thinking is beyond me. Whether it was the look in my eyes or the glance I made to the beast as Ivan spoke those words, I don't know. I got up behind Alsie and ran around him. Pulling my dagger, I jumped on the beast's neck and cut the mane from the beast from the top of the head to the start of its spine, right down to the bone of its neck.

"As I finished the beast stood up, with me still on its back. Fear ran through me, and I lost control of my bodily functions. Still, somehow, I regained myself and climbed back up his neck through the slimy, thick blood that oozed from the fresh wound I had just made. Holding on tight with the crook of my arm to one of the broken arrow shafts that still protruded from the base of its head, I shoved my dagger up and under his skull as far as it would go. He flailed his head from side to side once more and began to fall lifelessly to the ground. I jumped before it hit the ground and rolled, spraining my ankle. The mane was still clutched in my hand.

"Finat went to the beast and began chopping at its neck with his broadsword until its head lay separated from the rest of it. I crawled away from the beast as blood spewed from its open neck like a fountain of death.

"Alsie turned away from where he was and went to Ivan, to bind his wounds as he slept from the loss of blood.

"Minac wrapped the cuts on his legs that he had received from the rocks, and then he wrapped my ankle tight. Koreal had been hit by a wild swing of the beast's wing and had a few broken ribs.

"By the high glow of fresh torches we all stood looking at the beast that had fallen before us there. There in that huge cavern that was its home, it was smaller than we remembered it as it stood above us and screeched that last screech before Domatis's shaft found its throat. The wings of the beast were shredded, from the elven razors that had ripped through the thin, leathery, billows of skin that gave it flight. Its eyes were burned and blistered. That was what the big flash was that drew our attention. Ivan had used the flash powder that he uses to make his entrance. He burned the beast's eyes to confuse him. Alsie figured that he came upon the beast while he was sleeping."

Johuocin interrupted Anitae. "We have breakfast ready. Continue the story when we are on the road, small one. I'm sure that Alsie is anxious to leave, and we don't want to hold him up too long." Johuocin thought about how little time there was before solstice. If all went well for the captain and his party, soon after solstice, there would be war taking over the kingdom.

Johuocin/Marie looked down at the petite girl. She did look tomboyish, but it was impossible to picture her on the back of such a beast as she had described. Though, the self-admission of her reaction to fear added some credibility to the story. Quite honestly, most grown men would have such a reaction if put in that situation. Truly it was hard to believe that exaggeration had no entrance in her tale.

"Go, call the others now. I do wish to hear the rest soon."

"But I was just getting to the good part," Anitae whined as she stepped from the stool that placed her at chin level to Marie. "You must encourage everyone to eat quickly before I forget where I was." Off she scampered to call the others.

As they filed in, some were talking about Khibanhahm and spending the solstice there. It seemed the thought of solstice did not excite them so, but Khibanhahm lifted their spirits some. They laughed and joked as they ate, and none needed to be hurried with the meal. They were, as you would picture children, hurrying to some small adventure of the day, all but Alsie, who ate quickly, quietly, staring off at something in the distance.

As he finished his porridge, he announced it was time to go. Everyone pushed aside their bowls and went about their last-minute tasks, and they were out the door.

As they headed on their journey through the cold and dark before the dawn, Alsie pulled across his mandolin into his lap and began to sing.

> To a time so far away,
> Through which we passed a
> tender day,
> To a place we've been before,

A place we cherish to our core.
It was there the hand of fate
was kind,
It was there we found a peace
of mind.
It was there we found our secret
told,
A secret about the young, of old.
It is there we'll find our spirits
free,
It is there we'll go with friends
to see.

As the group traveled forward into the darkness of winter, Alsie sang the triumphs of their visit to Khibanhahm. Anitae moved closer to Marie to finish her story.

"Where was I? Oh, yes. Licking our wounds, so to speak." She looked at Marie and rolled her eyes. "We were pretty beat up, both physically and emotionally. Exhausted from our fear and fight, we sat upon the floor of the cavern. Many torches had been lit at this point, and we got a full look at where we were. The cavern was huge, though the beast looked smaller by comparison to what we thought at first. The mane of the beast was still gripped tightly in my hand. It was as though it held me instead of me holding it.

"I sat by Ivan as Alsie bound his wounds. Ivan lay unconscious and motionless. I looked at Alsie and saw the wear and worry on his face. 'Do you suppose he could have killed the beast if he were a mage?' I asked. Alsie looked at me and chuckled. 'Perhaps a very powerful one.' I looked back at Alsie and could not help but smile. Alsie has always made me smile when he would chuckle like that.

"I looked around the room and saw my brother and cousins as they bound their wounds and chided their pain. I saw the remnants of others who dealt with the beast, and I saw the marks in the walls from the claws of the beast that created such a place. Thoughts of what could have happened to some or all of us ran through my mind.

"The thing that happened as I spoke my next words shocked all of us, I said, 'I certainly wish he were one.' Suddenly the end of the mane crackled and burst into flame. It burned quickly and very hot. It burned, and I still could not let go of it. It burned over, around, and through my hand. When it was over, my hand was unscathed and opened. There was no ash or smoke or anything left of the mane. My eyes were wide, as were Alsie's, as I turned my hand over and over, inspecting it. My hand felt warm, but that was the only evidence that remained of the incident, and soon enough that too passed.

"After we got over the shock of what had happened, we all gathered together around the unconscious Ivan. He was injured badly it seemed, worse even than we had thought. He remained unconscious as we built a fire with the bones there in the chasm that was created by the beast that lay dead a few feet away. Alsie anguished over the fact that Ivan might not make it back to the village alive and what he would tell Avilla of her father's death, or how.

"The rest of us sat and waited, for what seemed an eternity, on Alsie to decide it was time to go. We all suffered our hunger as we waited. We were put off from eating the few pieces of jerky in our packs by the stench created by the burning of human bones and the fresh blood that had spilled from the beast that lay beheaded. That is, all but Finat. He always had less tolerance for hunger than the smell of blood. Finat ate without hindrance of his surroundings, almost as though the smell of blood made his hunger grow strong.

"Koreal and Avalaes, trying not to seem squeamish next to their younger brother, took a bite of jerky and found they could not swallow. They chewed the jerky until they puked.

"Finally, after several hours, Alsie decided we must move Ivan out of the cave and into the fresh air. Having no other way to move Ivan, we found a large section of the beast's sinewy wing and cut it away from him. After placing Ivan in the center of it, Minac, Soral, and Domatis took one side and Koreal, Avalaes, and Riman took the other and carried him out. Finat and Alsie took the lead, and Otinoe and I followed the bunch.

"As we started to leave the chamber, my brother motioned to me to fall back. As we did so, he mentioned the forepaw and eyes that Ivan had told the townspeople he would offer as proof. We let the others go ahead without notice of our absence.

"We returned to the chamber, where I detached the forepaw at the first joint nearest the end of the wing while Otinoe dug into the creature's skull to retrieve its eyes. After placing the eyes in the forepaw, we bound it closed with a thong made from a shred of the wing. Tying a rope to the end of it, we began dragging it out.

"It left a trail behind us in the dust of the cavern floor. One of the claws had sprung free of the bindings and had caught on something in the dirt and pulled it out.

"Now, Mother," Anitae moved closer and began whispering lightly, "what I tell you now must remain between us. Otinoe and I found something that the others know nothing of as yet. We know it is wrong to keep these things from our family, and that is likely why it is not yet been found out." Here she stopped and looked around to be sure she wasn't overheard.

"We heard the metallic clink as it was dragged behind us, or we would have missed it completely. As we turned, our torchlight hit it and sparkled off the surface so brightly that we were dazzled by its shine.

"Otinoe ran back and picked it up. It was a crown, covered in jewels and hammered of the finest dwarven gold Otinoe or I had ever seen. The light that reflected from it gleamed throughout the cavern, bouncing from one wall to another. So smooth it was that all the dust that may have touched it at one time had left its surface as it was picked up. The jewels were set so tightly in it that you could not tell where the metal ended and the jewel began, yet clearly they were not part of the other. Otinoe handed me the crown and went back to the place where it had been pulled from the dust. He began digging there with his hands. As he dug, he found more and more gold and jewels. Some were not as fine as others, but he did come upon three other items of the same quality as the crown—a golden chainmail cape with fine jewels woven into the mail in a fashion so intricate that they could be seen from many angles, yet so strong were the settings that neither Otinoe or I could pry them out; a simple gold mail kilt without ornamentation except for the jewel-encrusted sash at its front; and the last was a scepter with a heavy golden shaft and a red stone large enough to be fashioned to the shape of a miniature war hammer. These four items alone were too heavy for Otinoe and me to carry out, and they seemed to be more important than to be just booty in a treasure hunt.

"It was amazing for us to find this much gold and treasure in one place. Though it was not the most amazing thing we found there. Buried within the treasure were three eggs. They were black as coal at the wide end and fading gently to blood red at the narrow end. They were as large as church bells.

"Knowing we could not possibly carry out any of it in its entirety, we put it all back in place and buried it once more, all but three items: armor, crown, and scepter. These we moved and buried separately.

"After this we hurried to catch the others. We had taken more time than we had thought.

By the time we found them, they had set up camp outside the entrance to the cave, and Finat, Riman, and Avalaes were preparing to return and look for us.

"Dawn was come and gone by the time we came out of the cave, and Alsie stood glaring at us from the small clearing outside the opening. Ivan had begun to wake and also watched as we made our exit from the darkness, though his look was more of anticipation and impatience.

"Alsie almost immediately began scolding us for not staying with the group. Demanding to know what our need was for returning. Otinoe tried to explain to Alsie but was interrupted by an even more impatient and demanding Ivan.

"'You have something that is mine,'" he yelled, looking at Otinoe and me. Otinoe smiled and pulled forward the claw, proud that he had remembered Ivan's promise to the villagers. Ivan became enraged. 'No,' he said. 'I don't give a damn about the claw. I want the mane. Bring it to me.'

"Alsie looked at Ivan. He was taken aback by Ivan's scream.

"'Ivan,' he said, 'we don't have the mane anymore.'

"'What?' Ivan stood straight up. 'Where is it? Is it back inside? Was it left behind? Was it …?'

"'No, Ivan, it burst into flame in Anitae's hand. We thought she was burned by it. It just burst into flame for no reason.' Alsie just stood there then, in front of a wide-eyed Ivan.

"Ivan's eyes and face dropped then. He shook his head. Quietly then he asked me. 'What was your wish? Was it as trivial as I suspect it must have been at the time?'

"With everything that had happened since we left the town, and the treasure that had been found, and the eggs that still lay buried in the cavern, I remembered making no wish. 'I made none,'" I said.

"'You did,' he said. He turned and quietly limped away into the bramble around the clearing.

"Alsie watched as Ivan walked away, stunned by Ivan's depression after all that had happened. He stood puzzled by the mention of a wish and Ivan's confidence that one had been made. He called after Ivan, 'What wish did we have? Where would it come from?'

"The wish that was locked in the dragon's mane, boy! The wish I wanted for Avilla. The wish that was to make up for all the embarrassment I had caused a motherless child with a foolish father. The wish that was wasted at the hand of a little girl with the frivolity of finding newfound safety!' At that Ivan came back through the brush, coming to stand in front of Alsie and me. Glaring at us. Looking down at us as he stood there in his dirt and soot-smudged white robes. 'The wish,' he said, 'that comes to few people, a wish without restriction. The wish that is made from all the magic within a dragon before the dragon is wise enough to make the wish itself!' Then he raised his hand, waving it over Alsie and me, saying, 'If I were a powerful sorcerer, I would turn you both into beetles.'

"No sooner had he said that than it was that the two of us were crawling on the ground, and from what we were told, for that is all I have to go by, we were beetles. I remember nothing else from that time until the time we stood in Ivan's workshop at the back of his hovel.

"Otinoe said that he picked us up and placed us in a small pouch he emptied. They took us back into town. There, Avilla helped Ivan search the many books he possessed for a spell that would return us. Otinoe and the others had recounted everything from the entry into the cave until the mane burst into flame in my hand before anyone, including Ivan, understood exactly what happened.

"Upon hearing the story myself, I became depressed, knowing this was the second time I had wished without my knowledge. My depression did not last, however, for this was without malice.

"The village rejoiced at the destruction of Ivan's dragon and honored him with a great feast. (They did, of course, include us.) But the most significant thing was this: Avilla promised herself to Alsie. Not with

Alsie's asking, but on her own, in front of the whole town. She was twelve then.

"After the celebration was over, Alsie tried to explain that she could not make such a promise at her age. She would hear none of it. Finally, in desperation of our circumstance, he had to tell her everything about our age, our predicament, and our search. She would not believe him. So he told Ivan and the storekeeper, Imil, who told the entire village. Ivan searched for wish spells throughout his books but had none. The people there accepted us and treated us well. Avilla still refused to take back her promise, saying she didn't care about any of it. She was convinced that we would eventually find our wish and she would be there.

"This visit may prove to be both sad and happy for Alsie, reality being what it is. We promised to return in five years. Ivan promised to continue to search for a wish spell. For the first year we were away from there Alsie sang songs that lamented a love that would not be.

"The most weighing thing for Alsie, though, is that he plans once again to release Avilla from her promise. She is now seventeen, and he still appears to be the eleven summers old that he was when they first met. He plans to break his own heart for her happiness.

"Quite frankly, I see no other way for him to handle the situation unless Ivan has found a wish spell that would be effective. Ivan may be a powerful mage, but it is still necessary to have and learn the spells before he can use them. Discovering his own spells, or creating them, can take years upon years of experimentation and study.

"Otinoe and me, we did get a chance to ask Ivan about dragons and such. We tried to be inconspicuous about the egg thing. He knew nothing off hand, but he had a tome there that spoke of such things, and it says there that dragon's eggs are unstable and grow before they hatch. It said that they are odd shaped and then fill out. When they are large enough to hatch, they are buried and take about fifty years to be ready. That's why we told no one of the eggs we found. It makes the waiting longer."

Johuocin looked at the small girl-woman before her, awed by knowing the seasons behind this deceptive appearance of youth. She was older than Johuocin or Marie, yet she still appeared to be a child. The woman-child was filled with the wisdom and experience of time. She was filled with the dedication and patience of someone taught by trial, error, and never ending hope.

As Johuocin looked at Anitae, the look became a concentrated stare. The gaze made

Anitae uncomfortable and fidgety, until at last the girl looked away to avoid it.

"Why do you stare at me, Mother?" Anitae asked with a timid voice, still avoiding eye contact.

Johuocin realized then that his thoughts had drifted to a point of rudeness. "I'm sorry, child. I hadn't realized I was. I was only thinking how hard it has been for all of you, being children all these many seasons, having to deal with people who show no respect, though you probably have more wisdom and experience than they do."

Anitae heard that and grinned. Looking back to Marie, she even laughed a little. "Mother," she started, "think of this—as an adult you must first earn respect. Until you earn that respect, you are treated with distrust. As a child you are at least treated with courtesy and caring until you show arrogance or disrespect. Very few are threatened merely by a child's presence, and fewer still are those who would kill a child rather than chase one away. Many may wish to rob a child of something the child has, but none ever expect a child to win a fight for that item. We are the best at what we do, so we never lose.

"So, you tell me, Mother, of the two of us, which of us is better off?"

Johuocin thought for a moment on what Anitae said. All true, all wise, and the element of surprise on their side if they were attacked. A useful tool in any situation, wisdom combined with surprise. "That is a point well-made, child. The sight of you confuses my comprehension of your wisdom. Perhaps you hold an answer to my problems in the place you seek answers to yours."

Anitae looked away with quizzical disregard. There the conversation ended as the group rode further into the darkness of winter.

CHAPTER 15

Into the Darkness, Comes the Light

As the five traveled eastward toward the sea, clouds began to cover the sky. Gorn had rejoined the group as the moon of solstice came low to the horizon and its light faded into the darkness behind them. They continued forward toward their point of destination as the darkness swallowed their tracks and the stars were scarcely seen above. The further they traveled, the fewer stars they saw between the cloud cover. Soon enough they traveled only by presumption, with liquid faith in their hearts, a faith that evaporated a little with every step forward. The captain continued to wrestle in and out of sleep, oblivious to the problem they now faced.

The wind began as a cool breeze directly in their faces, and as they traveled it became bitter, biting their cheeks. As numbness came to Merson's nose and chin, he warned everyone to cover their skin against frostbite. Slowly it changed direction, coming from the south, blowing strong and carrying the clouds with it.

After hours of traveling under the heavy clouds above and no stars being seen to guide them, Merson came to a halt as he spied the first light of the sun coming over the horizon.

All but the captain pulled back their hoods as they stopped. A look of dismay came over their faces as they saw the sun rise directly before them. They had turned northeast; it was not the wind that had changed direction. Within moments the light was as bright as it would be that day as it fought its way through the clouds. A faint shadow could be seen to the east. High above the plains, the mountains before them overshadowed the miles before them. The sun would not light much of their way from this point until they reached the other side of the mountains ahead. By that time they may be in the total darkness of low solstice.

The bird that circled above them could be seen more clearly now as it spiraled higher toward the clouds. Gorn broke the silence of the troop as they came to a standstill in their dilemma. "It's the same bird that followed above me from the time we left the hovel of Harishe. I believe it's the boy's falcon."

"Why do you suppose he would have set that bird to follow?" Merson asked Gorn.

Gorn could only shake his head in query for the same answer.

For a while the party traveled silently as the light of the sun left them and darkness from an overcast sky once again became an envelope of uncertainty. No one was certain of the passing time setting their journey on a stretched path.

As Merson realized that they had gained some light from a clearing in the clouds above, he turned his attention to Riessa and the glass globe he gave her earlier. "Which way does the metal point, Riessa?"

"The same direction we're headed."

"Are you sure?" he exclaimed with hopelessness in his voice that rang out like thunder on a stormy night. "How long has it been like that?"

"I don't know. I forgot I was holding it. Which way are we going?"

"North. We must turn back to the southeast. We lost our footing in the dark and wind. We probably added a few leagues to our journey."

Riessa looked at Merson and Ben. She saw the worry and fatigue upon their souls. She pressed her horse to the captain's side as he jostled into wakefulness, nearly falling from his own mount with Ben preoccupied. "We need to get out of this wind and warm ourselves with a fire for a while. Something warm to eat wouldn't hurt either."

At that comment Ben looked up from the ground and took his brother's arm. "I could use the diversion myself. The cold has me lethargic. There's a stand of trees just ahead of us." He sat pointing to a grove of evergreens that came into view as they topped a small knoll. "How about it, Merson? Ory should wake soon, and a warm meal will help him gain some cheer."

Knowing that the party had already lost some ground on an uncertain path, Merson reluctantly consented. He warned, however, that the cheer their captain may or may not receive from a hot meal would probably be lost at the knowledge that time was passing.

As they approached the trees nearly half a league away, Ben raised his crossbow and shot, paying no attention to Gorn, who walked within inches of the bolt's path. Startled, Gorn jumped back and turned to see Ben focused on the ground ahead.

There, in the grass that peeked through the snow, flopped a cock pheasant spattering red flecks of blood over the ground, unable to recover from the wound caused by Ben's bolt having passed through its neck. The bolt from Ben's weapon had passed through and buried itself somewhere in the snow that glistened white in the darkness of winter.

Gorn ran ahead, catching the bird in his large hands and snapping its neck to put it out of its misery. As the others joined his position, he handed the bird to Ben, and they headed to the stand of trees together.

As they entered the trees, they looked for a suitable place to build a small fire and set the captain down from his mount. The stand was surprisingly larger and denser than what it had first appeared. As they found a suitable place to rest, Merson and Gorn began to gather dead wood and small branches to build a fire. A blanket was placed on the ground, and the captain was taken from his mount. Very little snow had reached the ground in the small clearing, and the smaller trees in the area were enough to keep the wind out. All in all, Riessa and Ben had agreed that they had been fortunate to find such a spot after all the trouble they had experienced on their journey.

Soon a fire had been started, and the group was preparing a meal. Merson took a large pot from a pack on one of the mules and began melting snow he had gathered from the edge of the clearing, where it had blown into banks during a previous storm. The group had depleted most of the water from their water jugs as they traveled through the cold, dry winds.

The captain rested comfortably by the warm fire as the rest of the group went about their business. Soon he woke to the aroma of pheasant roasting by the fire. Riessa sat near the fire, eyes closed, while Gorn lay nearby on a bed of evergreen branches.

"Merson," the captain called, "how far have we come?"

Merson was startled as he studied the star charts. He had not noticed the captain's wakefulness. "I'm not sure, Captain. We went off course when the cloud cover came up. I think we probably lost some ground, but we have been traveling near a full day without rest until now."

"How much ground have we lost, and how much time will it take us to make it up?"

"I'm still working on that, Captain. The clouds have an occasional clearing now and again, and I've been trying to find the correct chart angle." Merson tried to change the subject a little by asking the captain, "How are you feeling? Did the potion work as it was explained?"

The captain looked as if he had forgotten that he had been injured. He stood up slowly and stretched. He felt where he remembered the wounds to be and began moving his limbs and twisting his torso. "I'm surprisingly well. Nothing hurts or aches. And I feel rested and relaxed. However, I still don't remember parts of our journey. I feel ready to move forward."

Ben looked over at his brother. "I'm glad one of us does. I feel like I'm Gorn's age."

At that Gorn responded without moving or opening his eyes. "Careful now," he said in jest, "or you may not reach my age."

Ory looked back at his brother with limited patience in his eyes. He remembered back to the time when he and his brother were growing up in their father's castle, always comfortable and warm. Still, even then, Ben would find little things to complain about, especially near the end of winter when the food coming from the larder wasn't as fresh as it had been at harvest. Then he looked at what he had been through over the last few years and weeks and decided that perhaps his brother, too, had quite a bit to deal with, including his own wounds that had not yet healed.

"Don't worry, Ben," Orman Reglawr assured his brother. "You're next to take the potion. As a matter of fact, why don't you take it now? When you wake up, you'll feel fresh, ready to go again."

Ben looked at his brother like he was daft. "Oh no," he objected. "Not until I have a hot meal and my share of the pheasant cooking there. It was my kill, and the smell of it has been burning my senses ever since it started to braze."

Gorn listened and laughed as the two bantered back and forth for the duration of the wait as the pheasant cooked. To him, this was the way he had always heard siblings talk to one another.

The conversation took Gorn back to a time before he had lost his own brother, a brother younger than himself, who still lived in his heart and memory. They, too, would have moments of advice and resistance, much as these two brothers, who traveled side by side, and their father would speak with wisdom that neither could understand, nor, at times, would they even try.

Their father would say in his deep, smiling voice, "Throw your stones now boys, for later they will form a bridge for you to sit upon and laugh."

Gorn had only a partial understanding of that phrase until the two had finally reached a mature age and were able to sit and talk and laugh about the petty arguments they had once shared. The death of their father helped them to appreciate his words more than they had when he lived. The death of Gorn's brother helped him to appreciate the bridge they had built between them. For now, though, they could not sit upon it and laugh together. Gorn often sat alone there and smiled at the stones they had placed. Perhaps that's where he was when Riessa came to sit beside him and hand him a plate of food.

"… Don't know where we're going or how to get there, but he's mad because I lost our way by not keeping an eye on that silly contraption he handed me. Can you believe him?" Gorn had missed most of what Riessa was saying. She sounded as if she was mad, but he couldn't tell if she were mad at herself or someone else.

"What is your heart gnawing on, young one?" Gorn set down his plate and took

Riessa's hand as she set down her spoon. "Contemplate the philosophies gone before us and find peace."

"There is no philosophy in confusion, Gorn. I set myself into a valley of circles and find no straight path of escape."

"Ahh, remember now, all paths are a destiny and therefore philosophy has gone before you. We were meant to be in this place or we would not exist in ourselves." Gorn let Riessa's hand free to cup his own together. Holding his hands out to her, he invited her to look between his thumbs. "What do you see in my hands?"

Riessa moved her face to look inside. "Darkness."

Then he separated his large hands and cupped them around one of her small, delicate hands. "Do you feel the warmth within my hands?" She looked at him with confusion and fatuity over his incomprehensible exercise. Still she nodded in confirmation to his question. "Then think of this. If in darkness there can be warmth, then, in confusion there can be the existence of purpose, and beyond that, destiny. What have you always been taught?"

Riessa looked down as foolishness of her thought was revealed to her. Smiling ineptly she looked up at Gorn and said with a sigh, "The purpose of destiny is to create philosophy, the purpose of philosophy is to help us understand life's path, the purpose of life's path is to lead us to our destiny …"

Gorn smiled, "So all things ahead will come to pass." Gorn picked up his plate and spoon. "You will be a student of life, as we all are. What you learn is up to you." Then Gorn gave his respects to the forces of philosophy and began to enjoy his meal.

Riessa sat quietly next to him and finished her own meal.

After they had all finished their meal, Merson announced that he had found the direction they were after and they would be on course once again. No one spoke much as they picked up their gear and burdened their mounts. The captain tied his brother to his horse, and Ben took a half portion of his elixir. Gorn had talked Riessa into doing the same as they started off. However, she insisted on belaying the straps that would hold her to her mount. Gorn did not press the issue of binding her considering what had happened at the hovel of Harishe.

With Ben and Riessa quickly finding slumber even on the backs of their mounts, the five were underway. Merson had put away the star charts and had found a way to mount the directional device to the small forward crest of his riding saddle. As they started he decided he would entrust its use only to himself, mumbling, "I'll do it m'self."

The captain rode behind him, next to Ben, with Gorn and Riessa close behind.

Onward they traveled like this for some time, losing track of the hours that had passed. Ben and Riessa continued to sleep less restlessly than the captain had. The three men left with the charge of their safety traveled well, though Merson, the one with the least rest, wavered in his saddle from time to time. Little conversation took place as they traveled, for Merson was fading into exhaustion and Gorn could find little that the captain would respond to when he spoke. So it was as they traveled, each man taking care of his charge: Gorn, Riessa; the captain, his brother; Merson, the stars and his contraption.

Once again the hours seemed like days as they watched the light come over the horizon before them. Their mounts traveled more slowly, it seemed, as they felt the exhaustive effects of their journey of no rest.

As Gorn saw the light ahead, he shook Riessa, knowing that a day was all that was required for the elixir's rest. She did not respond. "Captain," he called, "wake Ben. Nearly a day has passed, and they have not stirred."

The captain shook Ben, also to no avail. "Merson," the captain called, with no response. Again he called yelling, "Merson!" and Merson jolted in his saddle.

Merson had fallen into sleep as he rode. In his waking he saw the light coming up in front of him, and his heart started to rumble like a great mountain ready to fall. His voice wavered as he tried to catch his breath, "Captain, I fell asleep and we are off our course once more. How long have we been traveling this direction? The sun should be to our left." The group stopped as Merson looked at his contraption on the saddle. "Wait, this cannot be; the metal still points in the correct direction."

The light continued to rise from behind the hill before them. Then Gorn noticed something. "Merson, shouldn't the horizon be farther off and not so low? And should the sun be reflecting on the clouds above us instead of trying to shine through from the other side?"

The captain turned to face Gorn, and then back to Merson. "Merson, Gorn is right. That light is traveling on the ground ahead of us." Some relief was in his voice as he spoke, coupled with confusion.

Then through the sound of the wind against their hoods they heard a low, methodical sound. It was like a battle chant with pipes in the background, mixed increasingly with the sound of clashing plate armor.

As they looked back to the lighted horizon, they saw a fearsome sight. It was a great ball of fire suspended high above a huge set of wheels, surrounded by a great battle force of dwarven warriors. Warriors were armed with spears, war hammers, and battle-axes. Their polished armor lit by the fire above showed their numbers to be four units wide of fifteen or twenty to a line as they came over the crest of the hill they marched.

The men stared, awestruck, as the first units passed the crest of that hill and the second units came into sight. No words passed between them as Merson lit a lantern and rode toward the battle force, stopping two hundred fifty paces to their forward and waving the tiny light high above his head. More awesome yet to the three men was when the entire force came to a single stop as the third line of units crested the hill. They had spotted Merson's insignificant light and were sending out a single delegate from each of the four forward units. They marched out evenly, converging and stopping fifteen paces in front of Merson as he dismounted and laid down his weapons in front of them.

The captain and Gorn quietly watched what went on in the field where Merson stood alone and unarmed in front of the delegates. He stood solitary before a great force of warriors, who shimmered like minions of a god in polished golden armor, covering what seemed to be a complete hillside and beyond.

Taken by surprise, the captain and Gorn laid down what weapons they carried as they found themselves surrounded by eight dwarven men dressed in black clothing and carrying black iron weapons. Still they did not speak a word. They only raised their hands open in front of them as evidence they were not armed.

CHAPTER 16

Destruction's Path

On the day before solstice, the children came over the hill outside of Khibanhahm just as the moments of light for the day shone across the village and disappeared. All seemed to look the same except for a new tower southwest of the village. The tower dwarfed all the other structures in the area, and at its top were windows all around that shone with the light from inside. The rest of the tower was dark, as dark as the lightless day of winter solstice, save a window here and there in its trunk.

Johuocin was feeling the strain of travel on Marie's elderly body, which he inhabited like a shroud for his continued shame. After midday the day before the coughing and wheezing came over him, and he could not seem to find any warmth at all. So the children, seeing Marie ill, set out to travel the night through to arrive at their destination and give rest to the woman they kindly referred to as "Mother." So, once again, as they came into the village of Khibanhahm they would seek aid and shelter at the inn.

The streets were quiet as they rode through the town. They saw only the light that peeked through the cracks of the shut-tered windows, the lantern that hung outside the inn, and the lights from the tower that loomed above the village to the southwest.

Alsie rode up next to the wagon, where Anitae sat driving the team that pulled it. "Doesn't it seem a little strange?" he asked.

"What?" asked Anitae, looking around. Then she noticed as she let go of the warm feeling of their arrival. Only about half of the buildings of the town had smoke coming from the stacks on their roof, and fewer still had any light behind their shutters.

"It is midday. Surely someone would be about, even the day before solstice." Alsie left the wagon and lowered himself slowly from his mount as he came to a stop in front of the inn. Looking around, he tied his horse to the rail and walked toward the door of the inn. On the door was a new sign. It read, "Welcome Poor Traveler."

Alsie tried to open the door, but it was barred from the inside. So he pounded heavily on it. Alsie was standing close to the door and was nearly hit by the sign that hung on it as Hafer Lotzman swung it aside to look out.

By that time the rest of the party had come to stand with Alsie.

The look on Master Lotzman's face was a combined one. Looking upon him, the party saw surprise, fear, joy, and sorrow. Quickly the sign was dropped, the door unbarred and opened. With urgency he waved the party through the door, and once they were in, he looked out to check the street before quickly shutting and barring the door.

Above the door and each window that the party could see hung a talisman of sorts. It appeared as an iron spider web with a crystal in its center. After securing the door, Hafer reached up and touched the talisman that hung above it. Then he sighed and turned to the party with a look of relief. "Why have you come here, dear friends? Would you have the terror leave his tower? Would you see your own end?"

To the party of venerable children, it was as though Hafer Lotzman were talking in riddles—riddles they could not answer. Then Marie coughed and hacked from their midst.

Alsie moved to the fireplace as he spoke and pulled out a chair for Marie to sit on. "Master Lotzman, we have returned as we said we would five years past. We need Ivan to visit the mother we bring, to help her regain herself and her health. Why are we welcomed with question? Why are you troubled to see us? And what is this terror you speak of?"

Lotzman walked to the fireplace and put more wood on the fire. Then motioning for them to sit, and rest themselves, he spoke with sorrow in his voice. "First I would offer you food. This I do so you know my joy in seeing you is not completely vacant." Walking toward the kitchen slowly, and with great weariness, he spoke more in exhaustion and concern. "Then as you repast, I will explain myself and my concern."

As Master Lotzman prepared in the kitchen his offering to them, the party shared looks of quizzical anticipation. Reflecting on Hafer's display of worry, each of them gained a quiet concern of their own.

Minac was the first to speak. He was always the one to split the silence when all had questions to distressing to ask. "Why do you suppose he has not sent for Ivan? The mother here needs a healer."

No one answered, for everyone felt they knew already. They knew that Ivan had let power bend his mind.

Hafer Lotzman returned to the room with a large pot of stew and a tray of plates, spoons, and mugs. Again Hafer left, returning quickly with pitchers of steaming spiced asra mixed with Josaberry wine. The aromas that filled the room, coming to the noses of those who had empty stomachs, gave priority over the confusion at their arrival. Hafer served each of them a hearty helping and went to stand by the fire with his back to them. After taking a short time to collect his thoughts, he began his oration of the events that took place after the time of their departure.

"I wish you had arrived earlier than this. I have been preparing a place for you to stay, in the hope that I could get word of your arrival quickly and divert you from coming into the town. The cavern where you killed the dragon has been cleaned and organized. The treasure the dragon had is still there and in a sub cavern among a small labyrinth of tunnels. We, the people of Khibanhahm, have been forbidden to touch it until your return. Ivan has tried to remove some of it and found he could not find his way out while it was in his possession. He would wander as if he were blind and not able to see his way to escape the dragon's lair. Ivan decided it was because this is what he did to the dragon, and somehow this is how the dragon's magic clung to him. (That was not long after you left.) The woman who suffered the loss of her daughter the day that Ivan went out to kill the beast was able to remove some coin. And a few others who suffered a loss at the dragon's pleasure were able to remove a little. But all who took from that cavern found they could take only that which would compensate their loss. Ivan said it was due to the magic within a dragon's treasure. Ivan deduced that the only others who may take from the dragon's treasure are his most formidable foes in life, those who killed him or have taken his most prized possession—his mane. Truly, this was found out by earnest need.

"Not long after you left, Ivan began creating new spells and looking for a wish spell for you. The supplies he needed were expensive and hard to come by. The town decided that we would plunder the treasure to finance Ivan's venture and research. It couldn't be done.

"After that the town decided they would try to finance Ivan. All agreed that Ivan should be the one to set the fees that should be paid by each of us because he knew best what the expenditures would be.

"At first the fees were small and no real burden on us. Ivan continued to take care of our healing needs and charged us nothing for that. In return we gave him an extra bit in the collections for him and his daughter. Avilla pushed him harder and harder to find the wish spell. Each passing season, she became more adamant and more intent on his quest for the spell. By the end of the second year of your absence, she had talked Ivan into allowing her to study under him as she was there all the time anyway, as his assistant. So her apprenticeship began.

"Avilla was a quick study. Soon she was past the first level of her studies and could easily cast spells that Ivan had worked for years to master and still had not mastered at the time you were here first. Avilla had such a drive for the completion of each assignment she was given by her father that at times she would have things accomplished before he would ask her to do them.

"Ivan was very proud of her. He would boast of her accomplishments to the entire town, whenever he took time to come here for a break or some food." Hafer's anxiousness broke for a moment and he nearly smiled. "I would feed him here for no charge. He was so amiable then." Then it was back to his task. "But Avilla was very insistent of his time. She would admonish him for taking a break from his work, calling him 'lazy' or 'inconsiderate'.

"Ivan could not handle her disapproval, as he would see her working and it seemed untiring for her, and she worked for days without rest. Soon she was demanding that he work alongside of her when she worked, never taking a break without her." He shook his head as his eyes met the floor in front of him. "I would take food to them and at times she would slam the door in my face.

She would be screaming at me, 'We don't have the time for that now!'

"Ivan soon began looking older than twice his years. Avilla went for days, even weeks, without so much as brushing her hair or bathing." Looking up at the young bard, he said, "Alsie, I don't mean to insult her, I just want you all to know what Ivan has been through." Then a moment of reflection came to Hafer, and he returned to his account. "Soon the expense of their studies became insurmountable. At Avilla's prodding, Ivan demanded more and more of our financial support. At first he promised great returns on the investment, and then when we had little or nothing more to give, he turned to threatening us with his powerful spells, carrying out his threats when he caught or suspected someone of withholding something.

"The people of Khibanhahm began stealing away in the middle of the night with what they had left. Sometimes they had only the clothes on their back. By the time Avilla had come from the laboratory to notice, half the town had gone, and many of the farmers had abandoned their farms. At that time she had achieved something that no other mage had achieved.

"Yes, this town knows firsthand now how long it takes for a mage to achieve his aspirations. And the lengths to which they will go. We have had many magical visitors here, all of them in awe of the accomplishments that Avilla has achieved at her young age and with her late start, none of them questioning her attitude or disposition because of her advancement. She, at the beginning of her sixteenth summer, had passed her seventh test of the magical order.

"Noticing the town stealing away, she set magical beasts to roam the streets at night. None dared leave in the day save a few of us who were given the amulets by Ivan before the terror.

"The amulets offer us the ability to pass through the streets unobserved by magic or those who possess it. If we hang them over the doorways and windows, the magi will pass without inquiry or entrance. I have one more than I need to cover all doorways and windows.

"The terror began that summer. Ivan found his daughter using spells and potions to keep herself awake to continue her studies! He knew she needed the rest she was missing. He knew she would go mad if she continued. Ivan switched one of the potions she had hidden away for a sleep potion. He intended her to sleep for a few days, a week, or perhaps even a month. The potion she was using to stay awake was intended to be used the same as the sleep potion he exchanged for it. A touch upon the lip and that was all that was needed. He didn't understand. He truly had no idea.

"A few days passed, and she still had not used the potion. Then one day he went to the storeroom in the lower level of the tower. When he returned, he found Avilla on the floor of the laboratory, fast asleep. He picked her up and moved her to her room. He then stopped his work for the day and went to bed himself for a good night's rest. In the morning he woke knowing that Avilla would sleep for the day. He dressed and went out for a bite of breakfast.

"He came in that morning alone. I thought it was a little strange. When I inquired of Avilla, he told me what he had done. He was in very good spirits. Better morale than he'd had for some time. When he finished, he returned to his studies.

"Over the next few days, he came in every day, still reporting that Avilla still slept, and still he was not concerned. Two weeks had passed, and still he was not too bothered by her sleep, but he reported that she called Alsie's name out incessantly. Then one day he came in, after another two weeks had passed. His face was white gray, like ash that had burned over and over again, with a numb look in his eyes.

"I inquired what was wrong. He only looked at me and put a small empty bottle on the table. Avilla had drunk every last drop from the bottle of potion he had left for her in that one dose. She slept. She called Alsie's name. He could not wake her.

"That was the summer before last. She still sleeps, and he works continually without sleep, looking for a way to wake her. She has no sustenance except what Ivan can induce her to drink as she sleeps. At one point Ivan made a special glass tube that would go into her throat to feed her so that she would not choke.

"She calls for you, Alsie, and this has been a wearing thing for Ivan. He blames you for her pushing herself so hard to advance, for her wanting to remain at work constantly and never to rest. For her pushing him so very hard to find the spell that you need, if such a spell exists. And he blames himself, for losing her to you.

"He has become very jealous of you, Alsie. He has set himself against you for what he feels you made him do to himself, this village, and for what has happened to Avilla. He also blames you for stealing Avilla from him. He has proclaimed that he could end all the madness if he could put an end to you.

"A few of us left in the village do not hold this to you. They understand a young girl's mind. Most, however, take Ivan at his word. They wish once more to live here in peace and joy and comfort. They believe it will be as it was before if Ivan is given what he wants. I hope you can understand what I am saying. Ivan has become the master, and the people of this village are his slaves. Not only do they long for the return of their peace; they also fear the punishment given to disobedient slaves."

Then he looked directly into Alsie's eyes. "You are not safe here."

As Hafer Lotzman spoke those last five words, the words rang through the minds of all there listening to him. Then he looked around to catch the gaze of everyone in the room.

They all stared at Hafer as if they did not hear, could not have heard, such things come out of his mouth. Their disbelief stopped them from the meal that was so needed and welcomed before he was half through his words. They sat to stare at him with their mouths agape, with the same disbelief they would have if one in the party were to strike out to kill another.

Alsie stood and faced Hafer. "What can we do? What can we offer Ivan to ease his burden? What can we do to comfort him?"

"He has been a year without sleep," Hafer replied, "turning to the potions that Avilla used to remain wakeful and at her work. From the look of him, his age is beyond seasons, and his nourishment comes from sources unknown to me. He no longer leaves his work for food. It is a pity that the power that was given him by Anitae's concern is now turned against you." Hafer continued, "And against this town." He looked around at the faces of the children and saw surprise. "Oh yes, we learned of that fact, through Avilla's admonishing of Ivan. He was a little discomforted by the fact that the town now knew where his power came from, but it did not bother him long. His only statement to that later was, 'Yes, it was given me by chance, but now it's mine.'"

Johuocin watched Alsie's face as Hafer finished the words he spoke, which came, from Ivan's mouth. Warmth left Alsie's eyes as shame took its place, and he stood. Without a word the man-boy turned and walked toward the door, his brothers and Anitae pleading with him and calling him back to the table. Johuocin worried about the action that Alsie's motions were leading to and called to him as the mother Marie wished to be. Still Alsie walked and opened the door, stepping out into the darkness and cold, disappearing into the street. Everyone there knew his destination: the tower.

Johuocin knew there would be only one chance for Alsie, one rescue. Taking hold of Anitae's arm as she stood next to Marie, he gripped tightly, with Marie's hand, to get Anitae's attention. When she looked at Marie, Johuocin moaned out to her, "Help me, I feel a spell coming on."

Then Johuocin slipped from Marie, leaving her to the confusion of being in a strange place with strangers all around and not knowing how it happened. Johuocin moved quickly toward, and then past, Alsie, trying to gain the common destination before anything befell the man-boy determined to gain forgiveness for the crimes that did not exist, even if that forgiveness meant his death.

CHAPTER 17

The Road to War

The Oschke Cree looked upon this party of five travelers, three of whom were in the uniform of the king's guard, the dwarves knowing well that they held the upper hand. Over two thousand strong, they marched, ready for war, all sturdy, stout warriors. The only concern they carried over the five was that one might escape and give the king advance warning and time to assemble something of his army.

The command general watched as his liaison officer and a group of four escorts marched toward the man who rode toward them, alone, as his companions stood fast in position. A scouting party had been dispatched to surround the party from the rear. The general watched as the man lay down his weapons and held his open hands in front of him for inspection by his officer. The escort remained steadfast, with red flags waving in the breeze as the man and his officer exchanged words. Suddenly a red flag was replaced by a blue flag, signaling friendly forces. Then a yellow flag was raised, signaling the existence of a messenger or liaison. Then a purple flag came up, to signal the arrival of an allied prince. This is when the general himself rode out to meet the party.

Proudly he sat upon the heavy steed, brilliantly dressed in his armament that was accented by colors of war, high upon the perch of his saddle, commanding a beast twice his own standing height. He brandished a long-bladed battle-ax. So polished was the blade that the stars themselves sparkled on its razor edge. The light from the fire behind him danced upon his armored shoulders with every step his mount placed on the cold winter ground, causing it to appear that his shoulders were ablaze. Sitting tall and straight on the back of this large horse, the general, though stout and appearing powerful across the shoulders, made a small target for any oncoming weaponry. His very presence commanded respect as he reached the place where Merson waited without movement.

Merson saluted the general in the fashion of Dwarves as the general's steed reigned to a stop. Merson stood motionless, the back of his fists held nearly touching his forehead, eyes uncovered, waiting for a return and release from his position until the general nodded in his direction. Words were then exchanged, and Merson motioned to his companions to come ahead. As the party reached them, the general planted the butt end of his battle-ax upon the ground and swung down from his seat upon the giant steed. Graceful and smooth was his movement, seemingly uncharacteristic of a dwarf. Speaking clearly in common tongue with little of the hillish accent of the dwarven speech, the general commanded the captain to dismount.

The captain moved from his horse and went to stand close in front of the general, well within the boundary of what he perceived as personal space. This was as Merson had earlier instructed him to do. As a sign of respect, a taller man standing close to the shorter man was to show trust and recognition of his personal stature. As uncomfortable as it seemed to the captain, not able to see the general's face very well, he would not grant ground between them.

"You are the son of Reglawr?" The general seemingly barked his question at the captain, as if he were annoyed at his presence.

"Yes, General, I am Orman Reglawr, son of Sesnic Reglawr."

"We were sent word that plans have changed. We are to attack before the solstice. You are late in your arrival. What was your delay?" The general barked out as he gave his reason for annoyance.

The captain stared off into the distance as he searched for an answer. There was no simple explanation and apparently no time for lengthy details. Yet if what his comrades and companions told him was true, it would certainly take a long time to explain. "Unexpected situations that will take some telling, I'm afraid."

"Yes, well, you will get your chance. Very few of the tribes have agreed to join this war because of your delays. We are going ahead to begin battle and put some pressure on the king and his troops. I will send an escort with you to the council to prevent any more of your *delays*. You can tell them of your stories, and may the gods help you to convince them to move with us. If not, it will be a long fight."

The general turned and signaled to one of his captains, who then pulled an escort from the ranks. Twelve dwarven men surrounded them and began moving in the direction from which the dwarven army came. The captain barely had enough time to remount and was allowed no more questions of the general.

The group had little chance to do more than exchange glances as they were escorted through the middle of the dwarven army between the columns. The giant torch fires were pulled by three teams of seven oxen as the light shimmered off the freshly polished armor of the dwarves. Gorn saw as they marched over knolls and hills, rank and file was kept, and the closed columns looked as if it were fine silk being pulled slowly over a woman's body, shimmering under the light of candles. Soon, they began to sound like a victorious army as the pipes began to hum and the pace was quickened by the beat of drums and the clash of metal as the dwarven warriors began to stomp their boots to the ground. Above the din of the clash and threat, the five could hear the chant of deep voices:

Oschke Cree
Da Louk
Oschke Cree

Trou Bok
Ilamon Ilamon ptoa ke
Ganviite
Atoschkaviite!
Teremon Honje riea Oschke
Cree!

The captain called to Merson and asked him to translate the words as they moved. They could barely hear each other through the rumble of the advancing force. Gorn could have sworn he heard Merson speak the words in a normal voice, and still, they could be heard plainly. He told the captain that the chant in common language was;

The people
are below you
The people
are above you

Fight hard, fight hard,
we are the rock.
Our blood does not flow
except back to the rock.
Your walls are our allies,
for they are the people.

As the group moved beyond the columns, they moved into the path of the traveling force. They were able to travel much faster in the compacted trail. The dwarven escort spread out from the party, and the leader reached into his battle pack and began handing out some type of biscuits to his men. He offered some to Merson, who took a few and broke them in half and handed half a biscuit to each of the others in the party.

A whole biscuit being about the size of a grown man's fist, Gorn could not help but chuckle as he turned that which was handed to him over in his fingers a few times.

Merson caught the sight out of the corner of his eye. He turned his face toward Gorn. "You don't think that will hold you then?"

"I would not venture to guess such a thing, but I must say that the crumbs that fall out of my beard are sometimes bigger than this." Gorn chuckled.

It was then that everyone noticed for the first time that the escorts they had would not be as tall as Gorn if one stood on the shoulders of another. Gorn moving along in the middle of the group appeared to be a giant even next to those on horseback, which none of the escort were.

The captain reached out and offered his half biscuit to Gorn as he pointed to Merson, who still had three full biscuits in his hands. "Gorn, you can have mine. I'm not that hungry. It looks as though you'd better keep them from Merson, though. I think he may just be missing the home cooking."

As everyone began laughing at Merson, he began to object with his eyes as he looked up from where the captain was pointing. "I wouldn't be quite laughin' yet. I would go ahead and eat those if I were you, and then you can poke all the fun you wish. I thought I was doing you a favor."

"That bad, are they, Merson?" Riessa chimed in.

"As a matter of fact, they are rather bland in flavor, but most people who eat them like them quite a lot," Merson shot back. "They seem so light and flaky and have a tendency to melt in your mouth. A little better when they are warm. Still with all their bland flavor and dry texture, it seems that they are very difficult to avoid eating after you take the first bite and before you've no more in your hand. Let me assure you that you each can have as many as you wish. Each of these fine escorts of ours has at least a dozen in their pack and will restock themselves when we reach our destination, so if you eat what you have and wish for more, please let me know."

Ben piped in, "Glad to hear you say that, Merson. I just finished the first piece you gave, me and I don't even think it was half. Could I have another? You're right though, even though they don't have a lot of flavor, they go down very well."

Merson gave each of the party a full biscuit at that point or at least everyone received a full biscuit in total. Except for the captain, who he told that they had better eat a little lighter, being that they had to do some more work as they traveled, trying to learn more about the meeting they would attend now that things had changed a bit. He tore a quarter off for himself and a quarter for the captain, and they ate as they talked and advanced.

As the party traveled, Merson explained to the captain the significance of the Oschke Cree already headed for battle. He explained that he would now share the floor with a silent ally. Now when the captain made his arguments for war, he would stand before ten kings with their advisors and one king, the king of the Oschke Cree, and his advisors would be seated behind him. He must step in front of the council without turning his back to the Oschke Cree before he asked their permission to do so and he must not turn his back to the other tribes ever in this meeting. If a tribe were to make the decision during the meeting to grant support then the captain would become the liaison between existing supporters and the new supporter to mediate ranking, positioning, and responsibilities. "Because there has already been a move to war and an alliance already set, it will make your job both easier and more difficult. Because the Oschke Cree have stepped forward first, they have labored themselves into the position of commander of the aligning forces. That will make it more difficult for you to convince the others that they should be willing to take lesser positions and responsibilities. You must choose wards of tactics, supply, forward intelligence, covert diversion, morale, reconstruction, and citizen influence.

"Remember that all of these are equally important as far as this effort is concerned. However if we manage to fill the first four, the others will be maneuvering themselves for citizen influence. Citizen influence will set the tone for the politics and has the greatest chance of profit setting. They are also in charge of rear intelligence, peace keeping, and prison camps. Your best chance is to show them that all of these positions are of equal value to them and not necessarily subordinate.

"The whole thing is easier for you because already having one ally aligned; most of the others will not want to be left out of the loop of acquisitions. The one thing you have to be careful of is not to get ahead of your allies as you build on the alignments. Each time a new ally signs on, you have to remember to include each of them in all the decisions about to whom and to which responsibilities each are assigned." Merson stopped here and looked at the captain to see if the captain understood what was being said or if the captain had any questions. The captain had been listening intently to Merson and seemed to be digesting the information well.

The travel seemed easier and faster in the wake of the compacted path of the army that traveled toward Eldwain. Far in the distance now it was becoming more and more difficult to catch a glimpse of the reflected light of the polished army. The escort seemed to move as though well rested and eager, almost dragging their charge. They would send out a scout every mile to run ahead, and then as they caught up with the scout, another runner would be sent, each in their turn and each with the same purpose. The party traveled at a steady pace until a rumbling was heard. And almost as if in a concerted effort, the rumbling began to come from all directions and yet all very close to the five people of the original party. All but Merson looked to each other to exchange glances. The captain wheeled his horse around as he saw pained looks on the faces of Ben, Riessa, and Gorn. As the rumbling grew it appeared that they were in greater pain. Each of them took off in a different direction, leaving the escort of dwarves and speeding into the darkness. The captain was calling after them and turning his horse this way and that, and then he noticed Merson riding steadily on with a smile on his face.

The captain moved up quickly to Merson's position, and when Merson saw him approach he smiled and said, "Biscuits."

Their eyes met, and they laughed.

Merson finally felt he had given all the information he could possibly give the captain, and the captain told him it was time for him to take his potion. The escort knew the path, and the captain needed Merson fresh when he went before the council.

There seemed to be a lack of joy for the group as they traveled. There was no banter back and forth, no conversation, no sound at all it seemed. Riessa had thoughts of her father with friends for the day but ultimately alone for the first time on winter solstice. She was the last of his blood family in a thousand leagues, and he was hers. It was a bit easier for her than for her father she was sure, because since the death of Gorn's wife, Gorn had spent this day with them every year.

The group had stopped only once in the last two days, and the leader of the escort had reported that they would soon be at their destination, Korfri. He had let them know that morning that they would arrive the next day before the middle of day. This was the day of winter solstice, and neither the escort nor their charges thought about stopping for rest or celebration in any way. They would have no daylight this day and no candlelight or light of lantern. This darkest day of the year would remain so in every way but one. The group moved toward their destination and did not falter in their purpose.

Ben, Gorn, and Riessa did not consume more of the biscuits than was absolutely necessary after that first day with the escort and had let Merson know that they did not appreciate the inadequate information that he had supplied them with that day.

CHAPTER 18

Facing the Unexpected

Alsie walked down the center of the street toward the tower without hesitation, without relegation, and without fear. As he came closer to his target, he looked up to see if there was any sign of Ivan in the tower window. He watched as the light faded from that high room above the village and again as it began to peek under the door at the base of the tower wall.

Slowly the door opened as Alsie approached, and there stood a shadow so narrow and frail, it appeared that a light breeze could break it to pieces and blow it away. Except for the robe he wore and the shoes that ventured from its tattered hem, Alsie would not have recognized Ivan. What a pitiful sight the magician was behind the threshold of the mud and stone tower. Alsie fought the sight, forcing himself not to forget a wish that was made so few years ago, remembering the wish that made Ivan a powerful magi and now, a frightful enemy.

Johuocin rushed toward Ivan, only to find himself repelled by an unseen force as Ivan turned left and toward him and raised a flat hand as if to push him away. Alsie jumped aside as if meeting the expected attack with a right side parry of his entire body to an unseen weapon. Then Alsie saw

Ivan continue opposite the direction of Alsie, raising one hand and then the other in an upward motion, rotating his hands in a circular fashion as if they were slicing into the air and pushing it at the same time. Ivan was moving toward empty ground, and yet he was full with motion in an attack or summoning of some kind. Alsie turned toward the action and waited. He stood as tall as his stature would allow, waiting to see what Ivan had to deliver toward him. It was then that Alsie noticed the torch that followed Ivan, just hovering there in midair slightly above the mage's head and shoulders. It burned bright, and as Ivan turned away from Alsie and the light was no longer directly behind him, Ivan seemed a little less frail and thin.

Johuocin was taken off guard, not knowing how the mage knew he was there, yet as Johuocin retreated, Ivan followed his direction. He had thought that he would invade the mage to save Alsie, and now he was faced with being propelled into full retreat. Not able to avoid the attack, Johuocin retreated as quickly as he could and was still feeling the repelling actions of the mage. When Johuocin was nearly back to the door of the inn, the mage finally turned in every direction looking for the invisible attacker, staying on the ready, waiting for the return.

"What color of night travels at your side, thief of dreams?" Ivan spat as he turned to Alsie. "What shade travels in this darkness that comes here with you? Have you no faith in my love for my daughter? Do you think you must come here with some conjured protector to save you from the wrath of a father's resentment and vengeance?" Ivan turned and walked back toward the tower door. "Come with me. She is here inside, I assume that is your purpose for coming, to see my beautiful Avilla."

Alsie tried to object to Ivan's ranting to no avail. He wasn't clear about Ivan's rants and even more confused by Ivan's open invitation to see the sleeping Avilla. Alsie followed as Ivan led him into the tower and up the stairs to the chamber above. Once there, Ivan moved to the side. Alsie saw Avilla lying there on a bed, pillow beneath her head, with her hair and clothing perfectly groomed. Her arms were at her side to her elbows that were bent, allowing her hands to rest together on her abdomen. She looked healthy if a little pale, and peaceful, with her eyes closed and her face without expression.

"This is what I have seen every day for some months now," Ivan said, looking only at Avilla. His voice filled with quiet despair and surrender. "I speak to her and receive no response, but I speak anyway. I never thought I could be lonelier than I was after I lost her mother. Avilla has surprised me once more and taught me that there is always a worse fate waiting to happen."

Alsie tried to speak but found that he could not. No sound would utter from his throat. Ivan smirked at him as he saw that he tried to speak and wagged a finger at him, pointing then to his own mouth as if to say, "Listen to me."

"You will not speak. I have been planning to say these things for some time, and I do not wish to be interrupted. Avilla was always good about listening and not interrupting, even before she slept. At least she was before you came along. She has lost but a short time in our lifetimes, but in hers it is a great portion. She has done this in trying to find a wish for you. You have no idea how accomplished she is as magi and chemist. I was sure she would surpass me in another year at the rate she was going. She was awake a great many months, and I had to do something. She was using potions to tend her wakefulness. It is your fault, you know, that I was not able to monitor and control her better. Now she lies here day after day, losing more and more of her life to dreams. At least I hope she dreams. She should have had a chance to finish her childhood and grow into a woman in a normal way. Now look at her—she is a beautiful young woman with no friends to speak of and no growing experiences to show for her age.

"That brings me to you. You are just the opposite. You are a boy with too many experiences to show for your age, or at least what people presume is your age. Do you think that she will still want you if you become the age you truly are? Well, I don't know about that. I do know that you need to make her happy if she ever wakes, and so I still search for wish spells. I write and I mix and I test and I toil over such things as this to give you a wish, because I know that if I can make one I can make another. But if I can make another, then I can make one wish for myself and I can wake Avilla.

"You should see some of the things I have created in my tests, aversions and manifestations, so hideous some of them." Now pieces of anger and spite started coming into his voice. "Oh, another thing I need to say to you is that you will probably have a chance to see some of the things I have created while you are here. I have done something for you. I want you to be sure of what your wish is before you make it, so you will be here with Avilla and me until it is found. Don't try to leave; you cannot. There is a spell cast on you much like the one on your voice now. Just as your voice cannot leave your throat, you cannot walk out the door of this tower."

Suddenly, Ivan seemed distracted and reminiscent. "Funny thing about those two spells, they have the same root spell. Spells are amazing. You can do any number of variations on the same spell using the root, and if one works well on a person then so does the other. That was something that Avilla showed *me*. She is an amazing girl, my Avilla." He gently smiled as he said this last thing and walked toward the window. He looked out the window and then directly down at the ground outside as he poked his head through. He had a regretful look on his face as he pulled his head in, slowly shaking it and looking toward the floor.

He looked back up at Alsie with a look of distaste and loathing. He mumbled something that Alsie couldn't quite hear. He pointed to the corner of the room, where another bed was and a chair. "That's where you will sleep. Being in this room with her may help you to remain focused on your task. If you need anything, just pull the sash by the doorway and you will be taken care of." At that, Ivan turned and walked to the door. Before leaving he turned back and said to Alsie, "You may speak now. I don't know if she hears us or not, but it certainly comforts me to speak to her."

As Ivan walked out into the stairwell, Alsie followed. Urgently, before Ivan started down the stairs, he called to the wizard. "Ivan, surely you know that none of this gives me anything less than heartache? You must know that my intention to Avilla was to release her from a promise made by a child. You must know that."

Without looking back, Ivan paused for a moment, and then started down the stairs without response. Alsie turned back into the room and walked to the window. Looking out he could see the lights at the inn peeking through a few small cracks here and there. He wondered what would happen when he did not return. He imagined that Finat would be short on patience and knocking on the door of the tower soon. It did not appear that Ivan had made plans for all of them to be in the tower, and he wondered what would happen as they approached the mud and stone tower.

Alsie turned back to where Avilla lay and looked at the young woman who lay before him there. She was no longer the gangly twelve-year-old girl he left five years ago. Aged beyond her years, she appeared to be a woman, not just a girl about to come of age. He wondered how she would feel about him now if she saw a reflection of the two of them side by side. He wondered what her reaction would be to seeing a similar sight involving two other people with the same appearance. And if he were of appropriate appearance for his age, what would be her thoughts then?

Alsie went back to the window and looked out at the town. There in the darkness he saw a shadow of what the little village once was, and there were few lights to tell him it was otherwise.

*

Johuocin retreated from the tower and Ivan in confusion. How did Ivan know he was there? How did he push him away? He came along with this group to allow the captain on his journey to complete his mission and to help this party take Marie to a safer place. He went with Alsie to try and assist in his safety and came up against a wall of unexpected resistance. What was he doing here? What use could he be to these people who had experienced so much more life than he? What must he do now?

He thought back to when he had chanced to help the captain's party. It was purely that, chance. If he had planned anything, it would probably not have worked out. They would probably all have died had he not given into temptation and reached out for Riessa. That same thing happened when he stood to greet her at her father's inn. Each time he had felt something deep inside himself, something he had not experienced before. It was something stronger than his resolve. It was stronger than his will to restrain himself. It was something he could not control that saved them.

Johuocin sensed a shadow, darker than night, coming from the southwest. It seemed to be getting smaller as it approached, smaller and darker. By the time it reached the foot of the tower, it was so dark it seemed to absorb any light around it. Suddenly, it was large enough to fill the street. The base of the tower could not be seen through it. Johuocin went toward it. If something that was not there could be heavy, this was it. The closer Johuocin came to the phenomenon, the heavier it seemed to make him feel. When he had gotten within a hundred paces, he could hear chanting from within it. Many voices, low and unrelenting, were making the same sound over and over. Johuocin could not make out the words. As he got closer the sound was inviting and seemed warm, or caused warmth to move through him, drawing him into the comfort of being wanted. As he got within fifty paces he could make out the words. The voices were chanting, "Be with us. We will have you. You are one of us. We are the warmth in a cold world. You belong with us." Over and over again he felt the words move through him.

As Johuocin got closer, he was drawn to the voices and began to see into the darkness. Hands reached out to him, wanting to take hold of him. Then he could see arms extended to him, waiting for him to accept their comfort. There was great warmth that felt deep, and the voices began to envelop him. He felt himself succumbing and began to yearn to be a part of the warmth. The closer he got, the more he wanted to be a part of whatever this was. It was then he saw the face of a young woman in anguish and torment. He began to push away the feeling, and the more he pushed, the more he was drawn to it. An ache started within him, causing a struggle of emotions and resentments and wants and needs. Suddenly he realized that, with all of these things, he was centered only on himself. Despairing in his selfishness, he could resist no more. He moved into the warmth.

*

In the tavern, the rest of the party waited. Finat, always being the anxious one, wanted to go to the tower and retrieve his oldest cousin and the leader of the group. Alsie had always been Finat's influence of reason. It made him even more anxious that Marie sat in the corner, not aware of the surroundings she was in, acting as if the group were beasts of an unnatural sort. She was screaming and demanding answers about what was happening. Anitae tried to calm her, tried to reason with her, but was not successful in her attempts. Indeed, she seemed to have the opposite effect.

Marie began screaming of her punishment from the gods—that punishment she insisted she so richly deserved for not minding the children left in her care by the gods. Soon she became catatonic and remorseful. She was totally unresponsive as she muttered under her breath and let tears stream down her face.

CHAPTER 19

Korfri, the Line Has Been Drawn

As the group entered the gates of the stone city, they were met by stares of contempt and disgust. Tired from the forced travel they had endured and the constant cold, there was still cheer to be felt by them knowing that they had met the end of this part of the journey. The captain and Ben were looking forward to a chance to warm by a fire and clean up a bit. Riessa was in awe as she looked around to see that the height of the walls that surrounded the city on the sea side were nearly as high as the mountain cliffs that completed walls around the city. Gorn had finally met his limit a half day before the arrival and sat down on a rock to rest and was promptly picked up and carried by all four of his limbs. He fought the situation at first, and was ignored, until he gave into the fact that he would be carried for a time. Amazingly he was able to sleep as he was carried and did not wake until the group stopped at the gates, where he was suddenly dropped with a tremendous thud.

He would have objected to the rough treatment, if only because he was surprised, had it not been for the total shock that he felt at the sights before him. The gate to the city of Korfri was at least ten times his height and fifty times his breadth. As he looked at it, the appearance was that it was solid stone and two arms deep. As it closed to the center, he saw only one guard push each half of the door as if it were made of thin rice paper. It could be seen they were cautious not to push to quickly as it swung on its stone hinges, and no grinding could be heard from the stone-on-stone connection.

The group stared with their mouths agape as they walked forward, eyes darting and heads turning from the high stone buildings to the mountain cliffs that were their backdrop and back to the activity that surrounded them. In the cliff sides there were windows carved out with the inhabitants hanging out and watching as they came through the open drill field of the fortress. Merson was providing some explanation of what the party was seeing as they marched forward, telling of private dwellings in the mountainside and deep within that provided the comfort and safety to the citizens there. The fortress at one time was the home to nearly three million, at a time before the elf wars. Great numbers were lost as battles raged on the open sea. Then one day the skies above the fortress turned black as the elves attacked from the high side of the cliffs. They had come in on sails that floated down into the city. Now the high side was regularly patrolled even though the war had been past many centuries. The kings avowed never again to be taken off their guard.

As they approached an inner wall with gates half the size of those they had previously entered, a new set of guards took over the escort of the party and led them to and across an inner courtyard that placed them in front of a large open hall. Though it seemed that the hall was at least a quarter mile deep, the occupants at the other end could be heard talking as if standing next to the party.

Merson looked to the captain and motioned toward the end of the great hall. "Looks as if they are not going to give us a chance to clean up. They are convening the Council of Kings now. We will be expected to present arguments at the time they are assembled."

Merson started interpreting, paraphrasing a little of what was being said, "They're not very happy, Captain. They were made to understand by their scouts that we should have been here days ago."

"Then let's not waste time trying to explain. I will apologize for informality and hope for the best." Orman Reglawr took the jacket of the king's guard from his back and threw it into a nearby fire pit as he started to the end of the hall at a quick pace, with Merson close behind.

As the others began to follow, they were stopped by two guards stepping in from the sides of the hall. Not one of them had previously noticed that the hall was lined down both sides by steel-clad dwarves with spears and battle-axes. They were lost in the height of the room and the mosaic of the walls that seemed to camouflage their existence in the space around and between the large granite columns that interrupted the open freedom of cathedral ceilings.

As the guards stepped out and blocked their path by crossing long spears in front of them, a female dwarf came from behind them, in floor-to-shoulder garments that looked like drapery hanging on a stump. She appeared to have smoothed and waxed her hair into curls and curled the beard under her chin to match.

She motioned for the group to follow her, and as she saw Riessa, it looked as though she had an expression of pity on her face. The group began to follow without question, with the exception of Ben, who was prodded with a spear point. Ben placed his hand on the hilt of his sword as he turned to the guard. At that he was surrounded by three more guards and the group came to a halt.

Gorn returned to Ben's side. "Hold on now," he said in his deep, rolling voice, holding his open hands out toward the little men. "I don't think we're here to start any fights with *you*."

Ben shot a look around in anger. "I will though if you continue to poke me with those things. I just want to know where we're going and why I can't join my brother. We've come a long way, and it's been a rough trip."

The woman who was leading them away turned back and addressed Ben and Gorn. "The council will only speak with the messenger and his interpreter. In the meantime I have been asked to provide you a place to refresh yourselves and allow you to ready yourselves for an audience with the king at his table. We will do our best to help you make yourselves presentable." Looking then back to Riessa and shaking her head, she said, "Not that this will be easy for all of you, but we will do our best."

Riessa looked at the woman and began to object. She raised her finger to point at the woman and was promptly tapped on the forearm by a spear. She took the cue to be silent, and the woman looked at her once again with pity in her eyes.

"I apologize for my forward speech, dear. It's just that, for a female," the woman dropped her gaze from Riessa, "you're just not a very attractive woman, and it will be hard to present you at dinner without a veil so as not to interrupt the king's dinner."

At this, Riessa allowed her eyes to open wide and her mouth to drop open.

The dwarven woman raised a hand in acknowledgment of Riessa's reaction, "That didn't help, dear." At that the woman turned and began walking again.

*

As Orman Reglawr walked through the hall toward the place of judgment, he felt a hand grab his forearm and turn him about. Here Merson stood close to him in resolve as he locked eyes on the man who would be presenting the case for alliance against Eldwain.

"Slow down, boy! You're going to make or break this alliance in about five minutes, and you need to breathe. Think about what you're gonna say, and hold onto the big picture. I don't know if you have realized it or not, but your father's the only one on the other side of Eldwain, and unless you're successful here with taking enough of Eldwain's resources off of the north of the kingdom, your father and all of those men will die. Respect is needed here, if not for these kings, for your father."

"Thanks, Merson."

Ory turned once again with resolve, but this time with focus, purpose, and calm determination. Thinking of all the information Merson had provided in the last few days, he walked toward the dais of the council, whose members had begun to take their seats. There he saw in the middle of the floor before them mosaic tile that appeared to depict molten earth. Around the circular depiction were thirteen symbols that appeared to be crudely carved in granite blocks that were seemingly out of place from the rest of the decor. Each of these looked like a crude representation of the tribal symbols on the backs of the council thrones. Two of the symbols appeared to be representations of two marble obelisks that were carved and placed to the right end of the line of thrones.

As Orman Reglawr reached the dais, he was led by Merson to stand in the center of the circular design in the mosaic tile. Then Merson took his place behind and to the right of the captain. All but one seat was occupied by the time he was in place. It was the third seat from the left and bore the sign of the Oschke Cree. At that time the king and council member that normally took residence there stepped from behind the seat and came down from the dais, followed by his entourage of representatives, to stand behind Orman and Merson.

The council member in the center seat stood looking down at Ory and ordered him to speak. Merson stood behind Ory, translating from the dwarf speech to a common tongue that Ory understood and he knew the kings and their staff also understood. When Ory began to speak, Merson immediately began to interpret to the speech of dwarves in loud and commanding tones.

"I am here on behalf of my father, Sesnic Reglawr, the people of Eldwain, and the interests of this honorable council. I believe we all share a common concern that can be overcome if we work together to rid ourselves of a tyrannical scourge that exists on this soil between the seas. It is clear to all of us that the old king of Eldwain is no longer among us, and his son has turned the purpose of the kingdom to his own selfish demands and wants. His people suffer, his neighbors suffer, and he has created and fed a prejudice among all men that serves no one but himself. My father speaks fondly of the old times when our communities, our peoples, shared free trade and strong alliances that served us all. I remember the times your people traveled freely and without fear throughout the lands. It was not so long ago in your times. To my people who are short lived, it becomes a myth, and that time is ever more difficult to regain. The small children of our people already don't know that past except in stories told by their parents. Some of our people twist stories to their needs. Those that thrive in your absence advance the prejudices of the king of Eldwain. They put fear in the innocent hearts of children that will grow into hate and root itself in the world of men. To you and your people, I am a child still today. You may talk among yourselves and say that this king will not last forever and the peace and freedom of the land will return to you still in your lifetimes. The lives of men are not so long as to see many kings of men in a lifetime. What one king of men can leave behind will take many generations to overcome, because fear and hatred are easy to perpetuate in the absence of contrary example.

"You may ask yourselves, 'What is the business of dwarves to control the happiness of men?' To this I say that the business of dwarves should be to rid the lands of prejudice while there are those who still remember the peace and congeniality of our cultures. I would say that it was a generational task to bring our peoples to the understanding of each other and that it takes little to tear this apart within a culture that is so long lived that some yet remember a time when understanding was not a consideration. It saddens me to know that it will take many generations of men to overcome the damage done to our camaraderie by one man if we do not stand and act together to return the freedoms we all once enjoyed.

"I will admit that many of you are right when you say the memory of men is short. But I would remind you, so are their lives. They do not have the luxury of waiting for change. Let me ask you: if they did have more time in this world, would it make it a more urgent task to stop this from continuing?

"The alliances of men cannot stop this king, and if we could, it would take many generations of men to put down the prejudices built in these short years. The Oscke Cree have joined us in our plight. I have not yet had the opportunity to speak with their king, but I will implore him that if we move forward and win this battle without you, win this war without you, we will, out of the charity of our hearts, allow you to share in our blood-won freedom."

As Merson translated that sentence, three of the council stood as if offended and yet confused. They moved together and talked among themselves. Many of the others sat forward in their seats, and their eyes flashed with anger as their teeth were bared. Merson placed his hand on Ory's shoulder as if to settle him. If he had seen the look on Merson's face at that time, he would have known the fear that lived in Merson as he said the word for *charity*.

"Thank you all for your time, and I invite you to join us in our fight, which already begins."

As Ory finished his speech, the center council member stood and motioned to the rear of the hall, and footsteps were heard as they came nearer. Then suddenly, a great, raucous laugh came from the king and council member who stood behind him. Then in the common tongue he hollered, "He stirs your passions now, does he not?"

The king came from behind him and walked about the circle, making eye contact with those upon the dais. "Without knowing your words, he has spoken to them." Merson translated once again as this chief of tribes went back to his native tongue. "You have spoken about your responsibility to humans and how the problems we see will pass with time. You have spoken of freedom and trade. You have spoken of the prejudices held against you.

"What you have not talked about is the responsibility you have toward the prejudice, toward the freedom, and toward free trade between our peoples.

"We fought with elfin kind over the question of silver and asteril. We overcame that and worked toward peace, only to lose it again when we were plagued by dragons. Not unlike us, the elves said that dragons were not their concern. Dragons lived beneath the earth and only came out to feed. Seldom did they feed on elf kind, or seldom did elf kind even see dragon in their lives. They fed on humans and livestock, which was no concern to us, and left behind great caverns for us to build villages and great halls like this. Then they began to feed on our children. It was then we bonded with humans over our common problem, and though we did not destroy all dragon kind, we drove them from our lives. The elves looked on the entire time and said among themselves, 'In time this will pass. What would it benefit to step forward as friends?' They knew they would live beyond the problems we faced."

Here the chieftain stopped and looked around. "Is it our intent to place ourselves above our friends when we know that time will eventually cure our problems, even if it does nothing for the problems of our friends? If so, then this man has offered you a great prospect. One in which you can remain here or 'in your place' and tend the fires while others die for your freedom, for your benefit. Their king only feeds on his own kind … for now. He was able to chase us out only because he knows that our attitude is to wait for the change we want."

The council magistrate stepped forward once again. "This man presumes to offer us charity where none is asked for!"

"Aye, he has." The king of the Oschke Cree looked out among the other tribes, finally meeting the eyes of the council magistrate. "But is it not charity if it is offered without participation in the acquisition? What if we go to war without you, and we lose? Do you not believe that Eldwain will see dwarven kind as weak and decide then to venture into our lands, while our numbers have been depleted? Do you not believe that you will be in war then with less to gain and still the same costs, or greater costs?" The questions resonated throughout the cavern, vibrating off of every wall and column until the silence became overwhelming. Not a breath or movement was heard, for what seemed to Merson and Ory a very long time.

Abruptly the silence ended. Movement was heard as three of the council stepped down from the dais and took a place behind Orman Reglawr, who had just now become a commander of armies. Merson was recording the chieftains who had stepped forward, and then more stepped out into the circle and took a place. Soon the last three to step into the circle were rushing into the circle, as if to avoid being the last.

Ory looked up to the dais, where only the council magistrate stood, staring down at his compatriots and cohorts. In seeing this, he remembered what Merson had said about all at the end would be vying for political power and it would be on him to make them feel their importance. He looked back to the magistrate, knowing that he was a great political figure for the tribes.

Among the noise and positioning going on about him, Orman Reglawr mustered a voice that climbed above the crowd and came down again from the ceiling of this great room. "Magistrate, would you command the rear efforts, supply, support, and prisoners of war?"

A smile crept across the magistrate's face and that of the first supporting king and council member. "Aye," his answer rang back to the ears of the crowd, and he stepped down to join the group inside the circle.

These men of war roamed momentarily through the crowd now formed on the audience room floor with great smiles, congratulating one another on a quick decision and step to action. Ory and Merson stood seemingly somber and dazed at the speedy, relenting decision, both wide eyed and breathless at the experience they had just been through. Merson eased toward the captain, now commander general, and whispered in his ear, "What in the stars just happened! One minute I thought we were done and the next we were, but we were not in the dungeons as I first thought."

"Merson, don't poke the bubble," the new commander said with a quiet sarcasm laced with fear. "We could fall a long, long way right now. We got away from Harishe … I think."

The magistrate stepped toward Orman Reglawr with an open hand. As Ory reached out, the magistrate grabbed his forearm and pressed Ory's hand to his own forearm. "What directives do you have for us?"

As commander, Ory stood tall and close to the magistrate and announced loudly,

"Assemble the armies. The council and I must meet in two hours, and I will bring what I have from my father." He looked the magistrate in the eyes. "Commander of Support, please have a room made ready. It must be large enough for each king and their one most trusted lieutenants, no more. We must have no echo in the room that will allow any to listen to the conversation beyond the room. I know there is great fealty in this place, which makes it all the more important to be close in our speech. Discussion becomes rumor, rumor becomes story, stories are told, and in the telling there is a lesson to our enemies." The chieftain nodded, and in making a motion, two of his people started off in the direction of a passageway. "Where may I and Merson refresh before the meeting?"

Before an answer could be made, the bearded dwarf woman appeared next to Merson and said, "Follow me."

As Merson and Ory walked in the direction from which they first came, they saw a flurry of movement from everyone who was in the room, going in every direction. A great energy was present that moved the light and air with efficiency and unexpected excitement. Whispers between groups as they met and passed each other were followed by looks of enthusiasm and determination. Soon they turned down a passage with less activity, light, and energy, causing the remembrance of their journey to Korfri and the realization of their exhaustion.

Merson looked over at Commander Reglawr, "Couldn't say three hours, eh?" He looked away, and the two followed their guide in silence.

CHAPTER 20

Seeding the Path to Justice

The warmth Johuocin sensed as he held outside the shadow began to feel like a thread being pulled through flesh—that uneasy feeling that grinds at the point of action but unnervingly tickles up and down the spine like sand working into the bone as flesh disappears.

It had been so long since he had felt his own flesh, and he thought back to the deal with Bolac once more. Johuocin had so much time now. Why did it always return to the regret of that deal? He longed for the day he would have no use for self-pity in a deal hastily accepted, but that was not this day.

This day, his thoughts went to his mother, who was alone, the constant cold he felt, the loss of his father, and the regret that he would never be a suitable match for Riessa. Easing further into the darkness, Johuocin felt despair become a part of him. Fingers of mist reached out to him and through him. The warmth he felt in being part of the mist began to burn like hot ember as it passed through him. Then realization set in. It was not burning. This was not warmth. This was like the intense cold of frost being touched to wet skin and being ripped away, like ice water being thrown onto frozen flesh then suddenly warmed with hot coals. Frozen flesh that was being thawed to quickly then held to the icy wind once again. Just enough warmth to avoid the numbing effect of the cold and so little that it would not prevent the bite of frost.

Johuocin thought, *This is what it is to have death without meaning, after a life without purpose.* Then he began once again to struggle away from the shadow that engulfed him. He pictured his mother, his father, Riessa, and all of the others he had been a part of or met since the beginning of his journey. Not one of them had been living without purpose. His father did not die without meaning. Johuocin knew he must pick up his lot and use it to meet whatever challenge would be ahead and provide what enhancement he could to the lives of others.

As he poured himself into this new pursuit, the chants turned to screeching, and the shadow moved to relieve itself of Johuocin.

*

Inside the tavern Anitae began to fret about the fate of her brother. It had been hours since his departure into the night darkness of the street that led to the tower. Minac stood at the shuttered window, peeking through the cracks in the old wood, unable to see anything except for the light that shone from the high windows of the tower. Finat paced the room, fondling the hilt of his sword, watching as Marie slipped into a manic, but unresponsive, state.

Hafer Lotzman came into the room with a cup of hot asra and offered the drink to Anitae for Marie. Anitae took the drink and tried to offer a taste of it to Marie, whispering to her, "Drink, Mother. It will warm you." After a bit of coaxing, Marie did indeed take a sip and held the cup in her hands as she leaned over, slowly rocking herself on the bench with her eyes darting from one to the other in the room.

Minac stepped back from the window and looked around at the group, who were becoming anxious as the time passed. "Hafer, are the streets safe for travel? Is there any reason that we cannot go to the tower?"

Hafer looked back at him with a worried look and put his hands in the air. "It is not safe to travel in the dark here, yet with Ivan distracted by Alsie's arrival, it may be safe to get to the tower. My question is, 'Then what?' What can you do just by getting there? Have you magic spells that will ward off the attacks by an angry Ivan? I don't remember this being any of your strengths. I don't remember this as something you can do well."

"Perhaps then, once there, I can sneak into the tower to see what is happening," Anitae chimed in.

Soral looked at her and shook his head. "No, sister, there's nothing you're doing wrong by checking on the safety of your brother. If Alsie is a prisoner, you're likely to be caught, and then Ivan will have two prisoners or worse yet, you get caught and Ivan still will have only one prisoner."

Anitae looked at her brother as if he were reminding her of a curse. She knew, however, that he only reminded her of the wish that was made, that she and Otinoe would never get caught doing anything 'wrong'. She knew that if she picked a pocket, broke into a home or business, or even decided to take revenge on someone, if it were not fundamentally wrong or if there were not a general idea that the thing she was doing was not right by nature, she or Otinoe stood a chance of getting caught. That was a lesson learned or decidedly learned after a few close scrapes with attempting to do things that no one disagreed with, even the offended party. That did, however, cause the twins to work on true skills of their chosen trade.

"What would you suggest we do then?" she spat at her brother.

Otinoe stepped over and reached for the cup that Marie held in her hands. Reluctantly she let go of it as she noticed that he had a warm pitcher of asra to refill the mug. As he refilled the mug, he turned slightly to address his sister and at the same time maneuvered his hand to drop a powder in the mug. "Obviously we cannot wait until daylight, given that it is the height of the solstice season." Turning back to Marie, he placed the mug back in her hand. "Here Mother, rest and find comfort," he said softly to her.

Riman and Domatis sat silently at the table with their friend Hafer. They looked on as their brothers Minac and Soral walked to each other and whispered intently, looking into each other's faces now and again in a quizzical craze. Then suddenly they turned to Hafer and spoke both at once. "Does Ivan have the supplies he needs to continue his work?"

Hafer answered with question in his eyes, not knowing what the two were getting at. "I don't know. It has been some time since he has come down from the tower. I have not seen anyone come into Khibanhahm except for you for some time. I would be surprised if he had all that he needed. I doubt that we have any way of getting the supplies before the renewing of the seasons." Then he looked down at the floor in his disappointment and embarrassment. "Even then I don't know that we will have the wherewithal to purchase them. We have been worried of the coming of spring for some time."

Domatis asked then as he stared intently at Hafer, "Do you suppose that Ivan could be bribed from his position in the tower? Do you believe that he has crossed the threshold of desperation that would allow an answer to his need change his disposition toward us, toward Alsie?" Domatis's dark hair and youthful look often made a poor pairing with his serious nature. It set people on edge and caused the hair to crawl across arms and up the back of necks. He knew it, and it made him maintain a quiet demeanor when he was not happy about the circumstance around him. That is, unless it would give an advantage, or he could not remain silent.

Domatis and his brother, Riman, were the smartest among the group when they shared their minds in discussion. Often they would assess a situation and know the minds of those they were at odds with, giving them an advantage in dealing swiftly with attackers and controlling authorities.

Riman was, however, less sinister in his presentation and those who heard him would take him less seriously. Riman, in fact, was so much the opposite of Domatis in presentation of himself that people who heard him would laugh at the threats or observances he made. This did not, however, bother him. He would frequently go on in his demonstrations to the point that people would get past the stage of laughter or amusement and enter a heightened state of annoyance. They would indeed begin to act hastily and without thought or consideration of the words Riman said, in an attempt to shoo away the pesky little boy.

The two were an unrivalled match for any mind games that others would like to play and would choose between themselves as to who spoke in order to make the situation what they would like it to be. They were as skilled with their mental warfare as they were with their bows, but this was a natural ability, not a magical one.

Hafer Lotzman rubbed the hair on his forearms as he stuttered his way through an honestly unsure answer, looking back at Domatis, "I d-don't know."

Riman looked around and hopped and moved in the middle of the room, turning and meeting the eyes of each and last his brother, saying, "I think he would, brother … if we offered in the right way. I think he would indeed. Ivan is a good man but prone to being the hero. If we offer him the chance to be the hero, the means to be the hero, he will consider his position. Reconsider his position. He will want to be Avilla's hero."

Koreal and Avalaes each stood. Koreal, having a more serious expression than usual asked as he looked to Riman and Domatis, "What did you have in mind? We know you have a plan. Just tell us what it is instead of this silly manipulation act of yours."

Domatis and Riman's eyes met, and they smiled slightly in the knowledge that they were in the den of their long time companions and family. Domatis spoke plainly then, "If we can get to the tower and get Ivan's attention, we will offer him some of the dragon treasure to support his need for supply and promise him what new sustenance we can. We came here to renew friendships, so, no deceit is necessary, and none will be detectable on our parts. It will then be up to him to either accept or deny our offer. If he is too estranged to us, too mentally predisposed, we may run into some problems. If he is not too far gone, however, we may find a bit of reason escaping his outlook."

A bit of hope returned to Anitae's face as she listened to her cousins, her brother's brothers. She looked to Hafer and asked, "What is the danger of traveling in the dark streets? Can it be done without too much trouble or risk?" As she said this, she saw Marie, out of the corner of her eye, begin to lean. She turned her attention to her brother, Otinoe. "What did you do?" she asked softly.

Otinoe looked back to his cousins and brothers. "We have bigger issues right now. It would have done the woman no good to have interruption in her care, and it would have done us no good to be distracted from our focus."

Minac and Soral chimed together, "Truth."

"Can we at least move her to a bed?" she asked, looking to the others.

Hafer, Koreal, and Finat moved to her side and carried her to the stair and up to a room. As they emerged, Finat looked down at Otinoe and asked, "How long will she be out?"

"Several hours. I have another dose if she wakes, but someone will have to tend her soon, in case she wakes."

Anitae looked at her slightly built brother and smiled. "Good," she said, "that one, will need to be you however. If I understand what Domatis is saying, the rest of us may need to be available to carry heavy objects and be ready to fight."

"What about you?" he objected. "You're no bigger than I and should have a better understanding of this woman than a man would!"

"But brother, we don't know exactly how far down the dragon spell will reach as to removing treasure from the lair. Remember, I was the one to remove the mane of the dragon," she said calmly and without hesitation.

Finat looked back to Hafer. "Is there a chance of safe passage, Master Lotzman?"

Hafer looked around the inn and counted on his fingers. Slowly turning as he looked from one wall to the other, he said, "I have a total of eleven amulets if I include the one that I carry for my personal travel, which will allow passage or protect the entrances to this inn. If someone stays behind, which I assume they will because of the woman, we have a total of nine if they move into one room that needs protection from two entrances ten if they move into a room that requires only one. That will, however, leave them in a position of not seeing into the street or to the outside. That can create a problem if you listen to the noises outside without a view."

Minac looked up at his sister from his seat on the floor near the fire. "What if we each just wore one of the medallions? That would give us freedom to move about and protection from these creatures we have not yet encountered."

Hafer looked down to Minac and then to Anitae. "I think that best be a last resort. How the woman would react to seeing some of these spirits in the room with her may send her into a greater state of confusion than any of you may have seen." He looked to Domatis. "Even you may find it hard to joust with the mind of a ghost. Sometimes it isn't about the fear you encounter so much as the reflection of what you may create."

Domatis looked back at Hafer and shrugged his shoulders as he turned and walked toward the fire. "Humph."

*

Johuocin suddenly realized that he was in the street, alone with no attacker, confronter, or demoralizer—except his own conscience. The light in the tower was still seeping from the shuttered window at its top. The darkness of winter solstice enveloped the rest of the town except for the light that came out under the door of the inn and through its worn and tattered drapery and cracked wooden barricades. The air was clear, and the snow tucked up against the base of the walks and buildings would offer some light reflection if there were any light to be shared.

Johuocin became gradually aware of the many amenities that the town must once have offered. The water troughs by the hitching posts, though empty now, once likely offered relief to travelers. He was sure the apothecary office once had a sign that hung from both ends and swung freely in the wind and was sure to offer a sense of advancement to visitors. Johuocin pictured a time when the sight of the inn would have been a warm and inviting moment of rest and revitalization to everyone who gathered here.

As he recognized the town for what it once was, Johuocin began to warm ever so slightly in his core. He turned back to the tower and moved toward the point of destination that was his earlier target and intention. He would, he knew, achieve his goal and attempt to offer what help he could to Alsie. Again he began to move toward the tower, this time rising ever so slightly upward, watching, focusing on the light from the window near the tower's top.

CHAPTER 21

Leading

As the men stepped through the doorway of the room that was their destination, at least six dwarf women stepped behind them, leaving the room. Looking around, Ory and Merson saw food, ale, two hot drawn baths, and the belongings that were previously on the horses they rode in on. One female remained just inside the door and motioned for them to partake of the amenities set out.

"Your friends have been led to the next room. If you need anything further, someone will be outside the door." Then she pointed to the divan in the room. "You will see we have left war robes there. If you would like to bathe and change, we will clean your clothes and return them after your meeting." At this she stepped out of the room and closed the door behind her.

The room was large, at least thirty steps by twenty-five, and was kept warm by a fire at the far end. Merson walked the entirety of the wall around the room, looking behind drapes and tapestries that were hanging on the walls. He looked in the closet boxes set at each side of the fireplace. He looked under the tables and beds and even tapped the floor in a few places to check for hollows. The whole time the new commander of the armies stood, becoming more and more paranoid with each of Merson's actions.

"You can't be too careful, Captain," he said. "You will have many kings trying to have an edge over others. Also, I'm not entirely sure that all of those that stepped in to help were not just trying to stay in the graces of others who were looking at them."

Merson took off his clothes and stepped into one of the baths that were in the room. Sighing when he sat down, as if he had never felt the pleasure of shaking away the cold so quickly and his muscles relaxing so thoroughly as he did. "You took a huge chance with that speech of yours. I thought I had failed in making it clear that these are very proud people. After I saw their reactions, I knew that you *had* gotten the message." Merson reached to a side table where a pipe and candle sat and lit up a bit of tobacco. Then he looked at Ory with narrowed eyes. "I'll have to watch you from now on. That statement about 'charity' was a little conniving."

While Merson was talking, the captain disrobed and stepped into the second bath. As he heard the last of Merson's words, he closed his eyes and sank beneath the water. He came up a moment later to hear Merson was still rambling about the meeting. He had no idea what he had said, and at the moment, he really didn't care. He was enjoying the feeling of washing away the grime from his recent travel, the feel of the warm water against his newfound scars, and was not about to start thinking about the filth that would soon pile on him as the armies went to war against Eldwain. The moment was all that mattered. In his mind's eye he was relaxing on a spring day with a picnic in front of him and a woman next to him. They were laughing and talking about nonsense. It wasn't until Merson started raising his voice that the captain realized the woman was Riessa.

"Captain! Commander! Are you ev'n listenin' to me at all?" He could hear the dwarfish brogue in Merson's voice, telling him that Merson was frustrated.

He looked up, meeting Merson's eyes. "Sorry, Merson. I believe I escaped for a moment to a time that I will never see."

Merson looked back with a bit of confusion into a face with melancholy and resolve. He did not wish to delve into the reason for Ory's mood. It was imperative now that the two move toward the instructions from Sesnic Reglawr. "Captain, if we are successful, there will be a lot of things that we will never see. There will be a lot of things we *will* see, as well."

Silence fell between them for some time. They got out of the bath and put on the robes that were left for them. The captain's robe, though clearly longer than a normal war robe, was a bit short. It was to meet the ground, as it was normally worn, the robe left the captain's ankles in clear sight until he put on his boots once again.

Orman Reglawr, son of Sesnic Reglawr, commander of kings, moved across the room to his saddle pack. He picked it up and dumped it out like a pickpocket about to assess his evening's booty. He held the bag in his hands after a short survey of the contents and then looked into the bag, where nothing else could be seen. Reaching into the bag, he scratched around a bit before pulling out a piece of hard leather that was lightly sewn into the bottom of the bag. Without looking at it, he threw it down and reached back into the bag, this time pulling out a piece of oil cloth wrapped around something. As he opened the oil cloth wrapper, Merson could see a folded parchment that had been stained by the oils that surrounded it. Folded many times before being placed in the wrap, it was now being slowly and carefully undone.

"What is this, Captain?" Merson asked.

"These are instructions from my father."

"What about the sealed scroll that you carry?"

"That is a letter from my father telling me to be steadfast and true to the cause and my king."

"You've read it already?"

"I wrote it. He made his mark upon it. Then the note upon the outside to open only when I have gotten to my destination was made to the outside of it."

The two men shared a knowing look. "A ruse then it was," Merson stated.

"Yes, in case we were ever suspected. I am sorry you were not told, but it was in the best interest of the mission. If we were suspected and searched by our ever-trusting king, he would find only an urging of loyalty from my father, and hopefully the search would end there. If anyone else knew, the secret may have been given away."

"Aye, it was a good plan. What if our packs were searched by the dwarves?"

"Merson, I would rather explain to friends our deceit to an enemy than explain to our enemy that we were traitors to his cause. The unveiling of the smuggled instructions would have gone toward proving my fealty to the true cause."

At that the two men looked down upon the table, where there was a map laid out outlining the attack routes and timelines.

"We are late, Merson, but not so late as I would have thought three days ago."

The captain studied the plans. He knew he must inform the kings of dwarf kind that the attack would be needed now. Three days in the direction of Castle Eldwain, there already moved an army of two thousand toward an army of seven thousand. Two thousand of those were soldiers on heavy horse. The closer they were to the castle, the more likely that Eldwain would be aware of their movement. If everything went well at the meeting today, there would be many sailing north this day toward the eastern coast. If the wind is with them, they will make up a day or a day and a half and march across the plains north of the Vergadain Mountains. They would arrive only a day behind the force already moving. By that time Reglawr House will be on attack, hoping for a successful trip by his sons. Not knowing any of the delays that were faced.

"I hope it is early enough."

"Aye, as do I."

The two men looked over the maps and plans. It seemed so short a time before there was a knock on the door, but Merson answered.

Before he could get the door all the way open, Riessa slid past him and into the room. She was followed closely by Ben. Gorn, however, had to have the door open so he could duck low enough to enter. "For such high ceilings, I wish the doors were taller! It's just not right!" he groaned as he came through the door.

Riessa walked quickly to the captain. "We have heard that war will be fought! You were successful in your speech, though a bit insulting is something else we heard.

When do we begin?" Riessa stared at Ory and waited.

Ben then got his brother's attention with an urgent, "Well?"

Orman Reglawr looked at his brother as if he were a misguided child. "What are you talking about? Aren't you tired from our recent experiences? Are you anxious to see and smell death? Because, frankly brother, I'm not!" He looked up to the tapestry hanging on the wall behind his brother. Pointing at the mural spun into its fiber with both hands open and grasping at something that was not there, he said, "Is that what you want?"

Everyone in the room turned to look. The colors so vivid and the scenes within it were so real, you would think that you were seeing it as it happened. Elves were coming to the ground as dwarves hewed legs off at the knees, swords going into the eyes of a dwarf and coming out at the base of his skull at the rear of his head. Children being shot in the back with arrows as they flew forward to the ground just outside their mother's reach. Mothers' bellies being split open because they were heavy with child.

Exasperated he yelled again, "Is this what you are waiting for?"

*

Looking at the scene, Riessa fell to her knees, mouth agape, eyes wet. Gorn shook his head and then looked back to the captain. "Is this not why you came here?" he asked.

Sharply the captain looked back to Gorn. "I just don't see a reason to be anxious. The letting of blood should be left to physicians. Soldiers and mercenaries have just been doing it longer."

Ben looked at Ory with disappointment. "It's not that we're anxious to be in war. We're anxious to hear what happened in the great hall. You may know what's going on, but the three of us were led off to a room where we were not privy to your presentation or the responses. We've got a vested interest in this too. We've been traveling with you in the same conditions."

Ory put a hand on his brother's shoulder. "Sorry, Ben, I forgot you really had no choice but to be here even though you had no idea about the plan when we started." He looked back to Riessa and Gorn. "You two, however, put yourselves into this without our request, and though you have been some help along the way, you have no right to push for information that is privileged to those who need it."

Riessa stepped back and grabbed Gorn's arm. "Fine, we'll leave and go back to where we came from as soon as we have rested." She turned with Gorn following her, his head shaking in response. As they opened the door, the captain called out.

"That is not necessary."

Looking back over her shoulder, Riessa said, "Yes it is. We have intruded long enough."

Merson stepped toward the door, but before he could reach them, they were out the door with the door closed behind them.

The three men stood watching the dead space for a moment. Then Merson chimed in. "I wouldn't worry about the whole thing. They couldn't leave even if they wanted to, at least not without us."

"What?" Ben asked.

"They can't leave without us."

Ory looked over. "Why do you say that, Merson?"

Continuing to look at the closed door, Merson added, "A little thing about security, not letting information leave before the army is dispatched. You know—little things like that." He paused for a moment to let them digest what was just said. Then he added, "If they become too insistent about leaving, they may be 'asked' to stay until after the war is well underway. Or until it's over."

"I suppose they'll be watched closely after that, if they are allowed to leave," the captain added.

"Aye, I suppose."

"The big guy may be able to overcome a few of them," Ben offered.

"Aye, a few, but with no weapons and nowhere to hide from weapons, what is a target of his size to do?"

"Ory? Merson? Should they be warned about what could happen?"

Orman Reglawr looked at his brother with a thoughtful look. "Let me think about that for a minute. No rush. They aren't planning on leaving yet."

*

As they closed the door behind themselves, Riessa began her rant. "Who does he think he is? Who put him in charge of the world? What makes him think that we have no right to be here, or no right to know what's going on?" She stopped and took a breath. They turned down the hall, walking toward their room. "We have worked at this just as hard as they have, suffered the same problems. Some of us have suffered more than they will know."

Gorn reached out and grabbed Riessa's shoulder. He stopped her and turned her toward him. Dropping on one knee, he looked her in the eye. "You know that he is right. We did not have to be here."

"Yes, that's true. If we hadn't been with them though, they might not have survived to be here either."

"We don't know that, and we never will. That is a question that is confused by the forces and powers of philosophy. Other questions you may ask are: Would they have been in the places they were had we not been there? Or would they have not been faced with some of these things had they not been friends to us? We can't answer those questions either."

"I can't believe you're defending them."

"I don't know that we shouldn't leave war to warring people. Perhaps it is best to part ways with those that have agendas of aggression. I think perhaps it is something of an influence on you to be in these situations that cause you to choose one side or the other. It is creating a place where you are offended by the confrontation of truth because it does not agree with your agenda."

"I don't have an agenda."

"Then what are you upset about? Why are you feeling slighted?"

Riessa stared back at Gorn as if he had accused her of a crime. Then realized he was right. Why should she be upset? She invited herself on this trip and then insisted in her mind that, because she was there, she should have a right to know the result of the journey. She placed herself in the river they traveled because she didn't know what was in the water, and now she wanted to know about the current that formed the bed of it. She felt unexpectedly ashamed of her actions and her demands. "You're right, Gorn, but what do we do now?"

Gorn stood and turned back toward their walk down the hallway. "I think that we need to think about this. It is not a journey we must continue together. Perhaps your father would be happy to see your return, or perhaps there are other places and times that would be served better by our decisions."

As she hurried to keep up with Gorn's strolling ambulation, she puzzled on the dilemma of what to do next. *Philosophy*, she thought. *What can be said that will answer all questions? Philosophy seems to be nothing but questions that never get answered.* Finally they arrived at their quarters. She went inside and sat in a chair that allowed her feet to touch the ground. There she sat back and closed her eyes as Gorn sat down at the fireplace and stared into the fire. Soon his eyes closed.

Just before Riessa fell asleep, she thought to herself, *How can one person make so much noise without waking?*

*

Ory, Ben, and Merson folded the map as a knock came to the door. They had finished studying the plans and discussing alternatives if there were disagreements to the instructions Ory's father had sent. Ory knew that the most important instruction was the last thing that was said: "Being flexible and having support is more important than having a plan that no one will follow."

As Ory, Ben, and Merson followed their guide to their next destination, Ben looked down the corridor toward the quarters where he knew he could find Riessa and Gorn.

CHAPTER 22

What a Dragon
Leaves Behind

Out the door and down the street in the opposite direction of the tower, Hafer and the group moved, staying close to the buildings and under porch covers whenever possible, trying to avoid the gaze from the tower window, trying to avoid attracting the attention of the creeping things that Ivan had set out to the little village of Khibanhahm. The village that once was a warm and welcoming place, full of personality and personalities, now seemed a cold and threatening place, barely tolerable to those who once knew its charm.

Darkness slowed their progress as they moved cautiously to the edge of the town. They dared not light a torch or lantern. Though it would speed their progress, it would also give them away as they retreated to the dragon's old lair. No one spoke. They simply moved down the street watching the person in front of them and the gestures from Hafer as he watched around corners and held in his hand the amulet at the end of the chain around his neck. Suddenly a light appeared at the top of the tower, and a great, booming voice seemed to fill the streets of Khibanhahm.

"You will not defy me!" the voice rang out. "You will remain where you are!"

Hearing this, the party ran away from the tower. They summoned every ounce of the panic they felt and pushed it into the energy they needed to move away from the light that now lit their path, away from the voice that commanded them to compliance. They found themselves on the outskirts and the voice stopped, though the light became brighter. They continued to run though they could hardly breathe. Finat and Soral took the arms of their older-looking companion and held him up as they ran. They ran until they could no longer run, until their lungs were burning from the constant intake and expulsion of the dry, frigid air of winter. They found a set of boulders to hide themselves behind so that the light from the tower would not hit them. Here they reached for scarves and placed them over their faces to muffle the sound of their breath. They began to take deep, deliberate, and slow breaths that moistened the scarves and made it easier to breathe.

The light continued. A slow rumble of the voice continued but was now too far away to be clear to them what was said.

As they caught their breath, Hafer ached out, "The amulets are cool … once again. Ivan's … terror … cannot reach us here."

Soon the group had come back to some capacity of travel and stepped from one set of cover to the next until the light was so dim it no longer cast a shadow. The group walked in silence toward the cave entrance that was their destination, always looking over their shoulders to see if the light still shone.

*

Otinoe was startled by the bright light shining through the cracked shutters and the booming voice in the air. "You will not defy me!" the voice rang out. "You will remain where you are!"

As he heard these words, he was sure that his sister and cousins had been found out, and he expected them to come charging through the door once again. Time passed slowly as he waited, but it seemed longer than it should be for their return. Soon the voices began to boom again, shaking the walls and shutters.

"Will you continue to defy my command?" The voice rumbled through the air like a thunder carrying the voice of the gods. "Stay or I will send you to the chasms from which you came, and there will be no return from the hopelessness there! You will find no solace in your entrance to the netherworld; you will find no peace!" The voice was one he had heard before but not so loud or overwhelming. It was Ivan. It seemed almost that he was commanding his sister and cousins to their very souls and threatening their last thread of hope. Still they had not returned.

Otinoe did not know what to make of it. Had they escaped, or were they trying still to evade the magic Ivan commanded? Or worse, were they lying in the street already hopeless in their endeavor?

Alsie jumped to the window in the tower room, when he heard the voice boom out. "You will not defy me!" the voice rang out. "You will remain where you are!"

He was sure his family was trying to come out to help him. He knew that they would not be able to find the patience to wait for his return. It was just as well, he thought. He would not be able to get away from Ivan on his own unless Ivan wanted him to.

As he looked out he saw nothing but the streets lit by a light above him. Then as he looked further, he saw nine figures running out through the streets toward the outskirts of town—faster he thought than he had ever seen them travel on foot. One of them was being carried by two others almost dragging him by the arms. But that was nine. Did they leave the old woman with Kale at the inn? Then they seemed to disappear in the shadows.

Alsie was startled by a second round from the voice "Will you continue to defy my command?" The voice seemed to come from the next room at the same time that it cut through the winter night. "Stay or I will send you to the chasms from which you came, and there will be no return from the hopelessness there! You will find no solace in your entrance to the netherworld; you will find no peace!"

Alsie ran to the door of the chamber. He beat on it with both fists as hard as he could, in an attempt to distract Ivan from his threats to his family.

The command stopped, and Ivan yelled through the door. "Is this something you're doing? Is this your shade that comes here?"

Alsie was confused. He ran back to the window and was startled yet a third time in minutes as a wisp of fog reflected the light and came through the window, blown by a fast wind that Alsie could not feel. Then it disappeared as it came into the room and was gone.

*

Johuocin rose through the space between ground and stars toward the window at the top of the tower. The shadow began to pull once again at Johuocin. It began again to call for him. Fighting the urge to join the darkness was easier now that he understood it better, now that he had tasted the other side of that cold and infinite depth. He struggled, with purpose and resolve, to reach his destination. The shadow beneath him began to screech in a thousand voices as it sensed Johuocin's determination and strength of will. A sudden jolt of cold came to the center of Johuocin as the shadow stretched toward him up from the ground then suddenly stopped as he heard a great voice, "You will not defy me!" the voice rang out. "You will remain where you are!"

An intense light that seemed to emanate to Johuocin, but not through him, came from the tower. It was impossible for Johuocin to sense where it came from. The shadow reacted to it by retreating fully to the soil beneath them. He heard the voice once again. "Stay or I will send you to the chasms from which you came, and there will be no return from the hopelessness there! You will find no solace in your entrance to the netherworld; you will find no peace!"

Then the voice was silent for a moment, and Johuocin took advantage of the moments of distraction he felt in the air. He pushed harder against the force of the light; he willed his way to pass beyond it. He saw Alsie's face as he heard the voice once again and entered through the tower window.

Ivan burst into the room and turned to a wall opposite Alsie. Ivan faced Johuocin. He stared at him and continued yelling. "What are you? Where, when did you come from?"

Alsie could not decide what to think of this. "Ivan, what are you babbling about? What do you see?"

Ivan turned back to Alsie. "You say you don't know about this creature, but it came with you. It was not summoned by me, yet now it pushes past my will to be in my home. You brought it here, so now you will tell me what it is."

Alsie responded with a look that Ivan could not deny was one of complete confusion, confirming that he knew nothing of the entity that Ivan saw at the wall.

Ivan moved around to the right of Alsie and just behind him. Placing his hand on Alsie's shoulder, he twisted something out of his voice that sounded like a garbled chant to Alsie. Then a smoke like vision appeared across the room from Alsie, and both Ivan and Alsie stared at Johuocin.

Alsie's mouth stood agape as he saw this hovering vision. It was the same vision he saw entering through the window just moments before. Alsie could feel himself shaking just the tiniest bit and grabbed the chair near his left hand to steady himself.

Ivan let go of Alsie's shoulder and moved toward the vision.

Alsie stood and watched.

Johuocin moved away from Ivan, not knowing what to think. Beyond Bolac, he had not yet experienced anyone who could follow him this intensely. He moved away as Ivan came closer. Soon he was moving back to the middle of the room between Ivan and Alsie. He had not noticed that he was moving into and through Avilla, who lay quiet and sleeping on the bed. Flashes of nasty things came to him as he passed through Avilla. He moved away quickly from her and lost track of Ivan. He tried to focus on what was there and found it left him feeling disgusted and reviled. Something was there in the place where Avilla lay. He realized then why he was repulsed. It tried to consume him, whatever it was. It began to grab hold of him in some way that made him feel ashamed and sickened by himself, as if he were not worth the existence he maintained. And still, it welcomed him as if he were a kindred force.

Johuocin recognized the feeling from a time long ago. He knew that if he had a physical manifestation at this moment, he would puke until the very bile of his gut left him. Remembering the first time he felt this feeling was an overwhelming force to his center. He had always thought it was just a bad dream, a nightmare, but as he now remembered he knew it was real.

Johuocin tried to concentrate in order to recall what had happened so he could overcome the memory and move past it. He remembered looking into the little boy's eyes and seeing hopelessness there. Wishing he could help him and yet feeling helpless himself to do anything. He watched unable to do anything as the boy was attacked with such evil, feeling the boy's pain and desperation. Anguished epiphany struck Johuocin as he realized the boy was a reflection.

"It's turned red, Ivan. What is it?" Alsie called out as Johuocin was about to move into him and Alsie was against the wall and cornered in retreat.

Johuocin became suddenly aware of his unintended movement and surveyed the room. He moved away from Alsie and up toward the ceiling. There he looked down at the others in the room while he shrunk away as much as he could. Ivan was conjuring something and waving his arms and hands and chanting. Johuocin could think of nothing else to do, so while Ivan concentrated on his casting, he moved suddenly into him and paused and then moved quickly out.

Ivan fell to his knees and was breathing hard. Alsie walked to him and helped him into a chair.

"Ivan, it vanished. It's gone. Are you all right?"

Ivan caught his breath momentarily and looked around. He took a few more deep breaths and said in a raspy whisper as he stared into Alsie's eyes with a cold hatred, "It's still here. I can feel it."

Johuocin was nearby watching, wondering how Ivan could see him. How could Alsie see him? Then he turned his attention back to the girl. He felt a need to help her, to free her from whatever it was that had a hold on her. Then he wished he knew more. He wished he could do something or ask questions or anything that would be of use. Outside of a physical form of any kind, as he was now, he was useless except to distract people who had a sense for spirits.

*

The group moved through the bramble by the wall, seeking once again the entrance to the cave that was the lair to a dragon that was once a fearsome scourge on the people in the area of Khibanhahm. They had traveled on foot in the cold for several miles and several hours to reach this destination. They began the journey poorly with a speedy retreat from the town and moved slowly and steadily after this, trying to regain their breath while fighting the fatigue of an urgent expedition. Midday the day before solstice, they had arrived in a place they expected to find comfort and reunion. Now, at the end of the eve of solstice, they found themselves in hope of rescuing a brother who is in danger of being punished for his nonexistent crimes, yet they are hours away from the place where they would hope to affect such a thing. They had no horses and no wagon to assist their effort.

Anitae reflected on their situation. *Great planning!* she thought. *We have to bring back enough silver, gold, and asteril to satisfy the wants of a tyrant, and all we have are our childhood bodies and our good intentions.*

Finat and Riman were at the lead of the group, searching for a path to the cave. Finat was edging through the bramble, hacking at it with his sword as Riman kept a keen eye to the forward area, watching for any sort of movement or life in the bush as they moved.

Riman hissed back silently, "I see a fire ahead." Then as Anitae moved forward next to Riman, he pointed out the place he saw the fire. As they looked deeper into the night, the light of the campfire showed two faces looking into the fire and flames dancing off of breastplates on their chests. As they looked more closely, they saw that the fire was just inside the front of a cave—their cave.

Anitae moved ahead to Finat and whispered to him. Finat moved aside, and

Anitae began to belly crawl under the bushes toward the cave. Hafer stepped forward quickly to try to stop her, but he was too late. Before he could get anywhere near, she was well on her way and heading to meet the two in the cave.

"What is she doing?" he asked.

Finat looked over at him. "She's going to steal something from them. I hope it's something that's theirs."

"I don't think this is the time for stealing something. If she gets caught, they'll kill her."

"That's why she's stealing." Riman added.

Hafer looked at them like they were daft. "So she can get killed?" he asked.

Minac and Soral chimed in together as they began to crawl under the bush themselves. "No. It's so she won't get caught." Dragging their bows to opposite sides, they began to move forward. They were determined to be ready if anything went wrong.

Hafer Lotzman was more confused than ever.

Seeing this, Domatis stepped forward to him, nudging everyone forward as he did. The group once again began to move toward the cave, and Domatis leaned over and got close enough for Hafer to feel Domatis's breath on his cheek as he said, "Otinoe's wish. It was that they never get caught doing anything wrong. It stands then to reason that if you don't want to get caught, you must do something wrong."

Slowly and quietly the group moved forward.

Anitae crawled slowly as she approached the cave. Once she was within a small stone's throw, she began to look for one. She heard the conversation as she got close. One of them said, "I hardly believe no one'd found 'ese. They stinks so bad. Can't waits to cook 'em up."

The other grunted and chuckled at his companion. Then he picked up a small boulder and threw it at him. The other caught it and fell backward, yelling, "Hey. Caref'l now. You don't want it to break before we wants it."

"Don't we wants it now?" the other hollered.

Chuckling a little, his response was quick. "Yeah, I guess we does!" With that he began beating the boulder against another.

There was a great cracking sound, and the rock split open. Something oozed from the edge of it and dripped a little on the ground. The one holding the rock put one half down and reached into the other half, pulling out a small, wriggling animal of some kind. It was hardly discernible. Looked a little like a large lizard.

"Who'd a thunk dragons eggs would taste so good, eh?" Then he put the end of the thing in his mouth and took a bite. With his mouth full and chewing, he garbled out as his dinner fell out in bits. "'Specially likes the pippin like dis one."

The other answered back. "We'll sav'a las' two fer brea'fast. Den we'll fig'er out how to get d'treasures out o'here."

Anitae was close enough to focus on their faces, and realizing what was being said, she panicked, *They found the eggs!* "Trolls!" she yelled back to her cousins. And as soon as she said it, she saw arrows flying from the bramble near her and into the arms of each of the trolls.

She heard bramble being hacked at with a sword, and no sooner did she turn over and look up than she saw Finat stepping over her with Riman behind him, arrow knocked.

Slow to respond, the trolls finally stood, each recognizing that the other had an arrow in their arm. Both pointed at the other at the same time, saying, "'Ey, you got a arrow." Then both looking at their own arms and looking out to the darkness. The one took a branch out of the fire and threw it into the bramble outside. They saw human children running toward them, and they both smiled and screamed, "Yummies!"

Running toward the children and the cave exit, they suddenly seemed to hit an invisible wall. Falling backward and rolling, they got up almost immediately and repeated the action. One looked at the other and yelled, "Toss the armor. It's part of the treasure."

As quickly as they could, which didn't seem very quickly, they removed the plate armor that they had taken from the treasure to wear for themselves. As they removed the armor, Riman, Domatis, Minac, and Soral all let arrows fly. The trolls pulled them out and threw them aside, only to receive another volley of arrows, which they did the same with. They were bleeding from all their wounds and had picked up their clubs as Finat, Avalaes, and Koreal stepped up and began hacking at their legs and hips with swords.

Domatis and Riman edged around behind them and began firing arrows into their backs. Domatis finally found a landing spot and planted an arrow just below the base of the skull of the troll Finat was hacking at. The troll stiffened and fell forward. Finat was not able to move out of the way fast enough, and his right leg was caught under the troll's shoulder.

Seeing his companion fall, the second troll stood straight and threw back his head. He opened his mouth and began making a sound like a war horn that echoed through the forest about them clear and loud until Finat threw his sword into the beast's throat, stopping the sound like placing a hand on the strings of a mandolin.

The beast grabbed the sword, pulling it free and causing a great flow of green oozing blood from the wound. He began swinging wildly with both the sword and his club. Narrowly he missed Koreal with the blade then he saw Finat stuck there beneath the lifeless corpse of his companion.

Finat struggled to escape the anchoring weight that held him, not yet aware that the troll was now focused on reaching him. The club came down beside him, creating a depression in the soil next to him that would have crushed his arm had the troll not been distracted by a poke from the sword of Avalaes.

The troll swung the sword toward Avalaes and hit him. Avalaes fell to the ground, bleeding from a gash at the side of his head. Seeing his brother fall, Koreal charged the beast with sword poised for a stabbing blow. Reaching his target, he pierced the abdomen of the thing and twisted. The troll dropped the sword and grabbed Koreal by the shoulder and threw him across the opening and into the cave just. Then the troll was hit by three arrows in the throat. Anitae had grabbed Avalaes and pulled him away from the action. Holding over his wound a piece of her tunic she had ripped from under her blouse, she applied pressure to stop the bleeding as he lay limp in her lap.

The troll grabbed the arrows with both hands and ripped them away. As he did, blood sprayed everywhere, and a great expulsion of air was heard coming from his throat. As the beast gasped for air once again, it became apparent that he would drown from the inhalation of his own blood. The beast fell to his knees and then backward, with arms flailing until he hit the ground in such a manner to look extremely contorted. As the beast struggled to regain himself, Hafer Lotzman snapped out of the fog of his shock. He picked up Finat's sword and ran toward the troll and hacked at his throat until the troll's head fell from its shoulders. Slowly the troll's arms stopped twitching, and it was most decidedly dead at the hand of an innkeeper. Hafer stood proudly by his victim as if to promulgate that he was the responsible party regarding the successful execution of the foe at his feet.

Those that saw his expression smiled and made no comment as they shared the knowing look of an inside joke.

Anitae was still tending Avalaes, who lay still and limp with shallow breath.

Domatis and Riman found a long, sturdy branch and rolled a boulder near to the side of Finat. They used the branch and boulder as a lever to lift the corpse that trapped Finat.

Anitae looked up from her charge and began yelling at them, "Be careful of that boulder! It is not what you may think it is! Treat it gently. Don't roll it, and bring it back into the cave!"

*

Otinoe and Marie were in the room for hours as Marie slept. Otinoe worried about his sister and cousins, not knowing what had happened. He had reckoned with himself that if they had been attacked and unable to leave town, at least some of them would have returned to the inn by this time. At any rate, if they had not returned before midnight of the day of solstice, he would have to make some effort to go find them or make the attempt to help Alsie himself. He remembered his past. When he was a young child, he would have been feeling the build of excitement by this time on the day before solstice. He would have been unable to sleep, and unable to concentrate on his chores and other things he would need to do.

Right now, he thought, he still could not sleep or concentrate, but it was for other reasons.

Marie began to stir. Otinoe grabbed the pitcher of asra left on the table and poured a mug full. Then he pulled out the packet of sleeping powder that he had in his pocket. If Marie seemed anxious when she woke, he would give her another dose of the medicine he carried.

*

Johuocin searched within himself for a purpose to his being. He watched as the stars passed through the sky and wanted to know what it was about the moment that he passed through Avilla that made him sense the feelings there so completely. He stayed close, hoping for an answer to come out of the darkness, leaving himself in thought and sickening curiosity.

CHAPTER 23

A Wish, a Hope,
and a Prayer

Ivan fell to his knees, shaking and weak.

Alsie, not wanting Ivan to fall further, tried to hold onto Ivan's shoulder as he reached for the chair that was nearby. Letting go momentarily because the chair was just out of reach, he was able to steady Ivan once again when he returned to Ivan's side. Helping Ivan into the chair, he asked, "Ivan when have you eaten last?"

"Days … no, weeks ago," Ivan said.

"How have you gone so long without eating? What did you eat?"

"I believe my last meal consisted of cheese, stale bread, and a sustenance powder mixed with asra. It was enough."

Alsie looked at him in disbelief. "That must be a powerful powder, Ivan. It's no wonder you look like a skeleton."

"The less you are, the less you need," Ivan responded.

"If you do not regain your strength, Ivan, we will not be able to help Avilla. Do you have food here I can prepare for you?"

"There are a few staples in the kitchen below. I don't know how good they are. I tried to keep them sealed, but you know how bugs are, especially weevils." Ivan stared at the floor in front of him.

As this was said, he heard the exhaustion in Ivan's voice. The look in Ivan's eyes was reminiscent to the times in the past when he knew Ivan had felt he had disappointed or embarrassed Avilla. Alsie knelt down in front of Ivan and looked into his face. "Ivan," he said, trying to get his friend to meet his eyes. "Ivan, we will find a way to help Avilla. All of us will. But we must rest and remain strong to do so. Our clarity will otherwise leave us."

At this Ivan looked at Alsie with sadness and exhaustion. "I am sorry, Alsie. I have grown to resent and hate you in your absence. I did not mean such a thing to happen, and Avilla would detest me for it."

"No apologies, Ivan. Just move forward. Now where is that kitchen?"

"Two floors down. There is a kitchen on one side and a laboratory on the other.

Avilla will be fine here. Help me to the kitchen, and we will talk. Solstice is about to begin, and we should move toward a new beginning and a new understanding as we regain the light."

At that, Alsie pulled Ivan's arm around his shoulders so Ivan could lean on him as they started down the stairwell to the kitchen.

*

Avalaes was not waking, but he was still breathing. Anitae had gotten Avalaes's bleeding to stop as she explained to everyone what she had heard. Then she quickly searched Avalaes for the dose of healing potion that each of them carried. She found it, but it was broken during the fight that had taken place. She quickly searched for her own and was able to get Avalaes to drink.

She bandaged his wound and helped to get him comfortable by the fire that the trolls had previously built.

Anitae had realized, as she tended Avalaes, the eggs the trolls were dining on were not those she and Otinoe had buried five years before. These resembled stone and had very little color. These must have been the immature eggs that were mentioned in the tome from Ivan's collection. They were smaller and not formed properly, as the other three had been. There was not enough light near to see into the cave where she and her brother had found them originally. She would need to check once everything had settled. She thought perhaps these would be enough to satisfy Ivan for a while.

Riman was about to carry out the egg and contents that had previously been broken when he was stopped by Anitae. "Don't throw any of that away. Find an urn in the treasure room and dump it in there and seal it after adding remains of the prehatched dragon that is around here somewhere."

Riman sat the shell down, and he and Domatis went to find the treasure and search for a container of some kind. As they walked away, Domatis commented, "Looks like puke to me, or at least *something* that was gagged up outside the backdoor of a pub."

They both chuckled as they walked on.

Finat came limping toward the fire and sat down next to Hafer, who had sat down as soon as the two troll corpses had been rolled a good distance from the cave opening. Koreal said, "It didn't help much; the blood was everywhere and stunk like a pig sty that had gone wrong through the summer." If that wasn't disgusting enough, he had to add, "You'd think that smell was because they never bathe or pick up a leaf when they're in the forest, but it goes deeper than that."

Soral and Minac wandered the cave to see if one rock looked different from another. They came to the consensus that they all looked alike. They looked just like the egg that had been broken by the previous occupants of the cave. They had wandered outside and found that there were three others that looked just the same as the one sitting next to the encampment.

Soral came back to the fire as Minac continued to investigate. "They all look alike on the surface. Even the shape of the broken eggs compared to the rocks are so random, how do you know which are eggs and which are rocks?

Anitae looked at him and said, "There has got to be a way. The trolls mentioned that they smelled different, that 'they stunk,' so there must be something. Did you smell them?"

Minac chimed in, "Our nostrils are burnt from helping roll those things away from here."

Soral stood in a spot at the back of the cavern where there was a depression in the wall that looked like a serving bowl. Hearing his brother's complaint, he mumbled under his breath, "And I ain't sniffin' nothin' else in here for a couple of hours."

From the treasure cavern Domatis yelled, "Soral, quit complaining. There's nothing to holler about in here."

The entire outer cavern echoed back and forth at least five times as he yelled. The cave was nearly unbearable with noise.

Soral retorted as the echo faded for the last time, trying to talk in a normal voice, "The only one yelling is you, and it hurts the ears. Don't you think our noses are causing enough pain already?" With the last of his statement he turned back to the bowl in the wall and they all had an echo of "… enough pain already?" pass over them at least three times.

Domatis stepped back into the main cavern from the treasure room. "You started yelling first. I was just responding."

Anitae spoke up. "I heard nothing from Soral until you started yelling, Domatis."

Soral walked back toward the fire. "But he is right, I did complain about the smell. I thought I was talking to myself in a corner."

"To yourself," Domatis scoffed. "I heard you clear in the next cavern. How can you say that you were talking to yourself?"

"I was whispering!" Soral exclaimed. "I was talking under my breath."

Hafer looked up from where he was sitting and listening to the two bicker about nothing. He remembered how he and his wife once did the same in their kitchen at the inn on a daily basis. He thought about having her there all the time with him and how the constant company of one another brought out the need to argue, just so they would hear one another's voices. Had it not been for their arguments, they would not have had a reason to speak. They knew each other and the way they each liked to do things so well that they would have had no other reason to speak. He remembered, too, that though they had an argument, they would not continue to be mad or angry with each other. They would say what they had to say, express what was bothering them, and walk away knowing they had been heard, and they knew they would have the same words another day. He missed her terribly. He missed the arguments. He missed not hearing her voice. He missed not seeing her smile each day, and the flash in her eyes when she was angry.

When she became ill, he took care of her like she was his life's breath. He enjoyed the time he had with her. She would often express the guilt she had for not having the strength to do for herself. He would assure her that it was a guilty pleasure he felt that he was allowed to take care of her. They frequently reminisced about their life together after she became ill. Hafer enjoyed those moments they could sit together, talk, and laugh after the inn's customers had been served. He recalled that talking to her about their life together was like stepping out the backdoor of the hot kitchen and taking a deep breath of the cool evening air. It was like feeling the coming of fall after a hot summer or a pleasant spring breeze after a long winter. He knew when they spoke that there was always love, always caring.

They had only been together for eighteen summers when he lost her companionship. He had not, in the twelve summers since, met anyone who could replace her, either as a friend or a partner. He would forever miss her, and she would forever be in his heart. He smiled about his life with her each day and shed a tear over her absence when his mind lingered too long on the happiness they shared. He still liked to say her name and often did so out loud, often talking to her and asking her advice, knowing that he would not hear an answer but knowing what she would have said. This had been his relationship with his Eleanor. He would have gladly taken her place or gone with her but knew that she would have wanted him to continue on.

Suddenly, he snapped back to the thing that made his mind wander to the subject of Eleanor. "Pot lids!" he said. "You're arguing because of pot lids."

Everyone stopped talking and looked at Hafer like he had lost his last marble.

Anitae spoke first. "I hope that the woman we travel with hasn't infected you with something. You sound like you've gone over the edge. What are you talking about 'pot lids'?"

"No, no!" he said, standing up and walking to the wall. "My wife and I started arguing in the kitchen one day because of pot lids." He looked at the wall very closely and then turned away to walk to the other chamber. He continued as he walked. "You see, she would complain about something, or maybe it was me. Well one of us, anyway, would complain, and the other would hear. We never meant for the other to hear at all, but we would, and then we would argue. It only happened when the pot lids were not on the pots and they were hung on the hook by the stove and by the block at the opposite side of the kitchen." He stopped at the other wall and looked at it carefully, and laughing he said, "Here it is, a pot lid!" The laugh and the words echoed back and forth a few times before everyone came to see what he was talking about.

As they stood staring at the wall in front of Hafer, Finat looked back to Hafer and asked, "What are you talking about?" Turning back to the wall he said rather loudly, "What pot lid?"

As the sound began to echo, Hafer touched the wall, and the echo stopped.

"This one," he said. "Not really a pot lid; just works the same."

He walked over about five steps and touched the side of the circle on the wall that ended in an abrupt edge. He was able to put his fingers just behind the edge. His fingers came out covered in soot and dust, and there was a slight hum that came off of the wall that echoed until he touched the inside of the circle again.

Pointing to the edge, he said, "You see here where it separates from the wall? You see how it is bellied in at the center? I don't know why it works, but it works like a mini-canyon wall and spits back everything you say into it. The bowl on the other wall catches the sound and does the same thing. If you speak softly next to it and it has another to catch it on the other side, it sounds as if you are right there when you speak." After looking back and forth a few times, he then spoke his conclusion. "The dragon probably used it to keep an ear on its treasure while she slept."

Riman, Domatis, Minac, and Soral all began testing the theory presented by Hafer. The entirety of the two caverns was filled with pointless noise, to the amazement of Anitae and the annoyance of Finat. Koreal was tied to his brother's side as the group studied and commented, joked and played. Avalaes still had not awoken and at this time was likely under the influence of the healing potion as he slept his way toward recovery. Finat finally became tired of the whole commotion and asked them all to settle down and help to discover which of the objects were certain to be dragon eggs and which were, most certainly, rocks.

Riman and Domatis continued on their quest for information about the reverberating walls but did so quietly between themselves in a corner. Finat did not press the issue with the two. One, he was just happy to have the noise stop. Two, he knew that many of the meetings the two had after discovering something new benefitted the group in some way later. Three, *he was just happy to have the noise stop.*

He and Minac and Soral were going from rock to rock trying to decide if there was a difference in the appearance of the surfaces of the rocks compared to what they knew were the outer shell of the previously cracked eggs. What they discovered was that the rocks were almost identical when the surface was dry, but if you wetted the surface of the rock and the shell, there was a specific and identifiable difference. The grains that were pressed together in the rock were closely held together with very little that came between the grains. The grains in the egg were clearly separated by a shiny or polished-looking material that was bluish black. If the egg shells were wet and held in front of the fire, light could be seen to some degree coming through that part of the eggshell.

With this, they were able to identify two eggs and several shells. The eggs seemed to be the same approximate weight as a rock of the same size and shape. Without the shells that had been known, the group acknowledged that they would not have known the difference between the eggs and the rocks. The group was unable to identify where the eggs were originally nested. Whether they were together or separate, if they were being kept warm in some way for the gestation period, or if they had been just lying about. They had no idea how to treat them now in order to preserve them. The remains of the dragon-ling that the trolls had not devoured were warm, but not the shell or the pippin of the egg.

"So, now what do we do with these eggs?" Finat asked.

Anitae was quick to answer. "We move them into the cave further and then we head back to Khibanhahm. Maybe they will interest Ivan enough to talk to us."

"What if there are more trolls about? We really can't risk leaving the eggs to be discovered," Minac ventured.

"We should bury them. The best way to hide a smell is to bury it in dirt," Anitae said. "The thing that attracted the trolls to the eggs was the smell, so we'll bury them just in case."

"Rest first," Finat added. "Once we've rested, we'll bury the things and head back to town. We'll have a busy time ahead of us.

I suspect that Ivan will want to come straight back without a break once he hears the news there are eggs here. And we need to get some gold and Avalaes back at the same time."

Riman and Domatis stepped out of the corner they were in and picked up two long spears from the treasure pile and started tying some rope from one to the other that created a litter of sorts that would allow them to drag whatever or whoever was on it. Riman looked at Hafer and said, "You get to pull, Avalaes. We'll make another for the gold."

Hafer nodded in agreement and lay down near the fire. On that cue everyone found a spot and tried to rest except Anitae. She made the excuse of being too nervous and got up to move about while the rest were near the fire. She took a torch further into the cave, where she was able to confirm the two burials of treasure had not been undone, and she started to dig a hole away from those two sites, that could be completed when the rest of them woke. She would not worry that the burial of the new eggs would disturb the previous work done by her and Otinoe.

*

Ivan sat on a stool as he propped himself against a wall while he finished a fresh biscuit and a piece of dried sausage. He looked uncomfortably full as he tried to swallow the last bite. The kitchen was warm from the oven that still had glowing embers in the fire chamber below it. He stared down at the floor as he placed his hands in his lap; a tear came from the corner of his left eye. He had a cup of hot asra sitting on a shelf near his right elbow, and the tear rolled down his face and into his beard as he reached for the cup. He took a drink of the asra and looked back up at Alsie.

"My heart has been withering from the absence of my daughter's smile, Alsie. My mind has been reeling in confusion trying to regain her. I have become a monster in a town that once showed tolerance to my silly antics and pretense of wizardry. I have unleashed terrible things in this place that are far too evil and threatening against those who have called me friend. I have become the dragon in this place. It may have been better to let the dragon live and kill us all, one by one."

Alsie placed a hand on Ivan's shoulder. He could feel the bone through Ivan's robes. More bone than flesh, Ivan felt the warmth of Alsie's hand quickly penetrate his arm. "You know, Ivan, you have the power to reverse what you have done. You have the strength in your heart and the knowledge in your mind to change the things that weigh on you."

Ivan looked back as if it were the end of all hope. "I don't think I can anymore. I think that I have opened too many doors to the other world and have forgotten to close one or two."

"Cheer yourself, friend," Alsie assured him. "You have those who would help you near you now. All you need do is to allow them the privilege of doing so."

Alsie and Ivan finished their asra and stared into the fire for a short time. As the quiet set in and comfort of friends was confirmed, Ivan found Alsie a bed for the night predicated on the idea that they would start fresh after some rest.

CHAPTER 24

A Conundrum of Conflict

As the three men walked toward the meeting hall led by their apparently assigned custodian, the dwarf woman suddenly stopped, turned to them, and asked if there was anything else that was needed by them in their quarters after the meeting. After receiving a response that nothing would be required other than a good brandy, she asked, "Who will be going forward into the meeting?"

Orman Reglawr answered quickly and directly, "We all will."

A look of surprise struck her face, and she stopped and addressed the commander. "It was my understanding that you asked that each sovereign enter only with one most trusted lieutenant?"

The captain felt taken aback when he realized the implications of what he had requested and his intention of entering the room with both Merson and Ben. "I understand. You are correct. I am, however, faced now with a decision I had not intended to make. You see, this is my lieutenant," he said, motioning toward Merson, "and this is my brother." He motioned to Ben.

"I see, Commander," she said. "Then I will take your brother to his new quarters, where he will meet his instructor."

Ory looked at Ben and then to the woman and asked, "What instructor?"

"Excuse me, Commander. Is there another brother of the Reglawr house?" she asked.

"No. What has that to do with needing an instructor, and what is the instructor for?"

The woman bowed her head to the captain and placed her hands in front of her face up. "I am sorry, Commander. I thought you were aware that the council had invoked the Rule of the Protected Prince when they first heard from your father about his plan to overthrow Eldwain. He will remain with us until the end of the war to learn about our culture, our customs, our laws, and our history." She raised her face to look at the captain. Her beard was ruffled slightly from the bowing of her head, and Ory could see in her eyes that she felt she had spoken of something she was not intended to speak about.

Ory looked at the woman and raised his hands in order to try and comfort her nerves. "Please don't feel nervous. What would have happened had Ben not been with me? What would the council have done?"

She once again bowed her head, "Commander, you would have been required to stay. You would have been given regular updates about the action at the front of the battles, but you would not have participated in battle in any way but to provide your input to the next action.

"The purpose behind this is to protect the interests of the clans and in the event of your father's death in battle and now yours as well. Reglawr house would have a prince to ascend the throne and remain as an ally to the clans. The protected prince will continue to act as the ambassador and liaison to the clans in the event of a successful end to the war, with you or your father remaining as the sovereign to the kingdoms of men upon this continent."

The woman leaned her head a bit to one side and looked upward to meet Orman Reglawr's gaze. Then with an apologetic tone she said, "Commander, please accept my apologies. I truly thought you were aware and am at a loss to know why you were not previously informed of the situation."

Ben stepped forward toward the woman. He was confused, he was incensed, and he was defiant to the idea. "I wanted to fight alongside my brother. I wanted to see the action in the front line. This is not acceptable. Is my father aware that this was the intention? I will not."

The woman stood silent, looking only to the captain. She stood as if Ben did not exist and made no attempt to answer.

Ory looked at her, seeing in her eyes that she heard him but was prohibited from answering him. "What would happen if Ben refused to submit to this rule? Is my father aware?"

She only looked back and said, "I know this is confusing, but I cannot speak more about this. I can find you someone who will. Please follow me." She turned again walked ten yards and turned through a doorway to a small room. Once everyone was there, she stopped. "Please wait here until I return." She walked out of the room, and the door closed behind her.

"Merson," the captain exclaimed, "what do you know about this Rule of the Protected

Prince? Is there an alternative to accepting the rule?"

"Captain, I don't think that they would entertain cooperation with your father unless he was aware and in agreement of this. It is an antiquated law even for the clans. I would never have imagined that they would have used this rule. It has been eons since its invocation, and it would have to have been a fluke that it was even brought up in a meeting. I would have to research it in their libraries to know if there are any alternatives."

Ben started walking around the room. "They can't do this. I'm not going to stay here, Ory! I want to be involved in the fight. I want to be part of the battle to free Eldwain from that tyrant!"

"Ben, what if our father knows? What if it stops the cooperation if you don't stay?"

Just then the door opened and a dwarven man with a scroll came into the room, followed by Granite Hammerhand. Ben looked at the little man. They had met before, and he grimaced. "I should have known you had something to do with this."

Ory looked over at Ben. "Do you know this man?"

Ben and Merson both chimed in at the same time. "Granite Hammerhand."

Merson finished with, "We met just before Rausche Laine." Seeing the captain's curious expression, he said, "Remember, he was the one who pointed us in the direction of Rausche Laine where we met Riessa and Gorn?"

Orman, not wanting to draw too much attention to the time he could not recall, tried to cover. Remembering the briefing that Merson had provided him about that time, he smiled slightly as he met the eyes of the dwarf, "Of course, it was a bit cold that night. And if I remember correctly, you were able to get some rest that night."

Hearing the captain's question about knowing him, Granite gained a moment of confusion and distrust. He gave up the thought, knowing that so much was happening now, smiled, and said, "Yeah, I did. It was the first in days. Left me quite rested lookin' back. It also left me with a sore wrist, as I recall. Your brother is a bit trigger happy."

"Well, I didn't get much rest that night! If you would have just been forthcoming with information, it may have been a bit easier for both of us," Ben responded.

Granite smirked and looked at him with a knowing arrogance. "Seems this is the second time you've been caught without enough information to be part of the conversation." Granite motioned for the man holding the scroll to hand it to the captain.

Ory took the scroll and opened it. Seeing first his father's signature at the bottom, he began to read:

Orman,

If you are reading this, you have reached the settlement of Korfri. I thank the gods for your safety. I should have told you before now, but I did not want this on Ouben's mind as you traveled forward. Our allies have an old law that I have asked them to invoke.

Here Ory stopped and looked at his brother and read the passage out loud then continued on.

> If you and your brother have both arrived safely, then it is my intention that Ben remains with our friends to become Liaison Prince unless it happens that you are injured badly and cannot continue. If for whatever reason one of you has not reached the settlement, then the other must stay. It is prime to our cause that when we succeed in our effort, we have both a leader and a liaison to ascend the throne. May the gods protect us from the one being both, but if this is what

is to be, then the one must be ready to step to the challenge. In this I ask that my sons understand my reasoning. It was not the idea of the clans to invoke this rule. I believe the clans were even surprised that I was aware of it. I apologize to you both for this unexpected circumstance, but there are reasons for everything. Please be sure that the rule is well read and studied by whoever is the liaison.

Your Father,
Sesnic Reglawr

"Ory," Ben whispered, "this isn't how I pictured entering this war, or how I pictured spending it."

Orman Reglawr looked at his brother in understanding. In many ways he knew how Ben felt, but he also knew that he was glad that Ben would not be exposed to the level of battle that was to come. He saw in his mind, all too realistically, the scenes from the tapestry that hung in his quarters, knowing this is what would be faced in the near future.

"Ben," Ory said, placing his hand on his brother's shoulder, "this is what our father has promised would happen. We will see this through and go forward with it for the good of all our peoples. You have no real choice in this. He is our father and has done well by us all of our lives."

Merson nudged Ory's arm. "We should go now. They will be waiting impatiently. You have encouraged the hearts of war in these clansmen, and it will serve us well to move urgently."

Orman looked back at Ben, meeting his eyes while talking to Merson. "Yes. We should begin, so we can get this over with." Then he spoke only to his brother. "We shall end this soon brother, and together we will change the face of this world."

At this the three men were led out of the room and started in two different directions. Granite Hammerhand followed Merson and the captain to the war room, stopping in the hall as they entered.

*

Gorn and Riessa sat in their chamber, eating and relaxing as they talked further about what would be next.

"War is not necessarily a place where your father will have you," Gorn said.

"Yes, that is probably true. However, he knows of my independent thoughts. He has not stood in the path before to stop my traveling forward." She looked about the room and felt a little uncomfortable. Everywhere she looked there seemed to be some reminder of the dissidence between dwarf and elf. She reached out for her cup of asra, and her hair fell forward across her face as she did so. Reaching back to place her hair off of her face, she traced her hand lightly across her cheek, over her temple, and drug her hair to rest behind her ear.

Gorn, seeing what she had done, became unsettled. He looked at her and reached to release the hair that was previously over her ears and let it fall into place. "You may want to keep your hair down and covering your ears. Or, if you can, put it in braids that will join in the back to keep them covered without fear of falling."

"What are you talking about?" She looked at Gorn as if he was a little daft. "I always keep my hair like this."

"Yes." Then Gorn pointed to the paintings and the stone carvings in the room. "Don't you see a bit of a theme here? If they haven't already noticed, you may not wish to tempt fate. If anything gives you away quickly, it will be those ears."

Riessa reached up with both hands and touched the tips of her ears. Nervously she said, "Hmm, perhaps we should think of traveling home, very soon. I have let myself become much too comfortable here."

"Yes, soon," Gorn said.

While Riessa was working on putting her hair into braid that she could draw together at the back of her head, a knock came at the door. She quickly secured what she could, and then Gorn called, "Enter."

Ben came into the room, closing the door behind him. Quickly he told the two of his new dilemma. "So I will be stuck here for the duration of the war and perhaps longer depending on the length of it all. I need to learn about a society that is as old as the dirt itself, and then I can go home."

Gorn nodded his head in understanding. "This seems wise on your father's part. His blood line is protected, his throne shall have at least one successor, and you will know your allies well if conflict between you arises in the future."

Ben just looked at him in disgust. "Yes, but I will be trapped here for years at best. What will I do here with nothing in common with a people who are indifferent to my race?"

Gorn looked at Ben and laughed. "I don't know that they are indifferent. They are going to war at your side, as your ally. There must be some interest in your wellbeing or at least in building relationships that will be ongoing. This appears to be your chance to make this a relationship of understanding and friendship. You have more riding on your shoulders than defeating a few soldiers in battle. Yours is to create a friendship and maintain it in peace when there are so many differences that could end it."

Suddenly a feeling of fear erupted inside of Ouben Reglawr that he had never known—the fear of failure in a task that was important to more than himself, his family, or his friends. This was something that would affect all of humankind if he failed. He fell to his knees, shaking and looking back and forth at Riessa and Gorn. "I can't. I don't have the smarts. I am not that person."

Gorn let out a great bellows of a laugh as he reached out and brought Ben back to his feet. "You can, you do, and you will be, Ouben Reglawr. This fear you have is from wanting to succeed while others are depending on you. This is your chance to step beyond what you feel are your capabilities. Truthfully, others often know more what we are capable of because they have seen us from a better perspective that we see ourselves. I'm sure your father has seen you step beyond yourself before or he would not have considered this as an option."

Ben didn't know why, but Gorn's words were reassuring to him, and he felt better about going forward. He knew now that it wasn't something he had to know about before experiencing the act. "Still a little scared," he said as he placed his weight on his own legs.

Riessa piped in anxiously. "You're scared—what about me?" she said as she pulled out one of her ears.

Ben's jaw dropped. "I'd keep that covered if I were you. They don't take kindly to 'your type' here, you know?"

Gorn and Ben laughed as Riessa gained an honestly insulted look.

*

Orman and Merson stepped into the war room, and all eyes were upon them coming from the shadows of the room. The new commander of the armies felt a sense of power and powerlessness all at once. He had instructions from his father as to what would be a good approach. However, if there was opposition to the plan, he knew he was on his own to form a new strategy. Right now he knew his best alternate strategy would be to involve the experience in the room, those who had fought for hundreds of years before he was even alive. As he looked to the table in front of him, a slimmer and younger-appearing dwarf rolled out a map on the table from one end to the other. Another put out a set of marker pegs with miniature standards poking from the top. They were clear as to what they represented, whether it was supplies or artillery. Orman pulled out a similar but smaller map from his breast pocket and lay it down on the edge of the great map.

"This, brothers," he began, "this is the plan that my father had envisioned. Let's find out how it figures into our current circumstance."

Nods of approval came from most of those at the edge of the table as they all began to place markers out to represent the available resources of their individual tribes. With little discussion or rumbling they placed them on the map where they existed at that moment. As they finished, they turned back to Orman, who surveyed the map and calculated the time it would take to put the resources in place.

King of the AnGrat was the first to speak. He was the supply chief and would be responsible for the timely delivery.

"This will take too long to make all the move of artillery to its destination effective. In some cases it would be better to move our men and engineers into place and build some of the equipment on site and then put it in place from there. The rope and spikes would be easier to pack in by heavy horse and wagon and then build the catapult we need just miles away instead of moving large armament over leagues. The existing can be set between our defenses and between going forward to the battle lines. Those that have gone in front of us will have brought what is needed to pick a fight and will need reinforcement before we can move armories to their aid. It is better to be there than it is to let our enemy get his bearing."

Orman Reglawr heard approval from those looking on in their grunts and shuffling of pieces and maneuvering of power, so he let the discussion and planning go on with little interruption. From time to time the plan would appear to stray from the immediate purpose, and he would call it back to order. By the time the session ended, there existed a clear direction of movement and attack that mostly mirrored the plan set forth by

Orman's father. Some groups were set to a speedier path to make up time, and an entire division was set to sail north before heading into the war. However, the plan was solid and would move forward rapidly.

At the end of it Orman stood over the map as the room went silent. He looked at the map and then surveyed the room full of men who were all four times his age at youngest and perhaps some were as old as twenty times his seasons. They stared back in silence as Orman's voice became raspy and low as the words flowed from his throat with stern confidence.

"Let's go to war." At that the room's occupants gave a great loud cheer and smiles flashed as hammers were raised high. It was as if a burden were lifted from everyone in the room.

No longer was there a question lingering about alliances. No longer was there the overwhelming pressure of "if." The decision made and direction given, and everyone who had stood by in silence, waiting for details, was now in motion as the great machine moved forward.

As he watched kings and generals move quickly to respond to the order to move ahead, he stood silent. At that moment Orman Reglawr felt a surge of power that sent fear racing through his mind and heart. He understood that there was no turning aside now. He knew that, though he may observe it in the lives of others, the world he lived in would no longer contain even a hint of innocence. He knew that the success or failure of this effort would forever hold his identity hostage, and there would be few who would know who he was before this moment took place.

CHAPTER 25

We Would Not Know Darkness, but for the Light

Johuocin remained in the room with Avilla, wandering in the space around her as he thought. She lay there with a look of emptiness on her face, and yet whatever was in her, whatever held her, tortured her. Johuocin felt the sense of pain as he passed through her. He felt a sense of what was there, and for a moment he felt it was a memory. He felt it was a memory that he had chased from his mind. Now with a separation from it, the memory faded, and he knew better than to believe in its existence.

Johuocin tried to remember the experience of waking from nightmares. It was all but impossible. He remembered the fear that startled him awake but was not sure of the lingering that existed. He could no longer recall many things his body went through when recovering from fear, grief, or any other emotion. It had been too long.

He remembered his time in Skillcore. He remembered the waking from that place and how it lingered in him. He remembered the disappointment of losing that moment with Riessa. It was real while he was there, but it seemed that the reality of it faded quickly without the race of his heart and the struggle for air his body would have gone through. He was back to reality ahead of the mage, it seemed. Of course, Harishe was distracted by his own entertainment, and Johuocin knew it was his own circumstance that triggered the wakening of Harishe. He knew that Harishe struggled momentarily, trying to hang on to the dream simply because he wanted to be in that place.

While in Skillcore, Johuocin knew, he too wanted to be there. It was easy to accept as reality because it was easy to be there. It wasn't the same as what he had just experienced, but it too seemed real.

This darkness took control of Johuocin. The dream made Johuocin a part of itself. It punished him for being where he didn't belong and called back to him, even now, to join it. Johuocin struggled in himself, wanting and not wanting to return there. He felt it was a deserved punishment for his sins against others.

As Johuocin hovered nearby, a tear rolled from the corner of Avilla's eye, and a grimace crossed her face. The darkness outside the window was great but seemed like daylight compared to what was in Avilla now. Johuocin felt the dread grow within him as he realized he would not be able to leave Avilla before he tried to help her. He hoped that if he could just go inside and wake her, that would be enough to banish it from her, enough to draw her back to reality. He also worried that going back might trap them both.

A fog rolled through the window and was lit by the fire in the hearth. Johuocin remembered the simplicity of being alive, of having a body that was his. He thought that there were some things that, as a whole person, you just couldn't do anything about and you would have no expectation of trying to help. There are some things that you would never know about. He was having the same internal conversation anyone would have that was about to do something that was a cause for fear: *What am I doing? Why? Should I just let it go? It should be Ivan's place to take care of this problem. He's the one who let it go this long.*

He was thinking all of these things as he moved toward Avilla. Then he thought them as he moved *into* Avilla. All of these things for a young girl he didn't know. Johuocin cursed the thoughts he was having, knowing that he would not be in this predicament except for the deal he made with the wizard Bolac. Had he still had a solid self, he would not have known of Avilla's pain and therefore not had a need to remedy it. Even with the knowledge of it he would not have the guilt that drove him to act—the guilt he felt in stealing the lives of others and the need to do penance for it. Yet, perhaps, this may be the place he was delivered to by destiny. Maybe this is the only purpose that he was to serve in this world.

Suddenly he was pulled into the darkness as he thought about his motivations being revenge and guilt. Had he always been so selfish that the only thing that made him act on anything was how the world affected him?

*

Otinoe, seeing Marie stir, set a chair next to the bed where she lay. She opened her eyes a small bit and looked over at him. After looking around, she tried to speak, seemingly asking after Anitae. Otinoe simply said she was out and about, and Marie asked quickly and in a panic, "In this cold darkness?"

"Yes, Mother," he said. "She is out helping a friend."

As he saw that Marie was not able to settle herself, he quickly poured some asra and stirred in the powder without her seeing. Then he poured a bit for himself. After Marie drank some from the mug, he set it back on the table next to the pitcher. By the time he returned to her, she was once again asleep. He covered her to keep her warm and resting.

Otinoe looked out the window once again, and the streets were quiet. There were lights in the tower at every window, and it caused a bit of a glow in the street between the inn and the tower. Otinoe saw no evidence of his sister or cousins and went back to the table to drink the asra he had poured for himself. He tipped back the mug and drank deeply as he sat in the chair next to the bed, thinking of their latest adventure in this life—thinking of how much things change from season to season and yet how much each of the venerable youth stayed the same. The thought made him tired. His eyes began to sag a bit, and he sat up in the chair, once again taking Marie's hand in his. He began to yawn and then looked over at the table where his mug sat next to the pitcher. Then he looked at the floor, where he heard the clunk of pewter on wood as he dropped the mug he had been holding and drinking from. *Oh no!* He was disappointed in himself for making such a mistake. Little he could do though. He fell into sleep anyway.

*

Anitae, Finat, Hafer, and the rest gathered their weapons and prepared for the trek back to the village. Then their brother, some gold, and the partial dragon egg were all placed on the litters. Minac and Soral pulled the litter with Avalaes out the opening of the cave, and Hafer took it over from that place, while the others carried bits and pieces as well as a litter of treasure toward the village of Khibanhahm.

Hafer pulled his burden easily through the path being trampled in front of him. They had harnessed Avalaes's shoulders to the top of the litter so he would not slide to the downside of the slanted carrying device. After traveling about a league, and Hafer running one leg of the litter or the other over a rock or scraping the base of a tree or bush, Avalaes began to stir from being jarred and shaken. He groaned as the litter dropped from the rock it had just climbed over and frost from a bush fell into his face. Anitae would check on him occasionally as he made his presence known.

There were no stirrings from wolves or other animals as they went on their way to the village. There was a thought from the group to stop and eat before reaching the town, but it was quickly dismissed by Finat, who knew their travel was already slow as they drug their cargo. He passed out some jerky and dry rolls. They stopped once to fill water bottles by the stream as they passed nearby. Soral broke the ice at the edge and placed a tube he had made from an old horn into the water. As long as he faced the low end into the oncoming stream, it would pull water out and work like a mill hose or a strip mining tube, depending on the force of the current pushing water into the horn. Using it prevented them from having to dip their hands into the cold water.

At what must have been midday, the light began to glow over the horizon to the south, making most in the group feel some melancholy as it was clear then that the winter solstice had passed without celebration or even any bit of cheer. The venerable youth all realized that the number of years that passed mattered not, for this was just another anniversary of their unfortunate contact with the Ocre king.

Anitae, in seeing the peak of light, offered a short prayer to the gods. "Bless our souls. It is good news that we still possess them."

Each in his turn raised their water to the sun and gave a solemn, "Aye."

As Avalaes's turn came around, he too agreed and then asked for water and to be untied from his uncomfortable situation. Cheer filled them all to hear him speak and to know he was once again among them. They stopped briefly as the party experienced their joy and moved things about a bit to spread out the load. Koreal was very pleased to have his brother with him. Though they spoke little, he reached out, slapping his brother on the shoulder and laughing as a great joy spread across his face. It comforted him to regain the confidence of his brother's health. The mood had changed dramatically as they moved once again along the path.

It had been a concern for all of them that they would one day lose a sibling or cousin before they were able to reverse their fortune and grow old like normal men and women. It often crossed their conversations that, while they may never die of old age, they certainly were not invulnerable to illness or injury. They all realized how lucky they were to have survived all these years after the curse. They often reminded themselves and each other so as not to become careless or overconfident. They held hope in that there would one day be a wish, or a spell, or a reversal of some sort that would return them to a natural order. Always searching for something that would allow them to have an ordinary life, yet always reminding each other also, they did not walk this place alone. Their concern for the circumstance of others was important to them, for this is how they were raised. This was the attitude of their fathers and mothers, and it had not yet failed them.

Philosophy or God? None of them had a clear vision of what drove them, but they all had a clear vision of what should be. They were as thankful to have a world to live in as they were that they were able to live, and they were aware of the significance of how each possibility was dependent on those things that they may never touch or see. There is magic in the wings of a butterfly that is powerful enough to blow a hurricane back out to the sea or lift it to the top of a mountain.

Their pondering and joy were enough to pass the time quickly. As they approached the town once again, they realized that the windows of the tower were all alight, and they covered the gold they carried so as not to create a noticeable reflection.

Was the light in the tower a good thing or a bad thing? No one was sure. It caused a feeling of anxiety in all of them as they entered the town, moving as quickly as they could toward the inn. The sun had already left them, and the darkness was no comfort as they scurried through the dusty, cold streets.

As they approached the inn, they saw a glimmer of light in the upper window flicker across a crack in the shutter there. Finat was the first to whisper in the darkness as they crossed the board walk to the door. "The light," he motioned to the window with his face. "I hope that says Otinoe is well."

Anitae looked to Finat and smiled as Hafer pushed open the doors and waved everyone through as he held them. No sooner were they through than Hafer closed the doors and lit a lamp. Placing his own amulet above the front door, he enlisted Riman and Domatis to assist as he checked the other rooms and entrances. Taking the amulets of each of the others in the room, he hung them by the openings as they proceeded. Soon they came to the stairs and hurried toward the top, calling to Otinoe as they approached the door of the room, where they had left Otinoe and Marie.

Otinoe woke to the sound of movement in the inn's main rooms downstairs. Feeling as though he had been drugged, he wasn't quite sure how to wake himself properly. He looked up from the floor, where he had fallen from the chair, and seeing Marie still resting quietly, he rolled up on one side and started crawling for the door. Soon enough though he heard his cousins calling his name, and he felt overwhelmed with relief and lay back down on the floor and closed his eyes.

They were open again as he felt Finat patting his face, calling his name. As his eyes opened once more, he found his sister looking down at him with one brow cocked high and her arms folded in front of her with a half-smile on her face. He knew that look. It was the look he got when she thought he was left in charge of something and decided it wasn't worth the details. He did what he has been doing for years when he received "the look"; he looked back at her, head cocked, raising both eyebrows and the corner of his mouth, shrugged his shoulders, and as he held out both hands, palms up. That was his admission of having no defense and no way to change what had happened. It was one of three looks he had developed over the years suited to dealing with his sister's levels of disappointment in him, one of three ways to say what he meant to say, without actually saying the words.

This was the one that came when no harm had come from his actions.

As Otinoe woke into clarity, he gave his explanation of being passed out at their return. "It really just comes down to picking up the wrong mug as I settled to watch Marie." Then looking around and seeing the group relaxed and dirty, he gave a sniff to the air in the room. Crinkling his nose and making a face, he demanded conveyance of their recent experience. "Now tell me why you all smell so badly."

Each of them looked at the others and realized what a great mess they must appear to be. The group laughed as they realized they were just relaxed and grateful to be in some semblance of safety and comfort and had dismissed the thought of how they must appear or how they must smell.

Hafer stood and walked toward the door to the room. "I'm going to the kitchen to start a fire and heat some water."

Riman and Domatis immediately stood to follow.

"You're going to the kitchen? Maybe we could help," Domatis chimed in.

"While we are there, perhaps you could show us your selection of pot lids," Riman intoned.

The group again laughed as the three walked out, taking with them candles and much of the light, and Anitae began to communicate the eventful journey of the trip to the dragon's lair.

As she spoke, Otinoe walked to the bed stand and lit another candle, still listening intently to his sister.

CHAPTER 26

The Cost of Redemption; the Difference Between Regret and Sin

Johuocin was feeling torn in this place. He was overwhelmed with sadness and confusion. He knew he purposely entered this place and had a reason to be here but was suddenly unable to focus on what it was. There was warmth that drew him toward a darkness looming in the distance, and Johuocin wanted nothing more than to go there. He had been so cold for so long, and the warmth beckoned to him. The darkness, on the other hand, was a great repelling force. Perhaps he felt this way because the darkness was, of itself, so very dark. Johuocin could not focus enough to remember darkness so solid ever in his existence. There seemed to be substantiality to this darkness. It was solid like a rock or a tree.

Johuocin moved closer. No. He felt closer. As he did, he corrected his thought. It was like water that allowed no light to pass into it or through it. Then as he felt distance close further, he felt reflections of pain. There was light moving toward the darkness that simply disappeared into it and was swallowed up by it.

Johuocin did not understand. He knew the nature of light was to be reflected or to wrap around objects or to bound through anything that was not solid. This darkness simply swallowed all light, never to be seen again. The reflections Johuocin saw in this darkness were not at all reflection. It was the pain locked in the souls it swallowed, souls that still carried the light of hope, despite the pain within them.

Johuocin felt closer to the darkness with each moment of greater understanding. Johuocin began to see faces connected to the pain. He started to feel the pain of his visions as if it were his own. He knew the cause of the pain as if he had been there at its inception. Now he knew why it was so real the last time he visited Avilla. This was the pain of punishment that came with not knowing the reason for the punishment. This is the pain that springs from not knowing for what sins to atone—knowing that a great sin must have been committed, for the punishment was great.

The more Johuocin watched the faces in the darkness, the more he understood. This pain was derivative of the innocence of children, children who feel they were punished by those they loved, without knowing their sins.

The warmth of this place emanated from the hope bonded to love—hope that they would be forgiven by those that punished them so they may deserve to be loved again. These souls were unaware they had done nothing for which to be forgiven, except the one sin they have committed upon themselves, their feeling of guilt for not deserving love.

Johuocin could no longer linger here as he felt this pain. He felt the need to move into the darkness to offer what solace he could to these souls trapped there. He moved forward to the pain, to the darkness, to the sadness, and was met with the denial of entry into it. He was pressed to it. He felt the need to stay and do something, anything, to free these souls of their burden. Yet there was only denial to his plight.

He felt the pain of each in its turn and yet all at the same moment. He tried once and again and again, conclusive that nothing could be done, until it was.

Still the need to do something was within him. He could not find a way to retreat from this task, this burden. A thought came to him to seek Avilla specifically. He searched for the thoughts of this one that he came to help. Yet none matched what he might know of this girl. He could identify many separate and individual children and then what seemed must be each individual child, but none were Avilla. If Avilla were not here, then where could she be found?

Finally in soulful exhaustion, Johuocin retreated from this darkness. He moved to a distance of feeling disconnected and withdrawn from the gravity of pain. He distanced himself into a moment of clarity.

Suddenly, Avilla was with him. She was a part of him. He understood her love for Alsie and her father and her drive to find a spell to return Alsie and his siblings to their mortality. Then he came to understand that she was drawn to the darkness as he was. As he recognized the pain, so Avilla did as well. Then he understood that she could have woken at any time and chose not to do so because of the souls locked in the darkness. It was as if they were one in thought. He felt her confusion of his presence. She wondered, was he a wizard or a ghost-ling? She wanted to know. Then a thought entered the communion of the two—as if it was always there, as if it were a piece of them both.

They sensed the edge of the darkness. Felt its coldness against them. Knew the warmth on the inside and called to the souls within—intent with love, understanding, and the message that they would always be remembered by them. They expressed the truth that was apparent in their mind's eye. They had done nothing to be punished. They exposed that the sin was against them and not of them. Abruptly Johuocin and Avilla felt the rush of release, of self-forgiveness and understanding and the love encased in gratefulness as the darkness no longer held these souls of innocence.

Then the great pain was changed. It emanated from whatever inhabited or made up the darkness. It became cold and anguished from within. In its selfishness and resentment, the darkness screamed the scream of banshees, the scream of wounded wyvern.

When nothing further was within the dark thing, Avilla woke, alone with the coals of the night's fire lighting her chamber and the stars lighting the night sky. She looked around to see no one, still knowing that someone was with her. She began to cry, tears of happiness and warmth. She felt the fire in her heart well out to the rest of her, knowing that those innocent souls were no longer tortured and she could return to her work.

Johuocin was near as she lay quietly, with tears running from the corners of her eyes, wetting her hair as color ran once again into her face.

Then he realized the cold that he had resented for so long was reassuring to him in some ways. He knew he was selfish in many ways, yet there were lines that he would not cross, things he would not do, to feel warmth. He was sure it was because he did not like the feeling of guilt it gave him. It seemed to him that he enjoyed his selfishness as it was. He was willing to complain about the cost but not willing to have others carry his burden of consequence, at least not for long. He wondered how it was that the dark thing had become what it was and where it began its journey of emptiness.

ABOUT THE AUTHOR

J. Elmer Tesch has been interested in worlds of fantasy since he was a young teenager, through both literature and games. He wrote this book as he thought about the role-playing games he created for friends when he was younger.